YANG AND YIN

YANG AND YIN

A NOVEL OF AN
AMERICAN DOCTOR IN CHINA

By ALICE TISDALE HOBART

GROSSET & DUNLAP

PUBLISHERS   NEW YORK

By arrangement with The Bobbs-Merrill Company

To
The Most Incisive of Critics
My Brother
EDWIN GRISWOLD NOURSE
who puts the achievement of a worthy
product above personal comfort or gain

FOREWORD

To THOSE of us who have watched it, tragic and beautiful and terrible has seemed the impact of West upon East—the blind drive of machinery into a civilization already over-stocked with man power, the forcing of impersonal business organization upon a people governed by personal responsibility to the clan, the onslaught of aggressive thinking upon the quietude of Eastern philosophies.

River Supreme and *Oil for the Lamps of China*, the first two in this series of four novels, dealt respectively with machinery and business organization. This novel, *Yang and Yin*, deals with Western and Eastern thought, the beauties and excesses of each, the impact of one upon the other. For its title I have used the Eastern phrase, *yang and yin*, difficult of literal translation, but meaning in its general sense, the two forces which create life. It is indicative of the West that I have reversed these terms, placing the active principle, *yang*, first. The Chinese place first the passive principle, *yin*.

With certain Chinese words I have sought through simplified spelling to remove the difficulties of pronunciation.

None of the characters in this book is taken from real life, nor is any institution described an actual one.

My gratitude is very great to many people who have given generously to me of time, knowledge and understanding. I can mention only a few. I wish to express especial apprecia-tion to Dr. Alfred C. Reed for scientific data used in this book; to Florence Ayscough MacNair for material on the old examinations and for the Song of the Carpenter, quoted from her book entitled *The Chinese Mirror;* to Mrs. Howell Moor-head for much of the material on opium; to Dr. J. C. Ferguson for his kindness in introducing me to Chinese scholars; to many Chinese friends, who, I think, would prefer to remain anonymous.

I wish to mention my secretary, Ruth Moore, for her loyal help and sensitive judgment on the later stages of the book. I owe much to the insight and knowledge of my friends, Helen Hendricks and Anne Stoddard, and to the understanding and wise guidance of my family.

CARVED on the old stone drums of China, inscribed in books handed down through thousands of years, traced on ancient dishes and on dishes made today, is a sign and a symbol. It is woven into fabrics, stitched into embroideries, blazoned over house gates, wrought into shop emblems, a circle, locked together within it *yang* and *yin*—*yang*, light, *yin*, dark, each carrying within itself the essence of the other, each shaped to the other.

Outside the circle is the octagon of the diagrams—eight groups of lines, broken and unbroken. Opposite the diagram for warmth is the one for cold. Opposite thunder, the arouser, is the wind and gentleness. Opposite Heaven is Earth—"Earth the tilled field that takes up the seed of Heaven." So on, endlessly, is the world divided between the creative and the receptive—motion and repose, man and woman, light and darkness, energy and inertia, active and passive, spiritual and material—*yang* and *yin*, forever opposed, forever united.

Man's mystic need is to keep their harmony. The law of the harmony is the *Tao*, unseen, all powerful, all pervading. The *Tao* is the undivided one within the circle.

We of the West have said that China has a system of ethics in Confucianism, a borrowed god in Buddhism, and superstition in Taoism. But beneath all three, secret and strong, runs this deeper imperative which keeps man forever seeking union with the creative forces of the universe—*yang* and *yin*.

YANG AND YIN

YANG AND YIN

PART ONE

I

THE abode of the ancestors was very still. It lay cupped in
the hills, a half-circle in shape, its straight edge held to its
straightness by the precision of the squared fields in the valley
below. From one of the flagged paths that set the valley in
its geometrical pattern, stone steps led to the gate of the enclosure. The ancestor of the Sen family five generations back,
for whom this land had been purchased, had his place in the
center of the half-circle, sheltered under a low, grass-grown
mound, which allowed him to communicate with Heaven and
Earth. His sons, grandsons, and principal wife lay in a
circle at his right. His other wives lay outside the coterie of
the family. Cypress trees rose tall and dark just above the
stone altar standing before the central mound, and from the
top of the mound itself grew a strong and vigorous grave
tree—the phaetinia.

The place was newly swept and garnished. Fallen leaves
and dry grass blades dropped by the poor when they had
stealthily raked the graves for fuel, had been brushed into the
corners of the enclosure. On the altar stood thimble-sized
cups of wine and rice and a pot of burning incense. The
air was filled with its fragrance. Faint smoke drifted up from
a burning pile of paper, shaped and colored like silver sycee.

Now in the late afternoon, as Scholar Sen and his son
bowed before the chief ancestor, a cypress tree cast the shadow
of its trunk upon the altar, but where it fell across the bent
and narrow figure of the man and the small one of the child,
it left no mark, absorbed into the black of their traveling
gowns.

Because of the boy's frailty, it was only today that he had

helped in the Sweeping of the Graves.   Though Sen, scholar and magistrate of the *hsien*, the district, was an old man, not for a long time had a son accompanied him.   Ten years ago, it had seemed that the family of scholars, dating back hundreds of years, was to be prematurely cut off by the death of his grown son.   Then, eight years ago, this boy had been born to his concubine.

As his son made the ancient kowtow at the graves of his ancestors, Scholar Sen found comfort in escape from the dread of catastrophe.   At last there was security for himself and his family through the harmonious communion of the living and the dead.   A son to worship and care for the ancestors, to bring them the fragrance of food, the smoke of spirit money, thus securing health and success for the living.

Sen felt no sense of separation from his dead.   The great ancestor, the generations of men lying to his right, himself, his living son, were but passing forms of the same substance, mysterious tides of life which flowed and ebbed, making the universe.

The rites for the community of spirits completed, Scholar Sen called to the chair-coolies to pack away the bowls filled with food offered to his ghostly guests, then went away down the steps leading to the dyke path, where his official sedan stood.   With a bit of rag the coolie tied the basket containing the spirit feast to a hook at the back of the chair.

"Lower the curtain to the second nail," commanded the Scholar, as he took his seat in the sedan and placed the child between his knees.

The chair-bearers lifted the blue-covered chair to their shoulders, moving quickly along the dyke path toward the city, a relay of bearers following, outriders on ponies before and behind.   The ponies' bells jingled.   Their hoofs clattered on the stone-flagged path.   There was the quick pat, pat of feet as the men broke into a run in order to keep up with the outriders.

Where his knees pressed the child, Scholar Sen felt the

fine, lean body; his eyes appraised the stoop of the narrow shoulders under the thin silk gown—the traditional shape and structure, the traditional posture of the nobles of learning.

At three, the child had had placed before him large ideographs of the language. A man must start early, if he is to master seven thousand ideographs. Nothing less would do for a scholar. In the child's fourth year, when his *amah* had carried him along the street, he had reached for the gilt ideographs on a sign swinging over a shop.

"*Ai!*" exclaimed the shopman. "A scholar! He brought them with him from another existence."

"Thou," his father now addressed the child looking silently out over the curtain, "note well the inscription above thee on the arch. Four hundred years the arch has stood there, memorial to a woman who remained faithful to her dead husband."

Clouds diaphanous as veils drifted up from the horizon, filming the sky. A light rain began to fall. It sharpened the fading green of the winter fields, the delicate new green of the willows, the dun-colored thatch of the peasants' cottage roofs against which the white blossoming pear was silhouetted. All the land bore signs of quickening.

The man became as silent as the child. By some delicate inner perception, he felt the rain touching to life the latent fertility of the earth. His spirit quivered to the union. The earth's spring conception was an experience stored in his memory, reaching back to the beginning of the race, when each spring the maidens lay with the youths on the fertile earth—"unions upon the soil, unions with the soil."

All at once, so it seemed, the massive bulk of the city wall towered above his chair. At its foot lay the moat, green-surfaced except for an ink-black pool here and there where the scum had been pushed aside when the peasants dipped their pails for water.

The chair-men's feet touched the bridge crossing the moat. Without looking, Scholar Sen knew. For most of the years

of his life, that hollow sound had signified that the journey
to the ancestors was over. The path was crowded with men
on foot and in chairs, returning from the day spent with
the ancestors. In the bottle-neck of the city gate, carrying
coolies, chairs, and pedestrians entering and leaving the city,
clogged the way. The magistrate's outriders pushed their
ponies forward. The sedan-bearers cried above the din of
many voices, "Open the way! Open the way!" and the
hsaio ren, the "little men," squeezed themselves back against
the damp masonry of the vaulted arch. Their heavy loads,
swinging from their shoulder poles, teetered precariously.

As the cavalcade passed out of the dark cavern of the
gateway into the city, Scholar Sen's serenity was marred.
Jutting above the low curved roofs of the native houses, he
saw a group of crude brick structures, with sharp-angled tin
roofs, and walls cut with yawning apertures. Vulgar in their
conspicuousness and ugliness, the work of a vulgar race of
coolie men who taught coolies to set aside the traditions, taught
women to set aside the sacred rites. His eldest son's widow
had run away to a place like this. He was filled with black
hate against these barbarians who had influenced her to violate
the relationship of woman to man, making the great Sen
family lose house reputation.

"Faster!" commanded Sen.

The chair-men, almost abreast of the gate in the wall that
surrounded these unsightly buildings, lunged forward, breaking into a run. At that instant, Peter Fraser, coming through
the open gate, made a sharp turn to the left. Suddenly he
felt a man's hand shoved against his chest. As he staggered
back, he saw the lead-coolie clutch at the poles of the great
chair he was carrying and lean against his shoulder yoke. His
strong and flexible fingers seemed almost to crush the smooth,
hard pole turning around in his hand. It looked as if the
man's wrists must break with the strain. The sedan steadied.

There was an ejaculation from the chair's occupant which
Peter, with his limited knowledge of Chinese, did not under-

stand, but he caught the note of sternness in the man's voice. Impulsively he stepped forward to accept his share of responsibility for the accident, as he would have done in his own country. But neither the gentleman nor the small, silent child at his knee, gave the slightest sign that he was seen or heard. Without glancing Peter's way, the Chinese gave the command to move forward.

Had the man meant to ignore him? Peter was inclined to think he had. He continued to stand thoughtfully in the street, his back flattened against the compound wall. He saw again in detailed clarity the elegance of the two figures, the refinement of their faces. Here was some quality of refinement not to be seen in his own people. Not even in the aristocratic classes of Europe, as he had observed them during his year of post-graduate study abroad, had he seen a face in which the refining process had been carried so far.

In his own people, struggle and pioneer hardship still kept the features vigorously angular. Abroad, the ideal of physical strength was kept, even for royalty, by means of games. Here in this country, where the cultivated man despised physical effort, it was natural that these men should have developed a more delicate structure than any woman of the West. Another thought crossed his mind. Could the delicacy lie in some quality of the spirit—some quietude that left the muscles of the face and body always in repose?

As the child's face came again before him, the physician in him awoke. The boy lacked something. What was it? The thin, oval face, with its quiet, contained expression, bore no mark of disease. No, nothing so definite. An absence of vitality—that was it.

A coolie, stepping quickly to keep the balance of the loads swung at the ends of his carrying pole, brushed the young doctor in passing, bringing him back to the moment. Peter looked at his watch. He must hurry if he were to get his daily walk on the city wall. Nearly four o'clock, and that meeting to attend at five. After that, he faced an evening of study

on the language. He was putting in longer and longer hours
of work, as the time for his examinations drew near.

As rapidly as possible, he wormed his way in and out among
the chair-bearers, load-coolies, and pedestrians who crowded
the alley-like street. By an act of will he tried to shut from
his mind the need for his skill which he always saw in the
little men, the *hsaio ren*, as he was learning to call the Chinese
masses.

He noticed that many familiar figures were absent today
from the shops. The man who hammered out brass kettles
was not here, neither was Wang, the shoemaker, with whom
he so often talked. Puzzled, he stopped to question an old
grandmother who sat under the eaves of her son's shop,
twirling a spindle, a fine, even thread forming between her
thumb and finger.

"*Ai yah*," she answered. "Do you not know that this is
Ch'ing Ming?" She went on explaining the matter of the
ancestors to him, for she, like many others on this street, had
come to count the young doctor her friend.

Almost immediately upon Peter Fraser's arrival in this interior city of China, the common people had liked him. The
members of the Mission, when they had first seen him, had
deplored his coming because of his red hair and the clear
whiteness of his skin.

"The Chinese call us who have brown hair the red-headed
barbarians. What will they think of him?" said Mrs. Baker,
eldest woman in the station. "You'd think the Board would
have realized he'd be conspicuous."

"His peculiarities won't matter to them any more than ours
do," Stella Perkins had answered. "To us he seems more different than he will to them. Somehow, I think they'll like
him."

She was right. The people of the city had given him no more
curious attention than they gave any other foreigner. Today,
in the matter of the ancestors, the old grandmother took for
granted his understanding.

But what was he saying? "If you would spend for your sick the money you use in making paper money for the dead, don't you think it would be better spent?" How could it be better spent?

As Peter moved away, she exclaimed to herself, "*Ai yah!* After all, he is a barbarian. He does not know that if one wishes health for the living, one cannot neglect the dead."

Five minutes later, Peter climbed the half-ruined ramp that led to the top of the city wall. Hands behind his back, head slightly bowed, he strode mechanically forward, his thoughts still in the city, unable to enjoy the solitude he had come to seek.

Even in that brief passage along the streets, he had seen on every hand the marks of disease. It was hard for him to withhold the gift of health he had for so many of these sick, and devote himself day after day to the language. The immediacy of the people's needs pressed in upon him, pulling his gaze from the empty spaces of the wall down to the man-filled streets and the no less man-crowded canals below him. He wondered with some anxiety if, during these months he had been giving himself exclusively to study, his hands had lost their cunning with the surgeon's knife.

Gradually he became conscious of the beauty of the delicate grey fog, indefinite, timeless, which enveloped the city. But even it created a warfare within him. The elements that made its beauty made for sickness. This splendid wall mewed up the air in the narrow streets, not allowing the vapors of countless steaming kettles, the smoke of chimneyless braziers to be blown away, creating this soft haze that made sickness almost universal. Rich, velvety shadows, half revealing the bent figures of men bowed to labor, lent false charm to what he knew was bestial toil. He ought not to love this scene as he did. But little by little his uneasiness left him.

He loitered now, stopping often to lean against the parapet. This ancient wall did not seem a man-made thing of brick and mortar. More like earth in the process of the centuries

petrified into the semblance of brick, but keeping the precious
life-giving properties of earth to nourish the swinging vines
and gnarled trees that grew on its perpendicular outer face.
Only the parapet, clean cut in its geometrically precise right
angles, retained a man-made look. But even it was crumbling
under the pressure of the creeping vines. He picked up a
bit, holding it between finger and thumb. Under his touch
it fell away into dust.

From the wall's lofty top he saw, encircling the horizon,
the mountains veiled in blue haze, one slender, aspiring pagoda
faintly outlined on a saddleback between two ridges. He
waited, hoping, as sometimes happened, he might recapture
the ardor of his original intention. He had come to this
country because he had wanted to make something real of
his life. He courted adventure, service, and some splendor
of the spirit which he felt he could not achieve in his own
country.

So far, he was simply a lonely young man, unable to find
a bond of sympathy with the others of his Mission. Mr. and
Mrs. Baker, with whom he boarded, annoyed him with their
religious patter. I He disliked their placid, satisfied faces, that
knew nothing of the warfare of the mind. Their very kindness to him seemed to make it worse. Berger, the head of the
boys' school, treated him with an air of condescension. Miss
Dyer, the middle-aged evangelist, sought to rule everyone
who came within her reach. Peter avoided her. And Dr.
Buchanan, whose work he was soon to take over, was old and
fumbling.

These made up his world, except for Stella Perkins, the
nurse at the hospital. Abrupt, often bitter in her speech,
frequently at odds with the Mission community, she sometimes gave him a glimpse of a gentler individual, her real self,
he believed, a personality which left him oddly disturbed and
happy. But she had not permitted him to see that person
for many days now.

The grey monotony of the sky began to change, until clouds

lay in long feathery lines like the great sweep of an archangel's wings. Peter was caught up into the magnificence of his faith—God transcending the earth, man made in God's image, God's especial care. And then, all at once, he thought of man as one of the Ten Thousand Things of the universe, which Wu, his language teacher, had taught him was the Chinese conception. It gave him a troubling sense of the immensity of that universe.

Strange diseases with their new suffering were beginning to cut into his acceptance of the Christians' traditional explanation of pain. The world at times no longer appeared ordered and planned, but an impersonal world, where disease and pain were natural. His God of compassion was daily blotted from his consciousness by the city's pageant of the diseased—men with white-filmed eyeballs raised to the sky vaguely searching out the way, men with the grotesque limbs of elephantiasis, lepers with countenances eaten half away. As spring had come, and the children ran half-clothed in the streets, he sometimes saw one with thin bony chest and distended belly, evidences of a disease he could not diagnose.

A premonition settled over him that the splendor of the spirit was not to come by the path he had planned. He drew back from some foreshadowed union with the city's suffering.

And then beauty like a sword cut into his forebodings. Out beyond the wall lay the fields. From the smoothness of immemorially cultivated fields, the grave mounds rose, tipped with long, thin spirit streamers fluttering white in the oncoming darkness. A pear tree in the angle of the grey wall cast its ethereal whiteness against the black waters of the moat. Peace entered him.

The mist-like rain increasing to a steady drizzle woke Peter Fraser to a knowledge of the hour. He hurried forward to the next ramp and down to the city. Everywhere was the bustle of home-coming men, back from their annual visit to the ancestors. All around was warm, human festivity. Looking into the tiny cubicles that did duty for shop and house, he saw in the flare of lighted wicks floating in oil, men feasting, and under the spirit tablets, food—a shared meal. The spirits still lingered among the living, in need of food and attention. The women waiting upon men and spirits had delicate tips of willow tucked into their nape-knots, and over each doorway hung willow branches—willow, sign of life, sign of fertility.

As he passed an apothecary shop, Peter's thoughts swung again in the orbit of his great interest. As if the God of Medicine sitting in his accustomed niche, or the stuff in the blue and white jars arranged so neatly on the shelves, could be of any use.

Ground lion bones to give men strength, lion hearts eaten for courage! Strange that the users of such nostrums should have been the first to discover a form of vaccination against smallpox by infecting well children with the virus of the sick. But they still used the crude method. Its perfection had been left to the West. Nobody knew when the Chinese had discovered that opium erased pain. But now opium was used to bring back youth, the passion of youth, giving to an old man the potency of his early years, that his women might bear him more sons—used also to free a man from his instinct to struggle, fabricating a life of ease.

Peter turned. He was in the wealthier section now. No tiny cubicles of houses here, spilling their life out on the streets. The long white walls stretched from street corner to street corner, a black lacquered gate occasionally breaking the white expanse. Peter thought again of the man in the blue sedan. Somewhere in this district, he must live, sheltered behind such walls as these.

Behind him he heard the tap of a blind man's staff, the tinkling of his gong—common sounds in this country. He was drawn back into his original absorption in the great surging multitude, a sick multitude, a hungry and cold multitude, caught in the clutches of its own anodyne—opium. Opium with its trick of destroying pain and hunger, only to bring its own hunger and pain. Everywhere he saw its ravages. Head down, his eyes on the worn stone flagging beneath his feet, automatically he walked on, until he came to the end of the streets of the rich, and turned into the Great Street, the main business thoroughfare. Coming toward him, he saw a foreign woman.

"Good afternoon," he said.

As he spoke, she tilted her umbrella back, and he saw it was Diana Moreland, a young teacher from another Mission, whom he knew casually. A long time since he'd met a girl on the street. The occurrence, commonplace at home, was a mighty event here. He forgot his driving urge to cope with all the disease of China.

"I'll come along, if you don't mind," he said.

But Diana Moreland stood silent, restraint in her manner. Then Peter remembered that unmarried men and women held no public communication with each other in this country. Although the missionaries had come to destroy the bonds which fettered the women of this race, they kept the ritual for fear they lose the confidence of the Chinese. They sensed some deep imperative which they did not understand, but which seemed to demand of them that they pay it respect.

So now, into the meeting of these two, filtered a strange, Oriental awareness of each other. They stood awkward and silent, unable to go on together, unable to do so strange a thing as not to. Then Diana, sensing the ludicrousness of the situation, laughed outright, breaking the spell.

"Of course. We're going the same way. Where else could we be going today? We'll have to hurry—we're late now. You go ahead, I'll follow. That will be all right." She spoke as one used to command. "Oh, no, it won't," she added, suddenly remembering that such was the proper procedure for the married.

Embarrassed, she resigned herself to Peter's polite suggestion that she let him walk at her side. But, absorbed in the contradictions of her position, she did not speak.

"After all," she thought, "I've broken the custom so completely by being on the street at all . . ."

The walking was difficult on the cobblestones which flanked the central flagging, and Peter, thinking little now of his unresponsive companion, dropped behind to the smooth center of the street.

She looked back. "I'm sorry. . . . It's rough, isn't it? If we walked more slowly——"

In a patch of light thrown across the dark street by the sudden opening of a gate, Peter saw her face clearly. Her eyes, intelligent, honest eyes. Brown, he imagined, black in this light, and full of warm concern for him. Suddenly he sensed a deep femininity in her—in the fastidious perfection of her dress, the grace of her hand clasping the umbrella handle, the supple movements of her slender body as she walked. He forgot the discomfort of the cobblestones and strode forward to her side. There was silence between them as before, but it held some unuttered consent to each other now.

They had come to their destination. The gateman, filled with the importance of the occasion, opened the gate at Peter's first tap. They passed up the walk and into the house. The door into the parlor had been partly closed for the prayer. They stood side by side in the hall. Diana's head was bowed, but Peter's was not.

He hoped she would look at him once more before she went in, but at the last low-spoken word, she stepped quickly into the room, taking a seat among a group of women. There were many curious glances for the two late comers, and on the faces of some a look of disapproval. He felt a wave of anger. No privacy in this community, and sometimes, he thought, no mercy. He slid into an empty chair near the door, took hold of the hymn book that Stella Perkins, sitting in the next seat, held out to him.

* * * * *

The Chinese servants in the kitchen, having a preliminary tea of their own, were enjoying the foreign sweet called cake. They were ensnared not by the strange rhythm or the unfamiliar custom of this singing, but by its note of urgency.

"*Ai,*" said one. "Their god is far off. They seek him."

"What wonder?" The speaker was an old man bent nearly double with a twisted spine. "They refuse the spirits the cost of offerings. Neither candles, nor incense, nor paper money. *Ai,* fooling the gods with singing, keeping the money for themselves."

"Thou," said a young woman in an unbleached homespun apron shaped like a butcher's, covering the front of her blue trousers and short gown, "thou, to speak so! Where is thy *tao li,* thy good custom, thou whom they care for? Wouldst thou have the new ones among us believe them stingy?"

As the hymn ended, with little rustles of contentment, the white people settled themselves for the reading. The curtains had been drawn, shutting from their thoughts the alien, wall-enclosed compound, the peaked gatehouse, the line of waiting sedans, the rain-soaked, corridor-like streets beyond. Almost was the scene as it would have been at home—the pictures on the wall, the neat rows of chairs, the table for the speaker with its pitcher of water and glass. All things familiar, lulling their minds into security.

The presiding officer was a thin-faced, slender American; the speaker, tall and slender, too, an aged white-haired English bishop. He caused an almost imperceptible catching of everyone's breath as he rose. Peter thought him very beautiful. He contrasted him with the Chinese gentleman he had seen earlier in the afternoon. There was breeding here, too, but the contour of the face had not been softened.

Peter's thoughts wandered to Diana. He looked across and saw her, her hands busy with some knitting. He understood that need to use one's hands. He looked down at Stella's lying quietly in her lap—oddly graceful in spite of their red-

ness and swollen knuckles—chilblains, he knew, brought about
by her work in the cold hospital wards. As his gaze rested
upon them, she knotted them into a hard clasp.

The bishop, forty years a student of Chinese, began reading to them, in all but faultless intonation, the statement of
their faith. This other language, although difficult for them
to understand, made them realize anew their religion's special promises against lonely selfhood—separateness, fear of
pain and death, dreads lurking in all men's minds. The human
craving to be loved and cared for was satisfied.

Diana Moreland lost that unhappy wondering as to what
the community would think of her coming to this meeting with Dr. Fraser; Mrs. Berger, the fear that she was going
to have another child—the doctor had said she was not strong
enough; Mrs. Baker, her anxiety about her children in
America; and Mr. Baker, his perplexity over the power the
younger men were getting in the affairs of the Mission. Peter
felt his last vestige of anger toward the community gone
from him. Stella's clasped hands relaxed.

Suddenly they were a mighty host who no longer sought
individual safety, the assurance for themselves surrendered if
they might bring their God to these people who knew Him
not. They did not detect the shadowy hosts come to this
country long years before—Mohammedans, Buddhists, missionaries also of spiritual certainty. In this Confucian country, already permeated with spirits, strange things had happened to those certainties.

The bishop had finished. A half-dozen men and women
rose. An Englishman wearing Chinese dress was given the
floor.

"In this connection the word *ming*, bright, I think is not
the best one to use." As he talked, on the palm of his hand
with his finger he drew the ideograph for *bright*—sun and
moon in conjunction.

So the discussion began. Who could arbitrate? No Chinese
were asked to come to these gatherings.

There was a restless moving of feet. One by one the women slipped out. Peter found his long legs cramped and his mind weary of this alien language. At last the presiding officer brought the meeting to a close. The double doors to the dining room were thrown open. Peter saw a table spread with a white cloth, women of his own race sitting behind silver urns pouring tea and coffee. As they entered the room, just as at home, young women moved toward them with sandwiches and cakes. He ate and drank, drawn into the warm companionship of his kind, the Chinese sick at last shut away.

"You owe it to the Chinese to start opium refuges. You British brought it to them in the beginning," he heard Dr. Buchanan, standing behind him, say.

"Don't forget the Chinese had a taste for opium before *our* countries—your own country is not free from blame—began selling it to them," a tall Englishman answered.

The color rose in Dr. Buchanan's pale cheeks. "I'll say *we,* then. Before *we* organized the business and made the evil popular. It was after *we* forced them to legalize the import of opium that they tried the dangerous experiment of legalizing the native stuff. Now they have both."

The men had raised their voices in the heat of argument.

"Careful—the servants might hear you," someone cautioned.

Peter caught Diana's glance. As once before this afternoon, there was unuttered consent between them. But as he moved away, he felt a curious resentment toward her. He had felt it toward Stella, too. They intruded on his singleness of purpose. He had thought of celibacy, as men often do, not because of his religion, but because by living alone he might attain the full growth of his unique self. He would be divided against himself if he loved any woman. Love, he felt, was a hard thing for those who took the time to think of it.

The party broke up late. The drizzle of the afternoon had turned into heavy rain. A long line of chairs moved out of the gate, for all the women were riding. Except for the bishop and Dr. Buchanan, the men walked. The hard heels of their shoes clattered on the paving stones as they kept pace with the chairs or followed behind.

The city was asleep, the shutters of the shophouses closed. Like passing through the corridors of a ward at night, Peter, the last of the line of men, was thinking, the streets so narrow, the people so near. He heard a child's cry, a woman's voice raised in startled exclamation.

They came into the street of the rich. He thought of the two elegant figures he had seen that afternoon. Somewhere within these high walls, they lived a life of which he knew nothing.

The young boy, Lo Shih, lay asleep in the outer court of the great patriarchal dwelling of the Sens. He woke, hearing a clatter as of great hoofs. The foreign devils! He shuddered, remembering the ghostly creature he had seen that afternoon in the street. Those round, pale eyes, the colored hair! Some spirit, uncared for by the living, taking his revenge on the living. The servants, his mother, and his grandmother had told him of such spirits and the harm they did mortals. Whimpering softly to himself, he beat his breast in the Chinese sign of fear. He longed for the comforting warmth of his *amah's* large body, to which he was accustomed. Then he heard a familiar sound—his *amah* stealthily lying down beside him, nestled his thin body inside her loosened garment.

In the apartment of Scholar Sen's mother, watched over by her sharp eyes, two men sat talking—Scholar Sen and the family's business manager who had just returned from a visit to the distant province of Szechuan to view certain ancestral lands.

"The crops are good?" asked the *lao tai tai*, the matriarch. "The family has need of much money this year. Masses for the dead master must be said in the next moon."

"Then the opium fields must be increased," answered the manager.

II

SHANGHAI belonged to Christendom. It had clean streets and parks. The Woosung River, on which it fronted, was filled with Western steamers and gunboats, white and gleaming in vivid contrast to the brown native sampans and primitive junks. It had Western-owned hospitals for the care of the Chinese sick, and two thousand dens, where the "foreign smoke," opium, laid siege to the Chinese strength. Along one of the main streets, shops flourished openly where a pellet of opium and a bed for the drowsy sleep it produced could be secured for a few cents. The opium trade, made lawful by war, brought great revenue to the Christian nations.

Here at the turn of the century, this city belonging to the Christian nations stood, with its modern improvements, its shrewd grasp on revenue, and its urge to serve humanity. Its exclusive white settlement had the longest bar in the world. The term "American girl," no American girl cared to use. Each night across the flat plain of the Yangtse delta, the city lights suffused the sky with a soft glow, penetrating a little the dark hinterland of China. Over the great valley of the Yangtse, each day opium poured out of Shanghai like a black wave.

Peter Fraser stepped forth into the streets of Shanghai an unshackled man. His examinations were over. Surprising and incredible result, the hospital in the interior city was to be his next fall, although, as the senior men of the Mission Board explained, he was not really prepared. Dr. Buchanan must go home for a rest. They were short-handed. It left no one but Peter to manage the hospital.

This released him from two more years spent exclusively on the language, from which it had seemed there was no escape. The thought of using his mind and hands in minister-

ing to the sick unleashed a pent-up vitality. That somehow
he must sandwich this study in with the heavy duties as head
of the hospital, did not worry him one whit.

As he rode in a ricksha toward the business district, the city
of Shanghai came sharply into focus. "What a splendid
Western city!" he said to himself, forgetting what a small
town it had seemed to him less than a year ago, when he had
come to it straight from America.

Reaching the Bund, he paid off his ricksha, and walked, delighting in the wide street, with shops on but one side. The
park across the way looked miraculously trim, with its closely
mowed grass and neat beds of flowers. Fair English children
were playing in the enclosure, watched over by their nurses.
Beyond, the scene widened out into the busy life of the Woosung River.

He stopped before the plate-glass window of the English
book shop. His salary would not allow any extra expendi-
tures. At the Mission press he could get the books he actually
needed, and at a discount. He turned resolutely away. Hence-
forth, a missionary's salary was all he could look forward to,
meted out, so much for a single man, so much for a married
one, so much for a married man with children. Growing
ability or growing responsibility would not increase the
amount. As he walked on, he realized as he had not before
what it meant to accustom himself to lifelong economy.

He took a ricksha for the hospital he was bent on seeing,
the best the city had, he had been told. As the ricksha went
on and on, he became perplexed as to his whereabouts. The
broad streets, the high walls, above which he glimpsed now
and then the second story of some Western house, told him
he was in the section of the city occupied by Western business
men. Well, now he was here, he would see it. He paid off his
ricksha and walked along the wide dusty road.

It was good to stretch his legs with no fear of running into
sedan chair or carrying coolie. How cramped and dark the
native streets of the interior city where he lived seemed now!

Occupants of rickshas and carriages glanced at him curiously, even disapprovingly. He began to feel awkward in the presence of his own countrymen. He was conscious that his suit was out of style and that he walked.

There was a clang of metal upon metal. A wrought-iron gate at Peter's right swung back, grating on its hinges. A middle-aged man, followed by a younger, rode forth. Their white hands lay nonchalantly on the arms of their rickshas. They were immaculately dressed. They glanced with disdain at Peter in his dusty shoes, his inexpensive suit.

"These damned missionaries," he heard the elder say. "Always pulling down our prestige."

Peter flushed hotly. Who were these men to show such superiority? He looked at the nameplate on the gate post. Everyone knew that name, for it stood for a fabulous fortune. Merchants of opium, these proud men. A robust anger rose in Peter. Prestige, indeed.

When he had left America, he had not thought of himself as a missionary, but as a doctor who saw in China an undeveloped field for research in certain diseases little known to the Western world. But even on the steamer he had found that all who came to give such service to the Chinese were tabbed as missionaries. At home, a man's religion was a private thing, his own concern, but in this outpost city of the Christian nations, he found it a tag, setting him apart from the other men of his country. Only the Catholic countries, it seemed, had respect for their Christian representatives.

He was puzzled. The money made in some of the very businesses carried on by Americans in China had made it possible for him to come as a doctor to the Chinese. Did business men in America, too, look down on him? Was it because of that enforced poverty of his? Did they think he could not be rich if he chose?

He called a ricksha, retracing his way to the Bund, and at last reached the hospital he sought. It was situated on a street familiar to him in all its details—as like as peas, this and the streets to which he had been accustomed all winter. A white-faced nurse showed him through the wards and at last ushered him into the main office.

The doctor in charge could talk of nothing but his new beds. "I've wanted them for years," he said. "Iron beds that can be kept clean. At last I've got them. The Chinese beds with their filthy cord bottoms are a thing of the past. It's a great step forward."

A lifetime of work, and rejoicing over beds! Peter thought of the deplorable technique he had seen in the hospital.

As he went away, he took oath with himself to hold to the standard he would have kept had he remained in America. He was going in for surgery. There'd be material for the medical journals at home. He'd make a name for himself, even if he were far away from the centers of modern medicine.

He reached Nanking Road, passed the hotel that stood at the corner, loitered for a moment at a flower stall crowded between the hotel and a British department store. Sprays of the *mei hua* with their waxy yellow flowers on bare golden-brown stems stood in glass bottles. Great bunches of English violets lay on the counter.

Two women were haggling with the Chinese flower vendor. As they turned away, empty-handed because they had been unable to lower the man's price, a ragged urchin pulled at the sleeve of one of them, holding up a bunch of violets. He got under the woman's feet as she tried to move forward.

"Twenty cents little money," he urged.

A white man, emerging from a near-by door just then, caught the boy and snatched his violets from him, throwing them into the street. "That'll teach you to bother a white woman."

The women bowed their thanks and passed on.

"A little marred. *Mei yu fatzu,* it cannot be helped," the boy muttered. He picked up the flowers and accosted another passer-by.

The scent of the violets reached Peter's nostrils. Diana

stood as a vision before him. He wished he could give her this great bunch of flowers. They'd die long before he had completed the canal trip back to the interior city. The boy was now offering them for fifteen cents. In America, they'd be too expensive for any but the rich. Impulsively, he bought them, went his way, holding the great bunch of violets, hugging the illusion of riches the flowers gave him. Lovely sensation!

In this plot of land where the Western nations held sway, wealth was not only desirable, but a mark of a man's ability. To strive for it is the normal thing, he thought, as he watched the well-dressed men and women who rode by him in rickshas and smart victorias pulled by fast-stepping Mongolian ponies.

III

Diana Moreland rose from her desk, cramped with the cold. These April days, even today with its sunshine, left the Chinese house which did duty as her school, damp and chill. The high compound wall that shut out any curious eye, stood close to the building. The latticed doors were pushed back, leaving the rooms open to the four-foot-wide court, but it gave forth only the dampness of past rains. The sun shone here only for a half-hour at noon.

She was annoyed with herself. Why had she told Dr. Fraser that he might call this afternoon? It had meant complications in the household and explanations to the other women. She was tired. It had been a hard day in the school. She thought with perplexity of the new girl.

Wearily she stepped through the doorway in the wall and out into the compound adjoining. The sun was here. An eager thrill ran through her. If she were to be ready when the young doctor came, she must hurry. She'd put on that silk dress she had brought with her from home three years ago. It was getting old, but the lace at neck and sleeves she liked for its delicate touch on her skin.

She reached the Single Ladies' house. No one was about. She ran up the stairs and into her room, throwing off her sweater as she went. She got out of her thick wool dress and woolen stockings. Some stolidity of her body fell away with the heavy garments. Her senses sharpened. She thought with pleasure of the young doctor, of his long, angular frame, his red hair that tumbled over his forehead, of the impatient, quick movement of his pointed fingers through it as he tossed it back from his eyes. His keen, judicial eyes . . . his full-lipped, ardent mouth belying them. She felt rebellion against this meager life of the Single Ladies.

For three years she had known the joy of complete absorption in work. First there had been the long, hard struggle for the mind's birth in these Chinese girls who came to her with the dull look of those in whom the mind is in embryo. She had known the triumphant sense of accomplishment when she saw the first stirrings of thought light up their black agate eyes. Breathless, absorbing days followed. The round, moon faces fined down, the thick, fleshy lips strengthened, the flaccid countenances took on elasticity, as thought quickened the flesh.

Again she experienced the joy of the artist as she thought of her highest achievement of all—the widow, Sen S Mo, first of the upper class to come to her school.

The disciplined woman of such intense effort stood away, surveying this other self dressing so eagerly for Dr. Fraser.

"Young unmarried miss," the gateman was addressing her in loud tones from outside the door. "There is a man sitting in the gatehouse who presumes to say he is to be taken to the house of the honorable unmarried mistresses. It seemed wise that I speak to the honorable young miss of the matter."

"Yes," she called out, patiently repeating her command given to her personal servant, Wang Ma, a half-hour before. "It is my wish that you bring the man to my house. Hurry! Do not keep him waiting."

"The honored teacher has spoken. I, her humble servant, will do this strange thing," he mumbled.

Entertain a young man—in these women's quarters! It was not the custom. It confused him, this following of the *tao li,* and not following the *tao li.* Yesterday she had been stern and had almost dismissed him, when she had learned of the note he was carrying to the school. Even a note, she had said, was against the custom. And now she commanded him to bring a man, not a note, to her own quarters. He walked slowly back to the gatehouse, thus delaying the evil as long as possible.

By showing great care in this matter, he believed he had

reinstated himself for the unfortunate affair of yesterday, when almost she had learned of the concubine in her school. He, the humble one, had been too rash in accepting money from the rich man to carry that note to his concubine. *Ai*, it was well that the honorable schoolmistress had seen him in the afternoon with the note, rather than when he came away from the school in the night with the girl herself, or when he had taken her back in the early dawn, after a night's revel with her master.

"How faithful the gateman is," thought Diana, as she gave a last smoothing to her hair. "I wonder if I misjudged him yesterday."

The door to the house of the Single Ladies stood open this spring afternoon of pale sunshine, and the clean frugality of the house struck Peter with its beauty even before he entered. The Ningpo varnished floors shone with a hard, red gleam. One brightly varnished Chinese tea table, flanked by straight chairs, stood against the white wall by the stairs in the hall. In the room to the right was a flat-topped desk, an odd, round-backed Chinese chair on either side. Upon it he noticed a cylindrical holder filled with brushes. He knew from his teacher that the holders of writing brushes were often works of art—all that pertained to the mind was worthy of beauty. Complete satisfaction possessed him as he looked at this one.

Over the empty grate, framed by a plain mantel, hung a Chinese scroll inscribed with bold and beautiful calligraphy. He wondered if this room were Miss Moreland's study. Not much like his, with his untidy heaps of papers, a cheap bamboo brush-holder he had picked up on the street for a few coppers ornamenting his desk. But he had one beautiful thing—the picture of St. Zenobius which he had brought back from Europe.

The gateman led him into the room on the left, tiptoeing ahead, making elaborate effort to leave no mark of his dusty cloth-soled shoes on the floor. A fire had been so newly lighted in the grate that the kindling still kept its natural

color. Smoke billowed up and puffed out into the room—a
cold chimney. How well Peter knew them! In the careful
missionary world, most fires were lighted just before the
guests arrived. As he sat down in one of the wicker chairs
that stood precisely against the wall, he felt a little depressed
by the feminine neatness of the house.

Then he saw Diana Moreland descending the stairs, soft
ruffles of lace at her neck and wrists, and the feeling was gone.
He had never before seen her without her hat. Her dark
brown hair grew straight back from her forehead, lying close
to her head in compact waves, seeming of its own accord to
be gathered together in a knot at the nape of her neck. It
gave her head a classic beauty. She was looking his way, but
seated as he was far back in the room, she did not see him.
With startling vividness he saw her face expressed a deep
privacy of the spirit. That expression had baffled and interested him before—an attribute of very feminine women.
It interested him now.

He was about to rise and go toward her, when he saw a
Chinese woman standing in the open door, and heard Miss
Moreland say, with elaborate politeness, "*Ching*, Sen S Mo,
chin lai. Please, Sen S Mo, come in." Polite refusal, then
polite urging on Diana's part. He was alternately hopeful and
despairing. Suddenly he was interested in the Chinese
woman—the first Chinese lady he had ever seen. The sound
of her name, with the soft slurring of the S into the final
syllable, was beautiful. She must be that widow, from an
official family, who had come to Diana Moreland's school
nearly two years ago. The incident still caused lively conjecture in the small missionary world—conjecture, elation and
gossip over her sudden appearance, her lovely garments, her
lack of money, and her evident separation from her family.

From his corner he studied her. So sophisticated in her
modesty, he thought—knowledge in the expression of her
eyes and mouth, in her dress, too. He sensed it was not
prudery which dictated the high collar giving just a glimpse

of her throat, the sleeves so closely drawn about the wrists, the thin gauze skirt veiling the trousers beneath, below which he caught a glimpse of her tiny, pointed, embroidered shoes. Those shoes the ultimate sophistication, he realized suddenly.

Heretofore, bound feet had seemed to him a deformity, pure and simple, a cruel practice, a symbol of woman's subjection. Those he had seen before had been the ugly, rag-wrapped feet of the poor. Looking at Sen S Mo's silk-clad feet, he realized that behind the custom lay amorous desire—the tiny feet, the swaying gait an achievement in sensual imagination. Shrewdly he began to wonder if the West had not misinterpreted the restrictions of Chinese women—the motive not subjection, but the heightening of contrasts to tease the senses. It crossed his mind that, if this were so, what amusement the Chinese must have at the white man's expense!

Sen S Mo was leaving, backing slowly out of the door with repeated words of farewell.

Diana came toward him. "I'm so sorry," she said. "I've kept you waiting. But Sen S Mo came in to ask me if I would go for a few days this summer to visit her mother."

As she shook hands with him, the delicate structure of her hand accentuating the strength of his, the fineness of her skin contrasting with the masculine quality of his, swept him into splendid excitement.

Just then the doors at the end of the hall opened and the other teachers in the school came in, the one middle-aged, with curious, seeking eyes, the other a neutral kind of creature who seemed neither woman nor man. "Tell us about Shanghai," said one, as soon as they were seated.

"Yes, do!" exclaimed the other.

You could not see a woman alone, it seemed. Diana's eyes met his.

The two, noticing the look which passed between them, sensed that mysterious rushing together of man and woman. They felt themselves rejected. Although by no word or deed would they have declared it, in their hearts they had offered themselves to the young doctor. Excited and wounded, they excused themselves and went away. Diana and Peter could hear rustling sounds in their studies down the hall. The doors had been left open to give propriety to the call.

Peter moved his chair nearer. "It's nice to have you to myself, Diana."

It was long since a man had called her by her given name. It sounded strangely intimate. In this community, so bound by the traditions of another race, a man did not venture lightly upon intimacy. Diana sensed intention on the part of the young doctor.

Peter saw the color rising in her cheeks and the quick flutter of the lace of her gown at the throat and where it lay crossed above her breast. Neither spoke. Burning, throbbing through her went an impulse answering the impulse in Peter.

With a quick movement, she rose and picked up her knitting from the table. What had made her surrender like this, at the attention of a man almost a stranger to her? Some inviolate self she had always possessed when other men courted her, was touched. Some dark, imperious self frightened her with its desires—desires which threatened the lovely achievement of her work. She drew back. Deliberately she set her mind on the perplexities of the day. The new girl, neither like the other schoolgirls nor like the widow, Sen S Mo. A kind of insolent superiority, an amorous sophistication about her, which made Diana feel like a child. In fact all these girls seemed more experienced than she.

Immediately sensitive to her inattention, Peter sought some way to bridge the growing separateness of their two selves. "I'm to take Dr. Buchanan's place next fall," he began. "It's rather a big undertaking, with so little knowledge of the language."

"Yes, it is," she answered. "But you've got Stella Perkins to help you. There's hardly anyone here, including the English bishop, who speaks Chinese as fluently as she."

The way she spoke of Stella Perkins carried to him, in

some indefinable way, her withdrawal from him. A wave of homesickness, which had been threatening him ever since his return from Shanghai, engulfed him. To be back in the normal world of affairs! Life filled with ambition, fame, honor, and love. Yes, love, not this thin substance that remained to the white man in this sex-conscious civilization, where a man neither embraced the Chinese idea of women's place in the universe, nor kept his own. He left soon.

After a few days his interest in Diana, still so delicate a thing, passed from him, leaving him with a vague sense of relief, as if he had been delivered from a relationship beautiful but binding.

IV

THE spring was far advanced. The expectancy of April, with
its ecstatic moment of conception, had changed into the long
days of the growth of life. The faint green buds of the weeping willows had burgeoned to a darker green, clothing the
trailing branches. Fresh clods of earth with which men at
the spring solstice had tipped the grave mounds, had been
blended by the rain with the old earth. Seeds of rice and
opium buried in the quickening womb of the soil, had alike
taken on life. The black waters of the rice paddies were
pricked with green. In the rich bottom land, the infinitesimal
seeds of the poppy had put forth their shoots.

The Chinese, mystified and reverent before the earth satu-
rate with life, felt it indwelt with spirits. Water, trees, and
every growing thing, had spirits. Man endeavored in each
act of his life to bring concord between himself, the sun, moon,
and the planets. Whether he ate or drank or tilled the fields
or spun the silk, there was the ghostly sanction of spirits to
be gained, that he might dwell in harmony with the universe.

More important than all were the spirits of the dead ancestors overlying the living, ever present in Heaven and Earth.
Each man defied the menace of cold and hunger to his own
body, that this not far distant family of spirits might not go
hungry and cold. So did each man take upon himself the
double burden, security for the living and security for the
dead—food, clothing, and money.

It was the fourth month, the Peony Moon, brave flower
of the vital principle, man. Beyond the city, at the Temple
of Spiritual Peace, the huge iron cauldron standing on its tripod in the open court, sent forth thin spirals of smoke from
the hot and heavy ashes of yesterday's offering. The tin
which silvered the spirit money was an unburned residue,

41

weighting the ashes so that smoke could escape only with difficulty in little jets.

As the sun rose higher, the flow of pilgrims through the entrance gate began. Flames leaped up in the cauldron. Beyond the uncurtained door in the dim hall of the temple, incense and burning tapers stood. A great bell tolled unceasingly. A god brought to China centuries ago from India was to be worshiped. The Lord God Buddha, worshiped with ritual, candles and incense, bells, drums, and chanting.

Mrs. Baker was giving a picnic—as farewell for Dr. Buchanan who was soon to leave for America. In all this great, rich floor of the coastal province, there was no bit of woodland, no unused field, except within the temple enclosures. Only the temple grounds and the graves escaped the peasants' careful tilling. The missionaries thought necessity was their reason for going to the temples, not recognizing that the color, the movement, the searching spirit abroad, drew them like moths to a flame. Only Miss Dyer, with whom Stella lived, had no use for temples.

As Peter looked from his window and saw the chair-men gathering below, and Mrs. Baker going out and in with baskets of food and bottles of drinking water, he felt a lighter mood than usual abroad in the compound, and he felt himself touched with vagrancy. The winter had been a rainy one. He had not yet made the day's journey to this ancient temple in the hills which he could see from his window far off on the blue horizon.

Since his appointment to the hospital, the compound had become his world—the arena for his achievements. Ordered and neat it looked, cut by flagged paths. The hospital and Dr. Buchanan's house, both soon to be his, confronted him from across the way. To his right, close at hand, he could see Mr. Berger's house and the boys' school, to the left, beyond a wall, the upper story of the women's building.

Below him was growing commotion. The chair-men had

slipped their poles through rings beneath the arms of wicker chairs, which the foreigners used in place of the box-like native sedans, and were deftly twisting cord back and forth like a cat's cradle, fastening yokes to the poles' ends. As they worked, they chattered of the queer creatures they were to carry. Mrs. Berger and the *amah* lifted the children into the seats built in deep wicker baskets. Mrs. Berger's fluttering, excited voice, speaking a queer, clipped Chinese that set the chair-men to mimicking her, mingled with the *amah's* and the children's fast-flowing words.

Peter watched his world gather—Mr. Berger come from the boys' school, Mr. Baker and Dr. Buchanan from the hospital. The women were already seated in their chairs. As Dr. Buchanan settled into his, the coolies tucked a rug gently over his knees. This action, seen many times by Peter, surprised and fascinated him anew. These pack animals of men, assuming suddenly the rôle of courteous gentlemen! With groans and grunts the men hoisted the chairs to their shoulders, and a coolie balanced the baskets, one containing the children, the other the lunch, on the ends of his carrying pole.

"Peter," called Mrs. Baker. "Where's Stella?" she asked as he came down.

"Walking with us. We're to pick her up at her children's clinic," said Peter.

The cavalcade moved slowly through the early morning life of the city. Tubs of fish and baskets of vegetables narrowed the narrow streets. To Peter's eyes, it was a great, grey city of the poor and downtrodden. Old customs, old habits held the people to a rigid pattern. Sons followed fathers who had followed grandfathers and great-grandfathers in the same trade, creating without creative flair. Everywhere, over the rigidity of age and poverty, sickness lay like a pall.

They reached a narrow corridor, the backs of shops on one side, the city wall bulking high on the other. Once this space had been the inner moat. But gradually, through the centuries, it had become a marsh, and then firm earth. They passed through the wall's inner gate. Deftly the chair-men made a swing to the left and passed through the outer gate.

"I wonder why they didn't build their gates in a line," said Peter.

"Another Chinese superstition," answered Mr. Baker. "Protect the city from evil spirits—they have to go in a straight line."

The cries of the bearers ceased abruptly. Peter looked up. Before him lay the still surface of a lake, fairy green causeways spanning it. Boats hung above their own reflections, and exquisitely arched bridges completed themselves in their reflected half-arch. That all this beauty had lain here just beyond the city wall and the close-packed, seething streets! It gave Peter something of the sensation he had had when the shabby coolies took on courtesy and gentleness. Some ancient, beautiful culture, gathering its waning vitality together, seemed to thrust its leaping fire through the crust of sterile decay.

The party was crossing one of the causeways now. On each side, the willow branches touched the water, swaying and dipping, like elaborate maidens caressing their own images. Berger stopped in rapt contemplation of them.

"You know, Fraser," he said, turning to Peter, "I've always thought the men acting women's parts in Chinese plays made unnatural, exotic gestures. Now I see they're natural. Look at that willow branch. That's where they got their swaying movement of the hands."

Peter felt a new interest in Berger. When had he escaped the strict missionary world long enough to attend Chinese plays?

They reached the end of the causeway. The dark brick core of a pagoda, long since shorn of its roofed galleries, cut into the landscape with strength and force, relic of a creative imagination now impotent.

Although Peter walked among the men, he did not join their talk. After a little, he dropped behind. Walking apart, he felt a high, lonely happiness. Occasionally he looked back to see if Stella were keeping up with them. She had dropped the restraint of the compound, for he could hear her singing softly to herself, and her face was alight. With each mile, her delight in the day seemed to grow. As he looked more and more often at her tiny figure, he felt his high, lonely happiness inadequate. The day held some undefined longing. . . .

They were in a fold of the hills. It was nearing noon. Widows' arches cast their narrow shadows straight down, fitting themselves to the steep sides of the dyke along which the path led. Suddenly there was the wail of beggars, and a stifled shriek from Mrs. Berger, as if wrung from her against her will. A leper, eaten with the dread disease, leaped in the path, thrusting his begging bowl almost in Peter's face.

"We're nearing the temple," called Mrs. Baker, turning in her chair to instruct Peter. "Beggars always collect here."

As if out of the ground, a host of beggars appeared, hopping on the path, crying, "Do good! Do good! Attain merit!" The sightless, the crippled, too broken with disease to rise, lay by the roadside, their begging bowls beside them, crying, "Do good! Do good!" Clothed in filthy rags, a child, hardly able to hold the bowl in its claw-like hands, lifted it on bony sticks of arms, beseeching Peter.

In spite of Mrs. Baker's high-pitched commands to give nothing, Peter emptied his pockets. The filthy crowd besieged him, clogged his way, ran at him from behind, ahead. Then, as suddenly as they had sprung up, they fell back. The party had reached the temple gates.

"What did I tell you?" said Mrs. Baker, getting out of her chair. "You shouldn't have given to them, Peter. It only makes them worse."

Still too shaken by that burst of misery, Peter did not answer, walking silently between the tall cryptomeria and camphor trees. He hardly saw the booths filled with things for use at the temple under the lee of a pink wall at his right, or the grotto and a running stream to his left.

Like some great army, the pilgrims moved forward, as if pulled by a magnet, up the steps, into the entrance hall, Peter and his friends with them. Around the central god, the crowd divided itself, moving to the right, to the left, placing incense before all manner of ugly and beautiful beings.

"Come and see them making their gods," urged Mr. Baker. "Imagine believing in a god you can make yourself."

"They've not only got clay feet, they're all clay," said Mr. Berger, amused at his own jest.

"Your god is made in your own image," said Stella, coming out of her absorption in the scene around her, and then returning into it, apparently not noticing the consternation created by her remark.

"Take me about," Peter begged her, confused by the moods of those around him.

"Here's the Goddess of Mercy. Isn't her name lovely? 'Hearer of the World's Cries.' And here's Ti Ts'ang, who takes special delight in delivering people out of purgatory. I'm quite fond of him," said Stella, as she separated Peter from the others, leading him about the entrance temple.

"What mummery!" he said at last.

"Not altogether," she answered. "It's all so human—the way they seek protection from pain."

"Why, Stella!" exclaimed Peter.

"Don't talk like the Bakers," she said, "as if all other religions but our own were pure evil. It's all right for *them*— they're old. But you, Peter, belong to this century. Don't be smug about the things of the spirit." Then, noticing the discomfiture of his expression, she added more gently, "Come. I'll show you Buddha."

As they stepped over the sill of the doorway from the grey cold of the outer temple into sunshine, Peter knew only that he and Stella stood there together, that together they made the three steps down to the stone-paved open space. The pilgrims were eddying around them, going toward the main temple, their bright yellow knapsacks catching the sun. High,

high above them, the blue sky, and all things reaching up to it—the temple roof with its curving upward fling, the encircling mountains with their upward thrust, a great iron tripod flinging smoke and flame upward, a deep-toned bell sending its sound toward heaven. Strong and deep, floating far off, touching the hills, coming back, like circles in a pool into which a stone has been dropped, the sound circled higher, filling the sky. Strong and deep, the bell tolled again.

On with Stella, up the temple steps with the pilgrims— women come to ask a son, men seeking help in divination, children riding piggy-back to the Buddha's feet to make their first bow of adoration, nuns with their yellow robes gleaming in the sun. Over the raised sill of the central doorway, high above the praying, beseeching crowd, the flaring candles, out of incense swam a great golden face. It was the Buddha, seated upon a golden lotus in untroubled golden calm. Some strange bliss of negation emanated from the placid lips, the downcast eyes. Nirvana—the blowing out of the flame called man, extinction of all that bore the character of life! Nirvana! Peter felt stubborn resistance, and then, discouragement. How could he teach people who worshiped that retreating spirit to thrust themselves into struggle, to investigate disease?

In the dim recesses of a temple guest room, Mrs. Baker spread a blue and white cloth over two square Chinese tables placed together. Out of the picnic basket she took sandwiches and cold chicken. A priest brought them tea in a cracked teapot, its wide spout brown with the testimony of many pourings.

Held almost against their wills by the color, the scent and the sound in the courts, the party gathered slowly, taking their places on benches around the long table, Dr. Buchanan in the seat of honor. Frail and old, he rose a little uncertainly to offer a blessing. But his quiet, serene voice filled the room, stilling even the curious Chinese, who crowded through doors and windows, closer and closer to the table.

"This third year of the new century has brought us peace. All thy children have lived together in peace. Teach us to forgive the year of persecution. It is the turn of the century."

When Peter looked up, he saw written in the faces around the table passions hidden from his sight until now—hate and fear, love and exaltation. Never before had he realized what the Boxer year had meant to this community. He had understood that nothing had happened here in this southern city. Now he saw that the persecution of other communities, and the months of suspense and uncertainty, had had their effect upon these people, even though none of their number had been killed.

He understood the frightened muffled cry of Mrs. Berger when the beggars flocked around her. Heretofore, he had thought of her as ineffectual. He saw that she was brave— a timid woman each day conquering her fear. Berger's eyes were lowered, his cheeks bright with an angry flush. Mr. Baker's eyes seemed to bore into him with a fierce scorn. What was hidden between these two?

He glanced at Stella. He was transfixed by her tragic expression of suffering . . . suffering held back by some terrible pride. He lowered his own eyes. Could it be that Stella . . . ? Stella had not always been in the city. She had come from a remote town where the fanatical outburst of the Secret Societies had risen to a fury of persecution. He had heard what had happened to some of the women. Could it be that Stella . . . ? Too horrible to contemplate. . . . Yet she nursed the sick of this country with unremitting care, with matchless compassion.

When Peter dared to look her way again, she had taken the Bergers' little boy, Timothy, on her lap, and was quietly helping him to feed himself. Only her trembling hands betrayed her emotion.

Night was settling down. The pilgrims and the picnic party had long since left. The trees stood dark on the slope behind

the temple roofs. From the hot and heavy ashes in the three-
legged cauldron, smoke rose in unwavering grey spirals, un-
shaken in its ascent by any stir of air. A grey hush lay over
the enclosure. Grey-robed priests moved without noise along
the verandas of the temple, advancing upon the central hall.
A visiting priest sat in the classic Buddha pose on a grey stone
lotus in the court. Moment after moment he held the attitude
of meditation. Within the temple, the everburning flame before
the great Buddha made a blot of yellow light—the only color.
The candles and incense had been snuffed out at the going of
the pilgrims, and carefully put away to be sold again.

The Sen family's long line of chairs entered the avenue of
cryptomerias, stopped at the outer temple.

The child, Sen Lo Shih, precious only son, walked with his
grandmother, as reverent in attitude as she, gravely making
his obeisance before the holy Buddha. His father had told him
that the Superior Man does not believe in gods. Confucius
teaches that all knowledge is within the breast of the Superior
Man, but for the women and the ignorant, there is this image.
But the men do not disparage this lesser faith of the women
and the *hsaio ren,* the little men.

"And," he had added, "I, too, find it well to revere Buddha,
lest, after all, he be a god."

So on the prayer mats, Sen Lo Shih and his father knelt
with the women.

In an upper prayer hall, near the private room of the abbot,
masses for the child's grandfather were being said. Twenty
thousand dollars had been spent by the Sen family. Besides
enriching the coffers of the priests, the money had given the
scene every beauty, every extravagant display.

Sen Lo Shih, in the midst of his people, watched gravely,
at first without emotion, the three priests in their gorgeous
and brilliant robes, sitting cross-legged, representing the triune
Buddha. But bit by bit he froze with terror as the chant told
him of the hungering, thirsting souls flitting through the
underworld.

The monks' supple fingers took on the agonies of those passing through the torments and terrors of hell. Those twisted, writhing hands became human forms—they were the bound, the tortured, the savage. They became fiendish tongues of fire. They shaped themselves into ice-cold rain. They moved portraying ever subtler forms of torture. The flickering fingers became man given over in abandonment to brutality, to endless transmigrations, coming back again and again to pain on the wheel of life.

The members of the Sen family were pale. Drops of sweat stood on their foreheads. Unbearable, almost, the agony, when the writhing fingers began taking on benign shapes, sprinkling water from the jar of the compassionate Goddess of Mercy, rice from the bowl of Sakyamuni. The filling of the hungry mouths of the dead had begun.

Sen Lo Shih in that evening tasted the torments of his dead and the bliss of their redemption, knew himself as their final hope in conducting them across the sea of hunger, thirst, and torment.

Twice now had he waited upon the ancestors—here at the temple and at their graves.

Throughout the service, Scholar Sen, lost in reverie, contemplated the Buddhist philosophy—the perpetual growth into decay of the universe, the universe produced by the thoughts of desire. Life an evil illusion to be escaped. Nirvana. The blowing out of the flame called man.

Outside the gates of the temple, the sick beggars, caught on the wheel of Karma, slept in their mat huts.

In the city, the air was stifling. Peter Fraser woke. The night was far advanced, he knew, without looking at his watch, for the noises of the city had died down. Only the pound of the presses hammering out spirit money, and the bark of wolf-like dogs roaming in packs, two sounds that never ceased. Far off, the deep note of a temple bell rose and fell.

Out of the scenes of the day, Stella's face came before him. He was filled with pity for her, and then he almost felt her presence in the room, proudly refusing his pity.   One did not pity a woman like Stella.   Profound respect took its place.

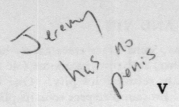

V

As THE summer heat settled upon the city, family by family the white people left for the hills. The schools and the churches were closed. In the hospital, Dr. Buchanan, Stella, and Peter were to take turns—Stella, Dr. Buchanan had said, would alternate with him during July and August. Peter was to be in charge during June.

June was the *Mei T'ien*, "rain a little each day." Through the veils of heated mist rising from the rice fields soaked with water, the sun sent its pale, hot rays, and each afternoon rain fell, coming down with a slow heavy movement, as if making its way with difficulty through the resisting moist blanket of air. The hospital was hot and dank. Fungus grew in neglected corners. Although there was no epidemic of cholera such as often swept the city in the summer, the wards were overcrowded.

The month was over, and Peter was on his way to the summer resort. This morning Dr. Buchanan had relieved him of his duties. Each labored step of the chair-men up the mountainside gave him cooler, drier air to breathe. For the first time in weeks, his skin was cleansed of the moist heat of the lowlands. The cool air flowed down upon him. His chair tipped backward as they ascended allowed him to look straight up into the blue sky. He felt a new rush of energy, and with it a sudden realization of his power. In the fall he would be master in his own right—have the hospital for his own.

As the bearers swung the chair outward to avoid a jutting rock, Peter found himself looking down upon the plain lying far below him. He was startled at the sudden vision of the important dead. Everywhere the graves broke up the luxuriant, growing rice. Like the dwellings of gophers enlarged

52

many times, the grave mounds rose out of the meticulously cultivated paddies. Strong and vigorous grave trees thrust their triumphant tops above the level fields of the living. The mere amount of space the dead occupied drove home their importance. He had forgotten them of late, in his absorption in the living.

The mountain's ascent grew more abrupt. The green trunks of bamboos hemmed him in. Cool, green light filtered through their branches. Suddenly Peter realized how tired he was—more tired than he had ever been in his life. He stretched out his legs, his heels on the edge of the sedan's footrest.

The way grew steeper. The bearers broke step in order to lessen the strain. In a small pavilion erected over the path, they set his chair down, mopped their steaming bodies with cloths already soaked with grime and sweat. Their over-developed leg muscles and chests told their tale. Peter decided to walk the rest of the steep climb.

And so they came to the main street of the mountain village, the stronghold of the Christian people—a Christian town owned by them, administered by them. No foreign business man could buy land outside the treaty ports, but missionaries could. The Chinese had granted this right to them, after Christendom's victory in the war fought in the interests of trade and the legalizing of opium.

The chair-men trotted along quickly now, like horses who know their stable is just ahead. Another ten minutes, and Peter was at the cottage of the young men of the Mission, the members of which were here from all over Central China. The place seemed deserted. Peter knocked vigorously. The chair-men ran around to the back, calling *"Hsiao I Sheng lai."* Peter knocked again. At last, a Chinese servant, his black eyes blinking as if he had just roused from sleep, came to the door. "Young medicine man who is expected, enter," he said.

His feet made a shuffling sound, as, with his slippers off at the heel, he walked ahead, leading Peter to a tiny room at the end of a long hall.

From its window he saw the green folds of the hills, the roofs of the cottages below. He could hear water somewhere trickling over rocks.

He was eager to see the town, the people. Picking up his tennis racket, he went out. He saw Stella standing on the veranda of the Single Women's house, as somehow he had suspected he might. It seemed natural that Stella should be waiting for him. He had seen a great deal of her at the hospital before she had gone on vacation.

She had given up the strict rule of dress adopted by the missionary women—high neck, long sleeves, after the Chinese custom. Her wrists and arms, as she leaned her hands on the railing, were small-boned and graceful. "She is beautifully proportioned," he thought.

As he looked at her small white-clad figure, set in the frame of the green hill, he suddenly realized that she was young. Always before he had considered her much older than himself, but now he knew that she was not. He had thought of her so because of her lock of white hair. Almost theatrical, the pure white line lying across the heavy masses of black looked today, with the sun shining on it, and the youth that this morning was in her face.

"Hello," he called out. "You're looking fine. Do you feel up to a game?"

"Yes. I'll come along, but I'm not in your class."

They walked together down the mountain path toward the grey cement squares of the tennis courts, which they could see below, set round with clumps of bamboo. There was some unresolved disharmony in Peter that always quieted to Stella's presence. He looked down upon her now, feeling that stilling of his spirit.

"Hospital all right?" she asked.

Her casual question seemed to take for granted his month in the disease-infested, stifling city.

"I've worked hard, Stella. It's been hot—unusually so, the Chinese say." He spoke protestingly.

"Yes, it has," she answered. "I never can be quite clear about it," she added, after a little pause, "our work, I mean . . . whether to write it in capitals or just small letters."

His sense of importance oozed away from him. She seemed always to demand some discipline of him for which he was not ready.

Looking into his eyes, Stella saw too late what she had done— widened the distance between them which today she had meant to close. She had spoken impulsively, when she saw he had discovered his power. He might consider power a fine thing. She knew it was not. Here in this group of white people, she had seen it fill men's lives, shutting them off from any deep human contact with the people. It would be a pity if Peter should lose that touch he had with the Chinese. Suddenly she realized that it was not for this reason she had spoken as she had. When he was with her, an unreasoned necessity rose within her to wound him if she could, in order to fend him off.

After the first set, Stella introduced him to a group of men, then slipped away. At noon, he went with the other men to buy tennis balls at the general store and post office, where, at this hour of the day, everyone came for mail.

As he looked around, Peter sensed an atmosphere of ease that he had never before experienced in the Mission community. Evidently Chinese customs were not kept up here, for the unmarried men and women were coming and going quite naturally together. Most of the women, like Stella, had given up the severe custom of dress. He saw Diana Moreland in a very becoming native blue linen with V-shaped neck and short sleeves. As he made his way across the store to speak to her, he passed Stella.

Stella sensed that she could have held him with a look, but she was powerless to give it. Instead, she let him go to Diana Moreland, watching the quick exchange of understanding in their eyes, clear, untouched by suffering. Then she went out, hurrying along the empty village street. If only she did not meet anyone! She struck into a lonely mountain path.

Her long-fought-for self-control was gone. She loved Peter . . . yet when he came near her, he was a horror to her. The agony and shame of the night in the camp of the Boxers she knew now were ineradicable. She wept.

Abrupt as birth, Peter's interest in Diana passed into love. While he stood talking to her, the innate caution of man before something antagonistic to him in woman was sundered. The incredible loveliness of Diana swept over him. As he went out of the store at her side, the village street, the mountains, the sunshine, were dowered with her beauty. Waterfalls, trees, held the spirit of Diana.

For Peter the days of the long summer were so heightened in reality that they partook of the quality of a dream. In a bamboo grove, they went often to sit in a hollowed place in the earth's surface. Between the green trunks, straight as Doric columns, the sun slanted, touching Diana's hair, the shimmering folds of her dress. Her eyes darkened with excessive inner light, about her mouth mysterious light. A Diana transfigured. His hand locked in hers spoke to him of what Diana yielded to him would be. And yet he delayed to ask her to marry him, fearful that he destroy his happiness. The summer advanced. The time for his return to the hospital drew nearer.

"Diana," he said softly one day. "Diana, you're like a goddess. Strange, though, you should have been named after one."

"And you, Peter—how are you named?" She looked into his ardent eyes, laughter and tenderness in her own. She leaned forward, brushing his unruly bright hair from his forehead.

With a quick, impulsive movement, he clasped her in his arms. She yielded her lips to his. He felt acquiescence suppling her body.

Finally she pushed him away.

"When can we be married, dear?" he asked.

"Married! Oh, Peter! Isn't it enough for you now that I love you?"

"No," he answered. "I need you now."

She hesitated. He sensed her withdrawal.

"You don't love me as I love you," said Peter.

"I do, but—— Your life will go on just the same whether you marry or not. It's my life that is going to be changed. And," she added, honestly, "I want my own life just now."

"I'd let you have it. I've no desire to narrow your life down to me alone," he said soberly.

Diana did not speak for a long time. Finally she said, "I can't answer so soon, Peter."

"But you're going away tomorrow."

"I'm not going far. Sen S Mo's clan lives at the base of the mountain, you know, and I'm invited for only a few days. I'll tell you when I get back. Wouldn't that do?"

"I guess it will have to," he answered, a little ruefully.

Late that afternoon, after he left her at her cottage, he went along the path to his own. Stella stood on the veranda of the Single Ladies' house, just as she had stood the first morning of his vacation. He had forgotten that today she returned from her month at the hospital.

"Come up, if you have a few minutes," she called out to him.

"Everything fine at the hospital?" he called back.

"Yes."

"Well, if everything's all right, I'll wait till another time, I guess."

He saw the look that passed across her face, but in his delight over Diana's love and the possibility that she would marry him soon, he did not realize that he had wounded Stella with his indifference.

In a flash of intuition, Stella knew that the time had passed when she might have had Peter, that she could not stay him as she might have that morning of his arrival at the mountain.   At the same moment that his indifference stung her, it took away her horror of him.   Now she reached out to him in terrible need.

VI

EARLY the next day, Diana took chair for the wayside pavilion where she was to meet Sen S Mo. All summer she had looked forward to the experience of visiting a Chinese family of high degree. But today she did not find herself eager for the journey. As she rode down the mountain, she was of two minds, one that wanted to go forward, one that wanted to go back and be always with Peter. The old, self-regulated Diana was gone—her former unity of self was no longer hers. If she only knew what she wanted to do!

But as she came to the low land with its familiar devitalizing heat, her languor was too great for her to wrestle with her two selves. She began wondering why Sen S Mo had wanted her to visit in her home. Of her husband's clan, Sen S Mo had never spoken, of her own but seldom. In the two years she had been at the school, she had never left it, spending even the summers in the deserted building. Was there some special reason that on her return to her family, she should ask a foreigner to go with her?

Just ahead, Diana could see a native chair standing within a tile-roofed pavilion. On the stone benches along the sides, coolies were lounging. That must be Sen S Mo's chair. Yes, she could hear the men call out, "*Wai kuo ren lai*, foreign one comes."

Her open chair was brought to rest by the closed one. As the front curtain was lowered from within, she thought she detected the slightest bit of disapproval in Sen S Mo's eyes. She supposed it was because of her curtainless chair. She realized too late that for Sen S Mo's sake she should have conformed to the custom and ridden in a closed one, on this visit to Sen S Mo's clan.

They skirted the base of the mountain, coming very soon to

59

a town.   Like a tunnel the street burrowed its way between massed shops.   Above was a roof of bamboo poles over which green boughs had been placed.   Diana enjoyed the open chair, for it allowed the cool, damp air rising from the wet paving stones to reach her, refreshing her skin, parched by the blinding glare of the treeless plain.   And then she was conscious that the men filling the crowded street had stopped to stare at her.   She lowered her head, realizing suddenly that in their eyes she was simply a female divested of the mystery of seclusion.   She had an unhappy moment of self-distrust.   Did she appear to lack modesty even in the eyes of Sen S Mo?

At the lead-coolie's tap, a black gate opened to them.   The two chairs were set down in a small court.   High, whitewashed walls surrounded them.   As the fat, comfortable gateman swung shut the gate, Diana saw over it, painted on the white wall, the *yin yang* symbol, the principles of life, *yin*, black, *yang*, white, each carrying within itself the essence of the other, each shaped to the other.

The gateman, clasping his two hands, bowed to Sen S Mo, eyed Diana with curiosity.   The place was very still.   But Diana felt enormous activity seething under the atmosphere of withdrawal and aloofness.   Sen S Mo took her hand, led her from empty court to empty court, over doorsill after doorsill, and at last into a room in one of the inner courts.   A curtained bed stood against the back wall, a square table and two chairs under the latticed window.

Although Sen S Mo went away, leaving her to wash and change after the hot ride, there was no privacy for her.   Women in trousers and coats, teetering on bound feet, seemed to spring up everywhere.   The bamboo curtain hanging in the doorway was continually lifted—a maid servant brought hot water, another, steaming towels, and other, simply idle women had no mission, evidently, but to observe her.

The hours of the day moved slowly forward.   Sen S Mo came often to ask if she were comfortable; the little creatures splitting tiny watermelon seeds with their strong white teeth chattered to her, fingered her, lifted her skirts to see her big feet, felt the strange fabric of her stockings, her shoes. Late in the afternoon, Sen S Mo entered with an *amah* bearing a steaming bowl of dumplings made from lotus roots. And later still, Sen S Mo brought her tea, "going-to-bed" tea, that quieted the nerves, she said.

Filled with sheer boredom, Diana went to bed early in the carved bed that was a room in itself once the curtains were drawn around it, saying to herself, "Tomorrow, I'll write to Peter, telling him of my safe arrival."

But in the morning she seemed paralyzed against any activity, even the writing of a letter. Idleness settled upon her.

Bit by bit she learned the life of the women's courts. She asked who the unhappy-looking older woman was, who came with the others.

A flippant young thing answered, "The head wife of the eldest son. She cannot bear sons. It is I who have borne him the son." She laughed, looking scornfully at the other. "Didst thou hear him pass thy door last night?"

Each time Diana saw Sen S Mo, she appeared to be less like the Sen S Mo of the school, more like these women of her clan. Although her friend did not tell her in so many words, Diana came to know that every pressure of the family was being used to force Sen S Mo to return to her dead husband's household. From her few low words, spoken from time to time, Diana glimpsed a little the magnitude of the Chinese woman's rebellion in refusing her duties as widow. And now she knew why she had been brought here. Sen S Mo gained strength from her presence.

As Sen S Mo sat with her one evening, Diana questioned her a little. "When you were a girl, Sen S Mo, did you live in this very house?"

"Yes. For seven generations my family has lived here, although we are Ningpo people." She took into her lap a child of ten. "I was always rebellious. This little girl is not. I used to take the bandages off my feet when they were first bound, and once I bribed an old servant to buy me paper and tools to make lotus lanterns for the lantern festival. I begged them to let me study with my brothers and cousins. They did, for a time. My father was proud of my poetry and my mother of my embroidery."

On the third day, Sen S Mo did not come until late, and then she spoke hurriedly. "My mother, the senior woman, desires to greet you."

Diana wondered, as she went with Sen S Mo. Had it been hard to win the head lady's consent for the foreign one to come into her presence?

The room they entered held a dozen women. By the latticed window sat Sen S Mo's mother, the matriarch of the clan, perfect in her conformity to pattern—shining black hair and nape knot, rice-powdered cheeks and serenity. If there had been struggle between Sen S Mo and this woman, there was no outward sign. Neither could Diana guess how the head lady felt toward her own presence in the household. Never, she thought, had she seen such serenity. And then, all at once, she knew the woman was vital to her finger tips. She had vitality enough to run an empire.

"Please, great teacher, sit, *chin dzo, chin dzo,*" the matriarch addressed her, ushering her to a round table set in the center of the room.

"I am not worthy . . . a lower seat," Diana murmured, knowing that, according to Chinese etiquette, she should demur. Finally she was seated, just as she would have been if they had taken their places immediately.

The feast began. The matriarch, when each new dish was brought, put her own chopsticks into it, taking out the choicest morsels and placing them on Diana's plate. The women talked little while they ate. Their sensuous enjoyment of the savory food engrossed them. But at last the *amahs* brought bowls piled high with rice, and passed hot towels. The women began talking among themselves.

Sen S Mo asked Diana if she would not like to walk about

the head lady's apartments. At her assent, they all rose, flocking around her. The room they entered adjoined the one where they had feasted, separated from it by a thin partition. It was two *jen* wide—two of the seven-foot wide spaces between rafter beams. A huge bed set against the wall, housed within a carved canopy, all but filled the room.

"Please enter," invited the owner and, taking Diana's hand, she led her within. A little wearily Diana whipped up her interest. A lacquered commode stood beside the bed. Trying to show polite curiosity, after the Eastern custom, Diana asked, "One sits here to dress?"

"To be delivered of children," answered the matriarch, and lifted the cover to explain the use.

Into these two rooms, thought Diana, the powerful head woman's life has been compressed. Here she has lived, here she will die, fulfilling her function. As she looked at this woman, she saw that the black, half-closed eyes gave no hint of spirit within. Her lips, as they settled into calm after speaking, were bare of any dreams that falsified the utilitarian issues of life. Diana thought she understood now why the Chinese were called a practical people. Materialism had here become the very vesture of the home. All that she had seen since she had come was intensified into meaning—the fleshy, flabby faces of the older women, the idleness, the children's frank acceptance of woman's relation to man.

Diana, product of the Christian tradition, with its emphasis on woman's high place, its sublimation of the physical, was revolted by what seemed to her dark, rushing forces, binding women to the physical. All the virginal innate in woman, intensified by that existence in the house of the Single Ladies, was roused. She must get back to the clean chastity of her own way of life, with its personal effort. Strenuous hard work was a cleansing fire. She shut her eyes for a moment, blotting out the matriarch and Sen S Mo. Her room at the Mission, its polished floors, its white walls, her dresser with its simple accessories, her iron bed with its white counterpane, rose before her—the door shut and locked against intruders.

Peter! She could not marry Peter. All marriage partook of the materiality she saw here, submission to physical purpose its core. She could not wait to free herself from him. As soon as she was back in the guest court, she dragged out pen and paper from her luggage, and wrote him, definitely refusing to marry him not only now, but ever.

In the night, Diana was awakened by such angry, furious voices as she had never before heard. She had been told that this serene race was subject to such outbursts. Could it be the head lady and Sen S Mo? Was it over Sen S Mo's departure with her on the morrow? Diana shuddered, drew the curtains of her bed closer, frantically trying to shut out the animal-like cries of the women echoing in the silent court.

The next morning as she finished her packing, she was again summoned to the apartment of the matriarch. Outside in a passageway, a table was spread and the children of the household were sitting about it on stools, bowls of soft boiled rice held to their mouths. Here each day they came for their morning meal, the daughter-in-law who accompanied Diana said, to be under the practiced eye of the matriarch.

"Foreign one comes!" shouted an *amah*, standing near the matriarch, who was seated at one end of the table. On her lap was a fat little boy, naked except for a square of flowered cloth fastened cornerwise over his chest and stomach. As Diana approached, she rose, giving the child to an *amah* hovering near. For a moment, the head lady's hand lay against his back, like the ribs of a fan, the long pointed finger nails reaching to the child's shoulders. She bent over him, nuzzling her head in the fat creases of his neck, before she turned to Diana.

When they were within the matriarch's room, again there was polite urging over the matter of where Diana should sit, but at last they were seated in the places decreed by custom for hostess and guest.

"That so honored a guest should leave without the attendance of my humble daughter is a disgrace, but she has put forth fire and is unable to go."

So she has succeeded, thought Diana. She was indignant. She would rescue Sen S Mo.

"I will wait for her," she said. "She is worthy of education and a life of her own."

The Chinese woman looked at her, not in the least embarrassed that Diana had seen through her subterfuge. "There is no escape from human relations. There is the *yin* and *yang*. It is idle to talk of freedom."

"Oh, but it is not!" exclaimed Diana. "In my country——"

"Have you children?" asked the matriarch.

"I am not married," Diana hastened to say.

"So it is true, what my humble daughter told me. I did not believe it could be true of one of your age. I will send a servant to accompany you." She clapped her hands. An *amah* appeared. "Send two servants with so honored a guest," she commanded.

Diana went away, believing that Sen S Mo could never pull herself free from submission to the clan. For Diana herself, no cost of loneliness seemed too great to pay for her own inviolateness of body and mind.

But as the summer drew to its close, she began to miss Peter. She frequented the tennis courts. She went to the post office at noon, thinking she might catch a glimpse of him. He seemed to have dropped out of the little community. Had he gone back to the hospital? She did not like to ask anyone. A vague sense of incompleteness grew in her into a definite need for Peter.

The longing would pass, she told herself, when she was once more at work. Since her visit to Sen S Mo's clan, she had looked upon her teaching of Chinese women almost as a crusade, but there were days when her ardor lagged a little. Then she would spur herself on with the indignant thought of Sen S Mo's fate. Undoubtedly she had been sent back to her husband's household.   How bitter would be her lot after her rebellion!

One morning she heard a stir outside her cottage—the grunt of coolies as they lowered a chair from their shoulders, the tap, tap that bound feet make ascending stairs.   Diana glanced out of the window.   Incredible sight—Sen S Mo was coming up the veranda steps!

Diana flew along the hall to greet her.   Here was the incentive she needed.   She was fired with enthusiasm when Sen S Mo said, "I have come back to eat of the new learning."

But of how Sen S Mo had managed her departure from her mother's house, Diana learned nothing.   When she sought to talk of her visit to Sen S Mo's family, hoping thus to lead up to the events of the last night, Sen S Mo's eyes seemed sealed over with incomprehension.   But her words, "We are now sisters," seemed to indicate that her break with her family was complete.

After Sen S Mo went back to the school, indifference to her work again stole over Diana.   She took to walking along the least frequented paths.   Her last day in the mountains, after she had finished her packing, she went out on the veranda, where her luggage stood, ready for an early start in the morning.   Many of the near-by cottages were already closed.   She felt isolated, desolated.

She struck out along the path taken many times that summer with Peter, reached the bamboo grove.   There was no sunlight in it now, for the sun had dipped behind the mountains.   The smooth green boles, roofed in by their intermingling leafy tops, were held in the embrace of darkness. Diana advanced to the hollowed place in the earth's surface, where she and Peter had sat so often.   Standing with his back against a tree, she saw Peter.

For a moment they stood apart.   Then Peter reached forward, drawing her to him, bent his head until his lips were pressed on hers.   Insatiable craving to submit herself to the dark abyss of union surged through her.

*   *   *   *   *

On the last day of Diana's and Peter's honeymoon, their house-boat moved slowly along the canal. The late October day held some clarity of light that gave each object a lucid beauty of its own. Grey and white villages, arched bridges, were touched with this clear light. The water was low in the canals—the fields were lost to sight.

Diana sat propped against the forward wall of the cabin. The luminous light seemed to hold her suspended in its tranquillity. Her whole body had acquired repose, a harmony which she had never possessed before. Her breath came in long, full movements, her hands lay on her lap, palms up, her fingers lightly locked. Her eyelids fluttered and closed. Content lay in every cell of her body. At the slightest movement of Peter within the cabin, through every nerve shot a thrill, exquisite, satisfying, bringing her into deeper and deeper harmony with herself. The memory of the nights since their marriage flowed through her—her own consciousness lost in Peter, caught up into his passionate love. She who had thought him something alien, had learned that he completed her.

The oars creaked in their rope locks, as the boatman manœuvered their boat out of the narrow canal they were traversing into the wide waters of the Grand Canal, the last lap of their journey.

"I've finished our packing," said Peter, as he sat on the steps leading to the deck and faced Diana. The house-like structure of the cabin hid them from the eyes of the boatman.

"If only it didn't have to end," sighed Diana. "Nothing can ever be like this first love of ours."

"It's only just begun. I'm sure there's much, much more than we have experienced," Peter answered. "Suppose it should be hard—you won't draw back, darling?"

There was a note almost of alarm in his voice, as if he saw some lonely road without her and could not bear it.

"Peter, I've given myself completely." And Diana pulled his head down on her breast.

VII

ALTHOUGH it was just sundown and the lucid light of the
October day still lay over the fields, evening had already come
to the narrow streets. Diana, from her vantage point in the
lead chair, looked with unseeing eyes on the scene usually so
interesting to her—the peaked roofs packed in a solid mass
on either side, the jutting eaves level with her eyes, the surging
human stream of men more machine-like than any machine,
seeming almost in uniform in their blue garb. Bit by bit
she began to notice that the rigidity of the daily pattern was
interlaced tonight with another. Piles of round cakes lay
on the counters of shops. Mechanically, she found herself
counting them . . . thirteen to a pile, thirteen to a pile—
pattern, pattern.

"What's the festival?" she called back to Peter, more because of the desire to hear his voice than to know.

"It's the Eighth Moon." Peter leaned forward, shouting
across the noises of the street, the cries of the chair-coolies,
"Open the way!"

"Of course. I'd forgotten," she called back.

She turned no more. With her outer vision she watched
preparations for the festival which brightened the streets—
last purchasers already in holiday attire bargaining for mooncakes, wayside merchants lighting peanut oil lamps which sent
smoky flares over trays of gaily painted moon rabbits. With
her inner vision she surveyed her new life about to begin,
which carried over much of the old. It could hardly be otherwise, for in the two years Diana had been in the city, she had
made ties that could not easily be dissolved. A relationship
once assumed in China carries life-long responsibility.

When Diana had told Sen S Mo of her coming marriage,
Sen S Mo's only reply had been, "Where you go, I will go.

The bond between us cannot be broken. We are now sisters."

Diana, who was to start a girls' school at Peter's Mission, had asked that Sen S Mo be its matron. But as no money was available for such service, the Frasers were paying Sen S Mo's tiny salary.

One other relationship Diana could not break. Her personal servant, Wang Ma, assumed that she would not be left behind. They had made her their head servant in place of the usual houseboy. She was also to do the work of coolie, and she would manage the man they would take as cook.

Diana's thoughts ran ahead of the slow pace of the chairmen, in her first wifely anxiety. Three was the usual number of servants among missionaries, two only if both were men. The business people often had eight or ten. She would have to crowd many small household tasks in with her school work, in order to give the servants time for their major duties. For the first time she realized how meagerly equipped they would be. In the desire of Peter and herself for immediate marriage, economy had seemed an unimportant detail. Now she glimpsed its submissions.

They came to the gate of the compound. A slight push of the head chair-man's hand, and the gate's two halves swung inward, for the wooden bolt long since had been pushed back by the gateman in anticipation of their coming. The full moon was hidden behind the hospital, but its radiance filled the compound. Only their own house, shadowed by the hospital, stood in darkness. A frugal dim light showed at the back.

As the chair-bearers strode rapidly along the walk, a hooded figure came down the hospital steps—Stella in her nurse's cloak. Peter called to the bearers to stop.

"It's nice to have you back," Stella said, coming quickly toward them. She rested her hand on the pole of Diana's chair, looked toward Peter. "I've told Wang Ma to have dinner ready for you."

The moon moved out from behind the hospital. Build-

ings, trees and flowers stood forth in unearthly beauty. As
the light fell on Stella, Diana looking down upon her had a
sudden intuition that Stella loved Peter.

Then Diana was absorbed in the details of her home-
coming—the chair-men setting down the chairs before the
steps of her house, Wang Ma standing in the doorway, a lamp
in her hand, to welcome them. But as Peter helped her out
of the sedan and his hand touched hers, exultation spread
through her veins. Peter was hers. She made the awkward
high step over the slanting side pole of the chair instead of
the easy low one over the yoke which rested on the ground—
the chair-men had a superstition that crossing the yoke would
bring them bad luck. She was oddly aware that at the same
time she sought to fathom her strange joy. That sudden
knowledge of Stella's love for Peter, a love that had no rights,
no privileges, had awakened some slumbering possessive being
in her.

"*Ai yah!* May you have a hundred sons," cried Wang Ma,
as excited and pleased as a child. Taking her place as both
servant and privileged character in the foreign household, as
she would have in a Chinese household, she ordered the bearers
off, Diana and Peter to come in, to wash, to see the clean
house.

Although for thirty years Dr. Buchanan had lived in this
house, it was empty tonight except for a few discarded things.
In the communal life of Christian Missions, where men and
women relinquish every distinction of money or ability, they
cling to their possessions as if they were their personalities.
When they go on home leave, they store their meager treasures
carefully away. In an upstairs room, Dr. Buchanan, in the
last days of the summer heat, had carefully placed the ac-
cumulation of thirty years, against his return.

"What an empty house," said Diana, as they walked through
the rooms. "More empty than a new one would be. Those
marks on the walls where pictures hung . . . this old couch.
See the faded places on the back and arms—tidies, I suppose."

"Haunted, I'd say," answered Peter. "I can feel Dr. Buchanan everywhere. I'm sure he's likely to rush at me from that closed room," he said, only half in fun, as they stood outside the locked door upstairs. "I'd like to do things differently at the hospital. You know, he was terribly conservative."

Later, when they were downstairs again, Peter drew her to him. "Do you remember our first meeting when we didn't dare to walk together because of the Chinese?"

"Even now we've got to be careful not to show our love before them," she answered. "Even before Wang Ma——"

"Yes, Dr. Buchanan," mocked Peter.

Diana placed her hand over his mouth. With the eager fervency of his mouth hidden, she had a startling impression of his keen, searching eyes. He took her hand away to speak, and then forgot to, as her arms locked themselves around his neck. And Diana forgot that penetrating, searching look, absorbed in the warm curve of his head fitting her hollowed hands.

There was a knock at the door and Diana drew away. She was thankful she had, for when the door opened, there stood Sen S Mo. Diana went now to the other side of the hearth, so that it might seem that Peter made no recognition of her presence. As she moved, she dropped her handkerchief. Peter stooped to pick it up from the floor, giving it back to her.

To Sen S Mo, it was as if a window had been opened, through which she caught a glimpse of a new relationship between man and woman. Only dimly she saw it, as through a glass darkly. The Chinese saying taught her by her mother came to her mind: "When man and woman lie in the bed they are man and wife; when they step down from it, the man is again the princely figure, the superior being." Now she grasped, through this foreign man's deferential care of his wife, a relationship between man and woman extending through each act of life. In the same moment it fascinated and offended her.

From outside came the sound of men's and women's voices, striking strangely on her ears. The door was thrown open and into the room came the members of the station, crowding around Diana and Peter.

"We've surprised you as we wanted to do," cried little Rose Berger, dancing about Diana. "We've got presents for you," she whispered.

"How nice of you!" Diana leaned down to kiss her.

The grown-ups stood in awkward restraint, waiting for the Chinese woman to go. In the pause, Sen S Mo moved forward, holding in two hands a round plate filled with pomegranates—round objects, symbol of harmony, harmony in marriage, the seeds symbol of productivity. Diana received the gift, and as Sen S Mo bowed and moved backward toward the door, she murmured, "Go slowly, go slowly," signifying she wished her to remain. But Sen S Mo went quietly away. She was alien to this group, holding something back until her going. As the door closed, and she heard the upward surge of their voices, a kind of shame flooded over her at this close association of men and women.

She looked up at the full radiant moon hanging high in the sky, typifying womanly submissiveness. This was women's festival night. As the passive winter drew on, the feminine principle came to its power in the universe. She thought of the house of her father-in-law, the court where the women even now worshiped the Silver Candle. She could see the old woman, her grandmother-in-law, swaying like a willow on her beautiful, tiny feet, go forward, kowtowing before the altar, and after her the other women of the household—the head wife of Scholar Sen, followed closely by his honored concubine, the mother of his only living son. But she, widow of his eldest son, was not there.

The habit of the selfless wife and the traditional allegiance to her dead husband were strong upon her. A new, terrifying emotion, experienced only since she had accepted the Western way of life, took hold of her as she stood in the middle of the

bare compound. Loneliness! In the patriarchal life of her
people, shut into the courts of the women, she had often
known boredom, and after marriage, fear, for her tyrannical
grandmother-in-law treated her as a slave, first because she
was childless, then because she was a widow. But even as
barren wife, as childless widow, she had been a part of the
fructifying universe, held deep in the stream of life. Loneliness was a frightening sensation.

Begging a few mooncakes from Wang Ma, she went to
her room high under the eaves in the house of the Single
Ladies. There she made her altar to the moon, knelt before it, hands clasped in the ancient gesture.

Once the door had closed behind Sen S Mo, activity broke
the bonds of Chinese decorum. Mrs. Baker covered the bare
boards of a scarred deal table lent the Frasers with her best
damask cloth. She shook out the folds with a sharp snap.
The room was quickly scented with *que hua* which Stella
brought in and laid in great masses on the white cloth. The
boy-cooks of the Bakers and Bergers appeared with steaming
dishes.

Wang Ma moved before them, a small compact creature in
blue trousers and coat, the pointed top of her apron, shaped
like a butcher's, pinned close to her throat with a gilded
safety-pin—cherished possession acquired from Diana's things
when she had arranged them in the bedroom upstairs. On
the high forehead of the married woman, with the hair plucked
away, she wore a black satin bandeau, fitting closely over
her ears. Her white stockings were immaculate, her pointed
shoes of shining black satin.

"Worthless one," she said in a high, sharp whisper to the
Bakers' young servant, "in this household we have *tao li*.
Place thy offering of meat here. And thou, Ting Ta Shih
Fu"—she turned with withering scorn upon the Bergers' cook,
following her to the kitchen—"ten years a servant of these out-
side ones, and you bring to the important occasion of marriage

a few coppers' worth of food bought on the street. Go quickly, and bring the thing called olives."

"There is but one bottle," ventured Ting Ta Shih Fu.

"Son and grandson of a liar, go, and return with two bottles!"

Mr. Baker placed two chairs side by side at one end of the table. "Come," he said, taking Diana's arm. "You're to stand behind this chair and Peter the other."

With fluttering hands, Mrs. Berger arranged a little pile of packages on the table before them.

Rose tugged at her mother's skirt. "I want to sit next her. It's my first white bride."

"Don't tug at me, Rose."

"I don't see what keeps Sophie," exclaimed Mrs. Baker. "We can't begin without her."

"Yes, where *is* Miss Dyer?" they all echoed, none but Mrs. Baker venturing on the intimacy of her given name.

"She said she'd be back from her itinerating trip in time," said Stella. "Shall I go over and see if she has come?"

"Why not begin without her?" volunteered Peter.

"Dare you?" said Mr. Berger, a faint hint of mockery in his voice.

"Listen—isn't that the gate bell?"

They heard the approach of a chair, heralded by the voices of coolies.

"That's Miss Dyer, all right," said Mr. Berger, as a deep-throated feminine voice was raised in command.

"Sh-h!" admonished Mrs. Baker.

The door opened to the short, solid figure of Miss Dyer, a pongee umbrella over her arm, its green lining showing where it flared out above the band holding it shut. A white pith sailor hat was set firmly on her head. The thick cork brim, lined with green, threw a heavy shadow over her eyes.

Diana noticed a moment's pause before, with what seemed to her assumed gaiety, they fell upon Miss Dyer, taking her umbrella, hat, and long coat.

"I was busy," said Miss Dyer, as she took her place at the head of the table. "I stopped along the way to preach the Gospel. The city has gone heathen tonight."

"It's made the streets brighter," said Stella.

Miss Dyer eyed her. "Heathenism is never beautiful," she said sternly.

In order to end the talk about the heathen, Peter picked up one of the packages. The present was from Miss Dyer— a passé-partouted picture of the head of Christ crowned with thorns.

Diana unwrapped a paper-covered book. "I've copied every recipe I've ever heard of for using native things our way," Mrs. Berger called out. "There's a recipe on how to use water chestnut so it tastes like corn." She leaned eagerly forward. "I've put down the cost. Three coppers will get you enough for a meal. And there's a recipe for——"

"Here, here!" Mr. Baker interrupted. "Not a present was to cost over ten cents, and see this." He picked up a pile of shining tin plates Peter had just unwrapped.

"It's all right," his wife assured him. "I had them made from an old oil tin."

"Quite suitable, quite suitable, my dear," beamed Mr. Baker. "Oil and the Bible, the two lights of Asia."

They all laughed at the well-worn joke.

"Open mine, open mine!" Rose in her excitement was kneeling on her chair, grasping one of two knobby packages left. "It's my moon rabbit," she volunteered. "My *amah* gave it to me." She was quite happy as Diana restored it to her.

Peter unwrapped the last bundle, revealing a small bronze figure of Buddha.

"Oh, how lovely!" exclaimed Diana.

Exquisite the filigree work making the petals of the lotus, the seat of Buddha. Lying in Buddha's lap his long thin hands, thumbs and finger tips touching, subtly suggesting repose.

"Stella, you didn't play fair. That certainly cost more

than ten cents. You can't fool me," said Mr. Berger, taking
the little figure, appraising it with the eye of the connoisseur.
"It's good stuff," he added, half under his breath, as he re-
gretfully gave it back to Peter.

"It was given me, so it didn't cost anything," Stella told
him.

"Images like that make good paper weights," said Miss
Dyer, glancing up from her plate. "Please pass me the
chicken." She went on with the business of eating.

As Peter again held the figure in his hand, he noticed neither
workmanship nor beauty. The passivity of the face struck
him afresh, rousing his aggressive spirit. Until now, the
meager gifts of the meager party had oppressed him. All
the evening he had felt himself twisting and turning, seeking
escape for himself and Diana. Marriage had brought to ach-
ing life the old ambition for wealth and fame.

Looking into the face of Buddha, he wanted above all else
to combat its expression of withdrawal from life, combat it
with activity. His eyes rested upon the picture of Christ.
Out of the confusion of wrapping paper and gifts strewn
about the table, the face crowned with thorns stood forth.
In spite of the cheapness of the reproduction, much of the
artist's conception had been kept. It held recognition of pain
and something more—a challenge to pain.

Diana had been watching him in his absorbed interest.
Was Stella's love for him quite without power? She was suddenly shot through with fierce determination to own him
completely. She reached out and took Stella's present from
him.

"It's getting late," said Miss Dyer.

"True," said Mr. Baker.

As Peter opened the house door for his guests, the orange
disk of the harvest moon stood forth in the sky. The group
was touched with mystery. Some haunting sense of forgotten gods stirred within them.

Rose, riding on her father's shoulder, held up her hands,

exclaiming, "There's my rabbit in the moon. My *amah* said so."

"See," said Stella. "The rabbit is sitting under the lovely cassia tree."

"No wonder the Chinese worship the moon," said Mrs. Berger. "I declare, I could tonight."

"Umph!" said Miss Dyer, and stalked away.

"It's tonight, isn't it, that the Chinese think the moon is married to the sun?" said someone.

"We mustn't keep you," they said, almost in unison, suddenly conscious that this was the last night of a honeymoon.

Peter and Diana stood together, watching their neighbors move down the moon-patterned walk—the Bakers arm in arm in the softened light blending and becoming one, the Bergers out of step, he appearing to walk on stilts, Rose upon his shoulder making of him a gigantic man, Mrs. Berger taking tiny steps, two to his one. Yet about them, also, was the mystery of oneness. Only Miss Dyer and Stella moved separately.

Peter drew Diana into the house, closing the door behind them. Through the uncurtained windows shone the moon—they walked upon its delicate shimmering light filigreed upon the stairs and upon their chamber floor. Standing at the window, looking out over the acres of grey roofs, blue-black in the moonlight, Peter had a sudden vision of the millions upon millions of Chinese courtyards where the moon, cool companion to the sun, was being worshiped tonight. All Nature he suddenly saw as the Chinese conceived it—two forces mated together, human beings one of the Ten Thousand Things following the fundamental law of the universe.

His hand upon Diana's shoulder slowly slipped to her waist, followed the long line of hip and thigh. Then they were locked in each other's arms.

Somewhere, far off in the ancient land, stood the altar of the moon hollowed to fit the raised altar to the sun.

VIII

PETER and Diana lingered a little over breakfast, their first meal alone in their own home. They could hear the lusty voices of the coolie boys in Mr. Berger's school chanting a Christian hymn. It came to an abrupt end, and in the silence that followed, Diana caught the tinkle of a gate bell.

"Is that the bell in the women's compound?" she asked, leaving her breakfast, going to the window. "It's always like this on the first day of school," she added, in answer to Peter's questioning eyes. "I can't eat. Suppose not a single girl should come?"

"You're offering them food and clothes," Peter encouraged her. "However," he added with a sigh, "even food and clothes won't bring women to my hospital."

"I ought to be at the school," said Diana.

"And I at the hospital," said Peter.

Still for a moment they lingered, their youth and their love calling to them. Through the clear October air the beat and throb of the ancient city reached them. Had they been here centuries ago, it would have sounded like this. The thin wedge of Christianity, seeking for centuries to thrust itself into this other way of life, appeared to have wrought no perceptible change.

Diana leaned forward, fingering the gift of fruit Sen S Mo had brought the evening before. "Pomegranates," she said. "I wonder why pomegranates——" As she lifted one, the bottom of the plate came into view. "Why, Peter," she exclaimed. "See, it's got the *yin yang* symbol."

They rose, Diana handsome, Peter possessed of a charm which made him seem so, walking together down the flagged path to the gate in the low bamboo fence that shut off their compound from the larger one.

"There's a closed chair going toward the women's compound. It must hold a girl for your school," Peter said. "And now I must go." And he turned left, taking the path to the hospital.

Diana, delighting in his strength and pride, watched him out of sight before she turned in the opposite direction to the women's compound and her school—a low, native building.

Sen S Mo was already there. Before her stood a girl clad in the coarsest of blue coolie cloth. She held in her hand no bundle. Obviously she had come because of the boon of clothes and food, obviously, too, without desire, sent there by her father. He had chosen the sanctuary of this school rather than sell her. Sen S Mo led the girl away to one of the bare dormitory rooms above.

A little later, as Diana passed along the gallery that ran in front of the rooms, she saw the girl sitting inert on the side of the bed. She stopped, held by some powerful intuition of the suffering ahead for the women of China in the hard birth of the individual. Some knowledge come to her since her visit to Sen S Mo's home, more definitely realized since her own marriage, told Diana that woman's submission to the family was not like a garment, as she had conceived it, easily cast off, but instinct pervading her being.

By afternoon there were five such girls. "All of them 'monkey-hearted,' " Sen S Mo said, using the term the Superior Man sometimes used for the *hsaio ren*.

As Peter entered the hospital, he could hear the Reverend Mr. Baker preaching to the patients in the waiting room. He went directly to the consulting room, and Stella called in a patient. There were not many this morning, as she had taken care of most of them.

"I thought this a good opportunity for you to get your office in shape. You may not have time later," she said.

"Why not?" demanded Peter, noticing with disapproval that once more the lines had appeared around Stella's mouth and eyes. "Neither you nor I should be worn out if we systematize our work."

But he was secretly thankful for this little respite. Now that the moment was upon him, he held back a little from plunging into the work that confronted him. Deep in his heart he knew that Stella was right. It was a task to stagger any man. Often they had told him how strong and vigorous Dr. Buchanan had been when he came to the hospital, and Peter had had a foretaste in the summer of the over-driven life of a doctor in China—he the one doctor in the province . . . one doctor for some forty million people.

He went down the hall which divided the dispensary and waiting room from the in-patients' ward, to the end where the ladder-like stairs led to his office under the eaves of the one-story building. A dormer window gave it light. He paused and looked back.

Stella in her white nurse's uniform was weaving in and out among the blue-garbed Chinese. A farmer, his smocked skirt belting in his top garment, stood bewildered in the middle of the hall. Stella's quick eyes took in the fact that he was frightened. She stopped to talk to him. Why, she actually had him smiling at the absurdity of a little boy so frightened of her white face that he clung screaming to the man who had brought him, and then, somehow, she had won the child too. Peeping out at her from the safe shelter of his father's legs, he reached gingerly for a bright red persimmon she held out to him.

Peter closed the door of his office behind him and surveyed the shabby room, the only new thing in it his medical books sent over from Mrs. Baker's, which had been piled in the corner. Opening the desk with the key Dr. Buchanan had given him, he found the cubbyholes stuffed with records of countless sick.

"I doubt if any of this is worth keeping," he said to himself, stacking the papers before him, "but I guess I'd better glance at it."

The Chinese names—Wang, Sen, Ho—kept passing and repassing before his eyes. With only a hundred surnames in use among the Chinese, the same names were bound to appear constantly. Such records as these were useless.

Then a notation at the bottom of a page attracted his attention—*If I could understand Chinese medicine, I could understand the Chinese character.*

"That's odd. I'd thought of Chinese medicine as a lot of superstition," Peter said to himself.

What had Dr. Buchanan learned of Chinese medicine? Nothing, was his conclusion after a half-hour's reading. He was about to give up his search when he came upon another footnote—*According to the Chinese belief, man's body is a compound of the* YIN *and* YANG. *Sickness comes when they are out of balance.*

Peter read the words again. Didn't *yang* and *yin* mean male and female? Upon what strange Eastern belief had he come? As he bundled the papers together, thinking sometime to examine them more closely, he puzzled over the two footnotes. They spoke to him of some definite philosophy of life. With his hands resting on the papers, he meditated, sensing as never before an intricate culture hidden beneath the poverty and sickness that he witnessed. His curiosity was roused. What gave to Chinese faces such contentment? How was it that disease and poverty had overtaken them?

Then he shook himself free of these absorbing thoughts. After all, what did it matter? His mission was not to study ancient philosophy, but to introduce modern scientific medicine, alleviate suffering, push knowledge forward. He went vigorously to work clearing out the desk, placing the bundle of records at the back of a drawer out of his way, and began sorting out his books. He was proud of his compact medical library. Then he set about planning a laboratory under the eaves. There must be a door leading out from the office, and another dormer window cut in the roof. He sent the hospital coolie for a carpenter.

IX

THE Frasers had neither much time nor money to spend on their house, but when furnished, it possessed a certain beauty. The house had been built on plain, ample lines, the rooms were big and the ceilings high. The very frugality of furnishings gave it restraint and an atmosphere of quiet.

They felt they could not afford rugs. But the floors, polished as only floors done in the hard Ningpo varnish could be, were dark mirrors reflecting facets of sun and lamplight. Wherever possible, in order to lessen expense, they used native furniture. Although made of a light-colored hemlock, it was as perfect in design as the costly Chinese blackwood. The tables were square, with straight, well-proportioned legs, except for the dining-room table, which was round with a flaring downward curve forming the upper part of the legs. The chairs had wide, shallow seats with backs straighter even than the chairs of America's Puritans. Like the floors, each piece of furniture shone with the high polish of the native varnish, proof against heat. Dr. Buchanan's old couch, of good colonial design, fitted well with the Chinese tables and chairs. Diana and Wang Ma recovered it in blue coolie cloth.

The white plastered walls were bare except over the two fireplaces. Over the one in the parlor hung the Chinese scroll Peter had noticed in Diana's study the first time he had called on her—Diana's cherished possession given to her by her Chinese teacher. Above the one in the dining room, hung Peter's picture of St. Zenobius—a primitive, simple picture, four times St. Zenobius appearing as he advanced toward the temple, healing the sick on his way, his gorgeous red robe four times accenting the greyness of the sick, four times accenting the whiteness of the Frasers' dining-room wall.

To the furnishing of the hall, Peter and Diana gave much

time, taking every pains to make it like a Chinese guest hall. They hoped to find entrée in time to the educated class, and here they would entertain them. The casual arrangement of their own parlor would offend the Chinese sense of balance.

Against either wall they placed a Chinese tea table, flanked by Chinese chairs made of satiny blackwood. That the room might not seem cheap and vulgar to the literati, they had relinquished their strict economy, and had purchased only such pieces as were used in the best Chinese houses. They got Scholar Wu to select fitting scrolls to hang on the walls. At first, the precisely arranged furniture made the place seem stiff and formal to them, but in time its balanced harmony became a pleasure.

Across the hall, opposite the living rooms, were their studies. Each held a table-desk and two chairs, one for the teacher, one for the pupil. Here they studied the Chinese language, read the Classics, Diana with dutiful regularity, Peter more brilliantly but less regularly. This literature, which, it seemed to him, had had nothing the scholar considered of consequence added to it for centuries, irritated him at times—a dead sea of thought, no invigorating inflowing streams of speculation, no new discoveries. Where was the adventure of the mind? He prodded Diana's reverence toward her study with his questioning.

Something of that conservative spirit which Diana showed in her study of the language clung about the house—something of the precise neatness which had oppressed Peter in the Single Ladies' dwelling. But little by little the rooms took on an air of masculine casualness—a book face down, a chair out of place, a litter of papers on his desk, ink, pen and paper left in the dining room—the only room heated. At first Diana was annoyed by these little disorders, then she came to love them as marks of Peter's passage through the house.

She welcomed, too, Peter's prodding of her mind, though

she never told him so. Hers was a silent acceptance of his gift to her spirit. But Peter was content, for Diana gave herself to him with intensity in the darkness of the night, and in the silence of those moments they seemed to know each other in the unfathomable depths of their difference.

X

WHEN Peter had been given charge of the hospital, Dr. Buchanan had warned him against innovations. He had not been long enough in the country, all the senior members of the Mission told him, to know that Chinese custom or superstition underlay details which on the surface seemed easily changeable. Let him learn the traditions.

From the first day Peter had entered the hospital, he had had to exert his utmost self-control not to show how the place offended him. "Why run a hospital at all," he said to himself, "if you're going to have no standards of hygiene or sanitation?"

The sick men, most of them from the poorest classes of Chinese, wore their own garments, and were wrapped in their own padded, often ragged blankets.

"Couldn't possibly keep those things clean," he had pointed out to Stella with fierce scorn, the minute he was out of earshot of Dr. Buchanan. "Certainly it wouldn't offend the Chinese to give them clean blankets?" he demanded of her.

"And the money?" Stella had asked.

But she loved his rebellion, though she surveyed with amusement the stiff carriage of his shoulders which unconsciously revealed it.

Now that the hospital was his, its condition irritated him the more. With nervous distaste he eyed the unkempt-looking patients, the disheveled beds, the bowls of half-eaten food on the tables beside the sick—extra delicacies brought in by some member of the family. Families, coming and going at all hours, seemed to be as numerous as the patients.

A month after he had taken charge, his love of efficiency conquered him. One morning he made the rounds of the ill-smelling wards with the unashamed nurse who awaited the

85

servants of the patients to carry away the night refuse. That it should be more honorable to allow untidiness, even filth, in a hospital, than to make use of one's hands—certainly there could be no idea worth preserving that upheld such a custom. It was simply bad discipline.

Feeling sure of himself, saying nothing to Stella, Peter called his three nurses together in his office. They sat up very straight, full of the dignity of their position—boys from the artisan class, once students in Berger's school, but too poor to go on with their education. Dr. Buchanan had induced them to come into the hospital as nurses, allowing them the long, blue gown of distinction, as in the school. They sat in a row, their neatly braided hair pulled tightly back from their shaved foreheads.

Slowly Peter felt his way in the language, trying to assemble the right words, seeking to inject into their minds the Western concept of hygiene—difficult, for his knowledge of their speech was limited. Besides, the Chinese language had no words which expressed scientific ideas. The oldest missionaries in the city had told him it could not be done.

Speaking very carefully, using many illustrations, he placed before these boys the hazard to the sick, even to themselves, in an unsanitary hospital. He spoke of germs and bacteria and the danger of infection. He explained the cleanliness that hygiene demanded. Then, at last, he came to the climax of his argument—the dignity of labor. A scholar, he told them, was not demeaned by labor. Rather a scholar gave dignity to the most menial task.

No change in the boys' expressions warned him that he had touched a hard, unyielding stratum of belief. Three generations of Puritan ancestors had sanctioned labor for him; generation after generation of ancestors, hallowed and worshiped, had disapproved of it for the Superior Man. As contradictory in China to say labor was for the scholar, as to say evil was good. Quietly the nurses left the room, the Confucian courtesy of seeming to yield preserved.

What did this foreign creature know of the distinctions of their culture, the necessity they felt to conform to the traditions if they, the sons of artisans, would be Superior Men? To them he appeared disorderly in clothes and manner. His quick, unmeasured step, his dress never precise, his unquiet eyes, his strange, bright hair through which he constantly passed his fingers. Like a skein of tangled silk it looked to one of the boys whose father was a silk weaver.

The next morning, Peter found an immaculate hospital. But later in the day, an old peasant, weak from an attack of dysentery, came to him grumbling that the nurses had made him rise early to clean his part of the ward.

Peter was indignant and he gave a direct command to his nurses. "This work must be done by you."

As he passed through the ward at noon, no nurses were about. Even the cook, he found, had left.

Peter was astounded and angry. Against all the rules of his profession to leave the helpless sick unattended! It was criminal. He hurried to the house for his own cook to prepare soft boiled rice, the customary food of Chinese sick. He himself was distributing it to the patients, when Stella came in from her clinic.

"If you had only told me," she said. "I could have arranged beforehand for this."

Peter did not answer. He was angry with Stella. What right had she to assume that it would be "like this"?

Out of China's jobless millions, he secured a new set of nurses. But these, too, under his strict discipline, left. Only after three trials did he succeed in getting men who would do the menial tasks. To his surprise, he found that he had dipped down into a society that did not live by *tao li*. That these men were without a sense of responsibility, he discovered when he sought to train them.

One night, finding no nurse about, he went the length of the ward, looking at each patient to see that all was well. In the last bed, curled up beside a patient, lay the night nurse, asleep. After that, it became Peter's habit to go soft-footed through his hospital at odd hours of both day and night. Many a menial task he did himself.

All through the compound Peter's rash act reverberated. At his house it brought difficulties. The cook left because he lost face serving a man who with his own hands not only washed the sores of the poorest coolie—that might be understood in a man wishing to attain merit—but he stooped to wash floors! This Peter had done once to avoid the danger of infection to the whole hospital.

After the departure of the cook, Diana helped in the kitchen, although Wang Ma grumbled at this last disgrace to a family of scholars.

Finally she said to Diana, "*Fei tai tai,* great lady Fraser——"

Diana corrected her. "I do not call myself a great lady." (The missionaries used the title of the people, S *Mo,* Mrs.) "*Fei S Mo,* Mrs. Fraser, is my name."

"I forget, *Fei S Mo.* But will *Fei tai tai* trust me to get a servant? A stout country girl can save *Fei tai tai* money. Two dollars instead of five paid the man cook each month is enough. One dollar for a coolie to carry water, one *Fei tai-tai* saves."

"Yes," said Diana, thinking it should be two dollars. "But I am not a *tai tai.* Remember when you get the servant."

So Wang Ma brought the stout country girl from her own town and trained her herself. That she bought her out of her own wages, that she was a slave in their house, Diana and Peter did not know. Wang Ma was pleased with her bargain. The girl was soon paid for, and then her wages were clear gain for Wang Ma.

Now did Peter feel the isolation of the compound, where each personality beat continuously upon every other, in an intimacy forcing each one into a defense of himself which accentuated his uniqueness. In the little circle of the compound, Peter found himself a breaker of custom. Mr. and

Mrs. Baker openly criticized him for his lack of respect to
Dr. Buchanan in destroying what the elder physician had
created. Miss Dyer denounced him as a fool for tampering
with customs he didn't have sense enough to know couldn't
be changed.

Peter appealed to Berger, hoping he would understand.

"I do not have to meet such a problem in my school.
Learning carries no menial tasks," was Berger's reply.

"There's plenty if you'd let them do it," Peter replied, not
a little nettled by Berger's superior tone. "You've got charity
scholars. The Mission's paying for them. Why don't you
make them work for their board? What'll they do when
they finish school?"

"Be teachers in my schools—pastors," answered Berger.

"It's all wrong," growled Peter. "You're getting an in-
verted pyramid. You need a wide foundation—a little learning for a great many—literacy well spread out. Send your
coolie pupils after two years out to the little villages to teach
primary classes. And you need to teach the dignity of labor,"
he added, still nettled.

"Anyway, you'll have to own," Berger answered, "that
my school runs smoothly."

Peter felt the sting of the words, but he did not suspect why
Berger was angry with him. By his action toward labor, Peter
had threatened the bigger, grander self that Berger was erect-
ing out of his old self—a man commanding servants, a man
above manual labor. When a boy, Berger had felt the humiliation of his position as the only one in his class at school whose
mother did her own work.

Even Diana, Peter felt, thought he had been rash. Their
love seemed caught up into anxiety.

Only Stella, who had prodded Peter ever since he had come
into dissatisfaction with himself, did not chide him for this
unprecedented drive for efficiency, although the constant
change of nurses increased her duties.

Worn down a little by his encounter with a force so unexpectedly powerful, Peter took his anger out on her. It left her helpless before the tumult in her own heart. Peter's anger was better than his indifference. That cold, ghost-like feeling of being no integral part of any life, which she had had ever since Peter's marriage, changed into one of significance. The listlessness which she had not been able to combat was mysteriously gone. With new energy she went about her tasks.

Peter had to own to himself that, instead of going forward, to all intents and purposes he had gone backward by his act. The boy nurses he had lost had been the first educated ones the hospital had ever had. After long effort, Dr. Buchanan had persuaded them to train as nurses. But although he was setting the nursing profession back to where it had been in the beginning, Peter would not allow the boys to return on their own terms. At least, the hospital came nearer the standards of cleanliness than it ever had before.

XI

THE landscape, sharp and clear in October, slipped back in November under the habitual soft haze of this semi-tropical land. In December, the delicate, slow drizzle of the winter rains began. The streets were covered with black slime compounded of rain and the dirt left by the feet of countless men acting as pack animals. In the houses—for even the houses of the rich were unheated—the air was chill and damp. Men, women, and children added padded garment to padded garment, and held in their hands to warm them tiny charcoal braziers through the filigreed tops of which a little heat escaped. The cold damp houses, the charcoal fumes from the little stoves, brought on many a case of pneumonia.

Sen S Mo, always in touch with the Sen family through a trusted servant, learned that for five days the precious only son had lain sick. For two days the house had been in turmoil. A half-dozen of the best native doctors had been called, but the child had grown worse. Soothsayers, workers of charms had been called, and he had grown worse. Servants moved back and forth going from the outer courts of the men to the inner courts of the women, bringing news of the arrival of priests to say masses, of tailors to make clothes for the dying boy.

Scholar Sen sat immobile as a statue by his table-desk in his own apartment. The sounds of the household making preparations for death came to him. This son, granted him so late in life, was to die. The serenity and bliss of union with the ancestors was again threatened, the immortality of the family in jeopardy. Hope was gone. Some evil spell lay upon the illustrious Sens.

Back in the servants' quarters, the wife of his dead son, so hated by him for her failure to honor the family, had returned, was in earnest conversation with his concubine, mother of the dying boy.

Sen S Mo spoke quietly, although agonizing fear gripped her. Suppose she should be found in this house of her husband's clan to whom she was an outcast! Suppose the matriarch of the family, her grandmother-in-law, the *lao tai tai*, should find her here!

At the sound of a woman's feet striking the paved passageway leading to the kitchen quarters, not only Sen S Mo but the honored concubine, the servants, and the slaves were held in a vise of fear. A serving maid entered.

"The old Buddha calls for thee," she said, addressing a young girl, the matriarch's favorite slave. "Hurry. She will not brook delay."

There was a sigh of relief like a breath of wind. The girl went out. For the time, the matriarch would not trouble them. Again they fell to their discussion, servants and slaves and Sen S Mo bound into the family not alone by fear, but by loyalty. Catastrophe threatened the clan.

"If the foreign doctor is called, the precious boy can be made well," Sen S Mo told them.

It was not hard for the concubine, mother of the boy, to believe that the foreign doctor was but another juggler with magic, and his might be the magic that would work. But no one dared approach the matriarch asking that the foreign doctor be called. Who, then, dared approach Scholar Sen, brave his anger, his scorn?

"He might listen to the boy's mother. Thou shouldst be the emissary," urged Sen S Mo, looking at the cowering concubine. "A curse upon thee!" she added sternly, "placing thine own fear above the life of the precious representative of the house! Go, I command thee!"

Sen S Mo sent a man servant ahead to see if the way were clear.

"*Lai, lai, ao sao!* Come, come, hurry!" he said on his re-

turn. "The *lao tai tai* sits in the young master's room. Old
Buddha will not see thee now."

"Go, and quickly!" commanded Sen S Mo, forcing the
concubine forward out of the door, going with her a few steps
along the passageway. "Fear not," she encouraged her, "thou,
the proud bearer of a son!"

"Yes, proud bearer of a son," murmured the other, still
propelled forward by Sen S Mo.

They reached the end of the passageway.

"I cannot guide thee farther. Go!" commanded the widow,
giving her a final push.

The woman's throat was dry with fright, as she entered
the presence of her master. "My lord," she said, brave with
the bravery of desperation, "there is yet one doctor in this
city the honorable one has not tried."

"Command him to come," ordered Sen. "Why has he not
been called?"

"He is the foreign one."

"Silence!" cried Scholar Sen. "I will not have the man's
name mentioned. The barbarian—he who drags down learning! Go from my presence."

"Thy son is dying."

"*Mei yu fatzu*, it cannot be helped."

"What does it matter that the honorable Sen despises this
coarse one? He only performs the menial task for the honorable son."

"I have sworn these barbarians shall not enter my house."

"Thy son is dying."

"I have sworn with the scholars, my friends, to keep these
barbarians who would vulgarize learning out of our families."

"Thy son is dying."

For a long time Sen did not speak; his delicate, long hands,
the sensitive finger tips protected by his long protruding
nails, moved among his books, his writing brushes. He spat
a little blood now and then, after the manner of scholars.
At last he spoke, frightening her with his harsh tone. "Com-

mand this vulgar one to come, then. But while he is in this house, it shall not know my presence."

The day had been cold and rainy. Diana waited for Peter to come in to dinner. She was worried. Early in the afternoon, Sen S Mo had asked if she might go away for a few days—affairs of the family. Her going frightened Diana, who knew more of the country than Peter. Her feminine intuitions were aroused. In this close-packed Chinese society, anything affecting one person appeared to affect all, and never did there seem a finale to any action. First the cook had left. Something in Wang Ma's manner had told her that he did so because Peter had set aside the proprieties at the hospital. Now Sen S Mo was doing such an unprecedented thing as to leave the compound. Was it, too, because Peter had broken custom at the hospital? Would she ever return? If only Peter were not so unbending. She herself was a little like the Chinese, yielding a little in order to gain a desired end. Those were women's tactics, and they were Chinese tactics.

She heard Wang Ma stumping noisily along the hall. She recognized the energetic thump, thump of her hoof-like feet, very different from the dainty tap of Sen S Mo's feet when she had come earlier in the afternoon. The door was opened and banged shut. Noise did not bother Wang Ma.

"*Fei tai tai!*" Wang Ma's voice was high-pitched with excitement. "There is a letter come from the great house of Magistrate Sen! A servant waits with a chair. Wang Ma, your slave, goes to the house of the sick to tell the master he must go with the messenger!" Wang Ma's voice now held deference, a note which had not been there for many days. Before Diana could speak, she had gone energetically out of the door, banging it again, shouting from the other side. "The honorable teacher must eat first. Wang Ma, humble servant, will see that the master comes to eat. Wang Ma will return quickly to wait upon the honorable ones."

Diana went to the door watching for Peter to come from the hospital, eager to know the details of this surprising event. The magistrate sending for Peter. A chair and a servant. In the dim light of a lantern she could make out the outlines of the chair—not an ordinary one from the chair *hong,* but a private one.

She saw Peter hurry down the steps of the hospital in the direction of the gatehouse. "Peter," she called.

He turned, strode toward her. "I can't wait a minute, Diana. There's somebody sick at the magistrate's. They've sent for me." His voice was full of excitement.

"Oh, Peter! I knew it would come. I'm so proud of you."

"Run in, dear—you're getting all wet." He kissed her, hurrying away.

Peter's first professional call among the literati, his first bidding to the courts of the Superior Man! Here was his opportunity. He saw his science, so little understood by the *hsaio ren,* meeting with acceptance by the scholars.

He had reached his destination—one of those mysterious black gates in the long white walls on the streets of the rich— closed doors he had begun to think would never swing open to him. Elation spread through him like a warm fire, as he watched the two halves of the black gate swing inward.

Peeping over the front curtain of the great chair, as he was carried within, he saw a crowd in the court, servants and grey-robed monks. A group of women stood apart, wrought to that high pitch of nervous excitement which he had learned to dread in the Chinese in time of crisis. They moved ahead of him, exclaiming, "*Ai, ai!* We prepare for his death."

Even with the urgency of this visit claiming his attention, Peter was struck by the grandeur and beauty of his surroundings. Two great horn lanterns decorated with red ideographs cast a lustrous glow over a spacious court and a carved marble spirit screen. As he followed his guide, he caught glimpses of court after court open to the sky. Rockery of strange shaped stones, beautiful as carvings, in one. In another, potted plants; in others, trees in studied groups. Each court was bounded by low buildings with narrow pillared verandas. The paper panes of the windows, intricately latticed with dark wood, glowed like mother-of-pearl.

At last Peter reached the court where the child lay sick. The room was full of women. A servant parted the bed curtains. The boy, so emaciated that his body made no appreciable bulk under the great quilts heaped upon him, stirred restlessly. His face was drawn with pain. With dull, unseeing eyes he regarded Peter.

Peter stooped, gently pulling the quilts away from the child's shoulders. The neck was purple where it had been pinched to drive away congestion—a common Chinese custom. Peter pulled the quilts a little lower. On the thin chest of the naked boy were the marks of acupuncture needles. This needling of the sick was a mode of treating disease peculiar to China—Peter had had patients suffering from such treatment and had seen elaborate charts indicating where it was safe to insert the needles, but he had only a hazy idea of why they were used.

The boy winced when he touched his scarred chest. Peter tapped lightly with his sensitive fingers, lowering his head to listen. Pneumonia, evidently. Could he save this child, hollow-chested and stupefied with opium?

As he took out his stethoscope, he heard behind him in a harsh, high treble, "No devil tricks!"

He turned. From the shadowy corner of the room, a shrunken old woman hobbled forward. She leaned heavily on a cane. Her hand, silver protectors sheathing her long finger nails, clutched the great carved bird forming the cane's head.

The women gathered around the sick boy fell back. A murmur spread through the room. "The *lao tai tai!*" Then all was still.

Pointing her cane at Peter, the little old woman cried again, "Put the evil thing away!"

Peter dropped his stethoscope into his pocket, not because of her command, but because he saw no one could succeed in opposing her. Greedy, tyrannical power was written in every line of her face.

Although the crisis was near, he took time to explain to the old woman each thing he did. She offered no further objection. Only once again she came forward, when the boy cried out as Peter bent above him adjusting a poultice, thrusting her face close to the child's, cosseting him.

Not trusting the women to carry out his orders, Peter decided to stay the night. For three days he scarcely left the sick boy, taking upon himself the careful nursing required.

Late in the fourth night of his watching, the native candles had burned low. The matriarch slept in her chair. Peter sat by the boy's side, dozing now and then. As he heard soft, slippered footfalls, he started awake. A Chinese gentleman had entered the room. In an instant Peter recognized the supreme elegance of the figure, the exquisite refinement of the face. This was the official who had so impressed him that day in the street. Evidently the gentleman was surprised to see him. A startled look broke up the immobile features, then slowly changed to an expression of such scorn that Peter felt seared by his contempt. With a dignified bow, the magistrate turned and left the room.

At noon that day, Peter returned exhausted. "I'll tell you about it later," he said to Diana. "I've got to have some rest first."

Diana tiptoed about the house, cautioning Wang Ma to be quiet. Suddenly she heard a *walla-walla* of voices outside the kitchen door. In a moment Wang Ma ushered in a strange servant carrying packages. "Presents from the house of the magistrate," she exclaimed importantly.

"For the foreign *I Sheng.*" The man spoke with evident deference and respect.

"Give him a dollar," whispered Wang Ma. "It is the *tao li.*

A servant of such an official bringing presents—nothing less than a dollar will do."

Peter came down, looking weary and discouraged, Diana thought. "Look, dear. Imagine. Presents for you from the magistrate. Shall I unwrap them?" she asked.

"Yes," said Peter. "If you like."

Two jade cups, a pair of dwarf peach trees, symmetrical and perfect in proportion, and a hanging of red silk with two grey cranes embroidered upon it—all, had Peter but known it, things expressive of the vital essence.

"Aren't they lovely!" exclaimed Diana. "Let's fasten the red hanging opposite St. Zenobius."

Peter watched her place the jade cups on the mantel under her scroll with its bold calligraphy, followed her to the hall carrying the peach trees.

"Put them here on these tables," she told him. Suddenly she regarded him. "If you weren't tired, dear, it would be a perfect afternoon. Three days is a long time to be separated. You're home . . . and these lovely presents. . . . I'm so proud of you, Peter. Tell me all about it," she urged.

Some security, gone from him in the magistrate's house, returned to him.

For days, the beauty of the gifts illumined the house for Diana. All the compound was impressed with their richness. When Berger saw the jade cups, his condescension toward Peter was changed to envy. Nothing in his own collection, painfully acquired out of his meager salary, could approach them. His constant study of Chinese works of art informed him that these cups were genuine treasures.

But the gifts meant nothing to Peter. He would have returned them if he had dared. Never had he believed that he could be the object of such contempt as he had surprised on the aristocratic face of that Chinese gentleman. Until now he had always thought himself superior to this race because of his scientific knowledge. Now he realized there was learning that could despise his learning—a way of life that saw nothing in Western science. In that house where he had seen sickness treated as in the Middle Ages, he was despised.

Peter tried to find out from Scholar Wu wherein he failed in the eyes of such a man. He learned that Sen, though a small official, was a prominent scholar of the city, honored even by the Throne for his calligraphy and painting, and because of his meritorious public deeds he had been given such high rank that he wore the Coral Button. But Wu did not tell Peter why he had been called to treat this important man's only son. He said nothing of the fact that Sen S Mo was a member of that family. Neither did he inform Peter wherein he habitually failed before them all. Peter never guessed that they disliked that very quality in him which had saved the precious son—his aggressive, fighting spirit.

Mr. Wu, though poor, was a scholar, and he held to the perfect Confucian etiquette, depreciating his own people, held to the Confucian ideal of self-blame. Scholar Sen had been rude, they were a rude nation. He expected Peter, according to the same etiquette, not to accept this humility, but to proclaim his own shortcomings. Peter, reacting to Wu's words according to Western thought, believed them.

Yet he could not get back the satisfaction he had previously had in his activities, nor his former certainty in his own way of life. He was disappointed, too. The road to the literati was as fast closed as ever.

XII

PETER had reached the path leading to his own house when Berger threw open his front door, hallooing. "Hey, Fraser! come over. I want to show you something." He ran toward Peter, hurrying him through the gate and up the steps of the Berger house into the cold parlor.

On the floor squatted a peddler. One by one he unfolded the four corners of a blue cloth, displaying a bronze incense burner.

"See its lines," exclaimed Berger, proudly, "and these characters on the side. It's a work of art."

"How do you know the man's not fooling you?" asked Peter. "Copied from an old piece, probably—buried it to make it look old."

"I know it's genuine," answered Berger. "I've studied bronzes for years. It will make my collection unique." He picked it up, caressing it with covetous fingers. "But I can't afford it," he added, as Mrs. Berger appeared in the doorway, anxiety written on her bird-like features.

"What do you think, Jessie?" he asked.

"Well, the children . . ."

"Of course, the children. We won't say any more about it." Berger's face took on an injured expression.

A week later, all in the compound gathered at the Bergers' house to discuss momentous affairs. As they took their places in a circle around the table in the dining room bare except for the jumble of Berger's curios, Peter noticed the bronze burner standing on the mantel.

Berger's eyes met his defiantly.

"After all, we decided it was such a good investment," Mrs. Berger hastened to say. "We could sell it in America for three times what we paid for it."

Mr. Baker tapped for order. "You all know the purpose of this meeting is to consider whether Wang An Fu, the shoemaker down the street, shall be admitted into the church. First, let us pray for guidance."

At the prayer's end, Miss Dyer asked, "Has Wang destroyed his idols and his ancestors' tablet?"

"I find him willing to do so," answered Mr. Baker.

"How willing? Willing enough to do it before the eyes of his neighbors?" urged Miss Dyer.

"Don't demand it," protested Stella. "You'll make him an outcast on his street—all over the city—if you do."

At her words, the group stiffened to attention. Until recently, the destroying of the household gods and the tablets had always been required of those who accepted the doctrine of Christianity. But lately, a few of the more radical and daring missionaries had contended that it was too harsh a custom. Others argued that membership in the church must be made hard. It helped to guard against "rice Christians." Stella Perkins had been quick to support the liberal outlook. Ever since, she had been regarded with suspicion by her more conservative colleagues, especially by the Reverend Mr. Baker and Miss Dyer.

"Stella," Mr. Baker now said, "you know they've got to give up such practices, or they aren't really Christians."

"It isn't the giving up I'm talking about at present," Stella answered. "It's doing it publicly."

"You ought to know that heathenism has got to be uprooted stock and branch," said Miss Dyer sternly.

"But don't you see," urged Stella, forgetting her disfigured hands, holding them out eagerly, as if she would tear down some curtain that kept the others from understanding, "don't you see what it would mean to us if someone asked us to deny our God?"

"But ours is true. Theirs is false." Mrs. Baker spoke in a shocked tone.

"The trouble with you, Stella," said Miss Dyer, "is that you

let the Chinese tell you about their superstitions. You've
filled your mind with their idolatrous ideas."

"I think Stella's making too much of the matter, anyway,"
Mr. Berger broke in. "I doubt if any of their religious ideas
go very deep with them. At heart they're materialists. Food
is really their god. Keeping Sunday free from profit will be
a lot harder for Wang than giving up his gods."

Stella looked around the room, her eyes appealing to Peter
for help. For a moment, he thought to support her in her
one-man battle. Then an armor of righteousness closed him
in. He felt more confidence in himself than he had felt
since the night he had glimpsed Scholar Sen's contempt for
him. His self-esteem, diminished by that contempt, was
subtly re-established, as he exerted his power over Shoemaker
Wang's beliefs.

Only timid Mrs. Berger voted with Stella against the measure. "I don't like to see people suffer," was her explanation.

Diana was secretly glad that she had not yet been formally
taken into her husband's church. It saved her the necessity
of voting.

Sunday was the day appointed to test the new convert to
Christianity.

Shoemaker Wang, who even before Peter spoke the Chinese
language, had recognized him as friend, was giving up the
old way of life of his own people, accepting this new way,
mostly because of his respect for Peter. This was the first
Sunday he had sat idle, set apart from all the busy life of
his street, losing the work he needed. One day in seven to
be kept free of profit for the sake of this new god. But even
that was overshadowed by what lay before him this afternoon—the burning of the tablet wherein dwelt the spirits of
his ancestors.

"They are but bits of wood," the Christians had told him.
He could reassure himself with these words; but when he
looked into his wife's frightened eyes, he felt the ghostly

displeasure of his ancestors who lived in the tablet. This terrible deed must be done publicly—so the Christians had commanded. He could hear their approach. The hard tap of their leather-soled shoes made an alien sound in the street used once only to the soft pat of feet, bare or shod in cloth-soled shoes. The Christians were there now, darkening the open front of his shop. The moment had come.

He rose, went to the sacred spot where stood the tablet, took it reverently in his two hands, bore it toward the waiting group. The gilt ideographs, the names of the ancestors, embodying spirits of his family, wavered before his eyes. As he advanced, the Christians moved back until half the narrow street was shut off, enclosed within the semicircle they made. Before him on the worn paving stones, he placed the spirit tablet. Went into his shop again, brought a few grasses piled up by the clay stove, carefully laid them by the tablet. Went again to the stove, lighted a paper spill in the dying ashes, bore it forward.

"Thou, thus to dishonor thy ancestors!" his wife cried harshly.

The child at her side shrank away into the shadows. Wang stood irresolute. The Christians waited. Behind their white, determined faces, he saw the curious, brown faces of his neighbors.

The lighted spill was burning down, touching his fingers with pain. He dropped it among the dry grasses. The flames licked quickly at the tablet, dimming the golden names. The black lacquered surface cracked, then split and curled, writhing as if alive, falling down into the flames. The wooden center glowed with white-hot brilliance. Wang gave a little gasp. The sky seemed to darken at midday. Then his vision cleared and he saw a small heap of ashes and, beyond the approving faces of the foreigners, the hostile ones of his neighbors.

The new friends moved forward across the ashes, shook hands with him, praised him for his bravery. Next Sunday he should be made one of them, accept that strange custom, baptism. Then they moved down the street toward the seclusion of their own compound.

Stella looked back. "Oh, how could you?" she cried. "I hate you all!"

Seeing the shoemaker standing alone, all his neighbors drawn away from him, Peter felt flooding over him the compassion he always felt for suffering. He checked it. He was certain that Christendom held exclusive knowledge of the needs of the spirit. But he did not join the others in condemning Stella for her outburst.

After this, Peter came to be a real force in the Mission. The other members felt greater confidence in him than before. His sense of power grew stronger as he expressed his right of decision in the hospital and in Mission affairs. But when he entered his crude laboratory, he was the searcher, filled with humility and longing.

Research! What could he ever hope to do in the few moments left for it? Deeper and deeper, Peter Fraser, as Dr. Buchanan before him, was pulled down into the mere relief of misery. He could not even trace the course of new diseases. The men who crowded his hospital came to him only when they were in the last stages of disease. Even if they came earlier, it would not make a great deal of difference, for he had no money to buy the instruments for diagnosis. The small funds at his disposal must go for apparatus for treatment and for medicine.

He could not even be scientific in his use of medicines! He had to buy the cheapest rather than the ones best fitted to the particular disease. Even bandages were a constantly pressing demand on his funds. As for operating—there wasn't a chance. They would rather see their loved ones die than be mutilated when they entered another incarnation. Peter felt like a man trying to stem the tides of a vast ocean—the ocean of sickness—four hundred million people who ignored the laws of health, who washed their clothes and food in the same dirty canal water, allowed their contagious sick to go everywhere, used filth to make plasters for sores!

What was this Christian religion that he professed, which drove him to give service to a people who did nothing for their sick poor? He was ill-supported by the business group at home, despised by the business group of his own countrymen here in China, who engaged in lucrative pursuits, many of them professing the same faith as he in a compassionate God. Some tenacious rootage held him to his task, making it impossible for him to leave these multitudes of sick to their fate. But he cried out in rebellion against such disuse of his talents. He was not willing to be thus expended.

Day after day the city wall became the arena of his spiritual struggle. He sensed a hardening process going on in him as he fitted himself to the cult of his religion. Was he slowly stiffening to its pattern? He felt sterility creeping over his life. Where lay that fecundity of spirit he sought?

He looked down at the winter fields, green and lush with the third fruition of the year. This old earth, still fertile after centuries of use, held to its fertility by careful adherence to the laws of nature. Was there as definite a law of growth for the spirit?

Diana was not conscious of his struggle. Never had he been so passionate a lover, whether because of the need for an inner harmony he did not possess, or because of the strange, inexplicable fact that spiritual ardor and passion often lie close.

XIII

With the giving of presents to the foreign doctor, Scholar Sen felt he had closed the way between his people and the barbarian come out of the West. The healing of his son by such a one was a matter to be forgotten with the passing of the old year. New Year was at hand, rebirth of life. Winter with the passive female spirit in ascendancy was waning; the male spirit would soon be potent. Again Heaven would mysteriously impregnate the Earth and there would be renewal of life.

New Year was not merely a time for a fresh start, as in the West. The day held something, too, of the joy of Easter, joy of resurrection. At this time, every man laid aside the continuous daily grind of toil, gave himself up to rejoicing. The people at the Mission found it hard to grasp the full significance of the festival spirit, but of necessity they resigned themselves to it and prepared to give up their study of the language, take a month's vacation from their work. All the twelfth month of the old year they felt the festival spirit gathering momentum, the East withdrawing from the West. Pupils left the schools, saying an important member of the family had died, or that affairs of the family called them home. As the old year drew to a close, even the very sick left the hospital. Some hobbled away leaning heavily on relatives, some were carried forth in crude litters made of an old door or cord-woven bed-spring. Down the steps of the hospital, out the gate, went the lame and the halt and the blind, drawn as by a magnet back into the ancient way of life.

The whole of the twelfth month in Scholar Sen's household was taken up in preparation for the coming month of celebration. Under the eye of the matriarch, new garments

were made for all the household, from the precious boy, Lo
Shih, down to the least slave; food was cooked for men, gods,
and ancestors, bodies ghostly and bodies real. As the first day
of the New Year drew near, fresh posters of luck were pasted
on door-posts and gate-gods on the two panels of the
front gate. Water was drawn from the well to last for two
days, the well sealed, its guardian spirit given a holiday. In
the great guest hall, a pair of gnarled and twisted pine trees,
emblems of long life, were placed, the branches casting bold
shadows on the white wall. Scholar Sen himself had seen
to the hanging of treasured scrolls which had been in the
family for many centuries. A few specimens of his own
beautiful calligraphy he had hung, too.

It was New Year's Eve. The old year, the twelfth month,
the Bitter Moon, was come to its end. In the vast patriarchal
mansions and the one-roomed huts of the poor, the doors had
been sealed until the morning, to hold good luck within, to
keep the seventy evil influences out. The East had withdrawn
into itself; its face was turned inward. The white people
scattered over the city gathered together that evening at the
home of the English bishop, feeling the necessity for one
another's companionship, sensing how alien they were as all
China locked its doors.

Diana and Peter going home from the bishop's party, walked
close to each other, each holding the other's hand, as they
passed from empty street to empty street, sounds of festivity,
firecrackers, tom toms, music, reaching them.

Shoemaker Wang was alien, too, shut out from the feasting
of his people, lonely, that night, as he sealed his door and
looked at the bare table which all previous New Year's Eves
had been bright with things of the altar, fruits, candles, and
incense. In his ears was the sound of his wife's bitter complain-
ing. "Calling thyself Christian! Destroying thy ancestors,
setting aside the duties of son! Thou, bringing poverty upon
us! Men go to others now for their shoes."

Why had the Christians demanded it? With perplexity this New Year's Eve he asked himself the question. The doctrines of his own people allowed him any private belief, Buddhist, Mohammedan, or Christian, if the ancestors were not neglected. But forever must be held that great abiding principle of duty to the dead. Why did the gentle Christ they told him of wish him to destroy the tablet? With a sigh, he opened his Bible, hearing in the huts to the left, to the right of him, sounds of festivity, firecrackers, tom toms, music.

Under the stars, in the central court of Scholar Sen's great dwelling, lanterns stood lighted in bamboo tripods, and high above the house from a tall mast hung the Heavenly Lantern. It threw its light down on the altar table, prepared for the first of the three great ceremonies rooted deep in the religious strivings of a people, who, reading their messianic hope backward, had forgotten neither jot nor tittle of the past.

On the altar were piles of apples and oranges. Between a pair of carved red candles stood a very old bronze pot. Incense burned within it, sending sweet-smelling smoke into the air. *As breath to men, so is incense to the gods.*

Midnight drew near. A salvo of firecrackers hit the air in a jumble of staccato sounds. Scholar Sen, high priest for his clan, walked reverently forth, reverently kneeling on the red silk cushion before the altar, his long slender hands like two halves close pressed in the traditional gesture of reverence. Three times he made the deep kowtow sanctioned by the centuries, bowing his head to the ground in worship of Heaven and Earth.

Again he came forth, in the name of the family to worship the household gods. These gods, theirs long before Buddhist and Taoist gods came to them—gods of the hearth, gate, and doors; god of the locality; god of the central hall; god and goddess of the bed. Again the aristocratic figure bowed to the ground in reverential kowtow.

And a third time Scholar Sen bowed—this time before the

tablets of his ancestors within the ancestral hall.   Cooked
food, its vapors nourishing the dead souls, stood before the
tablets.

And so at last to the evening's feasting, to which even
intimate friends were never invited.   A great gathering of
the clan, with the matriarch again assuming the place of importance, now that the duties of high priest were over.   The
child, Sen Lo Shih, sat at her side.

At the hour of the Tiger, before any cock had yet crowed,
Scholar Sen broke the seal on the gate, opening the door to
fortune.   And now that the New Year had come, he performed again the triple rites to Heaven and Earth, household
gods, and the ancestors, asking for protection during the new
year, even as a few hours before he had given thanks for
the past year's protection.   The circle was complete.

The first month, the Holiday Moon, was reaching its full.
Feasting, New Year's calls, theater going, gambling, filled
the days and nights.   All day and far into the night, the
young son, the precious son, Lo Shih, took his way from group
to group, welcomed, petted, by all.

Today he found his father sitting with a half-dozen friends
at a quiet game of *mah jong*.   He watched for a while, then
went on to a guest hall where his grandmother entertained
friends come to give New Year's greetings.   They, too, were
gambling—a silent, tense game that brooked no interruptions.
None but he dared interrupt when the matriarch was at the
gaming table.   He could do no wrong in her eyes.   He stayed
a long time, eating sweetmeat after sweetmeat which the
women gave him.

Tiring at last of the petting, he wandered away to the
ancestral hall, lingering in the doorway of the room, watching
the spirits of his ancestors at their feasting.   For nearly two
weeks now they had been visitors in the house.   On a square
table before the tablets stood food and five cups of wine,
five cups of tea.   Five hot towels had thoughtfully been pro-

vided for them to wipe their faces after the feast. Lo Shih saw five shadow men seated in the five chairs, familiar shadows before which he had bowed ever since he could remember, carried to this room first in his grandmother's arms. Even now he could feel her fitting his hands to each other for the kowtow, feel her hand at the back of his neck, pressing his head to the ground. Of late he had come here with his father, high priest of the clan.

Wearying of the ghostly company, again he wandered off through the entrancing maze of the garden. Steps led him down into the dark and damp center of a grotto, where he could dimly see the Goddess of Mercy carved in the rocks. Bending low to avoid the jagged points of stone, he made his way up the winding path leading out of the cavern. He stood in the pavilion at the top of the grotto. All the garden lay spread before him. He was tired. He clapped his hands. The *lao tai tai*'s slave girl, sent to attend him, appeared as if by magic.

"Tea, cakes," he commanded.

When he had finished his little feast, he strayed into a bit of garden outside the library. His ancestors two hundred years before had laid their harps on the stone table beside which he sat. It was they who had let the bits of calligraphy into the walls, ideographs beautiful as any painting, his father had told him. He went on into the library where the books were carefully stored in the wall cupboards, peeped into a little building beyond, where stood the God of Literature, then drifted again into the library garden.

Often his father came here to study an ancient grey pine. Sometimes it threw its black shadow against the white boundary wall of the library court. Sometimes it stood starkly forth without shadow.

Scholar Sen had painted the tree a hundred times. Still he was not satisfied; still he had not captured its entire significance. There was an old Chinese saying that the painter must have the bamboo in his heart before he can paint it.

For hours Sen would study the pine, then go away to his own apartment to paint what he held in his breast. Often he would abandon his brush, dipping the long nail of his little finger in the ink, making bold, sure strokes, bringing mind and paper intimately together. Yet he was not satisfied with his knowledge of the tree.

Sen Lo Shih seated himself on the bench, bent on imitating his father in his study of the pine. But after a little, he rested his head on the table. Late nights and continual feasting had taken their toll. The small reserve of strength he had gained since his sickness, was spent. He lay relaxed and quiescent, conscious only of the cold stone of the table against his cheek. His thoughts seemed to leave his tired body.

Floating outside his mind, hovering over him, was the foreign doctor, as he had looked that night when, waking suddenly, Lo Shih had seen the foreign devil leaning over him. He had been frightened by the grotesque white face topped with the ugly red hair, so near him. Then he had felt some strange new strength reaching out to help him. It had looked out of the creature's eyes. With that genius of memory of his race, sharpened and perfected by the daily memorizing of countless ideographs, Sen Lo Shih had held in his breast, ever since, the white doctor's look that willed him to get well. He had never seen such an expression before. He knew the expressions of reverence and meditation, but this new expression . . .

He was asleep. The delicate ends of his fingers were just visible below his long silken sleeves. His neatly braided queue hung down like a black rope, touching the ground. His thin face was obscured by the bulky shoulder of his padded gown. Only the thin curve of his cheek showed.

XIV

WITH the passing of China's New Year, the men and women of the Mission compounds of the city went vigorously to work. Peter Fraser had new plans for his hospital—more system, greater efficiency. In the gatehouse he had made a window like that of a ticket-seller. Old patients were given red cards of admission, new patients blue ones. Members of patients' families had yellow ones. In three streams the people went to dispensary and hospital.

Diana had six girls in her school this term—one from the artisan class—a step forward.

Miss Dyer was holding a second Bible class. Mr. Berger had forty boys enrolled in his school. Mr. Baker was finding Shoemaker Wang a veritable saint of old. Confucian gentleness and Christian mercy joined in him. Quietly he went about the city seeking out those who needed help. Whatever their trouble, he brought them to the Mission, believing that help would be given them. Sometimes it was difficult to keep faith with Christian Wang. He read his Bible with great literalness.

One afternoon in March, Peter was about to leave the hospital, when Wang, grasping the blue ticket of a new patient in his hand, came in leading a small girl.

"What's this?" said Peter, a little sternly. "This is not the hour to come with such a card."

"*Ai yah!*" exclaimed Wang indignantly. "That son of a turtle at the gate," he went on, "would have me wait until another day. I have told him that Christ said nothing of waiting until the morrow. *Ai yah*, that gateman, he is a stupid man! This girl child must be bought today. Her father must have money. He would sell her for a sing-song girl for four dollars. I offered him five. Here is the child."

"Why does he wish to sell her?" asked Peter.

"He is a smoker of the foreign dirt."

Peter winced at the reference to opium as Western, and took the money from his pocket.

"The child now belongs to the doctor." Wang went serenely away.

What should he do with her? Peter looked helplessly at the dirty, frightened child, her black eyes peering out from her matted, black hair. He guessed he'd better ask Diana, and he led her away to his house.

Diana was moved with pity and indignation. She rang for Wang Ma. With energy Wang Ma opened the door, then stopped.

"Wang brought her," said Diana, seeking to explain.

"That Christian!" exclaimed Wang Ma. "Without *tao li*, bringing such a creature to a scholar's house! Thy name?" she asked.

"Mei Ing."

Diana and Wang Ma scrubbed the little grey body, so crusted with dirt that they had to use lard instead of soap to cleanse it. They cut the matted hair. Wang Ma ordered her helper to go quickly and buy clean clothes. Then they dressed the child in a blue and white flowered coat and plain blue trousers.

In a few days she began to smile, in a few more she was naughty. When Diana was not busy at the school, she taught Mei Ing to sew. She delighted in her hours with the little girl on a footstool by her side. She even considered adopting Mei Ing. Many of the missionaries adopted waifs.

For the first time, she experienced love for a Chinese. Even Sen S Mo never roused such a feeling in her. It impregnated with new warmth Diana's delight in the molding of her school girls. She seemed to have a sudden understanding of them. And never had she had such results. The school girls, diffidently at first, then eagerly, came to call. They sat stiffly on the fronts of their chairs, sometimes not speaking for many

minutes. Then someone would venture a question. "Are
all the people in the teacher's country white?" they would
ask. "How did the teacher come to the kingdom of China?"
And over and over they asked about Diana's clothes. But
they never told her of their own lives, never let her pass the
citadels of their reserve.

Diana, made receptive by her love for Mei Ing, forgot
how clumsy these girls looked in their graceless padded trousers
and jackets. She began to think of them as individuals. One
had a pretty curve to her mouth. A girl named Mo Tsen
made her smile. She recognized in her that quality so marked
in Sen S Mo's mother. She was vital to her finger tips. She
will make a hard matriarch when she grows up, Diana mused—
unless she were tempered with a deeper understanding of the
use of woman's power.

Diana felt her own vigor tempered these days. A new
harmony had been wrought in her which held no striving—
such contentment as she had never before experienced. At
her first realization that she was to have a child, she had not
been certain that she desired it. Her life with Peter, their
sharing of each other's work, was sufficient. This new relationship of mother was an intrusion. And then, gradually,
without her willing it, body and mind felt profound satisfaction.

Peter's love for Diana was heightened. Into her face had
come an expression of great submission that startled him with
its beautiful maturity. Never, even in his first moments of
ecstatic love for her, had she seemed so mysterious and so
beautiful. He felt overwhelming tenderness toward her.

Diana sensed some new quality come into his love. The
knowledge that she was protected woman took definite shape
in her mind, bringing her its own contentment.

XV

MANY years before, Scholar Wu, the Frasers' Chinese teacher, had successfully taken the provincial examination, but the death of his mother, then his father, uncle and older brother, had made it necessary for him to spend many years in mourning, which, according to the strict Confucian ideal of filial piety, prevented him from going up for the higher examinations.

For the twelve years of mourning, three for each of his dead, he had eked out a meager living by teaching a school for Chinese boys whose fathers wished to raise their status by adding scholars to their families. Living outside all government in the quiet of his own tiny house and garden, Wu had grown each year more into oneness with the "immortality of great words," and the Confucian ideal of diminishing human desire in order to preserve the Heavenly Reason. As his son grew older, that he might have money for him to take the examinations, he had accepted the position of teacher to the foreigners. Instructor of one after another of them, he had found all alike belied his ideal of the scholar, the kingly man. All of them showed that striving which breaks the bonds of propriety.

But now he felt himself in a new attitude toward one of this race. Strangely enough, it was the woman who seemed to have acquired accord with the laws of the universe. As he sat opposite her these days, he gradually became conscious of acquiescence softening the angularity of her features, giving her face a refinement Western faces had heretofore lacked for him. Harmony, not striving, was the ultimate refinement.

In these languorous days of early spring, dozing a little as he intoned the language, he saw her face vaguely. Formerly he had been disturbed by her aggressive onslaught of questions.

115

Now dreamily her eyes wandered to the open window as she repeated after him the Classics.

He began to lose his antagonism for these uncultivated people, and he came to realize that they embodied certain Confucian ideals. Underneath their strident ways, they possessed gentleness and benevolence even for those outside their clan—that house of the sick which they kept for the *hsaio ren,* for instance. Sickness he had always thought of as a private matter. These people seemed to think they had responsibility to all sick.

Folding his hands in his sleeves, he moved from the study into the hall. The door stood open into the Frasers' private rooms, and for the hundredth time Wu surveyed the picture hanging on the wall beyond the eating table—a man in rich robes bending over the sick poor. He liked this picture. It had in it some element of his own country's art. The repetition of the figure of the red-robed priest told him in simple fashion the story. But, he felt, this picture should have been carefully put away, awaiting the moment and the kindred spirit when it might be brought forth and for an hour or two a day savored and honored. The perfect moment, the perfect companions. He paused in the hall to look at a picture of this people's great teacher among children. He felt a bond of ideals as he looked at it. Here was the gentleness of the Confucian ideal.

As he passed gravely out of the house and along the flagged walk leading to the gate, it came to him that he would like this man and woman to understand the Confucian ideal, see the ancient Confucian ceremony. Although women did not attend the rites, he believed this woman scholar might be admitted at his request. In this new quietness of hers he felt more in accord with her than with the man.

When he asked them, Peter and Diana were for the moment speechless. Although it was a spectacle every foreigner longed to see, no foreigner in this city ever had. Remembering the essentials of Chinese etiquette, the Frasers tried hard not to show their great eagerness, subduing their ardent youth to the ancient Eastern politeness, holding their features to a grave, expressionless calm. They quietly thanked him, first demurring, murmuring that he did them too much honor— they were not worthy.

But when he had gone, Diana exclaimed, "Oh, Peter! Isn't it wonderful! And you show no enthusiasm," she accused him.

"Yes, yes," he answered. "Just give me time to take it in."

Here, when he had not sought it, had come this touch with the literati. He had tried in so many ways to reach them, to have it always end in futility. What had he done that had suddenly brought this opening? He never guessed that it was Diana's harmonious accord with the universe which had opened the way.

When they told the others of the coveted privilege granted them, Miss Dyer and the Bakers wanted to be included. Then had come Berger, begging an invitation for himself and his wife. Three times the invitation was extended, until at last the whole compound was included, for the courtesy of the Confucian scholar demanded that what was asked for should be given. But Wu thought them greedy. It was like the "small men," the "monkey-hearted," of his people, who greedily insinuated themselves into every festival. But these foreign men claimed to be scholars, Superior Men, and that the ideal of their religion was disinterestedness, freedom from greed.

XVI

THE rain which had fallen all night ceased toward morning, but the sky remained overcast. In the hour before dawn, Peter and Diana came out on the veranda. The yellow light of kerosene lamps appearing in the other houses dissipated a little the sense of heavy night, and the doors opening and shutting broke the stillness. The gate bell tinkled. They heard Scholar Wu's voice. In the sudden flare of burning brands, they saw men's heads coroneted with heavy black queues, bent backs, hands clasped around poles, and the high narrow, box-shaped chairs, supported seemingly only by the air, outlined on the night. As an unseen hand swung a burning brand downward, heads, backs, and hands sank again into nothingness. The detail of men's feet and knotted bare calves took shape.

Silently the members of the Mission gathered, rode forth from the familiar compound. Diana drew her coat closely about her. She wished two could ride in one chair. She wanted to creep close to Peter. In this hour before dawn, her vitality, already drained by the new life within her, sank to its lowest ebb. No coat warmed her. The chill went deeper—chill of the spirit.

They entered an enclosure. The night still clung to it except along the approach to the temple. There, out of iron baskets, the first faint blaze of new fires rose. Over the stubble of recently cut dry grass, they advanced to the temple. Trying to soften the sharp impact of their shoes on the stone floor of the hall, they followed Scholar Wu within. On a great platform, they waited.

"See, there's the tablet," whispered Mrs. Baker.

The gold ideographs stood out in brilliant relief from the black lacquered tablet of Confucius standing on the altar.

Below on a table were offerings of fruits and vegetables. Before it, in open troughs, lay the sacrifice.

Mr. Baker and Berger shifted their positions a few paces to get a better view.

"What are those stone things over there?" Diana asked of Scholar Wu.

"Musical instruments used centuries ago. We no longer know how to play them."

Peter's eyes, accustomed now to the faint light in the vaulted room, saw a crowd of young boys facing the tablet—slender, beautiful youths clothed in rich ceremonial robes. From the vast enclosure beyond the temple came rustlings, as of an army moving stealthily into position. Scholar Wu stiffened into attention, then left them.

In the outer space the scholars were gathering.

Magistrate Sen saw the barbarians standing in the Confucian hall, the doctor among them. He felt angry fear. Ever since he had had this man attend his son, he had tried to justify himself, saying, "It is wise that we take from this common race such material things as medicine and firearms, but the Confucian ideal, the things of the spirit, need not be touched." Now here these aggressive barbarians stood, not far from the sacred tablet of Confucius!

Beyond the hooded gloom of the hall, beyond the wide entrance doors, Peter saw the faint light of dawn stir the darkness. Then flames leaped high in the iron baskets, putting out the dawn with their fierce light, making the world outside the radius of the flames black as ink. Somewhere from that outer darkness, a voice called. Peter felt Diana clutch his arm. He shivered, feeling in the call the utter loneliness of man searching for some hidden way.

Within the hall, the slow beat of drums rose and fell. The orchestra played its strange music. Feather wands in the hands of the crowd of boys swayed rhythmically, as they moved in a ceremonial dance.

"That's elegant!" Berger ejaculated in a sibilant whisper.

"Hush," said Stella.

Peter's gaze rested on the sacrificial ram, bull, and boar. The stiff legs, the raw flesh of the carcasses of the dead animals took on a more and more savage look, against the dignified setting of the restrained tablet, the cups of wine and rice, the thin elegant boys moving in beautiful rhythm. He was repelled. Then, like scenes from the Old Testament came to him. All men sought sacrificial atonement to bring them into harmony with God. The struggle of man to become one with the *Tao,* as the Chinese called it, led for all over the same road. |Religion, not sent down from on high, a perfect revelation to a special people, but a shared, terrible necessity in man to find himself a soul—the everlasting struggle of the spirit to penetrate the material. |

He was angry when he heard Miss Dyer say in an unnecessarily loud whisper to Mr. Baker, "Just as much heathenism in this ceremony of the scholars, as in everything else in China."

Into the hall, the five great officials of the province advanced, coming slowly, ten paces apart. Their dark ceremonial robes, faced with light blue, belted at the waist, stood out stiffly. Their long braids hung like lacquered black ropes to the hems of their robes. The colored buttons of their offices crowned their hats. Pacing slowly they came, their velvet boots moving softly over the stone floor. Outside, the scholars chanted the Ode to Confucius.

One by one each official came to the altar, prostrated himself, bowed his head until it touched the stone floor. Three times the abasement. Three times, walking slowly, ten paces apart, they advanced. Finally, taking from the altar narrow, beautiful boxes, the customary holders for rich silks, they went out for the last time. The flames leaped high in the baskets. The five officials and all the scholars crowded round, casting the offering into the flames. The silks, gorgeous and rich, unfurled, their bright colors meeting the orange flames. The wine of the offering sizzled and steamed, mingling with the flames' cracklings. *Blood of the sacrifice, the very essence of life given to the spirit.*

As the missionary group waited for Wu, servants entered, putting out the candles on the altar, slung the bloody sacrifice over their shoulders, ran off with it. Again Peter felt revulsion. His own religion was a thing quite different from this dark need for sacrifice, this savage offering. All religions except his own, false . . .

With the intuition so characteristic of men of his race, Scholar Wu, accompanying his guests home, felt their fastidious withdrawal. So again, the way closed between them. Peter was baffled. This unprecedented advance on the part of Wu had made him believe that he was at last to be accepted by the intellectuals. But on the day after the ceremony, when he sought to discuss the service with Wu, he found him more withdrawn than usual. Peter could hardly believe that the happenings of the night before had taken place, or that Wu had ever given them such an invitation, so fast closed now were the doors of his spirit.

XVII

To Peter the odor of opium was becoming the characteristic which set the Chinese apart from all other peoples. The smell of unwashed humanity was not peculiar to China, neither was the heavy smell of cities without sanitation. All these he had encountered in other countries. But the sweet, sickish odor of opium weighting the air was coming to stand in his mind for China. It laid its cloying perfume over the city. Often before one reached a village, it tainted the pungent fragrance of wet earth in the rice paddies.

Peter's attention was centered more and more on this phase of his medical work. The hospital might, here, he felt, do something constructive that would lessen the prejudice of the Chinese against the West because of its part in the opium business. In his laboratory he began to experiment on certain effects of the drug. Was there some chemical lacking in the Chinese, which, if supplied, would automatically cure the habit? He began, too, to keep careful records of all opium patients.

Dr. Buchanan had sought to cure addicts by substituting the eating of opium for the smoking of it, lessening the amount from day to day, until the victim was able to get along without the drug. The constant stream of such patients through the hospital, at first had pleased Peter. But as he learned more of the habits of opium addicts and how long it took really to cure a man, he began to be suspicious. His suspicions were further roused by Stella, who pointed out to him that there had been a sudden influx of such cases since he had taken charge of the hospital. "I don't know much about these patients," she said. "Dr. Buchanan didn't think it fit for a woman to have anything to do with them. But I think I've seen some of these men around the hospital before."

122

"Could it be," thought Peter, "that some of them aren't really cured, and are taking advantage of the fact that I don't know them, to get opium?"

Ling, a church member, had appeared particularly zealous in bringing men to be cured of the habit, during the first weeks Peter had had the hospital. "I, humble Ling, have been cured. It is well that such a miserable one devote himself to the cure of his friends," he would say, with great unction.

Peter had not liked the man, but he was important in the tiny colony of the church, so he had tried to control his dislike. Of late, much to his relief, Ling had stopped coming to the dispensary. But now, when Peter began to watch the men come for their daily quota of opium, he was surprised at how often he saw Ling—at the entrance to the dispensary, just turning the corner out of the street which passed the hospital, talking to patients in the ward.

One evening, as Peter entered the hospital for a last inspection, he found Ling in conversation with the night nurse. As Peter approached, the man shrank back out of the light shed by the kerosene lamp into the shadows beyond. Peter moved the lamp quickly so that he might see Ling's face. As he suspected—telltale signs of the drug addict! Bloodless cheeks and lips, waxy skin, the peculiar darkness of eyelids and temples.

After this, quietly, carefully, Peter traced Ling's activities. One day he uncovered the use to which the hospital and church had been put. Ling had been using the cure as a blind to secure the drug to sell. The church members in different villages were his salesmen. Ling was the business manager.

Peter had not been blind to the fact that some of the Chinese Christians were designing men, using the influence of the church as a protection against the law; but that the church and hospital were used for evil purposes had never occurred to him. Although opium was a universal habit, the Chinese looked upon the vice with shame. Already they hated the West for its part in introducing the drug. Many would believe—would wish to believe—that the church purposely sold this drug.

He saw but one way to correct the evil which he had unwittingly brought upon the city. He must stop giving out small quantities of opium as a cure for opium smoking, and he must take drastic measures with Ling and the other offending church members.

Peter had always felt that the sudden withdrawal method was the only certain cure. Now he was convinced of it. But it called for careful, exacting nursing. The heart had to be watched, and in the first terrible hours of restless craving, sedatives had to be administered; in the worst cases, hot baths must be given. For such treatment he must have the addicts in the hospital. But how could he manage it? He did not wish to mix them with the other patients, for he had learned that every addict was a kind of perverted missionary, wishing above all else to share his habit with others.

Then he had an idea. He would start an opium refuge. Not far from the surgical wing stood a low, native building, there when the missionaries had bought the land, occupied now by the household servants. Why couldn't each family use its own attic to house its servants?

The Bakers objected, because they said Dr. Buchanan, they felt sure, would not wish them to take servants into their houses. Mrs. Berger objected, because she said the children played in their attic sometimes on rainy days. Peter emphasized the loss of face to the Christian church in the duplicity of Ling. By night he had the consent of everyone.

Another day, and he had the building cleared of its occupants. He found it could be used temporarily without alterations. But if the same nurses and servants who worked in the main hospital were to work here, a covered passageway was necessary to protect them against the rain that fell so steadily during the winter months. Out of a small gift of money sent him at Christmas, which he had intended to spend on his laboratory, he built the passageway. The two buildings

were on different levels, which necessitated three steps, leading up to the hospital.

At last all was in readiness, and he made "Christian" Ling
the first patient, threatening him with expulsion from the
church if he did not take the cure.

Others, deprived of their daily supply of the drug, came to
Peter begging that they be taken in. Two weeks, and his
refuge was full. Peter sat up with these men, if the worst
hours of their struggle came at night, for he dared not trust
his nurses to withhold the opium they begged for. He feared
that his nurses and servants might even sell it to them.

XVIII

THE windows of his house stood wide open to the night. Peter, accustomed to being roused at any hour, was fully awake at the first hard pound of a man's fists upon the gate. Soon he heard a knock on his own house door. He called softly from the window to tell the man below that he was coming, hoping not to disturb Diana.

As he opened the door, the gateman said, "From the *wai kuo ren*, the foreign men."

In the light of the man's lantern, Peter read the letter sent him by the American agents of tobacco. One of their men was very sick, the note ran—cholera, they feared. Could he come immediately?

They lived outside the city by the Grand Canal, on land granted the foreign business men by treaty. The note must have been pulled up in a basket over the wall, for the city gates closed at dusk. He must go to the sick man in the same manner.

The descent was perilous. Vines and gnarled trees growing out of crevices in the wall threw the wicker basket this way and that, and tangled the rope—not too strong—by which the basket was lowered. When he reached out to free it, he found it was fraying badly. But at last he was down. He pressed the chair-men, awaiting him at the wall's foot, to a faster and faster pace. If it were cholera, there was no time to waste. A few hours and the man would be dead.

As the chair-men moved through the silent countryside, the acrid smell of the recently plowed rice paddies struck at Peter's nostrils—this black earth cultivated for thousands of years gave forth an odor unlike that of America's newly plowed land. He heard the croak of frogs in the rice paddies, and finally the chirp of birds in their first waking.

The chair-men halted, lowered the chair. A brick house loomed in front of him. One of the men of the company came out of the door to greet him. Peter felt strange. He had seen no layman since the fall.

He found the sick man little more than a boy, new to the country, and frightened. "This isn't cholera," Peter said gently, after he had made his examination.

At the doctor's words, fear died out of the sick man's eyes. The unknown world of death receded.

"It's a bad case of dysentery, though. That means a long fight for you," Peter added.

"That's all right . . . I can do that. But I don't want to die," said Randolph. Into his eyes again came fear.

Peter was oddly conscious that he had not witnessed such fear since he had left America. For so many months now he had been used to the Chinese acceptance of death.

Each day, until Randolph was out of danger, he made the long journey beyond the city. On his final call, he found his patient in the living room, his shoulders humped, his hands lying listlessly over the arms of his chair. Evidently lonely, was Peter's instant reaction. He thought of all the work he had yet to do that day, work put aside in order to make this visit. But he couldn't leave Randolph in such a mood. He began talking to him of the Chinese, of the funny things that happened at the hospital. Gradually the young man forgot the barrier of distrust that lay between missionary and layman.

"Do you smoke?" he asked impulsively.

"Yes," said Peter.

"Cigar or cigarette?"

"Cigar."

The young Virginian glowed with hospitality, brought out his finest brand, his gratitude to the doctor changed into respect and liking. He had found so many missionaries refusing to accept him because he sold tobacco. They considered smoking a sin. Narrow-minded people, all of them, had been his verdict. The missionary doctor was human.

Peter had not smoked for a long time. It was one of the things he could do without, in that careful balancing of his budget. He drew in with deep breaths the good tobacco, and drew in, also, deep drafts of the good companionship. He laughed aloud as Randolph told him of his up-country trips, of his way of getting on with the Chinese, of the sign language he had invented.

"They take it as a joke, and they like a joke. They're a fine people. There's a great chance for business among them." The ardent salesman in him now spoke. "We've got a slogan— *A cigarette in the mouth of every Chinese man, woman and child in ten years.* Think what that would mean in sales. Four hundred million of them, aren't there?"

Before Peter's eyes passed the long line of poor come to his hospital. All of them made more susceptible to opium because of undernourishment. The ravages of opium greater because of it. All of them now to be made to smoke cigarettes, so much more expensive than native pipe tobacco? Why? In order to fill the coffers of Christendom.

Was the negative side of Christian civilization, with its keen grasp on revenue, always to thwart its positive aspects, its gift of mercy? Trade was trade, he pondered, as he rode home, ruthless and self-seeking, whether for opium or other products.

XIX

A STRANGE gift had come to the hospital—money for a surgical building. The donor stipulated that none of the money was for equipment and that the building was to be exclusively for surgical cases and as large as possible. Peter had no surgical cases. And what could he do without equipment?

A bronze plaque with the inscription *The James Dalton Memorial* arrived, which was to be mortared into the wall above the entrance. Peter looked at it with a wry smile. Wouldn't it be ironical if James Dalton had made his money out of selling opium or tobacco to the Chinese? It would not be surprising. Missions were dependent upon business. Then all at once it struck him—was Christianity ruthless in its onslaught upon the East? He saw now what Stella had seen in the destruction of Wang's tablet.

Uncertainties seemed to attack Peter from every side since that first uncertainty came to him in the house of Scholar Sen.

After much consultation with all the members of the compound, Peter decided to place the new building between his own house and the hospital. Diana made the only objection to his plan. "I had hoped to have a garden there for the baby," she said.

"There doesn't seem to be any other place," Peter answered her. "But I'll tell you what we can do, in fact, what I had intended to do—put it as far back as possible against the wall of the compound to keep it from overshadowing our windows. That will bring it flush with the street and we can have the main entrance on that side, only a private one on this for my own use. That will leave a recessed space between the main hospital and our house. Will that do for a garden?"

129

"Yes," said Diana, a slight doubt in her voice. "It's a little public. But I can hem it in with high bushes,"·she added, brightening a little.

The surgical building was built, its outer wall taking the place of the boundary wall of the compound. Most of the first floor Peter made into one large room, with two iron grated windows and a door opening directly on the street. He meant to use this room as a waiting room for surgical cases. He wanted it easily accessible to the people. At the end, he partitioned off a space—his consultation office.

Peter found that as much of a ritual must be observed in the building of houses as in all other things in China. High above the squat main building, the scaffolding of bamboo poles rose, two stories high, and to the tips tufts of leaves were tied.

"Feng shui," the native contractor told Peter, when he asked the reason for the decorations, murmuring something about proper harmony in the universe that would bring the hospital luck. At least, that was how Peter interpreted the words.

"Useless," the contractor, a bent old man, said to himself, "to explain further." This breaking of the earth—a dangerous business which the foreign *I Sheng* did not seem to understand. Spirits from the shadow world disturbed, wreaking vengeance on the living. He had seen to it that the boughs hanging from the poles were large. Spirits would undoubtedly think this spot a grove of trees, not know that the earth was being disturbed. If he could only set the ridgepole with due ceremony— as the contractor for that new Chinese house across the way was doing. From his own scaffolding, he could see a carpenter walking along the plank under the ridgepole, casting the Dumplings of Good Luck to the four quarters of the compass, could hear his song:

"I trod on the nest of the Golden Pheasants,
The Golden Pheasants rose up, p'êng, p'êng, the sound of their
    wings.

That they flew to this spot and alighted is great good fortune.
I reach the eaves and pluck the Peaches of the Immortals.
Chang Pan, P'usa of Masons, has come to earth, Lu Pan,
    Patron Saint of Carpenters, snaps the twigs.
The posts must be placed truly when the fortunate day arrives.
I throw in the direction of prosperity and abundance.
To the South, the quarter Ping Ting, of Summer, of Fire,
    Burning Wood and the Flame of the Lamp.
To the North, the quarter of Jên Kuei, of Winter, Flowing
    Water, Waves and Brooks.
To the center of all points, the Quarters Wu Chi, of Earth,
    the Plains, and the Hills.
Fortunate people live where Fortune comes."

In most things Peter let the native contractor have his own
way, but when it came to the operating room, he sought to
have his. "There must be three large windows, placed where
they give the best light," he said.

"As *Fei I Sheng* wishes," murmured the old man, filling the
inch-large bowl of his pipe. *"Ai,"* he said, when Peter had
gone. "Better that I follow my own judgment as in the matter
of the spirits. One window is enough. Save a little money
thus."

Twice the wall had to be taken down before the contractor
decided on three windows, arranged to Peter's satisfaction.

But now the struggle of wills was over, the building nearly
complete, everything important as Peter wished it. He stood
in the door of the hospital a moment looking up at the blue
sky. Diana and he were going to inspect the new building
together. There she was, waiting for him.

"The contractor's made a terrible mistake," she explained,
as he came near. "He's laid the first floor too high. It isn't
on a level with the hospital."

"All has been done as the *I Sheng* wished," the contractor
said, surveying with satisfaction the new floor.

"But it's too high," protested Peter.

"It is a small matter, *ch'a pu to,* almost right. A little

matter of two feet. It is easily remedied," soothed the old
man, folding his hands in his sleeves. "A step or two—and the
small mistake is rectified."

"Almost right!" exclaimed Peter, as he and Diana went
away. "I hear it a hundred times a day. The *amahs* use it.
The servants use it. The nurses use it. Even Stella uses it to
soothe me. How can they ever get a scientific viewpoint if
they won't be exact? Besides, it's going to be awfully in-
convenient to have those extra steps connecting the two buildings."

"Why don't you have him take it out?"

"He wouldn't, except for extra money. At least, he'd
think he ought to have extra, and I haven't any. If I'd saved
what was left——"

There had been a hundred dollars left after he had accepted
the contractor's bid, which he had felt justified in using for
instruments.

The bell at the gate tinkled.

"I hope it's foreign mail. It should come today," cried
Diana.

Peter searched through the pile of letters the gateman
brought them.

"My things for the hospital are here. Here's the customs'
declaration. The gateman can go out and get them, can't he?"
Carefully he filled in the regulations, signing his name.

"Wait, I'll have Wang Ma send him," said Diana. "She'll
make the old man hurry if anyone can."

They spent a lovely hour sitting on the floor of the dining
room, enjoying the novel occupation of having packages to
open. Peter laughed outright when he unwrapped his sterilizer. "Look. You'd think I was going in for a hotel instead
of a hospital."

And he set down before her a huge steam-pressure vegetable
kettle. "It'll do the trick, though—be a little slow—take a
lot of time to sterilize bandages and sponges. What do you
think my colleagues at home would think of a thing like this?"

Diana settled back on her heels and laughed, too. Peter listened, delighted at her laughter, soft and filled with a kind of whimsical gaiety. For a moment, he felt some veil drawn aside, and the whole universe shot through with humor, just as sometimes he saw it shot through with beauty.

Stella came in a little later. "What's all the fun about?" she asked.

"Stay and have supper," said Diana, "to celebrate the sterilizer."

"If the Chinese knew that the sterilizer is a kettle for the cooking of food, they'd probably resurrect the old story about our cooking their babies for medicine. It wouldn't be hard for them to believe it—even after so many of them have been cured in our hospital."

At her words, Peter felt a sinister undertow of superstition dragging at their high gaiety. Then Wang Ma came energetically into the room, common sense written all over her flat features, and that sense of dark undertow was gone.

Mei Ing, skipping past Wang Ma's guard, ran toward Diana.

"Careful," said Peter, stopping her, afraid that in her eagerness she would jar Diana, still kneeling on the floor.

The Chinese child seated herself on a bamboo stool well beyond the reach of Wang Ma. Diana smiled at her. Mei Ing, with one quick movement, alighted at Diana's side, nestling close.

"Why don't you give her to me?" Stella asked Diana, as Peter picked up the pile of excelsior and wrapping paper and went out. "I'd like to adopt her."

"I suppose I'd better," said Diana. "Wang Ma's determined she shan't stay here. She says we can't afford it. And now that I'm to have my own baby——"

"Then it's arranged?" urged Stella.

She rose to go. Despite all Diana's and Peter's efforts to include her, the circle of their happiness was so complete that of necessity she was outside.

"Come, Mei Ing," she said gently. "You're to be my little girl."

From under her hair that lay in a smooth black bang touching her eyebrows, the child looked up with the old suspicious look. Stella knelt looking straight into her eyes. Suddenly Mei Ing smiled and placed her hand confidingly in Stella's.

XX

WHEN the building was completed, Peter laid his few instruments out in the case he had had a carpenter make. But he had no use for them.

"This is not good talk. If we die, we join our ancestors mutilated," answered his patients, when he proposed operating.

Peter thought he might accomplish his purpose by working with the native doctors. He had learned that the Chinese, much as in his own country, divided their doctors into two classes—the quacks and the respected doctors who had made a study of medicine and who were scholars. Would it be possible through Wu to interest one of them, at least in his surgery?

"Yes," said Scholar Wu, when Peter spoke to him of the matter. "I will take you to call upon one of the city's most famous. He is a scholar. Medicine is one of his many interests. He has studied deeply the *yin yang* principle."

When the day for the visit came, to give prestige to his call, Peter hired chairs for himself and Wu. The Chinese doctor, a thin, scholarly man, not unlike Wu in appearance, greeted them in the guest room of his house. Punctiliously, as a host should, he sat facing the south, Peter in the seat of honor at his left.

"I am a physician, even as the honorable one," said Peter. "Perhaps we could exchange knowledge and thus more quickly benefit the city. I have a cure for many diseases by cutting and removing diseased parts of the body. I should be glad to explain to the honorable *I Sheng* how it is done."

The Chinese gentleman fell back on polite phrases. After a little, he rose and brought a chart of the human body, carefully copied by himself from an ancient one. "Would

135

the honorable one care to know where it is safe to insert the acupuncture needles?"

Peter looked with interest at the lines running up and down the picture of a man, between them hundreds of minute ideographs, marking the place for the acupuncture needle.

"What is the reason for the insertion of these needles?" he asked.

"In nature, the vital essences, *yin* and *yang*, exactly balance. They ebb and flow in the body, as elsewhere. Sickness comes when they are out of balance. Then we seek to enter the channel and relieve the excess either of *yin* or *yang* with these needles of gold or silver."

"And how do you learn which is in excess?"

"By the fifty-two different pulses—slippery, fine, slow, hollow like an onion stalk, hard like a drum-beat——" The Chinese doctor, in guttural singsong Chinese, intoned the fifty-two.

Peter looked at the spatulate fingers of the gentleman before him. Indeed they must be sensitive to detect such innumerable variations. He was filled with a growing sense of the futility of such distinctions. As he glimpsed the tangled skeins of philosophy, knowledge, quackery, truth, and superstition, woven and interwoven through the centuries, that made up Chinese medicine, he wondered that the Western science of medicine should have penetrated even the little it had. He wondered that any of the Chinese ever came to his hospital, believing as they did in this idea of *yin* and *yang*— this balance of vital forces in the body. And yet . . . might it not be that there was a rhythm in man as well as in nature? However, as in the West a hundred years ago, theories accepted as dogma kept medicine static, precluding further progress by investigation.

He looked around the room. The shelves, reaching to the ceiling, were filled with bottles. "What are some of your remedies?" he asked. Although the Chinese doctor would take no interest in Western surgery, he might be willing to cooperate in the matter of medicines. It stood to reason that the Chinese, in all their centuries of experience with disease, must have discovered herbs and drugs which cured them of diseases peculiar to the East. All peoples possessed folk-medicines.

Smoothly, suavely, depreciating his own knowledge, the Chinese doctor told Peter that the Chinese were an ignorant and humble people, that he was not worthy to speak before the great teacher from the West on so learned a subject as medicine. He raised his teacup to drink. Etiquette demanded that Peter leave now.

After this, Peter found that opposition to him had sharpened. Wang Ma, who had constituted herself guardian of the family, told Diana of a rumor in the city that Peter was making himself a rich man, and that he sought to learn the secrets of the Chinese doctors. Inherited recipes for medicines families kept secret as the secrets of glazes were kept by potters. Then Peter realized that the Chinese doctor had misinterpreted his intentions, and also that this scholar and doctor saw medicine as business, not as service to mankind. One thing Peter was coming to believe—Chinese religion and philosophy held no idea of service.

XXI

THE summer was come. The hot rays of the glowing sun beating upon thousands of wet paddies, generated an intolerably brilliant blanket of moisture. It hung suspended between earth and sky, in the country forcing the fields to luxuriant growth, in the city lying heavy as wet flannel, absorbing the odors of decaying vegetables and night soil, drawing out like a poultice man's vitality.

The activity of the West ebbed away. The schools and chapels of the various Protestant Mission stations in the city were closed. The French Catholics carried on theirs through the summer. The door of the cathedral stood open. In the cool, dark interior, the yellow points of candleflames lit up the gloom, inviting men to enter and worship. Behind the small door let into the wall of the nuns' orphanage, just above a hollowed stone, sat a sister in black habit and coif, ready to open the door, if the bell above it tinkled, taking in the baby placed there. From over the wall, morning and evening, drifted the voices of Chinese orphans, singing masses.

At the American hospital, Stella and Peter relieved each other every fortnight, for neither could long endure the combination of heat and bad sanitation of the city. The other members of the station went away for the whole of the summer. Their houses stood empty, the blinds closed. The doors of the boys' school were locked, the windows shuttered. The new surgical building stood forth stark in its newness, empty and quiet. In the girls' school, Sen S Mo and an *amah* or two lived in native fashion.

Before Diana left, Sen S Mo had asked if she might have two stone jars once used to hold water brought from the canals. The jars had proved too small to hold enough sand and

cocoanut fiber to cleanse the drinking water, and had been
stored in a neglected corner of the compound. Diana was
glad to give them to her. Sen S Mo had placed one on each
side of the flagged path leading to the girls' school, superin-
tending the coolie in filling them with the proper slime and
water in which to grow the lotus, Sacred Flower of Buddha.
Soon the leaves floated green, like huge lily pads, upon the
surface.

Through the summer when the spirit of the white people
was gone from the compound, and she was once more in possession of an Eastern woman's leisure, Sen S Mo watched the
pink buds push themselves to the surface. Hour after hour
she gazed entranced as they unfolded into full flower, symbol
to her of purity—symbol of Buddha born into the defilement
of the world, but living outside the world. At night after
she went to her room, she took the Buddha pose, her legs folded
upon each other, her feet in their silk shoes resting like petals
in the curve of her knees, her eyes lowered. Quietude, keeping
the heart pure, that the lotus blossoms might not wither.

Through the city, the Rain Dragon was carried in procession. He that is of the *yang* essence, he who represents the
fecundating principle of nature, the Bringer of Rain. Clack-
ing gongs and cymbals attended him, echoing through the
quiet missionary compound.

In the sixth month, the Lotus Moon, the peasants decked
the Thunder God on his birthday with offerings of flowers,
inviting him to give the summer rains. In the temples at the
right of the Dragon of Rain stood the God of Lightning,
beating together the *yin* and *yang* mirrors. When the rains
at last came, the peasants stayed within their huts—when the
sky makes fecund the earth, man's delicacy demands that he
should not witness the mystery.

In the Lotus Moon the attention of all the city was centered
on the Flowers of Buddha. Out on the lake beyond the city,
pleasure boats floated toward the Lotus Island within the
center of which lay a pond, green from bank to bank with

lotus leaves. Men in gauze silk robes, in rapt contemplation of the pointed pink buds and cup-like blossoms, paced
gravely the stone-flagged walk that rose on piles out of the
stagnant water.

Lighted paper lotus were set adrift on the river. Ghostly
spirits of the drowned—hungry souls tossing on the waters—
seized the flowers, thus gaining rebirth in human form.

Autumn came with its tranquillity. The ponds lay in
smooth tranquillity, the lake lay in tranquillity. A soft breeze
blew against the golden heads of the ripened grain. In the
quiet air could be heard the soft thud of the bunched rice, as
the peasants beat it against the threshing boxes.

Sen S Mo, sitting in her room at the Mission, made lotus
blossoms out of stiff pink paper, set a candle in each, planning
to give them to her friend, *Fei S Mo.*

On the first afternoon after Diana's return, Sen S Mo carried
the gift to her. Touched by the gift, Diana drew closer to
Sen S Mo than ever before. Sen S Mo felt it, and asked a question she had long wanted to ask of her friend. "Have you no
figure of this Christ you tell me of? If your God came to
earth, surely you have kept His image."

"Yes," said Diana. "In my own church, the Episcopal
Church, there is such a figure." Strange, she thought, that
Sen S Mo should not have seen it before. She brought her
crucifix, and laid it in the Chinese woman's hands.

Christ, real now for the first time to Sen S Mo, a god
crowned with thorns! A god who suffered! Barbaric people,
who placed a crown of thorns on their god. Buddha wore a
crown of snails. As he sat in meditation on how to lessen
the woes of the world, they had crept up and formed a helmet
of their cool bodies to protect him from the sun.

For several days Sen S Mo was shaken, unable to forget the
touch of the cold ebony of the cross on the palm of her hand.
Then she found serenity in looking again into the calm face of
Buddha.

All through the first weeks of Peter's return, he found himself swept up into the all-consuming interest of the city—the Imperial Examinations. Teacher Wu spoke of little else. His son, a man of forty, was one of the contestants. Wu told Peter that the examination grounds, closed these three years, had been made ready during the summer against the coming of the imperial examiner and the thousands upon thousands of students. The official who had charge of the keys had stood before the locked doors, clad in his rich robes, the keys in his hand. Gravely he had handed them to a little old woman standing opposite—a midwife. Such was the ancient ritual by which learning was brought into the world.

On the fifth day of the Eighth Moon, Peter joined the throngs in the streets to see the great official chairs of the examiner and his retinue carried to the examination halls.

On the eighth day, he went again, when the students passed into the enclosure. For hours afterward, that great throng of scholars kept passing before him in retrospect, most of them middle-aged, some elderly, all thin-bodied, stoop-shouldered, their lives spent in preparation for the coveted degree.

As night drew on, he pictured them locked in their cells. At dawn, he woke. It is now, he thought, when the text for their essay is taken to them. For the nine days of the examination, he felt bowed under the weight of tradition—all the scholars of the nation, seeking in their thinking to conform to an ancient pattern. Where in this barren scholasticism could his ideal of speculative thinking be introduced? How force the seed of the West into this over-tilled field of the East?

He had no real progress to show for his year's work. It had ended in sterility.

XXII

DIANA and Peter threw themselves into Christmas plans with all the ardor of their youth and something more. They were touched with that wonder and excitement that hangs about the coming of one's first child.

On Christmas Eve, in the Christian compounds of the city, Protestant and Catholic alike prepared to honor the Christchild. At the cathedral, the child lay in his manger. At Diana's church, the altar shone forth in its silver and candles and white embroidered cloth. At Peter's Mission, on the chapel platform stood a lighted Christmas tree. Chapel, hospital, and houses had been decorated with holly, which grew wild in the hills.

There had been difficulty in securing the tree. The hillsides, centuries ago, had been denuded of trees. The only ones standing, outside the temple grounds and grave enclosures, were the mulberry, camphor, and tung oil, the products of which brought income, and which the owners refused to cut. But at last, Shoemaker Wang, happy as a child over this celebration that took the place of China New Year in his mind, found a cypress that could be bought from a grave plot which had been abandoned because of its bad *feng shui*.

At sundown, all work was laid aside and the compound gates tight shut against the busy life of the "heathen" city. The Chinese church members, wearing blue garments, new after the custom of their own New Year, had long before entered the chapel, fingered the tree, exclaimed over its beauty, and then seated themselves, the women on one side of the aisle, the men on the other, to wait patiently for the festivities.

Scholar Wu, who had accepted an invitation to the celebration given him in return for his to the Confucian service, sat in deep meditation among the men. As dusk fell and the

chapel grew dim, he heard under the chapel windows the high
voices of children singing in unison.

"Hark the Herald Angels sing"

He liked this singing together of the foreigners. He remembered the words of Confucius, speaking of music: *At the
commencement of the piece all the parts should sound together; as it proceeds they should be in harmony.* And the
strange gladness of the Occidental music touched him.

"Glory to the new-born King"

Kingship he understood. It lay at the very center of the Confucian belief. But across the likenesses of the foreign religion to his own, struck in jumbled confusion the differences.
This tree—what did it signify? And the cross—a king on a
cross?

Together Diana and Peter entered their own home. This
hour they had treasured for themselves. They had even succeeded in sending Wang Ma to bed.

For their Christmas tree they had chosen a Heavenly Bamboo, one of the pair that stood in pots on either side of their
house door. Peter set a match to the tiny red candles made
for temple use, which Wang Ma had bought for them, and
which they had placed on the table around the tree.

"It's as lovely as a fir would be," said Diana, looking at the
rough brown bark of the trunk stems, the clusters of bright
red berries against the shining green of the delicate leaves.

As the tiny flames multiplied, casting their light into Diana's
face, Peter was startled by her expression. Plainly, somewhere
back in his mind, something said to him, "Diana's labor has
begun." In his year of internship in America, he had seen too
many women in childbirth not to know that expression. "Are
you all right, darling?" he asked.

"Yes, but let me sit down," she answered him. "I'm tireder than I thought. I think I stood too long outside with the children, and the ground was cold." She shivered.

He brought a chair for her, gently helped her into it. "And now for your present, Diana." Eager as a boy, he took a little bundle from the branches.

"Peter!" exclaimed Diana, as she opened the package and found a Chinese ring set with the tiniest of pearls. "It's beautiful. But you shouldn't have done it. You've gone without something to get it."

"A man always gives his wife jewelry when his baby is born. I wish it were bigger—the pearl, I mean—but I couldn't manage more," he added a little wistfully. He turned away, concealing his emotion, saying, "Here's your mother's box. Let's open it next."

There was no response from Diana, and when he looked he saw she was gripping the chair-arms. Great drops of perspiration stood on her forehead.

"Darling," he cried, dropping down by her side. "What is it?"

For the moment, his doctor's knowledge had gone from him. All he could realize was that his woman was in pain and that he was powerless to prevent it and yet was responsible for it. Both were speechless, each shrinking from the sense of cold disaster which seemed suddenly to mingle with the warm stream of life.

"My time has come. There's nothing to be afraid of," said Diana simply. "The pain's gone, anyway."

Peter was all doctor now. "I must put you to bed at once." After he had snuffed out the candles by the tree, they went slowly up the stairs, Peter's support lessening that dragging weight within her. Gently, quickly, he got her into bed. Then he sent the gateman for the doctor who was to visit friends in the city during the holidays, and who had promised to take care of Diana. His boat had been due since early afternoon.

Wang Ma, hearing Peter's call for the gateman, came down from the attic, glanced at her mistress, then went out, shouting to her helper. "*Ao sao!* Hurry, Useless One. We must have hot water." Then she came back, taking her place by the bed, giving Diana her brown, strong hand to drag upon.

The gate bell rang. Peter listened. No sound of hard leather soles of foreign shoes beating against the flagstones— only the soft shuffle of the gateman along the walk, the hall, the stairs.

"The foreign doctor has not come."

"He can't get here now until morning. The city gates are closed," thought Peter. "And for over two years I have not delivered a child."

"All is not well," exclaimed Wang Ma.

Peter pushed her from the room, shutting the door behind her. "Diana," he said quietly, bending over her, "Dr. Smith has not come. Have you faith in me?"

Diana's eyes opened, resting upon him. "More than in anyone." Her eyelids dropped again and she was shut away into her struggle.

At once he was the clear-headed surgeon—the most promising man in his class. Quickly he made his examination. He would have to take the child. He must have help. He sent Wang Ma for Stella. He must have better light. He sent the gateman for coolies to help him move Diana to the hospital.

The compound, so recently filled with festivity, was still. The houses were dark. The candles in the windows had gone out. Only the gateman's lantern threw a dim path of light for the stalwart coolies carrying the improvised litter made of a camp cot. Peter walked by its side, holding Diana's hand. Wang Ma brought up the rear. So they entered the empty surgical building.

"Careful!" cried Peter to the coolies as they reached the stairs.

"It shall be done, *I Sheng,* doctor. Thy sick one shall know no jar," spoke one of the coolies, very gently.

In spite of his anxiety, Peter felt the wonder he used to feel when the coolies ministered with gentleness to Dr. Buchanan. It gave him a curious comfort.

He found Stella already in the operating room. Cool and efficient, she was making preparations.

The kerosene hanging-lamp with its huge reflector shone down upon Diana, but he steeled himself not to see his wife in the drawn and stricken woman on the operating table.

It was over. He had saved Diana and, almost by miracle, the child. No . . . not by miracle. He knew in his heart that he had done his work with utmost skill. He put the baby gently into the hands of Wang Ma.

"Wang Ma's baby," murmured the old woman.

Then he turned again, helping Stella arrange a bed in the operating room, for he dared not move Diana to the house and the rest of the surgical wing was cold. Together they lifted her, still unconscious from the anesthetic, placed her on the bed, drew the coverlets up to her chin. Peter knelt to tuck the blankets close. As he and Stella watched her for the first signs of returning consciousness, suddenly, without willing it, hardly knowing it, he leaned against Stella and wept. For one moment, his head lay next her heart.

Then, once more, he was all doctor, watching his patient for any change. He spoke impersonally to Stella. "She needs a stimulant. Will you get it, please?"

After Stella had shut the door, she leaned for a second against it, as if to steady herself, then walked with sure step down the corridor on her errand.

In the early morning hours, Peter, sitting at Diana's side, heard her speak his name faintly.

"Yes, dear. Everything's all right. It's a little girl." He motioned to Wang Ma, who reluctantly yielded the baby to him. He held the child close, so that Diana need not move to see her. "Look, darling."

Slowly, as if the effort were almost too great, Diana opened her eyes. A faint smile passed across her face. Then her eyes closed again. "You are willing ... that we should call her ... what I wanted ... Serena?" she whispered.

"Of course, dear."

Diana slept content. Weeks before she had asked this of Peter, giving as her reason that Serena was her mother's name. Deeper than that she wanted the name because it would remind her of those serene hours when she had carried the child.

XXIII

IT WAS as if Diana's travail had brought the sterile surgical building life. A few days after she was taken home, the first Chinese patient entered it. As Peter started for the hospital that morning, Ting Ta Shih Fu, the Bergers' cook, came in through the door at the back of the hall. His apron nearly touched the floor, so bent was he with pain.

"*I Sheng*, doctor, I have sickness. I would eat of your medicine." His hands grasped convulsively at his groin, as if he would hold himself together.

"Sit here." Peter bent over him. With his sensitive fingers he made a cursory examination. The man wore a crude native support which had not been strong enough to hold in rupture. "Ting Ta Shih Fu," said Peter, "I can save you, but not with medicine. I must cut and repair."

"*Ai*," said the middle-aged man. "Then I must consult my mother. Will *I Sheng* ask my master to permit me to leave his kitchen, go to her village?"

"Ta Shih Fu," said Peter, "there is not time to go to your home. No later than tonight you will die if I do not make the repairs."

Ting stood silent. Even as his agony gripped him, even as he faced quick death, his filial piety held him to that journey. This cutting was a diabolical business, sending him, if he died, to join his ancestors mutilated. He must consult the head of his family, lest he bring disaster upon his clan by such an act. "It is a small journey. Tomorrow I will again come to the doctor."

"Tomorrow you will not travel. You have but a few hours to live, Ta Shih Fu. Accept my help, accept life," begged Peter.

"It is not for me to decide. The old one must——"

Then, suddenly, Peter knew what to say. "In the absence

148

of thy mother, thou shouldst obey the master to whose household thou dost belong. To die is unfilial."

With dignity Ting at last spoke. "*Ai*, he is my master. What he says, I will do."

Peter could scarcely believe that he had won; but in a half-hour he was performing his first operation on a Chinese. The Bergers' coolie, Ting Ta Shih Fu's friend, stood wide-eyed in one corner of the operating room. Berger took on dignity in this rôle of responsibility, standing beside his servant, inspiring him with faith in Peter.

As soon as Peter took up the instruments, he forgot all but his patient and his own swift, skillful fingers. Elation stole through him. His hands had not lost their cunning.

The news spread through the city, through the countryside. The man Ting had been cut, sewn together, and made well. The sickness had been taken out. His friend, the coolie, had seen. Even into the rich quarters of the city, the news was carried. The tale grew as it traveled. The foreign doctor was a magician. Then a holy man. Then the God of Healing.

Here and there, a brave and daring man, suffering as Ting Ta Shih Fu had suffered, asked to be repaired. To Peter's surprise, the Chinese began to accept surgery. A practical people, they put aside superstition when they saw that "cutting" worked. They were used to powerful medicines that brought quick results; quick results they saw, they could get in surgery. Peter saw their minds take that abrupt jump of acceptance which had made medical history in the West.

Now for the first time he realized the great vitality of the Chinese race. Men with tumors so large they dragged on the ground, men in the last stages of cancer, lay and sat on the benches of his dispensary, groaning with gusto, insisting with gusto that he cut and cure. He felt that the inferno of sick, which he had seen thronging the road to the temple that first spring, had been transplanted to his consulting room. Some blessed him because he made them well; some cursed him because he would not. If he cured one, he could cure all, they argued. They could see no distinction among their diseases.

The narrow side street leading to the hospital became a thronged thoroughfare. The chairs and litters of the wealthy sick jostled the sick poor who walked. Street vendors set up their stalls narrowing the street; traveling kitchens fought their way into the mass. Sugar cane, water chestnuts and the bright red caltrop were hawked. Steaming dumplings and sweet potatoes tempted the waiting patients. Sometimes the street vendors crowded even into the waiting room. At the end of the day, bits of sugar cane and the peelings from caltrops and other nuts lay on the floor.

From Peter's hospital, the throng spilled itself over to his house. They came to bring little thank offerings—a chicken, a few peaches. They came hoping to see the doctor's child. Never had there been such a child in the city! The Berger children were dark-haired, dark-eyed, more like Chinese. But Serena had golden hair, blue eyes, and a fair skin. Always a faint, soft pink came and went in her cheeks.

Diana guarded her closely. "It isn't safe to have them near her," she told Peter.

"You might just hold her up to the window," suggested Peter. But Diana shook her head.

Serena's fame spread. Wang Ma told about her when she went to visit her husband's people. The girls in Diana's school told about her when they went to their homes. One day, Wu brought word that a woman from the educated Tang family would like to call and see her.

At last the formal hall of their house was to be used for the purpose for which it had been furnished. They had always thought it would be the men of the literati who would come first. Instead, it was a woman who had made the first advance.

Diana asked Sen S Mo to drill her in the correct procedure: how she should receive her guest, when to seat her, when to serve refreshments, and many other things.

The woman's chair was carried up the house steps and set down so near the open door that the poles extended into the hall. Thus the lady was not exposed to the vulgar gaze of the outside world, for she stepped from the chair directly into the house.

Diana led her to the seat of honor. As she stepped back to take the chair on the other side of the table, she stood paralyzed, realized that she herself was taking the seat of honor! This first call—so important. And she had made this unexplainable error in etiquette. She looked at the Chinese lady. Every line of her face expressed the woman of breeding who is certain beyond a doubt that the etiquette she is trained to is the only etiquette. Mrs. Tang would not forgive such setting aside of custom. This was the way the Chinese offered insults—pretending to be polite, hiding the insult beneath a show of courtesy.

Impulsively, she spoke. "Your customs, you see, I do not understand, but if Tang *tai tai* will come into my rooms, I shall know how to treat Tang *tai tai*."

There was a little silence, in which Mrs. Tang shrewdly measured this foreign woman. Suddenly she dropped her guard. "I like you. You do not pretend to what you do not know," she said. "Show me how you live. What is your *tao li?*"

Together they entered the dining room and Diana seated the lady at her right after her own custom and served tea after her own fashion. They talked of women's things, of their houses and their children. Diana told her the use of everything in the house, let her finger the table linen, answered when she asked its price. Mrs. Tang nibbled gingerly at the foreign cake, liked it, ate a second piece.

"*Ai!*" exclaimed Mrs. Tang.

In the doorway stood Wang Ma, Serena in her arms. Softly Mrs. Tang beat her breast with her flattened hand, the gesture of fear. To this black-haired woman come of black-haired people, the fair child dressed all in white resembled a *kuei*.

Kuei, who harm mortals, those uncared-for spirits who roam the world seeking human form.

Again Diana acted on impulse. She took Serena from Wang Ma and laid her in Mrs. Tang's arms.

"*Ai!*" gasped Mrs. Tang, flinching a little. Then she gave a soft chuckle of satisfaction at the touch of the warm child. Why, this was just another baby! She cuddled her close, and Serena, feeling about her the arms of one who knew how to hold her firmly and safely, smiled.

"I precious you," murmured the woman.

"Your children . . . ?" Diana began.

"Dead at birth. Not one have I left. Now there are others in the household who have given my lord sons." Her face set in acceptance of her fate. "*Mei yu fatzu,* it cannot be helped."

"It would have been so with me," said Diana, eagerly, "only that my lord is a doctor who can save babies. Let him deliver you of your next child."

For an instant, Mrs. Tang's face took on hope. Then an expression of suspicion crossed it. "I hear you have strange ways at this house of the sick."

"Nothing that matters," answered Diana. "Just a difference in *tao li.*"

"Like the seating of guests, only a difference in *tao li?*" Mrs. Tang looked down at Serena. "And beneath these skirts she is like our babies?" she asked. "The foreign doctor does not spoil a baby? I have heard——"

"I will show you," said Diana, and gently began to undress Serena. She took off the knitted white sacque, lawn dress, lawn slip, flannel underslip.

"Feet just like ours," murmured Mrs. Tang leaning close. "This, around the waist?"

"That is to guard against cold and to hold her against rupture."

"White, white, even her skin—but beautiful. Just like our babies, soft and warm." Mrs. Tang drew the blanket around Serena, hushed her until she fell asleep.

After the woman had gone, for a long time Diana held Serena close in her arms. So Peter found her. She explained to him how she had disarmed Mrs. Tang of her superstitious fears.

Peter was excited. "If we work together, we can break through the taboos that bind the women of China. The thing to do is to get the women to come and you do as you've done with Mrs. Tang—show them Serena." He was pacing back and forth across the room, rumpling his hair, planning as he walked. "It'll be just as it was with surgery. Once they see the sense of it, they'll come to me. With you and Serena to help, we can do it!"

"But I can't have the women come often," exclaimed Diana. "It wouldn't be good for Serena."

"My forceps are the only ones in all this province. And the women won't come to me! I could save so many lives—do away with so much pain!"

Diana looked away from him to Serena, asleep in her arms, her tiny mouth parted a little, sucking faintly. Diana was not yet accustomed to that defenseless look a baby has in sleep. "We're different, Peter. You can think of all the babies in China. I can only seem to think of ours."

"I suppose so," he answered. "But I wouldn't let any sick people come. You didn't think I'd do a thing like that, did you? I love Serena as much as you do."

"But how would you *know*? I don't want to take any risks."

Suddenly, Diana became conscious of a strange new look in Peter's eyes—as if he felt something alien in her. "Why couldn't we do this, Peter?" she hastened to say. "Perhaps here's our chance to win the upper class. Why don't we try to get a few of *them* to call on us and see the baby? We'd be beginning at the top to win the women."

So it was decided.

Mrs. Tang came and brought her friends. Gradually the women's fears lessened as they found nothing strange or terrible in the doctor's house. Diana took them from cellar to garret, explaining the use of everything. They liked best to have her show them the baby's things—her soap, powder, safety-pins, crib. Of the crib they did not approve. A baby should sleep close held against harm.

When in the Tang household a concubine gave birth to a girl, Mrs. Tang insisted the baby should have all the things Serena had. She sent to Shanghai for the same kind of powder and soap.

"First step toward proper care of babies," said Peter.

Once when Mrs. Tang was taken sick, Peter was called to the house to attend her. But all he was allowed to do was to take her pulse as she thrust her hands beyond the bed curtains.

Diana laughed, on his return. He looked so discomfited. His coat collar was rumpled and his pockets bagged like a small boy's. She went to him, smoothing his collar. "You are a dear," she said.

"More than usually so?" he asked.

"Yes—somehow more than usually so. But, Peter," she said gently, "you mustn't work too hard."

Sen S Mo, now a constant visitor in their house, one day said to Peter, "Why does not *Fei I Sheng* buy for himself the Seven Sick Ladies? Then, like our Chinese doctors, he would have plenty of women patients."

"What do you mean?" asked Peter.

"If *I Sheng* will let me, I will call a man that he may see."

Peter was leaving the hospital the next day, when a little old man, carrying a bundle like that of a curio vendor, limped toward him. "I have come to see the doctor. I have brought things to help him in his business."

Remembering Sen S Mo's remarks, Peter stepped back into the hall, motioning the man to follow.

Then the old man, squatting on the floor, his knees wide apart, the skirt of his cotton gown falling between, untied the blue cloth of his pack, handed Peter one porcelain female figure after another. Each lay so as to disclose a different part of the body. "If *Fei I Sheng* would buy a set, they could be of use to him when he visits sick women." He picked up one Peter had laid down. "A woman who has pain in the breast or in the stomach would like this one to show the doctor. Without disclosing herself, thus she could make known her sickness."

"No. I don't want them," said Peter shortly, and turned and walked away.

The man followed. "Very cheap. Help in business," he called.

"I said I didn't want them. Pack up your things and get out."

"Master no want? Very cheap," the man urged plaintively.

Peter strode out of the building. He was angry with the man. Speaking of medicine as a business! Angry with Sen S Mo. Did she really think he'd have anything to do with such claptrap? Hadn't she learned anything after living for two years next door to the hospital?

The gateman came toward him. "Did master see the man? Very precious, the man's wares."

"I don't want his things," answered Peter. His anger turned upon the gateman. "Don't ever let a man like that in here again. You ought to know better. How's your wife?" he asked, a change in his tone.

"A little sick," the gateman answered. "But very soon now——"

"Can I help?"

"My humble self would not bother the foreign doctor."

Again Peter's anger rose. Why were these people so stubborn? Why wouldn't they see what he could do for them? The gateman's wife had lost eight children in childbirth, and yet, now that she was again pregnant, she wouldn't even let Stella do anything for her . . . or Diana. Stella had given her quinine when she had had malaria, and had treated many small ailments. But she wouldn't trust Stella in the important matters. Stella had tried to find out what had gone wrong

when her other children had been born, but she could get
nothing out of the woman except that evil spirits had tor-
mented her. Diana, too, had tried, saying, "Before my baby
came, I was very careful. If you walked a little——"

"It is different with you," said the woman.

That night, as Peter came from his last inspection of the
hospital, he heard a woman's sharp cry. "Gateman's wife,"
he said to himself. "She's having trouble." He walked im-
patiently away to his own house, strode into the dining room
where Diana sat sewing. "The gateman's wife is in labor.
She needs help."

"But what can you do?" asked Diana.

"Nothing." He sat down, his beautiful, supple hands
clasped, hanging listlessly between his knees. "I suppose there's
a dirty midwife there. They do awful things."

"There's nothing you can do. You're tired. You ought to
go to bed."

"I'll wait a little."

It grew late. The noises of the city came now separate and
distinct. The confused jumble of street cries no longer muted
those two never-dying sounds—the bark, bark of wolf-like
dogs roaming in packs, hungry and lean, hundreds of them
giving chase to one with a bare bone; the pound, pound of the
presses beating out the spirit money . . . two sounds accenting
the stillness of the room.

"Listen!" said Diana, dropping her sewing on the table.
Rising, she went to the door, opened it.

A sharp drawn-out wail broke the stillness of the house.

"Oh, Peter," she cried, "you've got to do something. . . ."

He was on his feet. "I'm going to her!"

"If she should die . . . they'd blame you . . . Peter, should
you try——"

But he was gone out of the house.

She stood on the porch. It was too dark to see, but she
heard the slam of the hospital door, heard Peter running down
the steps. The door of the gateman's hut opened. In the dim

light thrown on to the night from within, she saw Peter's head and shoulders. Then the door was shut.

Suddenly it opened. Peter's tall form struggling with a Chinese woman was etched in the lighted doorway. Darkness again. From outside the gatehouse Diana could hear a woman cursing in Chinese.

The cries of the sick woman suddenly ceased.

Diana went back into the house. With her hands clasped in her lap, she waited. Suppose Peter couldn't save the baby, or even the mother. They'd say he had killed them. Her hands tightened in their hold upon each other. Why had she urged him to go? He'd been gone a long time. Never again would she urge danger upon him . . . if he'd only come! For the first time, this country seemed wholly alien to her. The endlessly pounding spirit-presses . . . the never-ending insistent bark of dogs.

She heard his quick step. He was there. He was excited. He was chortling with delight. "I've saved them both. They've got a son. You should see the old gateman—proud— why, Diana, what's the matter?"

She had thrown her arms around his neck and was crying. "I thought—you didn't come! It was so dangerous. . . ."

"But, dear, I was all right. I felt certain I could save her if I had a chance. When I was sure—that's when I put the midwife out."

"You didn't . . . "

"Yes. Had to. She wouldn't let me work. Well, anyway, I've christened forceps in this city tonight—used them to save a Chinese baby. Come, dear, it's almost morning. We must get a little sleep."

But for a long time sleep came to neither. Peter's excitement was too great, and Diana's anguish. Each had entered deep that night into experience. Peter, in the tense moments of effort, had lost the sense of his own entity, he an instrument through which life poured. Diana, in those same moments, sitting alone fearing for Peter, had felt herself, Peter, and their child an entity precious and separate.

The gateman walked proudly through the city, boasting in the tea shops of a son. "This foreign *I Sheng*," he said, "his ways are good. I alone of my friends have seen it, and thus I have a son."

It was not as it had been with surgery. Many of the gateman's neighbors blamed him for allowing a man to attend his wife in childbirth. But one or two men in the city, who wanted sons desperately, brought their wives to Peter.

Peter felt that if he were to make the most of this small beginning, he should have a women's ward. He begged the Mission to give him even a little money. Again, as with the opium refuge, he had to resort to a native building. He built it one story high on the other side of the gate, separate from the men's department. Now his hospital extended along two sides of the compound, an odd jumble of foreign and native structures.

The question of nurses for the women's ward was solved by Sen S Mo. "This thing which *I Sheng* wishes in his house for the sick, the care of women, could be done if he took widows. There are plenty who would come. I could control them."

"You!" exclaimed Diana.

"Yes. I should like to try the hospital work."

Diana trembled for Sen S Mo. In the school she had always been treated as the great lady, but in the hospital she would be in the impersonal world of science, where the individual subordinates himself to his task. Was Sen S Mo ready for such discipline? The men students had not proved to be.

Only a few weeks remained until the end of the term. Diana suggested to Peter that Sen S Mo take up her duties in the hospital after the girls' school closed.

"I need her, just now. Serena is still so small. During the long vacation, I can find another matron."

"Of course, dear," said Peter. "I've only one patient just now in the women's ward anyway."

"What my sister asks is granted," answered Sen S Mo when Diana suggested the plan to her.

In the final weeks of school, Diana tried adroitly to show Sen S Mo that this new individuality she had taught her had its own submissions.

At the beginning of the Great Heat, Sen S Mo entered the hospital. Following close behind her were three young widows, hair plucked from temples and foreheads—mark of the married woman. Walking stiffly on their bound feet, they went up the steps of the hospital into the presence of Peter.

But Diana's thought that Sen S Mo meant to care for the sick with her own hands was a mistake. Sen S Mo envisioned the care of the sick as the work of *amahs,* she their supervisor and superior.

"But it's a step forward," Stella pointed out to Peter, when he grumbled that it was bad discipline, "that Sen S Mo is willing even to come to the hospital. Let's see what she makes of it. Leave her alone until you return from your vacation," she begged.

Stella, in charge during the first of the summer, watched as Sen S Mo shaped the hospital to the ways of a patriarchal household. All the shrewd instinct of the Chinese housewife was evidently aroused by her new task.

"Young teacher," she said to Stella, "let me save you the trouble of carrying the keys to the rice bins. That I can do."

Soon Sen S Mo went through the women's ward like a Chinese matriarch, wearing at her waist the keys of rice bin and medicine chest. She had a desk set for herself in an unused corner. With all the power and ability of the head of a clan, she enforced her orders. Not only her widows, but the men attendants obeyed her. There was not a coolie on the place who did not fear Sen S Mo's displeasure.

"If she considers actual care of the sick a menial task, what does it matter?" Stella said to herself. "These widows of small tradesmen are humble because there is nothing for them in life. Them I can train to do the actual nursing. It's a beginning. Sen S Mo will change."

Peter returned from his vacation in the hills, filled with new vigor and determination. Stella showed him the hospital with pride. "It's never been so clean, has it?" she asked him.

"The actual nursing?" persisted Peter.

"With Sen S Mo taking over so much of the management, I have been able to do a lot of it, and I'm training the widows," Stella countered.

"You mean," answered Peter, "you're doing what Sen S Mo feels too grand to do."

"Peter," Stella cried out in exasperation, "do you think you can change this country in a few weeks? Efficiency isn't everything. You've been riding ruthlessly over customs ever since you fired the men nurses. You seem hard to the Chinese . . . without humanity."

Peter looked aghast. "Who are they to talk, when they don't take any care of their own sick?"

"I can't explain, if you don't see," answered Stella, defiance going out of her. "It's some human contact you're losing because of your insistence on efficiency. There's Wang"—her anger was rising again—"you haven't noticed what a hard time he's having among his neighbors."

Peter sat silent, his lips drawn in a fine line of pain and obstinacy.

"Oh, now I've hurt you." Filled with misery, Stella started to leave the room, then returned to the attack. "Can't you see? It's something the Chinese have that we haven't . . . respect for personality."

"Personality! Why, that's what we're trying to bring them."

"Yes, it's we who've developed the individual. And yet things like duty and efficiency come first with us. With the

Chinese, human relationships come first. For instance, this new rule you've made that the patients can't have their families with them except at special times. It's not that they won't accept it. They'd like time to talk about it."

"We haven't got time."

"That's just it." With these final words, Stella went out, taking with her Peter's self-assurance built through these days of growing accomplishment.

And now . . . he seemed hard to the Chinese! He had thought of his uncompromising attitude toward inefficiency as strength. Was there such a thing as compromise with one's ideal? The Chinese way that no ideal was absolute, that human relationship came first, he had always rejected. He had thought that the ideals of the West must crowd out those of the East. Perhaps the ideals of both, joined together . . .

He heard Stella's chair leaving the compound. He ought to go down and say good-by before she started on her vacation. But his heart was too sore against her.

It was a long, hard-fought battle with himself, but when at last he rose from his office chair, he had made up his mind to let Sen S Mo run the women's ward as she wished.

When Stella came back in the autumn, with pride he showed her the women's ward. It was full. The régime that Sen S Mo had established was acceptable to the Chinese.

XXIV

A GREAT drought threatened the land, and disease was spreading through the countryside. City and country were given over to propitiation. The spirit magistrate of the *hsien* was taken out in his high-backed chair to view the parched fields. Sen, magistrate of the *hsien,* saw that ram and bull and boar were cast into the river as offering. No life of any kind was used for food. The Buddhist vegetarian command, kept in theory in times of prosperity, was now rigorously adhered to. Even eggs were not eaten, for they held potential life. But the serene sky gave forth no rain.

Through the city, the Rain Dragon was carried in procession, he who is of the *yang* essence, the active principle, he who represents the fecundating principle of nature, Bringer of Rain. Gongs and cymbals attended him. Their insistent, brassy clanging echoed through the hospital as the procession passed the door of the waiting room, ajar, as always, to the street. Peter scarcely noticed it, so accustomed was he now to such sounds. His attention was on the message sent him by Stella.

"The woman we operated on yesterday is dead," she had scribbled on a piece of paper. "Please come quickly. I'm afraid we are in for trouble."

There had been deaths, of course, in Peter's hospital, since that day when he had had his first surgical case. Why was Stella particularly apprehensive today? He had taken the usual precaution—had had the woman's husband sign a paper saying they wanted him to operate.

Stella met him in the corridor. "This makes the third death in the hospital within the week."

"Yes," said Peter. "We've had bad luck lately. Of course, we hardly thought we could save this woman. It was her only chance, though.   I explained all that to her husband."

"I know," said Stella.   "But I never counted on the drought lasting, nor on our losing the child, too.   And it was a boy——"

As they entered the room, Du, husband of the dead woman, the irate mother-in-law, and others of relationship too complicated to decipher, did not rise in greeting.   They gave no salutations.

The insult was not lost upon Peter.   "You remember," he said, addressing Du, "it was at your request that I attempted to save your wife and child."

Du did not answer, but acting as if Peter were not there, walked almost into him as he left the room followed by his clan.

"If it only weren't for the drought," Stella said.

"What has the drought to do with it?" asked Peter.

"The superstitious see in the drought the anger of spirits. They may think us the cause."

"Just because that family acted as they did?   You're trembling, Stella . . . you're nervous."

Stella did not answer.

All day the bang, bang of the gongs beat upon Peter's nerves. Toward evening he went over to his house.   Diana would take from him his concern, as so often she did.   He found her giving Serena her bath.   The quiet scene, Diana kneeling on the floor by the tub, Serena plump and brown from her summer in the hills, solemnly squeezing a great sponge, quieted his anxiety.   Life slipped back into the normal.

Diana rose, lifting the baby to her lap.   "Peter," she said. "I'm glad you've come.   You make everything seem all right. Those gongs beating all day——"

That night Peter could not sleep.   He saw the people of the city, always close to starvation, taking every means to secure rain.   Men seeing Nature as some mysterious force with which they sought to bring themselves into harmony—never to probe its secrets, never to try to subjugate it.

*   *   *   *   *

There were few patients at the dispensary door the next morning. Peter told himself it was nothing unusual, but he knew better. A little later, Stella came to him saying, "Five patients have left the hospital."

"Did they have good reasons?"

"Oh, yes," said Stella. "Their *reasons* were all right."

Silently, they looked at each other.

When evening came, the hospital was empty.

Peter in his office heard soft footfalls coming up the stairs approaching his door. He opened it. He stood face to face with Du.

For an hour they sat in desultory conversation. More and more often, Du spoke of the ruined crops. At a sudden, startling bang of gongs, Peter looked down into the street, seeing a line of men, at its head a red chair carried shoulder high and in it the spirit magistrate.

"He has paid no attention to offerings. They are taking him out to view the barren fields," explained Du, with a giggling note in his voice. "But there is a greater evil. The evil spirit of sickness has entered the city."

"You mean the disease we have heard of in the country?"

"It is as thou sayest. Fires of cypress have been burning at the twelve city gates to keep the evil thing out. How, then, did it enter the city?"

Peter noted the familiarity with which the man had addressed him—familiarity that meant contempt.

"How did it enter the city?" Peter repeated the words. "I can explain that to you. From what I've heard, I imagine this is what we call typhus. Diseases that spread are carried by human beings."

"No Chinese would do this evil thing—carry disease. But, thou?"

Suddenly Peter realized where the man was leading him. He had destroyed the people's faith in the hospital. How much further had he gone? Perhaps he had already suggested to this fear-ridden city that the foreign doctor was the cause of both drought and sickness, cited the deaths at the hospital. Peter studied him for a moment. A shiver crept slowly over the whole of his body. Blackmail! That scourge held over the Chinese doctor, this man meant to hold over him.

"A little money——" Du began.

Even if he had money, it would not do to pay it. Then he would forever be in the hands of such men as this. No use to appeal to his own government. There was no foreign consul in this city.

How far would such a person as this go? *Could* he influence the city? "After all," Peter said to himself, "I'm pretty well known. I've a good many friends among the Chinese." Then he thought of Stella's concern. Stella was worried. He remembered the old ugly tales of foreigners cooking Chinese babies. He remembered the day the sterilizer had come and Stella's remark: "It wouldn't be hard for them to believe it, even now, after so many of them have been cured in our hospital." He remembered that sense of sinister undertow. He couldn't count on anyone in this nation being free from superstition. "I've got to gain time," he thought. "I've got to outwit him somehow." Aloud, he said, "A learned man like the honorable Du understands. Perhaps my honored guest would call again in the morning. We could make plans then."

"In the morning, then." Du rose and went out.

Peter tried to think. He had no plan for tomorrow. Should he take the other members of the station into his confidence? The Bakers were on home leave. Berger? No, he didn't believe it would help to talk to Berger. Miss Dyer?

Slowly he came to a conclusion. "I believe I'll go and see Wang." The simple, kindly Chinese. Brave, too. He got up, passed through the gate and along the street. The hubbub of the street was reassuring, and yet—did he imagine it? Did he imagine hostile glances? He reached Wang's little shop. It was shuttered. Had Wang gone away?

"Sickness within," said the tinsmith next door, "and sickness here," and he pointed to the shop across the way.

Peter knocked on the panel calling, "*Fei I Sheng* has come."

He could hear the murmurings of delirium within. But no answer came to his knock.

"Help me to get in," he asked the tinsmith, who stood watching.

The man turned away. Now Peter was certain. There was hostility. But he must get to Wang.

He called again. A shutter was slowly slipped aside, and Wang's little boy faced him. He saw Wang's wife sitting by the table.

"Thy father?"

"There." The boy pointed to the curtained bed at the back of the shop.

Hastily Peter drew aside the curtains. The shoemaker, he saw at a glance, was very sick. He was unconscious. If it were typhus, as he believed, careful nursing was necessary. Would the woman let him take her husband to the hospital? He asked her.

"Take him," she answered sullenly. "What good is he to me? See this shop." Peter looked around. "Everything we have has been pawned."

Under cover of darkness, Peter took Wang to the hospital. As he sat with him that night, he went over and over in his mind some way to deal with Du in the morning.

He had gone home for coffee and a little breakfast. Still he had no idea of what he was going to do. Wang Ma came in from the kitchen bringing a note. It was from Du, asking him to come to him. Sickness prevented him from coming to the honorable *I Sheng*, the note ran.

Was this but a ruse to get him to Du's house? thought Peter. And yet, if Du were sick . . . He'd take the precaution of telling Stella where he was going.

Stella was silent for a moment, her eyes lowered. "Yes, I suppose you must go," she said at last, looking at him.

A slovenly servant met him. "Follow," he said.

For a moment Peter hesitated. The place was a rather mean

affair of two courts. In a room off the second, the servant drew aside the slatted screen from the door.

"*Fei I Sheng.*"

Peter looked down at Du, sitting by a table. His shifty eyes were bright with fever. Peter glanced behind him. The servant was closing the door. As he turned to face Du, the man rose. Suddenly he fainted, falling in a heap at Peter's feet.

Well, whatever he had intended, he would not accomplish, thought Peter, lifting him and placing him on a bed in the corner. If Du had typhus, he could hardly be saved. This sudden collapse indicated the worst form of the disease.

That evening Peter called the members of the compound together. The circle was smaller than usual, with the Bakers on home leave. It seemed smaller yet because of the pestilence that pressed them close.

"It's typhus," he told them. "We don't know what causes it, but it's either infectious or contagious. We'll have to close the schools, give up all work except the hospital."

"How about our up-country Christians? Guess I'd better look after 'em," said Miss Dyer.

"It's pretty risky," said Peter. "If you're taken sick, there'll be no one to look after you."

"It wouldn't be the first time," answered Miss Dyer. "Anyway, I don't intend to be taken sick. Well, I guess I'd better get ready." She got up, put on her pith hat, which she had taken off when she came in, thrust her hands into the pockets of her long coat, and went out.

The light from the kerosene lamp set in the center of the round table, was reflected in the shining native varnish. All sat looking into it, as if it mirrored their future. Above the mantel, St. Zenobius in his red robe leaned over the sick.

Peter could do little unless people would come to the hospital. He went up and down the near-by streets, trying to persuade the sick to come; but those who would not he cared for as best he could in the dark little huts, and, finally, when the well fled in terror before the demon of sickness, he and Stella carried food to those who could eat.

Early one morning before anyone was stirring, Stella's *amah* came stumping across the compound, knocking wildly on Peter's house door, crying, "Come quickly! My mistress is dying."

Peter, on the couch downstairs, snatching a few hours of rest, sunk in the heavy sleep of weariness, awoke slowly. As he realized the import of the woman's frightened crying, he felt a sudden apprehension of the unknown, a sudden dipping down under the ordered surface. How had Stella taken the dread disease? He did not know.

He was up, dressing and running toward the house of the Single Ladies, leaving the *amah* far behind. He seemed to the *amah* to cross the space with one magical leap of his long legs. Hobbling, crying, she hurried after him.

Peter stood for a moment gazing down upon Stella, so worn with the strain of nursing. Her hair fell around her flushed face. No longer was there just the white band across it; grey had crept through it all. Her hands picked at the bed covers. Her mind was already cloudy. He wished Miss Dyer were not up-country. She could have cared for Stella here at the house. Well, he'd have to take her to the hospital.

"*Amah!*" he called.

"*Lai la,* coming." She panted up the stairs.

Together they wrapped the sick woman in blankets, preparatory to taking her to the hospital. Peter lifted her in his arms. There was no need for help in carrying her. He realized now that Stella had not been well for days. That sudden trembling of her hands, her apprehension over so many things. The thought crossed his mind—perhaps this accounts for her apprehension over the Du matter.

All that day he felt that dipping down under the ordered surface into the unknown. Despite his science, when it came to this disease, he stood where the Chinese stood. He did not know its cause. Centuries ago in Europe, they had called it gaol fever, because people in the jails had had it. Men then thought the foul smell of the jailed carried the disease. Through the centuries since, in places where there was drought or war or great poverty, it had broken out. He stood helpless before it.

Night came. He could no longer neglect the sick outside his hospital, those neighbors of his on the near-by streets. He made ready to go.

Diana was standing in the window upstairs. Now that her school was closed, she was giving her full time to Serena. Sometimes she felt guilty that she could be happy with so much misery around her, but never before since Serena had been born had she been free to devote herself to her without the distraction of school. But today, Stella's sickness had brought foreboding and fear.

She scarcely saw Peter now. Day and night the sick claimed him. There he was, leaving the kitchen door, taking a short cut to the gatehouse. His suit was wrinkled. He had evidently slept in it. The curious peak of his shoulders which she loved was accentuated into the stoop of a desperately tired man. He stumbled as he walked. With a sudden impulse she put on her coat and hurried out to the gatehouse.

"I'll take Stella's place. Wang Ma can care for Serena," she said, and slipped her hand into his.

"It's not safe, dear."

"It's as safe for me as for you. If you go, I'm going too."

They stood together waiting for the gruel to be brought from the kitchen, looking into each other's eyes. The mystery of disease brushed them with fear.

"No, Diana. I can't let you go. There's Serena."

Convulsively they clasped each other's hands, then, taking the rice kettle, he went out alone into the gathering darkness.

This night Peter went among the sick and dead with no sense of superior knowledge. He was not different from these other men, whose usual cheery common sense was just now submerged in gripping superstition. All consciousness dipped down into ancient racial experiences, where the evil spirits of disease brushed their dark bodies against man. As he held the lantern high above a sick man, Peter was startled to hear him say, "This is Buddha man."

As the winter advanced, the epidemic subsided. Both Wang and Stella lived. Of the cause of the disease, Peter knew no more than before the epidemic. Typhus gave evidence of being contagious, yet the facts often seemed to dispute it. One of the women at another Mission, who had not left her house for days, had died of it. In a third Mission, there had not been a single case. The Berger children and Mei Ing Perkins, who had twice escaped the vigilant eye of Mrs. Berger and slipped out into the street, had not taken it either.

Believing in the all-important stream of life, the Chinese wasted no time in barren grief. Wives and concubines were taken in order that there might be sons in families depleted by the epidemic. According to Confucius, the greatest sin, greater than adultery, was to leave the ancestors unattended. Early and late the people labored to meet the demands of the living and the dead. Birth was the ecstatic concern of the teeming millions. At the time of marriage, no symbol of fecundity was ignored. The right food was sent by relatives and friends. About the marriage bed embroideries to induce fertility were hung. Stitched into the hangings the mystic knot, the swastika, modifications which had been made in the *yin yang* symbol during the centuries.

In the Mission compounds there were many vacancies in churches and schools. It was difficult to fill the gaps left by death. Shoemaker Wang, although only an artisan, was unanimously chosen as native pastor of the chapel to fill one vacancy.

Only Peter's superb health and his ability for organization had made it possible for him to keep up with the extra work. The hospital had lost two nurses. Stella's convalescence proved a long one.

For several weeks they feared Miss Dyer had been one of the victims. They could get no word of her. But one afternoon, Rose and Timothy Berger ran across the compound chanting in unison, "Miss Dyer's back, Miss Dyer's back." From the hospital came Peter in his surgical gown, out on the porch came Diana with Serena. The Bergers appeared from here and there. They watched Miss Dyer, sitting erect in her open sedan, ride into the compound. As she got out, her friends crowded around to greet her. She was thin to the point of emaciation and looked unutterably weary. But she spoke with her old asperity. "You act as if I'd never itinerated before."

None ever knew the story of those weeks.

Relieved of anxiety, reaction set in, and everyone's nerves were on edge. The slightest difference of opinion brought on resentment, which gradually focused itself upon Stella. To all appearances well, she had what seemed to the others unaccountable fits of depression and bitter self-denunciation— a denunciation which often included the other members of the Mission. At such times, she questioned their right to impose themselves upon the Chinese. "Why should we feel we know more about God than they do?" she would ask.

Heresy to Miss Dyer. Even the easy-going Berger thought she went too far. Peter believed that Stella's moods were due to the ravages of typhus upon her nervous system. He was finding shattered nerves one of the aftermaths of the disease. But he, too, was at the breaking point from overwork, and neglected to emphasize to the others the need to be patient with her. By this time, Stella's remarks were being whispered about in other communities of the denomination all over China.

But at last she was able to take up her work. With her return to the hospital, a great change came over her. Sudden joy, like a rebirth of youth, claimed her. She was dowered with vitality, intoxicated with the return to service. Miraculously, it seemed to Peter, the hospital work was lightened for him.

Once more he was free to go to the city wall—the first time in months. He found a sunny corner made by an old watchtower jutting out at right angles from the parapet. He fitted his back into the angle, his long legs straight out in front of him, his hands resting on clumps of grass. The last year's hard stubble and the soft blades of this year's spring growth touched the palms of his hands as he rested there on the cold earth. The sun moved across him, warming first this then that part of his body. Renewal came to him, a tapping of some hidden source. His mind moved here and there, and at last settled on his new happiness. Diana was pregnant again, and they both looked forward to having a son. The dark happenings of death receded. Only this hope in new life remained.

Diana was lost to all else but life forming within her—not as it had been before Serena was born, not that harmonious contentment. The child beat vigorously within her womb. She knew her son before he was born. She laughed with him and talked to him as she felt him struggling in the secret center of her. She and he, she felt, could never be entirely separate.

XXV

WINTER was gone. Seeds sprouted in the earth. New life stirred in the wombs of women. Western thought, long dormant in the mind of the East, gave sign of quickening.

China, for centuries shut off to herself, sterile in her separateness, was stirring under the touch of Christendom as once she had stirred under the touch of India. Two thousand years before, Buddhism had engendered within her creative life. This strong and different thought, impregnating the Confucian moral concept, had brought China to a high pitch of creation. There had been discovery and invention. Her sculpture and painting bore the imaginative impress of the union.

But the energy of life had gradually died away, leaving only a rigid cultural form; under the stagnating forces of use and wont, China had again set to a pattern. Now Christendom was cleaving that stiff matrix with the sword of its energy.

For a long time, Chinese scholars here and there over the Empire had been contending that unless decay was to come to China, the new learning from the West must be taken in. The Empire was shrinking. China was powerless to resist the virile, "earth-hungry" nations who were taking her land—powerless because she was weak, disorganized by graft and dishonesty among her officials. Many men bought their degrees, many officials grew rich using their positions to rob the people. The Confucian ideal of governing by virtuous example was no longer a vital principle.

The more radical among the reformers had thought to hasten change by destroying the old order. They had failed. But now, suddenly, the Throne itself commanded reform.

By decree of the Vermilion Pen, the Empress abolished the old Classical training of the scholars, ordered that the ex-

amination halls be destroyed, Western learning taught, schools
set up in Taoist and Buddhist temples for the *hsaio ren,*
women educated.   There were many in the Empire who rejoiced, but more who mourned.

Scholar Wu was bewildered.   "My son—what is there left
for my son?" he asked, as he sat opposite Peter.

"A place in the New China," said Peter gently, thinking
with sympathy of the long years of study, the long preparation, at last the coveted degree—and now the coveted degree
made worthless.

Teacher Wu spoke harshly.   "Had you not come, the old
system would be working perfectly.   We are not fitted for
your culture."   He looked at Peter and then at himself, as if
seeing his delicate person clothed as Peter was clothed, rough
wool garments in place of soft silks, stiff cuffs coming down
over his hands.   "Even though we are friends, if I could take
you and your race and cast you into the four seas, I would
do it."

"So does even gentle Wu feel toward me," thought Peter.

As for Scholar Sen, when the news was brought to him of
the decree abolishing the examinations, he gathered his friends
together in his guest hall.   His anger broke the bounds of
propriety.   He cursed the barbarians, bringers of destruction.

About the vaulted room hung scrolls bearing quotations,
wishing Sen prosperity and long life.   They had been given
him by the scholars of the city on his fiftieth birthday.   The
celebration, held only a week ago, had been a time of great
rejoicing and feasting.

These scholars had exchanged terse and quickly turned
phrases of wit and humor.   There had been a contest in the
writing of couplets and a little gambling over a finger game.

The crowd of scholar officials were arrayed in stiff satin
gowns, dull purple and subtle shades of grey, squares embroidered with pheasant, wild goose, mandarin duck, according
to rank, on chest and back.   Their silk trousers were neatly

bound at the ankles with black satin bands, their white cloth stockings fitted so smoothly they appeared to be made on the foot. Their black satin shoes fitted snugly, too. Their foreheads were neatly shaven, their hair drawn back into braids that fell, strong and black, down the backs of their gowns. Their hats were crowned with the buttons of their rank, white crystal, sapphire, coral. Instead of the gilded button of his office, Sen wore the Coral Button of the first rank, because of meritorious service.

These scholars represented a culture that they believed could never be bettered. For many centuries, China had proudly held to this culture. That the creative fire which had leaped and flared centuries ago in their country was again manifesting itself in the outside world, they did not see.

The eldest in the group, whose white thin goatee marked him as a very virile man, for most Chinese had faces smooth as a woman's, spoke. "Western learning belongs to the workshop."

"It cannot be that our divine ruler would set aside learning. The examinations in the Classics done away with, the examination halls torn down! This is to destroy ourselves. Good government is synonymous with the scholar," mourned the man sitting in the seat of honor.

"Only with self-cultivation can a man rule others. Western learning has no discipline. There is no knowledge in the man who would tear the universe apart," said a stout and very old gentleman.

"The West needs science because it supposes human nature is imperfect and therefore seeks to gain something from the outside. For us who know that good is already within us, it is as Buddha said—like begging for food with a golden bowl," exclaimed Scholar Sen. "Let us pledge that our sons shall be held to the rigid training that we received, that they may carry on the Classical tradition. If the horses of government are untrained, we shall ride on the wind."

"Let it be done!" they cried together.

Scholar Sen clapped his hands and a grave old serving man appeared. Quietly he listened to the master's order, went out, returned, bringing the writing materials. Each man opened a vein in his wrist and wrote his pledge in blood.

Scholar Sen's only son, Lo Shih, loitered in the court outside the guest hall. He had grown thinner and more stooped, more perfect in scholarly posture, during these three years of study. He was eleven, now. He heard the angry excited voices. Curses placed upon the barbarians for the evil they had done the Empire. The examination halls to be torn down! Where, then, could he take his examinations? How could he, Sen Lo Shih, become a great official? He spat, and placed his own curse upon the only barbarian he knew—the doctor, the light one, with the flaming hair, the pale eyes.

XXVI

REBIRTH! Whence was to come vigor for rebirth? With despair and horror, China faced her doom, poisoned and weakened by opium. The craving for opium wrought into the very bone and blood of the nation. Rich men and officials smoked the imported product, the middle class used the native stuff, the poor smoked an unspeakable mixture of pipe-scourings and charcoal. Coolies transporting the sticky substance scraped the gummy residue from saddlebags for their use. Women sitting idly in the inner courts deadened their ennui with opium. Babies were given a whiff to ease pain or hunger. The unhappy, the hungry, used opium, the effete used opium. Famine followed in its wake, for the delicate poppy took the best rice and vegetable land.

Misunderstanding, suspicion and hatred over opium tore West and East apart. China hated the West's aggressive trade in the drug. The West pointed its finger of scorn at China, despising her for the habit, saying, "We only meet the demand. The demand comes from the Chinese themselves." That it had been difficult at first to get opium into the currents of Chinese trade, they ignored—trade pays no homage to morals or humanity. The West feared for its revenue and hated China's resistance. China feared her own impotence and raged at her destroyer. The shuttlecock of fear and anger year after year had been tossed back and forth.

Men of both East and West fought to end the vice; men of both East and West sought to keep the vice. Finally, East and West made a bargain.

China pledged herself, through a period of ten years, to a yearly curtailing of the poppy crop in her own countrysides; Indian opium, the greatest import, was to be gradually reduced during that period. It meant for China, if she kept

177

her word, suffering; for England, it meant the complete un-
balancing of her Indian budget. A group around the Throne
in China, public opinion in England, brought the thing to
pass.

Hatred dies slowly, suspicion even more slowly. China
doubted that the West was in earnest. The West did not
guess that China was in dead earnest.

The decree for the eradication of opium had gone out in
the autumn. Not until the planting season for the poppy
should come, not until the individual stores of opium should
become exhausted, would there be struggle. That time was
now at hand. Many wealthy must be impoverished. The
conflicts between officials and farmers would be bitter. Men
would die crying for the drug. Men would do vile deeds
in order to sell the drug. Many would pay the death penalty.
The country would drip blood. According to the ancient
code of family and village responsibility, innocent and guilty
would suffer alike.

The viceroy of the province where Peter lived had not
acted quickly. Perhaps the stroke of the Vermilion Pen was
merely a face-saving gesture to the West. But by spring he
knew that the edict was more than a paper sham. When he
found that the death penalty for growing, selling, or using
the drug, was being enforced, he set about the intricate business of reform.

He commanded that all officials and teachers in schools
throughout the province must stop the drug within six
months. He ordered the farmers to limit the poppy fields.
He closed restaurants, hotels and wineshops which provided
couches where the drug could be smoked.

Along the streets where opium dens had flourished, Peter
began to see building after building where the shutters were
never taken down. In the pawnshops, opium pipes and lamps
lay in great piles—beautiful pipes of jade and cloisonné,
higher piles of cheap wooden pipes. The poor could not get
the drug—it was costly now.

Opium-cure shops sprang up. Fake cures—opium in disguise.

A long line of miserable, emaciated beings stood outside Peter's refuge each morning, waiting for it to open. Peter steadied their hearts with stimulants, quieted their nerves with belladonna, gave them the encouragement of his own strong will.

A few smokers and sellers of the drug were executed, their heads hung at the gates of the city, like those of common criminals, their property confiscated. Men from a better class began to come to Peter.

One morning Peter recognized an old patient, a simple countryman. "Thou?" he asked. "A needer of the cure?"

"No. But I eat bitterness. My family . . . my son. My village has been burned. Some did not conform to the law—planted the poppy in excess. For them the village perished. I, only, have escaped."

"And you need help?"

"No, I Sheng."

"You came just to tell me?"

"Yes, to tell you."

Rich and poor, they came in greater and greater numbers, for one reason or another. Peter's refuge would not accommodate them all. He managed to rent a two-story building across the street. Out of the slender funds allowed him for upkeep, he took enough to build a bridge, leading from the second floor of the surgical building to the second floor of the new refuge. His hospital now resembled an old house with a series of haphazard lean-tos.

The West is without the cardinal virtue of benevolence, the Chinese said. Large shipments of morphine to take the place of opium were coming into China from America. And in Shanghai, in the International district, in licensed dens, the Chinese could smoke opium in safety. Peter was sore at heart.

It was only an occasional moment he had with his teacher, these days. Peter had snatched a half-hour and gone to his study one morning.

"*Fei I Sheng* is very busy helping my people," said Wu, as he made his customary formal bow.

To Peter, the old man's greeting was like a blessing.

XXVII

SCHOLAR SEN had rejoiced in his heart over the opium decree. Here was a way for his country to gain in strength and power. He did not dream that the first great struggle would be with himself. Striving always to be the Superior Man, he had known no excess. In thirty years, his daily quantity of opium had never been increased from one pipe a day, smoked in the evening. Never had he suspected that he could not give it up at any time.

Today he called his head servant, issuing orders that none but the *lao tai tai,* his mother, should have this smoke. It was permitted to her because of her great age. All other opium pipes, including his own, were to be destroyed.

Night fell. The hour for his pipe passed. A faint restlessness settled over him. Restlessness was repugnant. Serenity was the necessity of a physique impoverished by years of excessive study, serenity the necessity of age, serenity the lode star of his spirit.

He slept fitfully, his dreams filled with subtle torments of restless activity. He woke. His pipe . . . where was his lamp . . . his pipe . . . his servant to prepare the pellet? Worthless one! He clapped his hands. His trusted servant appeared.

"What does *lao yeh* wish?"

"My pipe . . . and hurry."

"The *lao yeh* gave orders to destroy the pipe."

He remembered now. He was humiliated before himself. He was not the Superior Man! But no man should know. Outward form of serenity should be kept. With proud hauteur, he rose. "A light in my study," he commanded.

He opened one of the Classics which he had been reading for the hundredth time. He drove himself to the task of punctuating it after the manner of the scholar—small neatly made red circles. Now did he know his great humiliation—he, the master of calligraphy, whose firm strong strokes were known in a half-dozen provinces, could make only quavering marks. Secretly, he burned the book.

In the early morning, he sent for his son. Lo Shih was long in coming.

"Why dost thou delay?" asked the father, surveying the lad. There was no intimacy between these two. Their relationship was one of etiquette and honor.

Lo Shih knew he had failed in the matter of etiquette. "I have been with *lao lao,* grandmother," he gave as his excuse.

"Sit here at the table. Show thy facility with the brush."

Lo Shih seated himself, pointed his brush, straightened his arm for the bold, sure stroke. Not perfect, the control of his arm and hand. He had stopped training of late. *Lao lao* had said now that the examination halls were torn down, it was unnecessary for him to study—"My little leaf, it will be easy to buy official position for thee."

"A son of a calligraphist, making scratches such as these!" Scholar Sen held up the lad's work. "Spending thy time in the women's courts!" Then he paused, remembering it was the matriarch who spoiled Lo Shih, fondling him, over-feeding him, and claiming he studied too much. Scholar Sen said no more against the women's courts. He had forgotten himself. Filial piety demanded he pay respect to the ways of his mother.

He dismissed Lo Shih. A strange faintness . . . his heart . . . pain in his groin. He must have opium. Every pore of his body was a hungry mouth, sucking at the air, gaining nothing. He went to his bed, drawing the curtains close. All day his will held against those crying million mouths of his body. Another night. Food . . . but he could take no food.

The light was just coming, touching the drawn curtains of his bed. A bowl of water stood near. He let the tips of his long, sensitive fingers rest in the cool liquid, and at last he slept, his dreams full of quiet pools, lotus flowers swimming on the surface.

He woke exhausted. Tenderly the old servant gave him tea to drink, holding the cup to his lips.

A man servant came along the gallery, crying, "The master is summoned to the apartment of the *lao tai tai.*"

He must go. This was his filial duty. Honor and etiquette demanded it. Slowly, carefully, he made his way to his mother's apartments, bowed before the tiny, tyrannical creature. Her sharp eyes sought out his condition. Yes, the rumor that had been brought her was correct. He was not strong this morning. She would not ask him to be seated.

"What is this the business manager tells me, that we must curtail our opium, grown in the fields of Szechuan?" she cried, feigning ignorance of the imperial decree, feigning ignorance of previous discussion. "It is monstrous! No other crop can be transported across the country so easily. No other crop brings so much money."

Her son swayed a little as he stood before her. "This year a third must be given up," he said. "Next year, two-thirds. Men are being executed who do not obey."

"But it can be arranged," she said, speaking in cajoling tones. "Thou needst give no order. Suggest to the business manager that he speak to the tenants of caution—hide the opium fields behind fields of tall grain—perhaps a little money to the local officials."

"The Superior Man does not let the white robe of his honor become spotted with black," answered her son. "Surely it is not the honorable one's wish."

Then the old *tai tai* was angry. She lifted her cane, pointing it at him. "Bah! Because of thy silly white robes of honor, thou wouldst set aside the needs of the family! Stupid one! Dost thou not see that the foreign devils plot to take the trade away from us . . . their opium sold in place of ours? Thou wouldst let the foreign devils ruin us!" Her voice rose in a harsh, high treble. Her eyes narrowed. "Where

is thy filial piety? I am the head of this household! I say
to thee, give the command!"

"If it is the honored one's wish," Scholar Sen answered
her wearily, "let it be done. Only enough for income this
year. Another year we must obey the mandate."

He bowed, went out, his hands folded within his sleeves,
his head lowered. He was trembling. His mother's room
had been filled with the sweet odor of opium. The ravages of
his abstinence were great. He must have quiet. He was not fit
for strife. He would go for a time to the Buddhist monastery
in the hills, where he often went when the bickerings of the
clan became too much for him.

The long journey took him far to the south of the province
into Buddhist country—tall mountains, high passes, old trees.
As ancient writings were preserved in the monasteries of
Europe, so the monasteries of China had preserved trees.
Here grew the cryptomerias dating back to the T'ang Dynasty,
trees a thousand years old, temples and monasteries hidden
among them on the mountainsides.

The magistrate's chair-coolies climbed slowly, carefully,
to the highest temple. There, with the great trees looming
up behind him and the plain lying far below, he rested in one
of the guest rooms. The room was stored with quiet. As he
sat eating the vegetarian meal brought him, he heard in the
dusk the soft footfalls of many priests, treading the stone
corridors leading to the main temple.

In another day, the world receded from his memory. Hour
after hour, he held himself to meditation. Longer each day
he took the Buddha pose—legs crossed, feet resting upon
thighs, back flattened—practicing breath control and the turning of his thoughts inward. Making the heart empty, eating
the spirit-power of the receptive, he entered into contemplation.

XXVIII

WINTER lay again on the land. Late each afternoon, Peter left behind the driving, exhausting work of the hospital and took retreat upon the city wall. It was the only place now where he could find quiet.

Even his study was invaded by demand. He was using it now as his office. As the time passed when an official could lawfully smoke opium, officials unable to stop the habit had come asking for private apartments in the hospital. Peter turned his office and laboratory over to one after another of them. Now the life of the hospital spilled over even into his study. The nurses came there to ask questions about their work. Patients he did not wish to see at the hospital came there to consult him, tradesmen to settle hospital accounts. A young student from Berger's school worked there most of the day, earning his tuition by helping with hospital accounts and records.

Peter loved this old grey wall, the patterned fields beyond, and the thin, tall pagoda standing on the saddleback between two mountain ridges. But even the ancient wall was changing. Not far from where he walked, it had been pierced to let the railway into the city. The gash, covered with fresh mortar, was raw and unsightly. The wall's solitude usually brought him peace. But today it brought him no peace.

Fear nagged his thoughts. Diana was nearing the birth of their second child. She was not well. He told himself that everything would be all right, but his knowledge of medicine told him that what had happened before might happen again. And then there was his burning desire for a son. He would wrest from God this boon of a son. He got his way in so many things in this hospital world where he was master, he hoped to get this too. Yet deep in his heart, he felt that he had lost the spiritual significance of Christianity by such an attitude.

As he strode along the wall, his anxiety for his wife took the form of irritation at himself. Failures in his conduct troubled him—anger with his nurses and Sen S Mo over their inefficiency, rebellion over his poverty, and the continued fret that he had no time for research.

Mid-winter had come. The house was full of soft bustlings—the poking of the kitchen fire, the placing of dishes on the unpadded dining table, near by in the bathroom, the sound of water poured into a tin tub, Wang Ma's heavy step, her guttural Chinese, Serena's voice raised in objection, the child's chuckles of satisfaction at the splashing of water.

All these sounds enhanced Peter's well-being, as he sat by his wife's side. He was experiencing that pleasant sense of complacency that comes after straining one's self to the utmost to get what one wants and winning. Diana had had an easy time. His son had been born after brief labor. He was glad that no other doctor had been available. Secretly, he had wanted to be the first to touch his son.

A three-cent oil lamp, placed on a table in the hall, sent faint light into the room. Bending over them, he could just see the faces of his wife and child. Intently, Peter regarded his son. Red hair, like his own, and a fighter from the start! All the dreams of his own youth he transferred to this boy.

"Peter." He said the name softly. He was very happy that Diana had chosen *his* name for the baby.

Gazing at her, he felt ecstatic delight. Her thick, curling hair, even now when it was let down, fitted her head like a shimmering cap. Her face against the pillow showed the lovely profile of cheek and chin. Her lips lightly touched the baby's head as it lay close against her face. He thought she slept. Her eyes were closed and her breath came evenly.

Diana was not asleep. She was spent by the long effort of conception and birth. But as she lay there, even in

her weakness, she felt her mind clearing after the months
when she had lived caught in some web of the physical. Something of herself had gone in the years given over to creation.
She did not wish to be consumed . . . she was more than the
fructifying creature. She felt the need to replenish mind
and body.

The child stirred. Convulsive joy seized Diana. Her
son . . . some re-shaping of her spirit, stronger now than it
had been after Serena's birth, urged her to live completely in
her children, separate for a time from Peter. Unless they
meant to have children, there should be no union, she said to
herself, taking refuge in the religious concept held by the
missionaries, making her withdrawal a right thing to ask of
Peter. . . . They should have no more children. Truly, they
could not afford it. She laid her hand on Peter's. "Wang
Ma left the baby here while she cared for Serena."

"Yes?" said Peter, startled to find Diana was awake, surprised, too, at the significance she seemed to be trying to
put into the simple words.

"I can just manage to keep up my work and care for
them," Diana went on. "We don't want to be like the
Bergers, do we—more children than we can care for?"

"Of course not," said Peter in consternation.

"It lies with us, Peter."

"Yes?"

"But, Peter, union is not blessed except——"

Peter sat very still. This union with Diana . . . had it,
then, been to her only the desire for children? This union
that to him had meant a profound spiritual experience? Then
he did not mean completion to her as she to him. It was
only the children. . . .

He felt separate, fragmentary. Was there no complete
union? Was there, then, only a constant duel of the sexes,
so that even in him there was something that Diana would
ward off? As he looked down at her, desire for her filled
him. He wanted to lose himself in her. He could not ac-

cept her decision. He sat still, held in the vise of his separate self.

Diana watched him. The demands of both husband and children were too great. Withdrawal was a necessity for her. "Peter," she cried.

The rhythms of life flowed differently in man and woman. He of all men should know this. He was a physician. He knelt by her side, entering into covenant with her, in his first submission to her needs.

As the weeks passed, the satisfaction of motherhood, the lovely sensation of her son's lips pulling at her breast, held Diana to a high pitch of exaltation and completion, but left her drained of strength. It held her love for her husband ever below the point of desire; she rejoiced, believing that she had spiritualized their union.

Peter's days took on a new intensity. Diana marveled at his splendid drive. Never for an instant did his interest or activity flag. After dinner, before he hurried back to the hospital for his last inspection, instead of sitting quietly by his hearth as he had been wont to do, he put in an hour of study on the language. Diana, coming in to say good night just before she went up to her children, thought him deeply absorbed in his work. As she stood by his side, her hand on his shoulder, she had no understanding of the magnitude of his sacrifice. His poignant love for her, his overpowering passionate need of her, were held under.

XXIX

THAT year, as winter passed into spring, the dissatisfaction of the Mission with Stella's beliefs reached a crisis. Ever since her sickness of last year, her sayings had been passed from mouth to mouth, growing more outrageous, more strange, at every repetition. A meeting was to be held in Shanghai to consider whether or not she should be expelled from the Mission.

Peter and Miss Dyer, chosen as members of the examining board, went down together on the train. Stella herself had gone a few days before. For most of the six-hour ride, Miss Dyer read a book, Peter looked out the window. The unaccustomed motion of the train lulled him. From the cheerful good nature and the hubbub of a Chinese village all around him in the train, replica of that life which daily submerged him, he was released. Squared fields, farm huts under clusters of bamboo and mulberry slid in and out of his vision as in a dream.

As the train neared Shanghai, Miss Dyer closed her book with a snap. "I hope, Fraser," she said, "you're going to see this business straight—not let your own interests interfere with your duty. There's a right and a wrong to everything."

"You mean I need Stella at the hospital, and it might interfere with my judgment?"

"You've got to think of your faith. It's not an individual matter. I like Stella well enough, but that's not the issue. Friendship hasn't got anything to do with it."

"What has, then?" asked Peter.

"What has! Your duty to God."

Peter was silent. Anxiety for his friend closed round his heart.

189

A grave group, representatives from every station, the missionaries gathered in the house of their senior member. The long, oval table, the sober men and women sitting round it, the white-haired man at one end with a gavel before him, Stella's slight figure standing to answer, gave the air of a courtroom to this Christian gathering. Peter lowered his gaze. He noticed Stella's hands, those expressive hands of hers, so scarred by chilblains, and yet still strangely beautiful. They were clinging to the edge of the table. He had seen women in childbirth clutching thus. He dropped his eyes still lower, not to see his friend in such a plight.

"This is a difficult task, Miss Perkins," said the chairman of the meeting. "We are not unmindful that once you did great things for your Lord, but now it has been brought to our attention that you said Buddha is Christ for the Chinese. Did you say that?"

"Yes." Stella's quiet voice as she answered gave the lie to her clinging hands.

"Then you lessen the divinity of Christ."

"I do not think so."

The ring of triumph in her voice made Peter look up. He was startled. A kind of glory hung around her. Her hair, touched all over with silver, looked like a nimbus of light around her head. And her face . . . it was filled with an intense vitality. She seemed to be tapping some hidden, energizing force. Why, she possessed that fertility of spirit he himself had so often sought. He looked around at the others, expecting to see wonder as they witnessed what he was witnessing, but disapproval filmed all their faces.

He did not hear the questions that went on and on. He was absorbed in the memory of that day in the temple, when he had first become conscious of what had happened to Stella in the Boxer year . . . Stella, her eyes dark with suffering . . . Stella, as he knew her in the hospital, filled with a compassion that could not be stayed . . . Stella, as she had looked a few moments before, her eyes drenched with light.

"You have been quoted as saying you feel ashamed of yourself as a missionary."

"Don't *you* ever . . . at any time?"

"Did you say that the church of Christ might disappear sometime, and it wouldn't matter?"

"Not quite that," answered Stella. "I said it wouldn't matter because Christ would still be among us."

"Miss Perkins," the chairman asked, "would you like to leave before we vote?"

"I will stay."

"Very well. Those who feel Miss Perkins is unfit to represent our Lord, will say so in a written ballot we will now take."

"Wait!" cried Peter, getting to his feet. "I know Miss Perkins better than any of you do. Take all these years in the hospital . . . she's done more good than any of us! Why, she's——" he faltered. They, too, had looked upon that light in her face and had not seen it. What good to tell them then? "Look here," he said. "The Chinese need her . . . the hospital's understaffed, anyway. We'll have to cut down on our work. . . ."

"We can't take such things into consideration, Dr. Fraser," said the chairman.

The room was very still. Only the soft swish of paper, as the secretary of the meeting distributed the ballot slips . . . then the thin scratching of pens and pencils . . . the almost imperceptible sounds the slips of paper made falling in a wicker basket the secretary passed around . . . the tiny thump of the basket against the table as it was placed before the chairman . . . the slip, slip of paper against paper as he sorted the ballot. He rose, all the bits of paper in his hand, except one which still lay on the table.

"The vote is against you, Miss Perkins. I wish to say this: perhaps in our own country where God is known, this would not be necessary."

There was a hubbub of voices. The meeting was breaking up.

Suddenly Peter realized that Stella was not in the room. He hurried out. She was not in the hall nor on the street. The missionary hostelry was not far away. He'd catch her there. But when he reached it, they told him she was not staying with them this time.

Where could she be staying? Unable to let her go like that, alone, Peter walked up one street, down another, the futility of his quest slowly settling over him.

As he walked, his habitual response to misery made him conscious of his surroundings. "This International Settlement has mean, ugly streets," he said to himself. The sweet smell of opium was all about him. Here were the licensed dens of Christendom, where the appetite punishable by death in Chinese territory was kept alive, given protection, under Christian flags.

As Stella had said, what right had they to speak of God to the Chinese?

He wished he could find Stella. That impression of light and glory hanging round her was gone. He had only the memory of her clinging hands.

Oblivion seemed to close over Stella. She left no forwarding address at the Mission. A strange Chinese came to the compound with a note from her, asking that her possessions be given to him. Money was enclosed for the support of Mei Ing, sufficient to care for her until she was old enough to be betrothed and married, or to teach in the school if she preferred. This money was put in Peter's care. It was not a large sum. A few dollars kept a Chinese girl in the school for a year. However, he felt that the sum represented most of Stella's savings.

"Where is thy mistress?" he asked the bearer of the note.

"Not my mistress," he replied.

"How is it then that you come to get the foreign one's things?" demanded Peter.

"This humble one was sent by a member of the village."

"What village?"

The coolie feigned not to understand the question.

"Is there a white woman in your village?"

Again real or feigned ignorance. Peter was baffled.

"Well, here, anyway," he said, scratching a note on a piece of paper and handing it to the man. "Put this with the things of the honorable Miss."

"As the foreign *I Sheng* commands," said the coolie, submissively, and lifted to his shoulder the carrying pole with Stella's boxes suspended at the ends.

Peter never knew whether the note reached her or not. No answer came. He watched the sailing lists in the Shanghai paper, but did not find her name. Inquiry from the Mission brought the information that she had not drawn her passage money, to which she was entitled.

No one mentioned her at the Mission. Even Diana and he, after the first evening of his return, when he had poured out the whole tale, seldom mentioned her, as the subject was painful to both.

Peter had not realized before how much the smooth running of the hospital was due to Stella. It was necessary now to put Sen S Mo in charge of all the nurses. And he had to take upon himself such matters as checking the outgoing and incoming laundry. Neither had he realized before how many menial duties Stella had performed, many of them growing out of reforms he had made in the hospital. This checking of the laundry, for instance, had come out of the fact that he would not let the patients use their own dirty clothes in the hospital. A splendid idea. But Stella had been the one to see that the bed robes did not disappear.

Great as was his need for her in the actual work of the hospital, he was experiencing an even greater need for her presence. He needed her mind in consultation—that feminine intuition which, up to now, had informed all his decisions, making him more effective in his work as surgeon and doctor. A relationship delicate and uncharted gone out of his life. This friendship with Stella . . . something quite different from his love for Diana, who stirred his senses and quickened his pulses.

That summer, without relief, Peter stayed on at the hospital. Often he heard the phrase, "Sister to the Goddess of Mercy." He thought at first the patients called upon another of the gods of their vast pantheon, then one day he learned that they were speaking of Stella—that they called her this among themselves—the secret name the foreigners were not supposed to know. The Chinese, shrewd in their estimate of character, gave each foreigner a name portraying his true nature.

What did the Chinese think of Stella's expulsion from the Mission? With their ethics of personal responsibility to friends, how did it look to them, he wondered?

XXX

THAT winter a new vigor possessed the land. The two years in which China had dripped blood to cleanse herself of the poison of opium, were beginning to bring her strength. The vitality of peasants and artisans was no longer sapped. Opium was too expensive for them. The need for Peter's refuge was lessening almost daily—scarcely a coolie now who came for the cure. The refuge on the compound he had turned into an annex to the women's ward. The one across the street he used as a private refuge for the rich. They could still buy the expensive, imported opium, and many, even among the officials, kept reverting to the habit. But the evil, always looked upon with shame by the Chinese, was becoming a greater shame, and no one wished to be known as an addict. There were women, too, coming to him, who asked to be cured. These he handled in the women's ward.

Tales of greed still reached Peter's ears. Men secretly sold and grew opium. But more and more was the government closing in upon such.

The new learning was gathering impetus. Temples had been turned into schools for the *hsaio ren*. As Peter went about the city, under the shadow of the ancient gods he could see the boys of the neighborhood bent over slates making the difficult ideographs. Men with high degrees, like Scholar Wu's son, taught them. Far down the street above the hum of voices and cries of coolies, the boys could be heard chanting the Classics.

To the Mission schools came now, without urging, the girls of the better classes. The Chinese schools, discarding the old ways, had discarded seclusion, too. The Mission schools were stricter. Chinese gentlemen felt them safer places for their daughters. At the opening of the term, Diana no longer, as on that first morning after her honeymoon, left her breakfast untouched. "No need to worry," she said happily to Peter, "the school will be crowded." Perhaps she would not have worried anyway. She lived in her son these days.

Even Diana's care for Serena was overshadowed by her care for her son. "Serene"—Wang Ma never called her anything else—was "Wang Ma's baby." She was quiet, like a Chinese child. Small Peter did not win the old servant. He was always wriggling, twisting in her arms. But Serena sat upon her trousered lap quietly.

"Wang Ma feed you, Wang Ma's baby." Jealously, the old woman guarded her, too, against the growth of the mind. "Wang Ma's baby." Listlessly, Serena lay back against her, letting Wang Ma feed her, dress her—Wang Ma, important with the pride of the service.

Diana, coming from her duties at boarding school and day school, would find them like this, a lovely picture, maternal devotion in every line of Wang Ma's body, her smooth black head bent over Serena's gold hair. The child's hair was neither light brown like Diana's, nor fiery red like Peter's. It partook of the quality of both.

But "Pete," as they were beginning to call the baby, had his father's hair and his turbulent spirit. He would accept no service from Wang Ma, struggling alone to sit up and, as the winter went on, to stand, getting support from the bars of his crib. Even from his father he refused all aid, except in trying to walk from him to his mother. When he heard his mother's voice, or step, he cried, demanding that she carry him, feed him. So it was, in one way or another, Diana's attention was concentrated on her son.

XXXI

As Sen S Mo's power in the hospital grew, more deeply did she dip down into the experiences of her race. The spirit of the matriarch grew stronger and stronger in her. In place of the clan she placed the hospital, giving it the same allegiance, demanding of it the same bending to her will. Men and women obeyed her. She began to find her bound feet a hindrance to her energetic supervision. She came one day to Peter, asking that he unbind them for her.

Never could she quite separate herself from her husband's clan. Through an old servant she learned of its intricate life. He came in the fall bringing her *que hua* for her hair, the waxy, scented blossoms picked from the great tree in the old matriarch's court. He came in the winter bringing her lilies, their bulbs set in stones, planned to bloom at China New Year.

Endlessly the two talked of a thousand happenings in the Sen household, of cousins and uncles, of children born to concubines, of the matriarch's tyrannical ways, of the precious son, Lo Shih, growing up to take the place of Sen S Mo's husband, the son of the first wife. Had Sen S Mo's husband lived, had she borne a son, sometime she would have been the matriarch in the vast household—a household growing very rich, these days, the old servant told her.

"It is whispered," he said, "that the matriarch has managed well. *Ai yah*, this humble one knows nothing, but it is whispered"—he leaned nearer—"opium brings a big price, these days. . . . *Ai yah*, this humble one knows nothing. Our face is very great. The Sen household is rich—greatly, greatly rich."

"But tell me of Lo Shih," Sen S Mo commanded. In her mind, he stood as the son not granted to her. How many

197

offerings she had once made to *Kwan Yin*, Goddess of Women,
for a son! *Mei yu fatzu*, it was not to be.

The old man went garrulously on. "A great scholar, Lo
Shih. Small master's shoulders bent almost as much as big
master's. Very learned. When the examination halls are
built again, the small master will take high degree, in time,
be a great official.

"Very elegant, Lo Shih. The braid of his hair hangs almost
to the hem of his gown. His fingers sensitive . . . sensitive . . . never blunted by short nails. *Ai*, the young master
is beautiful to behold."

At last Sen S Mo would slip a little money in his hand,
saying, "Come again when thou hast more to tell."

Peter asked one day who the old man was who came so
often to sit at Sen S Mo's desk.

"An old servant, bringing news of my family."

Peter thought she spoke of her own clan, whom Diana
had visited. "They are well?" he would ask.

"Well, *Fei I Sheng*." Never did she tell him more.

Would he ever be admitted into intimacy with any Chinese,
he wondered? Was it possible for West and East to know
each other? There was Mei Ing Perkins, adopted as a tiny
girl—the same withdrawal in her, despite her Western ways
and Western living.

He would come upon her jumping rope with the Berger
children, boisterous and happy as the Bergers themselves. She,
in fact, was the leader among them. Rose and Timothy would
docilely hold the rope for her while she jumped, seeming never
to tire. The Chinese trousers she wore made it easy for her
to run in and out. She jumped high, her two short black
braids bobbing against her shoulders, her voice raised in
raucous command.

But when he tried to question her about the packages which
came to her so regularly, she retreated into Eastern reserve,
staring up at him with impenetrable black eyes.

"My mother sends them," she would answer him.

"You mean Miss Perkins?"

"I mean my mother." The mask of her childish face was as perfect as Sen S Mo's.

On her table, in the room at the school where she lived, Diana told him, she kept a snapshot of Stella.

"My mother," she said, when the girls asked her who it was.

XXXII

THIS year, March brought spring, as sometimes happened in this semi-tropical land.

"Diana," Peter begged, "come with me to the hills for a whole day. When have we had a day to ourselves?"

Diana thought of the azaleas covering the hills, the willows putting out their delicate tracery. Why, she, too, wanted to escape every duty, even the precious duty of caring for Pete!

Partly because of the expense of chairs, partly because it gave them more companionship, they walked. Eagerly, they came to the city gate, stepped forth. There lay the still surface of the lake, green causeways spanning it, the half-circles of the bridges completing themselves in the reflected half-arches. For a few coppers they hired a boat to take them across the lake. They sat side by side, trailing their hands in the water. Pilgrim boats drifted by, filled with men and women in indigo-blue garments, yellow knapsacks across their shoulders.

The boat bumped against the landing. They found the way more crowded than usual. Long lines of coolies thronged the narrow path, *ti 'ao*ing mammoth logs, tall as masts, a hundred coolies to a log, chanting, stepping to the chant. Slowly the logs were borne forward.

"*E-ho-eh! E-ho-eh!*"

Laboriously they were bearing the logs from the sea into the hills. Logs brought from America—a shipload full, some for a new Christian school, and some for the pillars of the great Buddhist temple which had been destroyed during the Tai Ping rebellion and which was now being rebuilt.

Along the sides of the path, as before, lay and squatted the sick beggars—more of them this year. Now that there were so many workers at the temple, more money would be thrown into beggars' bowls for merit.

"Do good! Do good! Attain merit!" wailed the beggars, leaping around Peter as they had on his first visit. But the old horror did not come upon him. That stream of people through the hospital, whom he had cured, was a cloak of achievement protecting him from this suffering.

When he and Diana entered the temple, and he saw through the drifting clouds of incense the face of Buddha, downcast eyes, placid lips, Peter's own negation stole over him. These months when he and Diana had denied the senses— the triumph of spirit over the body.

Late in the afternoon, they left the temple, found an unfrequented path and wandered back toward the city, hand in hand.

The day had been hot and the water buffaloes were soaking themselves in the ponds, their noses and curved horns lying upon the grey surface of the water. The grey tiled roofs of the villages nestled deep in the mulberry groves. The grave trees were in full blossom, and their compact clusters of flowers made a white pattern in the compact domes of leaves. The evening glow came into the sky, touching its grey silver with rose. Around them were fields of clover, a cover crop to be plowed under to nourish the ever-producing earth. The grey peaked roofs of the grave houses and a faded red temple wall broke the pink sea of clover. Through the open door of a wayside shrine, sacred to the earth gods, they saw a candle's red flame. On a hill stood forth the white walls of a Catholic monastery. The gold cross on its steeple shone bright in the final slanting rays of the sun.

Diana and Peter lay long that night, their hands twined together. Peter, tired by the physical effort of the day, feeling no need for that stern watch he had kept upon himself for so long, drew Diana to him. She lay in his arms, wholly confident of their strength for self-denial—self-denial striven for in all religions—some balance sought between the material and the spiritual. "Only fools waste the precious seed of the body: the conserved seed brings creative power," says the Buddhist doctrine.

The jumbled noises of the city did not die down, for the night was warm. The pound, pound of spirit-money presses, the bark of dogs, blended with the hum of a million voices, the high squeak of the one-stringed violins, the laughter and moans of the great city. An ocean of sound, out of which the quiet compound with its faint rustle of bamboos rose like some island of bliss. The smell of its lilacs lying heavy on the air set their senses to delicious ecstasy.

They drifted into languorous dreaming that was neither sleeping nor waking. After the long abstinence, Peter's lonely separateness seemed slowly to dissolve in Diana's embrace. His body merged in the warmth of hers, that moment by moment molded itself more completely to his.

Suddenly his lips were clinging to hers in a great hunger. Union. All else in heaven and earth fell away into cloudy nothingness, out of which their love rose like a plume of light.

Slowly, reality asserted itself. Diana and Peter, so confident of their wills, defeated, humbled before themselves . . . but at peace.

XXXIII

IN CELEBRATION of the splendid record his province had made
in stamping out the native opium in three years instead of the
allotted ten, the viceroy was giving a feast on the island called
"The Heart of the Lake."

An invitation came for Peter one afternoon in early September. The long narrow red envelope, with the black ideographs of the doctor's name on it, was brought to him at
the hospital. An invitation from the viceroy himself! Recognition of the fact that he had cured the man's only son of
the opium habit.

Peter paused in his work, thinking of what this celebration
really meant. Not in ten years, but in a little over three, the
Chinese nation had succeeded in practically stamping out
native opium. Recently a British inspector had traveled over
the poppy-growing provinces. In this province he had not
found a single field of poppies. Fields of nourishing rice
grew in their place. If all China could reach this standard,
Great Britain would keep to her promise and in seven more
years stop entirely her imports of the drug.

Peter felt certain the Chinese would accomplish this great
moral reform. The government, he understood, was closing
in around the last offenders, determined to stamp out the last
fields of poppy. No longer should the beautiful white and
pink blossoms disfigure the land.

As he fingered the viceroy's invitation, Peter felt a boyish
eagerness to share his honor with Diana. She had recently
returned from the hills. Her presence after the separation
of the summer was still a conscious delight, not yet a pattern
of every day. He ran up the steps of his house, seeking her.
She was not there. He glanced out of the window into
the garden—that secluded little plot entirely hidden from

the rest of the compound. At the garden's front, in order to shut it off from the constant stream of people passing along the main flagged walks of the compound, Diana had planted a hedge, letting it grow as high as her head. The house and the hospital sheltered it on two sides, the bamboos grew tall at the back. Diana called this spot "the nuns' garden," after one she had once seen in a convent school for girls in Shanghai. It had always been her place of retreat.

Yes, there she was, with the children. It was a warm, still September day, and she wore a dress of light blue native linen—the shade he liked best. She was sitting on a stone bench. Behind her rose the green bamboo boles. The sun was low. The trees cast a protecting shadow down upon her and the two children. Sunlight stood in a corner of the enclosure.

Serena, dressed in light blue, sitting very straight at her mother's side, was gravely listening to Diana reading aloud; Pete, in darker blue, on Diana's lap, was pounding with his heels on the stone bench and on the book with his fist, trying to attract his mother's attention, pointing at the alluring sunlight into which he was never allowed to go without his sun helmet, which he did not like to wear. The light brown of Diana's hair, the soft gold of Serena's, and the red of Pete's, accented the blue-clad group.

Peter was secretly glad that in a few months they were to have another child. He wondered if Diana were glad, too. She had never said. Always, Peter carried a little fear for his children, in this land where disease stalked so unchecked. Unconsciously he had come to feel safety in numbers, as the Chinese did.

As he went forward, the picture was broken apart. Diana rose, and with a strong, vigorous movement, swung Pete to her hip. Serena held up her arms for him to take her.

He handed the red envelope to Diana. Her companionship wrapped him round, as he saw her quick understanding of how much the invitation meant to him.

"I wonder," he said, after a little, as he sat beside her, Serena on his lap, "if any of us can even imagine what this triumph has cost China. I wonder if we as a people would have been willing to pay such a price. Strange, isn't it . . . Christendom says it would cost too much to stop the import at once?"

Wang Ma appeared in the doorway, dressed in the indigo cotton of the people. Her unbleached apron covered her ample front. Clapping her hands, she called loudly, "Se-rene! Pe-et!"

Serena got obediently down from her father's lap, but Pete took firm hold of his mother's skirt. Wang Ma stumped across the garden, crying, "Wang Ma carry small master. Wang Ma make him very good chow."

But the child motioned her away and started out alone, stepping precisely, a little uncertainly, for he was slow in learning to walk. Wang Ma followed, holding Serena's hand.

The garden was very still. Peter lingered, loath to go back to his work, far from finished for the day, enjoying this moment of companionship. A little breeze carrying the scent of *que hua* went through the garden. A knowledge growing in Peter for a long time took definite shape in his mind. He loved this country. By a thousand interweaving strands of experience, he was bound into it. The sound of the city, once a meaningless jumble, spoke to him intimately of men whose daily struggles he shared. And interwoven inextricably into the identification of himself with this nation, was his identification with Diana.

With one of her rare and lovely gestures of affection, she lifted his hand, kissed the palm, then fitted her fingers between his. Peter sat very still, feeling as never before their ever-deepening relationship, the harmonious blending of their two selves.

Diana felt the bulk of his man's fingers between hers. Intuition told her that because she was his beloved woman, in some mysterious process of union, this strong man submitted himself to her. Yet when she had made the gesture, locking her hand into his, it had been wholly because of her need of him.

The house door opened. They drew apart as they saw Sen S Mo framed in the doorway. Through all the years of their marriage they had recognized the Chinese idea of propriety.

Sen S Mo was hurrying, although perhaps it only appeared so because of the greater ease with which she walked on her unbound feet. She had on the leather street shoes which she had recently purchased. They were oddly shaped to cover the high instep, which feet once bound never lost. Peter was a little surprised to see Sen S Mo wearing them, for this was not her afternoon off.

"*Fei I Sheng,*" she addressed him, "may Sen S Mo have leave to go away for a few days? There are affairs of the family."

"Of course, Sen S Mo," said Peter. "I'll arrange things." Instantly he rose, his work again claiming him.

His duties kept him late. Now that he did not have Stella, any emergency fell squarely upon his own shoulders. To spare Sen S Mo even for a day was difficult. The lights were out in the compound and his own house when he felt free to leave for the night. He would not disturb Diana, but would sleep on the couch downstairs.

It seemed to him that he had just dropped off to sleep, when he felt someone stealthily shaking him.

"The great doctor is needed at Magistrate Sen's," whispered Wang Ma.

So, after all these years, he was to go again to Scholar Sen's! But he found no great chair awaiting him at the gatehouse as on the former occasion. A shrouded figure spoke. "I, humble servant of the Sen family, will direct you."

As they passed through the sleeping city, and the servant chose back street after back street, Peter began to suspect some hoax was being practiced on him. This was not the way to the Sen house through this mean part of the city.

As they reached a guttering street lamp, he took a step forward to the side of his guide to get a good view of the man's face. After that, he followed without hesitation. No one would doubt this man. He had that peculiar look of goodness and devotion so noticeable in many Chinese faces; Wang Ma had that look. Something else struck Peter, too. Long accustomed to the decorum of calm practiced by this people, he was startled by the naked tragedy in the old man's face. "Let us hurry," said Peter.

They had reached one of the high-arched bridges over a canal. Up its long flight of steps the man went, almost as fast as a chair-coolie would have gone, Peter following close. A moment they stood at the top to catch their breath. Looking down, Peter saw the hooded city of junks. Then they were making the descent, were down. The man darted to the left along the canal's edge. Peter had to take its precarious footing a little more slowly. When he again caught up, the man was scratching with his fingernails on the closed panels of a mean shop, whispering into the crack between panels. One slid quietly back, and Peter saw Sen S Mo standing in the narrow opening.

"Thou!" exclaimed Peter. "What do you do here?"

"I am a humble member of this scholar's family," she said with great dignity. "We have need of your help." She stood aside for him to enter.

He could see little at first. The stub of a candle burned feebly in the closed room. Sen S Mo lighted another. Kneeling on the dirt floor of the miserable hut, a thin and beautiful youth faced a tier of boards placed one above the other separated by heavy blocks. On each plank lay a figure seemingly in deep sleep. All were dead.

It was a moment before Peter recognized, lying on the central plank, the man he had but twice met—Scholar Sen. The fine and delicate features, the nobility, the calm—yes, Scholar Sen. Just above him lay the tiny old woman who had watched him so closely that night years ago, when he had attended the sick boy. Even in death he saw her imperious will in the set of her chin and her lips. He shuddered slightly at the gluttonous look of power in her face.

The others—who were the others? How came it they were all dead? There was no mark of sickness upon them.

"Will the physician help?" Sen S Mo asked. "Lo Shih will not go unless someone promises them burial. He wants only to see them buried. Then he, too, must die."

"Sen Lo Shih!" Peter looked again, still not recognizing the child he had once attended in the stony, silent figure of the kneeling youth.

Bits of the story Sen S Mo whispered to him. "The *lao tai tai* was a wicked woman. She it was who brought the great Sens to this."

Gradually, out of Sen S Mo's fragmentary whispers, Peter pieced together the story. Opium raised on the family fields in far-away Szechuan because the old mother demanded it. Her crafty defiance of the law, her gloating delight in the outwitting of inspectors and officials. Her greed tempting her to greater risks as the price of opium went up. And last night, because of the crimes of his family, Scholar Sen had received the official command to kill himself—the purple cord, mark of honor sent him by the Empress—because of his meritorious degree spared public execution. The *lao tai tai's* fierce, wild denunciation of her son and the family, accusing them all of extravagance, of duplicity, of traitorous acts. The family was disgraced. Face was gone. The wild scene of frantic women and frightened men, as the *lao tai tai* drove them to the killing of themselves. The well full of the bodies of the concubines. Then her own suicide by swallowing an overdose of opium.

"Only Lo Shih remains, and I who am cast out of the family. The *lao tai tai* commanded Lo Shih that he, too, must end his life. He waits only his final duty, to bury these."

Peter was shaken. His own belief in the sacredness of human life made him recoil from such destruction. Some profound negation existed in the thought of this people, a dark unconquerable force that brought them so often to self-annihilation.

All his energies rose to fight it. This boy could be saved. He must find a way to help Lo Shih bury his dead and then get him away. Out of his slender stores, he must take the money for coffins.

"If I provide coffins, you and the boy are responsible to me. You must obey me."

"Yes, master."

"I will arrange it," said Peter.

"No, no," said Sen S Mo, fright in her voice. "It must be done secretly. Let me arrange——"

Peter sensed another element in the tragedy, some vengeance to be wreaked on the family that it would be idle for him to try to fathom, retribution paid by the entire clan. Sen Lo Shih, even Sen S Mo, perhaps, would not be safe in this city. To save them he'd have to send them away to another province. But first there were the dead to be buried.

"Where is the burial ground?"

"Reached by junk," said Sen S Mo, laconic now, after her sudden whispered outburst.

"A junk here tomorrow night," promised Peter.

"No," said Sen S Mo. "It is better that I arrange for the junk. This trusty man——"

The next night under cover of darkness, Peter went again to the sordid room. How Sen S Mo had arranged it he did not know, nor did he ask. Sen Lo Shih, clothed in white sack-cloth, knelt before his coffined ancestors, no sign of emotion on his proud, thin features. Reserved, haughty, he followed the last coffin down the steps to a boat on the canal, took his place within it, kneeling again among his dead.

The junk knocked its way through the massed boats to the water gate, with Peter standing at its prow to allay suspicion. At dawn when the wicket was raised, the hooded boat, with its dead, slipped quietly out of the city.

"We shall need *Fei I Sheng* no longer," said Sen S Mo, when they had gone a little way.

"After the burial," commanded Peter, "thou and the boy are to come back to us. By that time I can arrange to send you to another city, another province. The boy would be safe in a school there?"

"Yes, honorable teacher. In seven days we shall return."

It was evening. The seven days were over. Peter and Diana sat in his study. Would the sense of honor by which these people lived force Sen Lo Shih to the last step? Would the *lao tai tai's* command be stronger than any effort Sen S Mo could put forth? Sen S Mo, returning to her clan after so many years; Sen S Mo whom they now knew had defied the old matriarch. Sen S Mo, who called Diana sister, and yet had never told them that she belonged to the great Sen family. Neither had Wang Ma nor Scholar Wu ever betrayed the fact of Sen S Mo's relationship to the most illustrious Sens in the city. How could they tell what these people would do? How little they knew them. How could they know them?

Peter looked up. No knock at the door had announced them. There was no need. The doors to his study stood always open for the Chinese to come and go as they would. Sen S Mo stood there, marked with the indomitable will of the older women of her country, the heritage of matriarchs. Sen Lo Shih, clad in a common blue gown of the people, followed her, unresponsive, remote, negation written deep in his face, in the posture of his body.

This strange room woke in him consciousness. It offended him to stand in the house of the hated foreigner. Until now dulled by the catastrophe that had come upon him, he had been oblivious to all but his dead and his commitment to them. Now, startled, he saw the face of the foreign man. So had he seen it when as a child, aroused from stupor, something in that face had willed him to get well. Something in it now willed him to live.

"Sen S Mo, you must stay and rest," urged Diana, seeing how haggard her friend looked.

"It is better that we go immediately, my sister," Sen S Mo replied.

"You are too tired."

"*Mei yu fatzu*, it cannot be helped," said Sen S Mo.

Peter placed the money for the journey in her hand. "You are to go to the province of Hunan. Ask for the foreign *I Sheng* at the Mission there. Give him this letter."

Sen S Mo took the letter, carefully secreting it and the money in the breast of her black gown. Turning to Diana, she said, "My sister, we must go now."

The two went, silently as they had come.

Peter and Diana sat for a long time looking at each other, saying nothing.

"Perhaps we ought not to have done it," said Diana at last. "Our own children——"

"But what else *could* we do?" Peter spoke with a little helplessness in his voice, adding, "And what am I to do at the hospital without Sen S Mo?"

On the day of the celebration over the eradication of opium, as the party drifted toward the little island called "The Heart of the Lake," Peter kept thinking of the Sen family. He was wondering how many other clans had been wiped out as they had been.

"China has dripped blood to do this," the English inspector said to him. "A costly reform—perhaps you don't realize it."

"I think I do," said Peter. He glanced at the viceroy, who was politely depreciating his own people, saying, "The reform—it is nothing." What did he think of those seven years which the West exacted as necessary to complete its part of the bargain? His face gave no sign. He was the suave and polite host.

XXXIV

Peter and Diana were to go on furlough in the spring. Peter sought in these months only to establish firmly what he had already done, against his absence.

November came. The travail of new birth was upon China. No longer would it be delayed. The Mission schools that Scholar Sen had so scornfully thought of as coolie schools had impregnated the nation with revolutionary thought: the equality of women, the rights of the common man. The youth trained in such schools were filled with the hope of government by the people coming to this land. There was talk of revolution. Antiquity sanctioned rebellion against an unrighteous monarch. Confucius sanctioned rebellion against those who no longer governed by virtue. As so often throughout the two thousand years of China's history, the people were about to exercise their prerogative—pull from the throne the Son of Heaven.

Their leader, a man educated in one of their own schools, returned from his exile abroad. The overthrow of the Manchus, their rulers, for so many years the usurpers of the Throne, must be the first objective. Province after province declared independence. The little Manchu garrisons, stationed for so many years in provincial cities, fed and housed by the people, weakened by idleness, were unable to defend themselves.

For two days fear had held the city tense. There were those who remembered the last rebellion when the city had been razed to the ground. What would happen this time? The rich people fled. Great patriarchal families, men, wives, concubines, and children, stowed themselves away in junks, houseboats, and in compartments on the one train a day going to Shanghai. The poor hid behind shuttered shops.

All day the Mission compound had been tense with the premonition of disaster. The fathers of the girls in the school, elegant gentlemen, came for their daughters. Diana saw beneath the decorum of their etiquette. She had thought only women wrung their hands, but these silk-clad men wrung theirs and wept in fear. Diana quieted the girls and their fathers, superintended the departure of each chair. At last the school was empty, except for Mei Ing Perkins, who had no other home.

"Come, Mei Ing," said Diana gently. "We'll go over to my house." She put her hand on Mei Ing's shoulder, leaning upon the tall girl. She felt the weight of her unborn child. If only she could get home and lie down!

In spite of all Peter could do, patients left the hospital, even those who had just been operated on, some on mattresses swung between poles, others staggering forth on foot, staffs to support them, buoyed up by the incredible strength of fear. At China New Year, Peter had seen the hospital empty itself, but never before with such haste. As the last patient passed out of the gate, he followed, stood for a moment looking down the street. Never, even at New Year, had he seen the city so deserted.

Miss Dyer came toward him, the only figure to be seen, pith hat, long coat, umbrella hooked over her arm. She advanced calmly. "You're a fool, Fraser," she said, "not to have got your family out. The city's as panicky as an ant-hill that's been stepped on. I'll bet Berger's gone. Showed sense, this time."

"Well, it's too late now," Peter said. "Anyway, all the boats and trains—I couldn't take Diana into such a jam. She's safer here. Besides, you know that we, as foreigners, will be given every consideration—the revolutionists want us for their friends."

"Have it as you will," said Miss Dyer, and stalked away.

Toward morning, Diana's third travail began, premature travail brought on by the effort of the day. Peter blamed himself that he had not saved her from the strain, but there had been no time to help her in the stress of his own work.

There was fitful firing far to the north in the city, but Peter did not notice. Again he must deliver Diana of her child. She seemed to him to have entered into some deep pre-occupation which he could not penetrate. It was as if she went inward for some force of which he was ignorant, so that this life separating itself from her should be sent forth with her strength, until it could create strength of its own.

The child was born—tiny, perfect. All his energy was galvanized into saving the frail girl thrust into the world too early to make her own struggle. He loved her with a passionate love as he nestled her in his hands, holding her close to his own body for warmth. He felt himself in some mystic touch with creation—sharing with Diana its ecstasy, but not its pain.

At dawn, suddenly, Peter realized that the intermittent sounds of guns had ceased. He heard soft footfalls on the stairs. The gateman came in to show a white band around his sleeve. "The government of the people has been born in the city," he announced proudly.

The nation was in the hands of the revolutionists. The Manchu dynasty, old and crumbling, under the pressure of in-trigue and lust, had fallen away at a touch. Democracy, and without bloodshed. All Christendom applauded.

But the months following appeared to be a kind of after-math of lethargy. The revolution so easily accomplished seemed waiting for something to give it vitality. Peter, like others, often wondered if it would live.

During those first weeks of its life, Diana scarcely left the baby's side. She had had no need to give to her other children, healthy and strong from the very first, such all-absorbing care. It gave a new emphasis to her motherhood. The secret life of her womb was going on outside her this time. As she sought to duplicate the ever-flowing nourishment and warmth that she had given subconsciously to Serena and Pete, her whole life was impregnated with the anxieties of her motherhood. In these months she leaned upon Peter, drawing from his strength, his skill, his gentle care, the help she needed.

One day in early spring, as they stood looking down on the baby, at last out of danger, Peter said, "We've been drawn so close through her—I'd like her to be named after you, Diana."

"I had thought——" Diana began, and then broke off. "Yes, it would be nice to have her named after me."

But Serena and Pete were already calling her Mei Mei, the Chinese for Little Sister. The name held some subtle charm as it was pronounced in English—May May.

Change was already coming to the city, when, in the last days of June, the Frasers left for America. The houses of the Manchu city, that little garrison of a vanquished conqueror, had been torn down and new government buildings built on the land. In Peking, in the Forbidden City of the Son of Heaven, the first president of China lived.

PART TWO

I

"Is THIS China?"

"Why, yes, Pete, it's been China ever since we got off the ship yesterday," answered Diana.

The Frasers were standing in a little group on the station platform, waiting for the train which would take them back to their station.

"But," protested Pete, fixing accusing eyes on his mother, "you said China was beautiful."

"Just wait," answered his father. "You haven't seen it yet. Don't you remember it, Serena?"

"No," answered the little girl. "It was a long time ago."

"We were only in America a little over two years," said Diana. "Mei Mei was the only one who was a baby when we left." And she stooped over Mei Mei sitting in her lap and kissed the top of her head.

"Here's the train. I'll take Mei Mei. We'll have to hurry or all the seats will be full." Eagerly Peter led his family toward the third-class car, with all the urgency of his own anticipation. After two years, he was back in China, back at his work!

Jostled and pushed by the crowd, they reached the third class, only to find every seat taken.

"We'll have to try the second."

In the second class, Chinese gentlemen were making themselves comfortable. Peter looked hopelessly about. A man just removing his long gown, preparatory to stretching himself out on the seat for rest, saw the foreign family, bowed and moved across the aisle. Peter bowed back his thanks.

A brass gong clanged and the train moved out across the

216

flat fertile coastal plain, quiescent under its tawny growth
of rice. Willows fringing the fields trailed their delicate
branches in lace-like grace over the undulating grain. At
each leisurely stop, the hush of the fields penetrated the car.
The heat and light of the September day hung about them,
motionless and golden.

"It's the same China," mused Peter.

As the afternoon wore on, the children grew restless.
Serena and Pete, energetic after the way of American children,
ran up and down the aisle. The carload of Chinese looked
curiously at them. They returned to their mother's side.
Mei Mei pulled and strained in Diana's arms. "Down, down,"
she begged. Peter coaxed her to him, walking back and forth
with her.

Serena fell asleep, her head in Diana's lap. Pete sat wide-
eyed and quiet on her other side, staring at the Chinese around
him. Mei Mei went to sleep on her father's shoulder. Very
carefully, Peter got his long legs under the table running between the two seats, and, sliding slowly over to the window,
looked out. No, he had not missed that first view of the
remote blue hills.

During the two years in America, the encircling hills, as he
had seen them so often from the city wall, had become to him
the symbol of something his own land failed to give him.
With all his love of energy, he had found the energy of
America almost sinister. If China's passivity had led to stagna-
tion, the West's activities held elements of chaos. Men who
had not felt the discipline of scientific effort rushed the newly
opened gates of power which the hard work of scientists had
flung wide, and carried away the spoils.

Diana's eyes were upon him. Oblivious to the watching
Chinese, he and she joined hands under the table, and together watched the tranquil scene with the enchanted vision
of their first days of union.

The train servant passed along the aisle, with his great
brass kettle, dextrously swirling hot water from its long

spout into the passengers' tea pots. There was the sibilant sound of many mouths sucking in the hot drink.

A frightened whisper came from Pete. "I don't like all these Chinese around me. Why don't they go away?"

"Hush, Pete. You mustn't say such things," said Diana.

Breaking into sobs, the boy buried his head in her lap, his bright hair confused with the soft gold of Serena's. With his violent little fists he struck the soft flesh of Diana's thigh. Diana turned from Peter. With one hand she tried to capture Pete's beating fists, with the other she stroked his hair.

Peter marked how tired she looked. She had never quite recovered from Mei Mei's birth, and those trying months that followed. And the two years in America had been hard, with the constant demands of the children, and no servant to help her.

"You're tired, darling. Come over here by me, Pete," said Peter.

Diana looked up. Then she drew Pete to her shoulder, nestling her head against his. "He's all right. He doesn't tire me." Every line of her face, every line of her body, bespoke enthralled devotion to the clinging soft touch of Pete on her shoulder and Serena on her lap.

Peter looked away to the hills, which now stood all along the horizon.

Suddenly the city wall reared itself out of the flat fields, bulked itself against the brilliance of the evening sky. The vines and gnarled trees growing from its outer face, took shape. Then the train seemed to run straight into the wall's medieval strength. The windows darkened as in a tunnel. An instant more, and the station's lighted platform slid slowly past the windows.

A bedlam of noise broke round them. Coolies poured through the doors, snatching at luggage, determined to make a few coppers. The native passengers elbowed their way among the shouting, gesticulating coolies. Serena woke, looked wonderingly about. Pete, lips set, picked up his small suitcase. Mei Mei still slept peacefully on her father's shoulder. With one hand he pulled their luggage from the racks. He called to the coolies. The Chinese words came familiarly to his tongue.

They were on the platform trying to keep themselves and their luggage-coolies from being forced apart in the jostling crowd. Through the turnstile Peter manœuvered his family. Chair-men besieged them, also ricksha men, new to the city since they had left, besieged them. Serena and Pete clung to Diana. Mei Mei woke, smiling down on the crowd.

Then suddenly, in their midst was Wang Ma, shouting, "Sons of turtles! Do you think we ride thus? We are important people with our own chairs!"

She swept Serena and Pete into the circle of her arms. "Wang Ma's babies," she cried, reaching for Mei Mei. A moment more and they were seated in their own sedan chairs. Wang Ma arranged them—Mei Mei with Diana, Pete standing between his father's knees, and Serena on Wang Ma's lap in the last chair.

Darkness had come to the city. The men stooped, lighting brands of rushes. They turned into their own street. The shopmen came out, bowing the familiar bow, hands in sleeves. "The man with the Buddha heart has come back."

The gate of their compound swung to the touch of the head chair-man. High on the shoulders of the carrying men, they rode through a lane of blue-clad friends. The torches swung high, lighted one face, then another. There stood the old shoemaker, Pastor Wang, in his long gown. There was Mei Ing Perkins, grown into a big girl of fourteen. There were a group of girls, Diana's old pupils; a countryman, a patient of Peter's, clutching his offering of a squawking chicken. There was Teacher Wu, and with him a middle-aged man. At the entrance to their house, a group of white friends gathered, crowding about them as they entered.

Diana sat on the old couch, her children around her. Peter stood near.

"Glad to have you back," said Miss Dyer. "The school's yours tomorrow, Diana. I want to get back to my itinerating."

The English bishop addressed Peter. "How was the train trip? I prefer the quiet and dignified houseboat. The train in its haste seems vulgar."

"Perhaps," said Peter. "How is your son? Is he in England?"

"No," replied the bishop. "He lives in quiet seclusion within his own compound. He does not like the New China."

"Is it, then, so different?" asked Peter.

Others crowded around, Berger pathetically glad to have them back. "The wife's in the hills," he said. "Want you to come and look at her, Fraser. She's not well." He lowered his voice, as Dr. Smith, who had taken Peter's place during his absence, joined them.

Teacher Wu came forward, introducing his son. "A teacher perhaps the great doctor can use for his children. The son of my unworthy self is gentle, and could teach the small hands to shape the ideographs."

"The son who, under the old régime, might now be a great official," thought Peter.

The guests had gone. As Diana rose, she saw Sen S Mo standing in the doorway. The aristocratic Sen S Mo, her placid lips, her calm black eyes unchanged, even when she bowed to Diana, saying, "We have come back, my sister. This is a new government."

Following Sen S Mo was a young man. Sen Lo Shih. Peter could never forget that face, so definitely had it been engraved on his mind on the night when the boy had knelt with his dead around him. The lad's face was hardly less tragic now than then in its profound melancholy.

"I hear *Fei I Sheng* has brought no nurse back from America," Sen S Mo began, when they were seated.

So Sen S Mo expected her old place at the hospital, thought Peter. He couldn't go back to that. The day for untrained widows was over. Students, now, for nurses, Dr. Smith had told him. He was relieved to hear Diana say, "Perhaps my sister would help me in the school. I need you, Sen S Mo—with the children taking so much of my time."

Sen S Mo bowed her consent.

"And you, Lo Shih?"

"I would enter the boys' school," he replied.

As Peter and Diana bade these last guests good night, they felt as if they had never been away. The needs of those around them were already their needs. They were home.

But in the morning they felt themselves strangers. New China was sharply defined. Diana's school, in her absence, had become popular, even smart. When Peter entered the hospital, at first all seemed the same. The *amahs* toiling along the corridors with great cans of hot water, the familiar steps to the surgical ward, the winding passageway to the opium refuge, and the bridge across the street—even the old sterilizer, its valves working less competently now. Familiar patterns in his mind. But the student nurses moving through the wards with notebooks under their arms, a class of girls, a class of boys—these things had scarcely been dreamed of when he left. Dr. Smith was justly proud of this achievement.

That afternoon, as Diana and Peter walked through the city on the way to the lake, Western enterprise met them everywhere. The humpbacked bridges with their flights of steps had been rebuilt. The new ramp-like structures of cement made it possible to have wheeled vehicles in the city. The hard labor of chair-bearing was disappearing—taking its place the hard labor of ricksha-pulling.

The Manchu section of the city, razed to the ground at the time of the revolution, had wide streets and tawdry copies of Western buildings.

"Oh, Peter," said Diana, "how changed it is!"

"Let's hurry and get out of this," said Peter. "We're near that nice walk by the wall."

Already in their imaginations they were there, the wall

bulking in a black mass to the left, silence and expectation their companions as they advanced slowly to the city gate. Sudden and exquisite thrust of beauty—the lake clothed in soft haze, green causeways like fairy green spanning it.

"Here's the turn," cried Peter. He stopped.

The section of wall which had formerly hidden the lake from sight, had been taken down. Through a modern park, without the pleasure of surprise, they advanced to the lake. Here, too, the ancient bridges had been replaced by modern ones.

"Of course, taking down even a part of the wall has let fresh air into the city. It's a good thing," said Peter sturdily.

But each had his moment of doubt. Was what they were bringing to China good? How could they know? For a moment even Peter would have stepped back into the safety of tradition away from the hazards of change.

As they stood there, he thought of Stella. What did she think of all this change? Strange, the sudden vivid impression of her. He looked around, half expecting to see her, but there was only a group of students in foreign dress walking languidly through the park.

"Come," he said to Diana. "Let's go home."

In silence they turned back into the city.

"Look," said Diana. "That must be the house where the bishop's son lives. See, its upstairs windows are all shuttered. They told me last night he has hidden himself away there with the Chinese Classics. He doesn't want to see any of the changes."

In the days that followed, the whole family found themselves not a little homesick, whether for America or for old China, Diana and Peter were not quite certain. But Serena and small Pete knew. They missed America. That one precious year of school in America! Serena longed for the rows of little girls like herself and the fun. As for Pete, he was continually running away hunting for playmates, shak-

ing his fists angrily at the compound wall which hemmed him
in. He was indignant. He, a boy, forced to go to a girls'
school, his mother's school for girls! He was too young to go
to the boys' school, Diana thought.

The compound was very empty just now. The Bakers had
had to go home for Mr. Baker's health, and Miss Dyer, the
day after their arrival, had started on her itinerating—an
ambitious trip this time. She would be gone three months.
When Peter went up the mountain to see Mrs. Berger, he
found that she had tuberculosis, as Dr. Smith had said. He
insisted that she spend the winter there. So there were no
children for Serena and Pete.

Diana wondered about the angry Pete, the silent Serena—
a strange Serena since her return. One day Diana found her
lying on the bed letting Wang Ma dress her. When she
spoke sharply to the child, Serena appeared to emerge bewildered from her languor, almost like a Chinese child, with
that dull look of those in whom the mind is asleep. Gradually
the children developed a patience such as one often sees in
sick children, accepting the hard fate of loneliness mysteriously
thrust upon them. Sometimes Diana wondered if she should
not have left Serena and Pete in America. But they were so
young. Better, she told herself, for them to be without
friends than without their parents. It never occurred to her
to let them play with Chinese children. It was not the custom
among the missionaries.

Finally the Frasers were entirely alone on the compound,
for Berger, too, went to the mountains, unable to bear his
empty house, daily becoming more uncomfortable. He had
dismissed one servant after another because they squeezed,
until only an old coolie remained. Every extra penny he spent
on old bronzes. In order to buy more, he decided to eat
nothing but Chinese food. At last, sick and miserable, he
consulted Peter.

"The change from wheat to rice in your diet is too drastic."
And then, seeing the man's misery, Peter added, "Why don't

you go up to the mountain? I'll look after the school while you're gone."

The leaves of the bamboos were dry and brown. Berger shivered in his thin overcoat, as the chair-coolies carried him higher and higher up the mountain. He was discouraged and uncertain of himself. All that great personality he had been building had crumpled. Since Jessie had been in the hills, some richness and warmth seemed to have gone out of him. When she was with him, he did not know where he was strong and where he was weak, her strength and weakness flowing around him until he felt completed.

"*Ao sao!* Hurry!" he commanded the chair-men, as they paced along the main street of the empty summer resort. There ahead, on a little promontory, looking down on the valley, was his cottage. With one bound he leaped the two steps of the porch and was at the door, calling, "Jessie, Jessie!" Held in her fragile embrace, he was again strong.

The children crowded around, catching a new spirit of gaiety in their mother. Poor little things, she hadn't been much of a mother lately. Then, when her husband told her of the bleak house, the bad food, she was contrite indeed. And when she saw him wolfing his dinner, she decided she would go home.

"But are you well enough?" Berger asked.

"Oh, Bert, see how well I am!" and she moved gaily about the room. His need of her had made her strong.

The children clapped their hands. "We're going home!" they cried.

"Well, we don't have to decide now," said Berger. "Fraser's tending to my school for a little. I need rest."

II

THE attitude of the New China toward Western civilization was one of appreciation and admiration. At times Peter felt humbled and even frightened before the Chinese acceptance of the West. It was too close to worship, too blind an adoration. Once before Christendom had stood in such a place. In the seventeenth century, the Jesuits had come, bringing their religion and the best scientific knowledge of Europe. They had helped in the adjustment of the calendar. They had brought greater accuracy in astronomical calculations. The Chinese scholars were deeply impressed then with the learning, devotion, and beautiful gentleness of the Fathers. They desired Christianity for their own country.

Then while the churchmen quibbled over the word to be used to express God, Christianity, for lack of nurture, died. Two hundred years, and new heralds of the West came—not gentle Fathers of the Church this time, but pirate traders in opium. The Chinese lost faith in the West. But along with the traders, missionary scholars had come bringing science and medicine and had fought against the evils of footbinding and opium. And now again Christianity injected its ideals into China. Again China bowed in recognition of democracy and science. Would Christendom be equal to the test this time? Often Peter feared it might not.

In this New China, everyone wanted to study science. But the young students thought they could learn chemistry, physics and physiology by rote, as they had learned their Classics. Experimentation meant work with the hands. It departed from the traditions.

Berger had deferred to the boys in the matter of laboratory work. But for Peter, there was no science without experimentation. As he stood among the boys at the laboratory tables, conducting an experiment, he studied Sen Lo Shih, among them. Fastidiously the boy handled the test tubes and bottles of chemicals with his delicate fingers. Something almost supercilious in his expression reminded Peter of Scholar Sen, his father. Peter paused in his demonstration. Lo Shih should know that science was worthy of the best minds. All the boys' black heads, including Sen Lo Shih's, were bowed over notebooks, meticulously writing down the experiment.

"Sen Lo Shih," said Peter, "are you simply going to accept what I say? Have you no questions, no doubts?"

Sen Lo Shih slowly raised his head, and for a moment Peter saw keen interest in the black eyes, before the face again took on superciliousness. A secret thrill shot through Peter. Had he wedged open the gate of speculation in Lo Shih's mind?

From then on, he hardly noticed the other boys. Let them learn this science by rote, according to the old Chinese customs. Sen Lo Shih he would stir to the scientific attitude. "Perhaps I can make him a research worker," Peter said excitedly to himself.

As he left the school, he passed through the playground where a football game was in progress. He almost wished the boys wouldn't attempt this masculine game. It seemed to accentuate a certain femininity in them. They were moving languidly over the field, holding up the skirts of their long gowns. Passing through the gate, he stopped a minute at the entrance to the girls' compound. He heard the clipped Chinese, "*Ih, erh, san,* one, two, three." Solemnly, the girls swayed, bent, and stepped to the young Chinese teacher's command. In their short jackets and trousers, they could have stepped out more freely than the boys, if it had not been that most of them, in childhood, had had their feet bound. And even the little girls, who had never had their feet bound, patterned their walk after the traditional gait. Still, it was smart in the New China to make physical effort.

Was this New China, perhaps, merely an imitation of

Christendom, not a rebirth after all—the form without the spirit?

He swung along the central path toward the hospital. The outer gate opened and a long line of chairs moved into the compound. Foreigners. Then his heart contracted with anger. Berger, the children, and Mrs. Berger! He had told Berger that under no conditions should Mrs. Berger attempt a winter in the city. "What did you do such an idiotic thing for?" he asked, striding up to Berger's chair.

"Better for her here than up there all alone," Berger answered defiantly.

"You see, when Bert came, we begged him to let us come back. Oh, there's Diana!" Mrs. Berger began to cry, the tears rolling unheeded down her cheeks.

"Never mind. You're here now." Diana gently took the baby from her. "You're tired after your long ride." But she knew that Mrs. Berger needed a woman about. She, too, felt warmed by the presence of another woman.

Peter's protests died on his lips as he saw Serena and Pete come racing down the path, Serena smiling, the baffled look gone from Pete's face. They came to a halt, sudden shyness overtaking them as the chairs were set down and the Berger children got out—Rose, Timothy, and three small girls like steps.

"You must stay with us until they get the fires lighted in your house and it's thoroughly warmed," said Diana, taking hold of Mrs. Berger's arm.

They gathered in the dining room. Wang Ma brought tea.

"It's so good," sighed Mrs. Berger, hardly knowing whether she meant the tea or Diana's presence.

Serena surveyed first the three smaller Berger girls, then Rose. Rose smiled. Serena walked over to her.

"I'm seven," Serena announced.

"I'm eleven."

But what did four years' difference in age matter? They liked each other.

"Hello," said Pete. Putting his hands in his pockets, he walked up to Timothy, a head taller than himself.

"Want to see my knife?" asked Timothy. "Good knife."

"It's all right," said Pete, looking it over with a judicial air. Peter placed an extra lump of coal on the fire. Wang Ma brought in the lamp.

"Look here," said Peter to the two boys, "I'll teach you how to play mumblety-peg . . . but we can't do it on the floor, can we? Wait, I'll get a board."

Soon the two men and the boys were kneeling, intent on their game.

In the days that followed, everyone seemed completely happy, the lonely mountain erased from the minds of the Bergers, homesickness for America from the minds of the Frasers.

Mrs. Berger seemed to gain rapidly. Berger felt justified in his judgment. He was glad they had defied Dr. Fraser. Lying quietly in her bed, Mrs. Berger could hear her children and husband going about the house.

Diana's motherhood seemed a little in abeyance these days, a happy accompaniment to her union with Peter.

Serena's sober contentment was unmistakable.

"My Ko Ko," Pete called Timothy. Ko Ko, Elder Brother. Marching head up with Ko Ko, he braved all those chattering, giggling girls at the school.

The two boys learned to bribe the gateman and get out into the street, timing their wanderings to the hours of the day when their parents were occupied. At large in the city, they entered a secret, thrilling world of their own, filled with hazards real and imaginary.

On Saturday mornings they followed the Bergers' cook to market, keeping a discreet distance so he should not see them. They followed patients from the hospital into dingy alleys. They followed Sen Lo Shih as he left the school. Far across the city he went, to the streets of the rich. Then he turned suddenly, and they lost him. But just ahead they found a small gate, half tumbled in. Fearfully at first, then more bravely, they squeezed through it. They were in a courtyard overgrown with dry weeds. A Chinese kitchen, the mortared-in pots rusted, the clay stoves broken, ran along one side. A tile fell and a furry animal scurried forth. Fox fairies, about which Wang Ma had told them! They shook with fear.

The next time, they discovered a garden court. An old grey pine threw a black shadow against a wall. There were stone benches and a round table. Just the place for picnics and all kinds of adventures. For weeks, they lived an enchanted life.

One day, they saw a little spiral of smoke rising above the wall. A bottle-shaped doorway blocked with boards hid what lay beyond.

"Let's play we're the robber kings sneaking down on a village," said Timothy, whose father was reading to him *The Three Kingdoms*. "We see the smoke of the house fires. We run down from the mountains."

"I'm the robber chief," said Pete, strutting back and forth. One garter had broken, and his stocking hung around his ankle. He was using his sun helmet for a breast-plate. "Break the barrier!" he commanded.

Timothy, a gentle boy who always gave way to his vehement companion, advanced at Pete's command, an army of men, striking with a stick against the boarded-up doorway. A loosened board fell with a clatter. Pete, close on Timothy's heels, jumped through the open space into the court beyond, then stopped.

A black piece of wood with bright gold characters stood on a table in a room the front of which had been destroyed. Before it, silver paper shaped like money was licked about with flame. On the stone floor knelt a Chinese.

"Hello, Sen Lo Shih," cried Pete, friendly as a little dog. There was no response from the kneeling figure.

"I say hello!" called Pete again. He ran toward Sen Lo Shih, touching him on the shoulder.

Sen Lo Shih looked up, dazed. Then he turned golden yellow with anger. The boys started to run, but they were not quick enough. Sen had hold of them.

"Bear witness before Heaven and Earth, Sun and Moon, and all the other deities and demons, that you will never tell that you saw me here. . . ."

They bore witness.

"If you come here again, you shall be cursed with chronic sores!"

"If we come here again, we shall be cursed with chronic sores."

Then he let them go.

Sen Lo Shih had come to his father's house with the command of the *lao tai tai* still strong upon him, the responsibility to the vital dead. No longer could his duty to them be put off. He must take his own life. But now his anger was greater than his commitment to death.

That night, when Pete's mother came to hear his prayers, he almost told her of what had happened. He wanted her comfort. But then, if he told her, he and his Ko Ko could never wander again, and, too, they had sworn by a terrible oath not to tell.

"Is Sen Lo Shih going to come to our house any more?"

"Why do you ask?"

"Oh, nothing," said Pete. "I just wondered. Is he going to come here ever again?"

"Why? Have you been teasing Lo Shih?" asked his mother. Once she had caught Timothy and Pete mimicking the Chinese boys, as they held up their long gowns on the athletic field.

"Oh, no," said Pete. "But, mummie, wouldn't you like to sit by me a little while? You haven't seen much of me today."

He was standing in his bed. Diana caught him in her arms, lifted him and laid him down. "My darling," she whispered, burying her head in his neck, touching the soft flesh with her lips, making him wriggle with laughter.

"You tickle," he gasped, and forgot about Lo Shih.

III

JANUARY and February had been sunny. In March the spring rains began. April, and still the grey sky. The weeping willows put forth their buds. The pear threw its white beauty against farmhouse and grey city wall. The rich black earth nurtured its third crop of the year. The rice in the seeding beds grew luxuriantly. The people of this fertile valley paid toll for the long, slow rains which gave life to the strong earth. Tuberculosis took its thousands.

The slow drip in the eaves told Jessie Berger, waking in the blackness before dawn, that another sunless day was before her. But some strange life filled her. She was going to get well, not leave the children and Bert. She could hear their quiet breathing if she held her own breath—that short, precious breath of hers.

Dawn had laid its grey light in the room when Berger was awakened by broken murmurings. "Jessie . . . fever," he said to himself. But when he touched her, her forehead and hands were cold. He brought blankets from his own bed, until she lay under a mound of them, but still her hands were cold. He was frightened. Her half-sentences had turned to incoherent mumblings. He went in where the children slept, waking Rose.

"Who's talking in such a funny way?" she asked, only half awake.

"It's your mother. Wake the children."

She woke Timothy, and together they struggled with the underdrawers, the long stockings of the younger children. She led them into her mother's room. Frightened by the odd sound of their mother's voice, they hovered near Rose.

"Her feet!" Berger cried. "They are cold, too."

"I'll warm them, father." Rose chafed them, tried with

her small warm hands to cover them. "Help me, brother," she begged Timothy. "My hands are too little."

Thus Peter, called by the servants, found them. But all his knowledge could avail no more than Rose's unskilled hands.

A sad and helpless household after Mrs. Berger's death. Rose tried to be mother to the younger children and to manage the household. Each morning she put on a long apron of her mother's and went to the kitchen to interview the cook.

"Ting Ta Shih Fu," she would say, sitting gravely upon a chair he solemnly placed for her, "in the absence of my mother, I will command thee."

"Yes, missie," said Ting Ta Shih Fu. "My unworthy self made bold to buy a chicken this morning in the market."

"You may cook it," said Rose. Then she paused, thinking for a long time. The old cook in his big white apron, stood waiting. "I can't think, Ta Shih Fu. What else could we have?"

"I think, missie, perhaps, a little potato."

"Oh, yes, Ting Ta Shih Fu."

But in spite of all the efforts of Rose and Ta Shih Fu, things did not go very well.

Diana had wanted to take the Berger baby to her house, but that would leave the other children without an *amah*.

At last Berger decided he must take his family home to America. The Mission felt it was the only thing to do. He had no sooner decided, than he began to get ready.

The house seethed with activity. He must take all his curios with him. He'd pay back the money he had borrowed for his trip by the sale of them. Boxes stood about and baskets of rice husk for packing. One vase, his most valued piece, absolutely without doubt an authentic Ming, he told everyone, he packed and repacked for fear it might get broken. Finally he decided to carry it in his hand.

The day came for departure. The children stood in a little group on the veranda, waiting for their rickshas to come.

Rose and Serena were holding hands, whispering last farewells. Pete stood with his hands in his pockets, looking at Timothy, now and then winking back his tears. Berger came out, the vase wrapped in a ragged paper in his arms.

"Better let me tie that up for you," said Peter, who had just come over from the hospital.

"Never mind, it'll do," said Berger.

The ricksha-men came through the gate, their voices raised in a hubbub of chatter.

Amah sought to thrust the baby into Berger's arms.

"I've got to carry the vase," said Berger. "Give her to Rose."

"I've got the big incense burner," said the child. "You couldn't get it in the last box. You said I was to carry it."

"Give it to Timothy," commanded Berger. "Hurry—get into your rickshas. Come, Rose. Come, Janie. Leonora, you get in with Timothy."

Rose leaned over the arm of her ricksha, clasping Serena's hand.

"Good-by," called out Pete in a loud tone. "See you sometime in America, Ko Ko."

Berger with his works of art and babies disappeared from their sight.

The compound looked empty and deserted.

Diana, watching her children after the Bergers had gone, saw that Serena was not greatly unhappy without Rose. About her was something of the acceptance of the Chinese. Perhaps she had learned it from Wang Ma. But Pete could not be comforted for the loss of Timothy. He was like some bright instrument broken.

"He'll forget soon," said Peter. "Aren't there some little boys at the other Missions you could ask over, Diana?"

So Diana gave a party, asking the twelve white children of the city to an Easter egg rolling. Among the bamboos and in Mrs. Baker's rockery, Serena and Pete hid the eggs.

"See," said Peter. "He's forgotten already."

And Diana thought so, too, as she watched him among the children, bearing himself proudly at this, his first party, obligingly showing his guests where the eggs could be found.

The sun that had shone uncertainly all the morning, had come out strong and brilliant, dispelling the last cloud in the sky. The long spring rains had brought the compound unusual beauty. Foreign lawns with their clipped, even green were difficult to grow in China, but this year the grass looked as compact as a carpet's nap. The roses on trellises hung in great clusters, red and pink and yellow over the high pillared porches. The bamboos at the edge of Diana's closed-in garden had put forth new sprouts. Some were still sheathed, some had cracked their sheaths and stood forth in their first vivid green. The dragon-eye shrubs threw their red elephant's-ear leaves against the grey compound wall. The light colors of the children's clothes made spots of blue and pink on the lawn. Their voices were shrill and sweet. From the chapel came the sound of Chinese voices practicing the songs to be sung on Easter Sunday. "Christ is Risen, Christ is Risen." Piercing and sweet, higher and higher. They died away, lost in the pound of the spirit presses, the high squeak of wheelbarrows, the chants of heavy-laden men.

A couple of days later Peter came in through the kitchen of his house on his way to a room on the third floor which he had made his study, since the house had become so full of the voices of children and the work of the hospital. He found the door to the back stairs locked.

"Thy son wills it so," said Wang Ma.

"But why should you let him?" he asked, realizing what the extra steps, necessary because of this locked door, cost Wang Ma with her bound feet.

"The man child wishes it."

Peter went around to the front stairs, trying the door on the landing which led down the back way. It was unlocked.

He looked in. There on the top stair which widened out a little, was a cunningly constructed warm nest, lined with soft silks—an old dress of Diana's, a quilt covered with *mien dz,* that unevenly woven cheap silk made from the broken inner threads of cocoons, softer than any high-priced silk. Pete lay curled up in the darkness, asleep. It reminded Peter of Mei Mei on the night of her birth curled in the soft wool in which he had placed her.

"Why do you come here, Pete?" he asked him, lifting him to his lap.

"It's because I hurt."

"In your tummy?" asked his father.

"It's Ko Ko." And then, in a flood of words, Pete poured out the story of his wanderings with his hero.

"Pete," said his father, when he had finished. "A man can't hide. You have to fight."

"Am I a man?" asked Pete.

"Yes. Suppose we two men go for a walk on the wall?"

Very proudly Pete walked by the side of his tall father, out the gate, along the street, up the crumbling ramp to the wall's top.

"Why did God take Ko Ko's mother and make Ko Ko go to America?" Pete asked suddenly.

Peter did not speak for a moment. Here on this wall many hours he had paced, seeking to find an answer to the problems of suffering. How, then, should he answer Pete? But he did not have to.

The child's attention was caught by an old man who had brought his bird to the wall for a sunning. He squatted by the cage, sitting comfortably on his haunches, as the old man did. Peter stood watching.

"Why does the honorable one bring his honorable bird here?" Pete asked gravely.

"He will not sing unless the sun warms him."

"Has the honorable one cicadas, too, to sing for him?" Pete asked.

"And to fight, too," said the old man. "Mine win much money for me in the yearly tournament of insects. For a little money, I would show thee."

Pete turned a vivid, happy face up to his father. "Can I . . .?"

Peter took some Chinese coppers from his pocket, handing them to Pete, and then stood looking down on his son squatted by the tiny cicada cage.

"*Ai yah!*" cried Pete. "There they go at each other!"

Peter bent lower, finally sat on the ground, his long legs doubled under him, absorbed as his son in the battle.

The sun sank lower, shone in their eyes.

"Why, Pete!" he cried, looking at his watch. "It's past supper time!"

They hurried down the ramp, hand in hand.

That evening Peter told Diana of the nest on the stairs Pete had made for himself. A secret joy pierced Diana. She knew what he sought. He was circling blindly back, hunting the warmth and safety she had given him before his birth. That possessive motherhood that always felt a little stab of pain at any indication of her children's growing separateness from her, was satisfied.

IV

IN THE hundreds of years disease had stalked unchecked, the Chinese had developed certain immunities, built up special resistance; but the white man, with his precautions, had no such immunity. In the first processes of any betterment, man, about to step forward, for one dangerous moment stands between the primitive shelter of the past and the scientific shelter soon to be his. Life goes out quickly for the white man in the East.

Peter no longer had that fear he once felt for his family. He had been lulled into a sense of security that his skill was sufficient to keep harm from his own. He guarded his family against epidemics, watched that no infection should come to them through their food. He taught them the laws of sanitation and hygiene.

Spring was passing into summer. In a few weeks, as soon as Diana's school closed, she and the children would leave for the safety of the hills.

One hot, damp morning that presaged the *Mei Ti'en,* the "rain a little each day," Wang Ma called to him as he was about to go to the hospital. The old woman would not relinquish "her baby" long enough to come properly to him, but standing at the top of the stairs, the child in her arms, she hailed him. "Serene sick."

When he went up, he found Serena, beads of perspiration standing out on her forehead, moving restlessly in the old servant's embrace, first laying her head on Wang Ma's shoulder, then on her arm.

"Perhaps she is restless because she is so uncomfortable," thought Peter, although fear stabbed his heart, for restlessness was one of the symptoms of dysentery, and there was dysentery in the city. The child's pulse was frequent, small and feeble—the typical pulse of dysentery. He questioned Wang Ma. Yes, beyond a doubt, dysentery.

"Why didn't you tell *Fei S Mo?*" he asked her, "before she left for the school?"

The old woman did not answer him, holding the child closer to her.

Hastily he wrote Diana a note, telling her simply that Serena was not well. He did not want to worry Diana—it looked like a light case. "Give her to me," he said, "and take this chit to your mistress."

Now that he had Serena in bed, her restlessness was gone. Gently he drew a thin blanket over her, for even in this heat, there was danger of a chill.

"Sen S Mo, you'll have to take charge here," said Diana. As she turned her desk over to Sen S Mo, she realized how capable the Chinese lady had become. For the first time she saw Sen S Mo as she really was—a woman of power and ability. She need not give the school another thought. She hurried home.

Serena waved brightly as Peter left the room in search of the other children. He found Mei Mei in the garden. "Run up to mother," he said. Pete had already left for the boys' school, where, since Berger had gone, Peter had placed him. He sent for him. The same things Serena had eaten, the other children had eaten, too. The possibility of infection hung on the hazards of chance. All he could do was to attempt to check the disease.

Diana would let no one else attend her sick child. That night she sat by Serena, gently replacing the blanket again and again, as the little girl, restless and in pain, threw it off. She rose often and went into the nursery, where Mei Mei and Pete slept. The room was still. She could vaguely distinguish the white masses of mosquito nets hanging from round hoops suspended from the ceiling. Quietly she stood by Pete's bed, Mei Mei's crib, peering anxiously through the veil of the nets, alert for any sign of sickness.

Toward morning, laying her head on the pillow beside Serena, she slept, lightly, one hand holding the blanket over the child. Suddenly she sat up. Pete was calling her. She hurried across the hall to reach him before he got out of bed, but he was already halfway across the room. In the grey early light, she saw him. He had caught up his nightgown in one hand. How he hated that nightgown, handed down from Serena! "Girl's stuff," he called it. He stood in the middle of the floor, the despised garment, girdled with a string, held high so that he could run.

"Mother, Ko Ko isn't here. Where's my Ko Ko?"

Diana caught him.

He struggled. "Where is he?" After the old fashion, his violent little fists pounded the soft flesh of her thigh.

Diana's heart stood still. As she held him close, she felt the heat of his body. Pete sick, too!

"Peter!" she called, anguish in her voice.

With one spring, Peter was out of bed.

In the morning, Diana gave Mei Mei into Wang Ma's care, but the old woman could not quite relinquish "her baby." Often she stood in the doorway, Mei Mei in her arms, looking anxiously toward the bed where Serena lay.

All the time Peter could spare from the hospital he helped Diana tend the sick children. He bathed them, lifted them for her, aghast when he saw how white their bodies were. They were depleted by the long winter without sun, the continuous diet of cooked food, not equipped for the hard fight with disease. Diana saw it, too. Had she given more time to them? Had she neglected them—left them too much to Wang Ma? With intolerable remorse she asked herself was it Peter's fault? Both of them too absorbed in work?

The days dragged on. Nothing Peter could do served to stay the disease. Day after day the fevered children tossed in a mild delirium, then shivered in a cold sweat.

White friends and Chinese wanted to help. Mrs. Tang sent a native remedy for the little white child she had held

so often. Sen S Mo took the dried stamens of the lotus and
made an astringent after an ancient formula known to her
family, and brought it to Diana. Miss Dyer, back at last
from her long itinerating trip, sent bowls of strong broth she
herself had made. Mei Ing Perkins, who secretly, silently,
worshiped the fiery Pete, brought funny grotesque dolls she
had knitted. From the women at the other Missions came
offers of help with the nursing, but Diana would not let them.
Pastor Wang sat in the study, quietly praying.

At last Serena lay in a drowsy sleep; but there was no healing in that sleep. That night she died, slipping away in spite
of all Peter's skill and Diana's will to keep her. Together
Diana and Peter laid out their first-born.

In the early dawn, Peter went down to the garden. The
fierce heat had stripped it of flowers. He looked around.
Surely there was something . . . Out by the front door, he
came upon the Heavenly Bamboo in their blue pots. He
picked the evergreen, delicate leaves. Going back upstairs,
he laid them around Serena. As he stood with Diana looking
down on her, he felt Diana sway. For one moment she leaned
against him. Then she stood erect again. "Pete——"

Together they went back to fight for him.

Wang Ma stole into the room, dropped on her knees by
the child, beating her head on the side of the bed. "Wang
Ma's baby, Wang Ma's baby," she cried.

"Try, Pete," said his father, calling on the child's will to
help. "Try to get well."

"If I could see Ko Ko!" Pete threw himself forward. "Ko
Ko!" he cried, then fell back. With one quick sweep of her
hand, Diana ripped the mosquito net loose where it was
tucked around the bed, threw it up over the frame above,
reached for his hands, felt his forehead.

"My God!" she cried. "You cannot do this to me," and
fell upon the body of her son, drawing him to her, seeking
to give him life.

The net's white folds, caught over the frame above, slipped

slowly down, falling in a cascade of whiteness around Diana
and her son.

Out beyond the city in the Christian cemetery, in a fold
of the hills, Diana and Peter laid their children, a cross at the
head of each.

As they came back to the house, Diana turned sharply, crying, "I can't bear it!" Peter led her to the couch, his anxiety
for her crowding out his own grief.

Wang Ma stood in the doorway watching. Then Peter
heard her going energetically up the stairs, coming down again
quickly. He looked up. She had Mei Mei in her arms. Evidently she had waked the child, for Mei Mei's feet were bare
and one cheek was rosy and moist where it had pressed against
the pillow. She was rubbing her eyes sleepily. He put his
finger on his lips signaling for quiet, but Wang Ma, paying
no attention, set the child down.

"Go to mummie. Mummie wanchee you," she commanded,
in her few words of English.

Mei Mei ran across the room and hurled herself at her
mother, crying, "Wake up!"

Diana opened her eyes. She took the child into her arms,
pressed the warm little body to her, holding the tiny feet in
her hands. "Why, Wang Ma, Mei Mei shouldn't be without
her stockings. Get them at once." There was decision and
interest in Diana's voice.

"Yes, missie." Wang Ma went to get them, nodding sagely.

Peter realized the native woman's wisdom. But what neither
of them counted on was Diana's complete absorption in the
child. That night she had a cot placed for herself by Mei
Mei's crib, and sent Wang Ma to the servants' quarters. Wang
Ma, who had been the trusted caretaker of all three children,
banished from her place as privileged servant!

Night after night, Peter, lying awake in their room that
was now his alone, would hear the voice of the little girl. "I
want to come into your bed, mummie."

"Yes, darling." Diana's voice vibrating with tenderness.

Stealing across the hall at dawn, he would find Diana with Mei Mei curled in the right angle of warmth and protection made by her body, her arm stretched along the pillow.

Night after night as he lay in the dark alone, the physician in him reasoned and analyzed, saying, "This is shock. Give her time." But the man Peter cried out for his place in his wife's life.

Diana made no mention of going back to the school. She seemed almost to have forgotten it. When Sen S Mo came to see her, bringing some problem that had arisen, Diana gave listless attention. Except when Mei Mei was in her arms, she sat grieving. Sen S Mo was shaken by her friend's hopeless grief. Again she saw desire as the Buddhist sees it, as evil.

Teacher Wu was shocked at Diana's struggle to wrest herself apart from the inevitable consequences of life and death. She, who at one time had seemed acquiescent to the law of nature! The man of Confucian faith made an instinctive preparation against death. Such spiritual therapy the white woman seemed to know nothing about.

Diana's first wailing grief the Chinese had understood. But what they could not understand was her continued rebellion, her fierce resentment against fate. Catastrophe like this which had overtaken these foreigners, lay always near at hand for them. Perhaps in suffering, as well as in disease, the Chinese had built up immunity.

Peter grew more and more anxious. Diana had a low grade of dysentery, dangerous only if, depleted as she was by the hard work of nursing, she were further depleted by despair. He would think her cured, and then some special anxiety over Mei Mei, a little confusion or conflict, and she would be in bed for a day. Finally, she had an attack a little more severe than the others.

Just before sunset one evening, Peter left his many duties in order to see that she did not get up to care for Mei Mei. He told Wang Ma to bring a tin tub into Diana's room, so that she could see Mei Mei bathed. Wang Ma grumbled, and tried in a half-dozen ways to circumvent him. However, the tub was at last brought, but on the pretext of getting a toy the little girl wanted, Wang Ma picked up the child and went out mumbling, "Wang Ma know what to do for her baby."

Diana, listening for every sound from the other room, detected the careful pouring of water. In a moment she had her feet in her slippers. Peter pressed her gently back on her pillows.

"I'll see where they are," he assured her.

He found the two playing a game of quietness. Mei Mei had her finger on her lips. Her brown eyes sparkled with delight, as Wang Ma very carefully poured water into an enamel basin.

"Come, dear," he said, and took the small protesting hand in his. He spoke sharply to the old servant. "Wang Ma, do as I told you."

At last the child was asleep in her cot close to Diana. Even then Diana watched her anxiously.

"I think you ought to go to the mountains now," he said. "Get Mei Mei away."

"I couldn't go *there*. Last summer——"

Peter was silent, remembering last summer with the cottage filled with his children's voices, Serena's slow throaty tones, Pete's excited treble.

"No, of course not. Somewhere else, then?"

"If I could go to the seaside," said Diana, "the sea would do Mei Mei good."

He thought quickly of his all-but-nothing bank account. The sea was far away. Aloud he said, "I think we could manage it."

"Yes, I'd like to take Mei Mei right away. I'm afraid for her here."

After she had fallen asleep, he sat on in the growing twilight, studying his wife. Her abundant hair lay in damp strands against her neck. The low fever that burned in her cheeks accentuated the dark hollows around her eyes and the thinness of face and neck. A great wave of tenderness swept over him. He saw her as she had been that summer he had courted her. How strong and beautiful she had been then! And he had vowed if she would marry him that, although life might be hard, there should be equality between them—the personality of Diana bowing no more than the personality of Peter to the submission of marriage. Futile vow that he could not keep. With each child, some bit of Diana's strength had gone. In a sense, for each one she had given her own life. Yet sometimes he envied her that creation. And now both of them robbed of that for which she had paid so high a price.

V

THE summer seemed unbearable to Peter. The sun beat down on the white walls of the hospital; his consulting room was stifling. He had to will his feet to take the two extra steps up to the surgical wing, the three steps down to the passageway that led to the women's building.

After the sun had set and there was some measure of coolness, he paced the city wall, longing to know, as he had never longed before, the meaning of suffering. Until now, all his questioning had been over the suffering of others. Now he sought explanation of his own and Diana's pain and loss.

One evening he stayed longer than usual watching the hills fade into the night. In this dark and bitter hour, he grieved. And then, with startling vividness, out of some closed chamber of his mind, Stella stepped forth, as he had last seen her . . . surging up through the suffering in her eyes, something she knew but could not communicate. He turned wearily home. The barrenness of grief settled over his work.

Miss Dyer was staying in the city this summer conducting a short-term class for country women. She and Peter were the only foreigners on the compound. Her shrewd, hard facing of facts made her impatient with his listless inattention. "Exaggerating his trouble, as if no one else in the world had ever had any. He'll soon be like a lot of other missionaries— ineffective, the kind foreign business men say can't succeed out in the world," she thought wrathfully to herself.

What he needed first was plenty of real food to fill out that lean frame of his. Miss Dyer liked good food herself, believed it had spiritual substance. Starving himself since his wife had gone away, not keeping Wang Ma up to the mark! Wang Ma was sulking over something—mad, probably, be-

246

cause she hadn't been taken along to care for Mei Mei. It was time somebody took Fraser and his household in hand.

Walking solidly in her flat-soled shoes, she opened the closed door without knocking and stepped into Peter's office.

He jumped from his chair, startled. "What do you want?" he asked harshly.

About as she'd suspected. Evidently had had his head on his desk, doing nothing.

"I came to say you're having your meals with me after this. I've sent Wang Ma off to her own village for a rest. The Chinese haven't got much stamina—three children, the cooking, and no one much to help her—on her feet all day—she's tired out. Lunch is at twelve. Don't be late."

Peter winced at the mention of his children, and then anger flared and flamed within him. What right had this Dyer woman to interfere with his personal affairs?

Stout, middle-aged Miss Dyer looked with satisfaction at the angry man. "Don't forget . . . twelve o'clock," she said, and went out.

From each well-prepared meal Peter came away stronger and seething with opposition to her narrow views. He went to sleep at night vowing he'd never go to her house again; he woke with new arguments in his mind with which to combat her.

"Why don't you go in for research?" she said to him one evening. "Do something that will get you somewhere? Find out the causes of some of these Oriental diseases, instead of using yourself up and dying before your time, like Dr. Buchanan, trying to cure each poor devil after he gets sick? You're smart enough to get to the bottom of things."

"Of course I'm smart enough," Peter flung back at her. "But just when have I had the time for research?" He checked himself. If he had failed in the great objective of modern medicine, he wasn't going to tell her. "How do you know I haven't?" he demanded. "I've kept careful records of all the opium addicts that have passed through my refuge—

those who've been really cured and those who've returned to the habit. I'm working on a theory," he went on. "Men don't smoke opium for pleasure entirely. They've either got malaria, or they are insufficiently nourished. We've got to cure the underlying cause."

"Humph! I could have told you that. I can tell you something else," said Miss Dyer. "You put the power of Christ into them and they'll conquer."

In spite of his old distaste for what he felt were glib words, he was buoyed up by an idea Miss Dyer had given him. Why fuss along with this study of opium? Had he stumbled into that danger to the scientist—the meticulous recording of data to no creative purpose? His old ambition came back. Research—he believed at last he had his opportunity to do an organized piece of work. Another doctor was taking over the hospital for a month, while he went on his vacation.

He'd use the time to start his research on a parasitic disease of which he had always had scattering cases, but of which there had been more and more as the fame of his hospital spread and patients had begun coming to him from the canal district to the west. The disease was caused by an intestinal fluke. A cure was known, but, more often than not, the patients returned reinfected. No drug had been discovered that could safely be distributed among the people. And no one had learned how man became infected.

Since early in the nineteenth century, European doctors had been interested in intestinal flukes. Some forty years ago, a fluke which infested sheep had been studied and its life cycle recorded; snails had been found to be the intermediary hosts of the parasite.

"It's quite possible," Peter said to himself, "that snails are the hosts for this fluke, also."

He would go to the canal district from which all of his cases came, and see if he could get some clue to the problem. At least, it would be a start in research on one major disease of China.

Two weeks later he hired a boat and started out. It was hot in the low junk. The sun beat down on the rounded matting top, and from a thousand wet rice paddies moisture rose, sucked up by the sun. Between earth and sky hung a gossamer mist which wrapped its tenuous folds about the valley. Men naked to the waist worked with slow, languorous movements in the paddies, weeding the rice, or stretched themselves on benches in a narrow bit of shade under the eaves of their houses. Babies with nothing on but the ring of safety about their necks, slept in the dust near the house doors. The dogs lay on their sides, legs extended, their tongues hanging red against the black skin of their lower lips as they panted for breath. Ducks floated listlessly on the ponds. Even the chickens neglected to scratch the earth for insects and stood, motionless, eyes glazed, wings drooped.

The fields of rice grew thick and lush.

Peter lay on his cot, listening to the soothing creak of the stern paddle in its rope lock. Hot as it was, the air was fresher than in the city, and he was rid of Miss Dyer. And somehow, mysteriously, that paralysis of grief was gone. He had work to do. He felt new life.

Toward sundown, the boatman anchored for the night in a narrow valley. No breath of air reached this pocket in the hills. Mosquitoes settled down in hordes. A half-hour of this—even the time it would take him to get the simplest food together—and Peter knew he would have enough mosquito bites to give him a fine case of malaria. To crawl under his bed net in this breathless heat would be intolerable. He glanced longingly at a ridge of hills. High up, he saw a small temple. Buddhist priests were always hospitable.

"I'll be back in the morning," he said to the boatman. Rolling up his mosquito net, not stopping even for food, he started off over the worn stone path which led toward the hills. A half-hour and he had reached them. The climb was steeper than he had expected. He dared not stop to rest—his clothes were soaked with perspiration. As he followed the winding path, he began to fear he had missed the temple. He could no longer see it. Then all at once it stood boldly forth. It was not as he had thought, small and insignificant. Its beautiful curved roof-lines rose one after another on the mountainside. From all directions paths converged into one wide way leading to its great entrance gate.

Weary as any pilgrim, he made the last ascent and entered the empty front court. He heard priests in an inner room intoning the evening prayers. He feared to wait until the service was over because of his wet clothes. In this mountain air, they already clung to him clammy and cold. He moved across the court and knocked gently on a closed door, hoping that someone of the order might be within.

The door was opened.

Peter was speechless. He had expected one of the ignorant, degraded-looking priests whom he knew so well, to whom it would be easy to offer a little money for a night's lodging. Instead, there stood before him a man of evident culture. Rarely had he seen a face of such grandeur and nobility. He could not offer this man money.

"I have a boat yonder in the valley," he said, after a moment's hesitation, "but it was stifling—I thought perhaps I might find lodging here for the night. I am a Christian missionary," he added. He had felt impelled, for some obscure reason, to make this last remark. Now that he had made it, he realized he had never called himself that before—simply, physician.

"The highest court is vacant. There you can be quiet," replied the priest. "Come," he added, and himself went before, moving silently.

The room they entered crowned the mountain-top. The latticed windows in the farther wall had their paper panes rolled up. The whole earth seemed spread at his feet. The room was empty except for a square table and two chairs standing under the windows. Upon the table in a bowl of water floated the five-fingered gourd called Buddha's Hand.

"I will send one to attend you," said the priest. Then he went out.

Peter realized now that this man must be the abbot of the order.

A young priest brought water for bathing, a simple meal of vegetables, and later, a bed which he placed in a corner.

Peter was sitting in the gathering dusk listening to the temple bell, when the abbot came again.

"We are two priests," he said. "I have read of your teacher, and perhaps you have read of mine. We are Ch'an Buddhists here. Your religion and mine are not unlike. We call your Christ a Buddha."

Such a concept was startling to Peter, but as the abbot talked, he felt the sense of brotherhood which had come to him at rare moments through the years. For a long time the two sat silent. The bell's deep tone filled the lofty room, died slowly away in the valley, rose again, deep and strong around them. The young priest brought a candle. Peter's mood changed. He felt inclined to argue with the abbot. He challenged the Eastern way of life, its acquiescence.

"And your way of life," the abbot asked gently, "leads you where?" He moved the candle so that the light fell full upon Peter's face, upon its lines of grief. Long the abbot looked into his eyes. "Together, perhaps——" With his rosary twined around his fingers, he locked his hands in an expressive gesture.

The abbot rose, passing from the room. The padded soles of his shoes made a soft sound on the stone floor.

Soon there were light footfalls, and the young priest entered carrying a closed box which he placed on the table. "The abbot has sent you the temple lark. On no account open the box in which the cage is set."

For what purpose had the abbot sent the lark shut into the box? thought Peter, as he examined it. There seemed no tiny crack for air. Fearing that the bird would smother, he arose several times in the night, moving the box a little. Each time there was a faint rustling. Finally he fell sound asleep.

When he wakened, dawn was in his room and the first sweet notes of a skylark's song came from the closed box. They grew full and more vibrant. For an hour the lark sang his ravishing sweet song. Suddenly he stopped. In a moment the priest came in. Lifting the cage from the box, he carried the bird away.

Peter washed and ate, then went quietly down the mountain to his work.

For two weeks Peter pushed his little boat up this canal and that, staying a night here and there with old patients. Now again, as in his first experience with this people, the drab veil of poverty parted for him. An ancient and beautiful culture showed its still-flickering life. No matter how poor the little hovels, the courtesy of the gentleman was there.

As he went through the villages of this rice farming district, he was appalled to see the extent of the parasitic disease he had come to investigate. The children running half naked in the summer heat had thin, bony chests, stick-like arms, distended bellies—evidence of starvation, a symptom of the infection. Men and women showed in their faces the same evidence of starvation. As he sat in tea shop and farmhouse, he noticed how languorously the people moved about. He looked with pity on men, women and children taken with sudden, griping pains. Tons of medicine would not have cured them all, and unless the cause were removed, it would be useless to cure them. They would shortly be reinfected.

He had only one clue—snails. Did snails carry the infection to human beings? If so, how did the parasite get from snail to human food? It was safe to suppose that some food grew in the same environment in which the snails flourished. There were the water nuts, of course. But people in the city ate water nuts, and rarely did he have a case among them.

Day after day he went from canal to canal, studying all growing things. One day his boatman took him along a canal fed by fresh water from a river. Peter found the people in this area well and vigorous. Whatever carried the disease probably did not live in clean water. There must be some connection between the disease and stagnant canals.

At last he came to a small city where everyone bore sign of the disease. He decided to make his study here. That night he anchored his junk on the edge of the city, hoping not to attract quite so much attention as he would in the thickly packed center. The moon rose, casting an enchantment over this stricken city. Again, as when Peter first came to China, he felt warfare within him. These canals were breeders of disease, but in the moonlight they were long lines of shimmering beauty. The white plastered walls of the houses, studded with dark timbers, rose ghostly and mysterious on either side. The broken and worn stone steps, leading down to the water, took on beauty, too.

He sighed, then went into the junk, lay down under his mosquito net.

The size of the canal area, roughly estimated, must embrace about sixteen hundred square miles. Somewhere between a million and two million people, then, must be infected by this fluke. He put his mind to the plans for his research. He would take back specimens of plant and animal life of the stagnant canals and study them during the winter.

The next morning, he bought native wooden tubs, hired a countryman to help him—an old patient of his who lived near by—and set to work to drag the canal with a net.

"As *Fei I Sheng* wishes," the peasant said, when Peter explained to him why he wanted the canal dragged. But he thought to himself, "The disease is in the stomach, not in the canal. *Fei I Sheng* has medicine to eat. But if the *I Sheng* wishes it——" Gratitude to the doctor made him loyal even to this silly activity.

Into the peasant's net came small fishes, more than one kind of snail, and the broken stems of water plants. Peter wanted their roots. This canal was too deep to reach down and pull them loose.

"Fu," he said, "do you know of a shallower canal? See, we don't get the roots."

"*Fei I Sheng*, beyond my village there is such a canal. Through that bridge." And he pointed ahead to what looked like a rounded shadow.

"*Lao dah*," called Peter to the boatman, asleep in the stern. "Row the boat ahead."

The boatman grunted, twisted his queue around his head, took up the long oar. Late that afternoon, as the sun stood low, they came into a canal hardly wide enough for the junk to enter and very shallow.

Peter lay sprawled face down on the deck, looking into the water, stagnant and green but clear, seeing all manner of plants growing on the sides and bottom of the canal. He had pushed his helmet back so its brim rested on his neck, protecting him from the hot tropic sun. His sleeves were rolled up. He had on an old pair of patched khaki trousers.

"A scholar conducting himself thus!" thought Fu.

Very carefully, Peter pulled up the plants, handing them to Fu to put into the tubs. On the bank stood groups of curious peasants, little naked children. With his face not more than six inches from the canal, Peter saw their shadows lying on the water, and the shadow of the junk. Ahead was more than a shadow, a black mass. He reached out to push the junk clear of it. His hand touched a sunken boat, roughened with growth. He studied the mass which came off in his hand. Tiny snails, such as he had not seen before.

"Fu," he called, "look at these snails. Do you have many of them around here?"

The peasant took them. "In the caltrop ponds I have seen these tiny snails. In the mud at the bottom—when I walk in the pond to pick the *ling*, they lodge between my toes."

"We'll finish here," said Peter. "Then we'd better look at one of these ponds. Can you take me to one?"

"As *Fei I Sheng* wishes," said the peasant.

On the last day before Peter had to go back, Fu took him to

one of his own caltrop ponds. Water chestnuts and caltrops were ripe at this season.

"Snails destroy my plants," mourned Fu, and he brought Peter one of the fleshy stalks of the water chestnut, showing him where the snail had tunneled it.

"Umph!" said Peter, and he grew excited. Here were snails, and here were foods eaten by the people. If he could only find out the connection! He felt sure there was a connection.

As the junk moved slowly along the canals, taking him back to the city, Peter studied his problem. Had he got all the plants? Had he got the right ones? Had he got every kind of snail that lived in this region?

He must have someone to assist him. With the hospital work, it would be impossible otherwise to keep the continuity of the experiment. One of the nurses? They were all too busy. There was Sen Lo Shih. He remembered that look of interest in his eyes. Until the school opened, he might be willing to help. He was living in the boys' dormitory this summer.

VI

On the still canal, Peter had had no inkling that Christendom had gone to war. But news of it had reached the city. Sen Lo Shih and his young countrymen, so ardently trying to copy the West, knew it. They who had found it difficult to enter into the age of machine civilization which changed so radically their habits, now took shelter against this aggressive life, despising Christendom for its manifestation of violence. The inferiority they had felt before the West's knowledge of science, was suddenly changed to superiority. Christendom, taking on such heroic proportions in the East, had pulled itself from its pedestal.

Sen Lo Shih, sitting in his room in the empty school building, read avidly all news of the war. His lips curled in scorn at the spectacle of countries who dated their civilization from the birth of the gentle Christ, who proudly called themselves by His name, making ruthless warfare on each other. Ironical beyond measure—each side called upon that same God, in the name of this Christ, to help them!

As soon as Peter was back, the tides of sick threatened again to immerse him. He hardly had time to get his specimens into proper receptacles. As for an artificial pond, for several days he had not time even to see a mason about it.

It was not until the end of the first week that he found an opportunity to hunt up Sen Lo Shih. The boys' school looked entirely empty, every window shuttered. Evidently Lo Shih was not here. Disappointed, Peter was about to turn away, when he noticed a blind on an upstairs window slightly ajar. He tried the door and found it unlocked. Sitting by a table in his room in the empty dormitory, reading a Chinese newspaper, was Lo Shih.

Now that he was here, Peter felt doubtful about asking the young man. As he rose to greet Peter, despite his ordinary dress, he appeared elegant and fastidious, the typical Chinese gentleman, about him the aloof dignity of his father.

"I should have gone first and seen Sen S Mo. She might have persuaded him," thought Peter. But his great need crowded out his hesitancy. "Sen Lo Shih," he said, "I have come to you for help. I am trying an experiment in my laboratory which I cannot carry on alone. I'd like to show you what I am trying to do, if you would come over to the hospital with me."

Together they walked across the compound, Peter tall, propelled forward rapidly by his great objective, Sen Lo Shih, short and slender, walking with the composure of the traditional Chinese scholar, able in his heart today to despise as a barbarian this man who had twice willed him to live. Uncontrolled, aggressive Christendom. Uncontrolled, this ungainly man, who strode forward without quietude.

"You see," said Peter, showing him his rows of native clay pots.

Politely, without show of interest, Sen listened to him, looked at snails and plants. How break through this indifference to the speculative mind which Peter believed he possessed? Turning impulsively to his microscope, where under a glass slide he had fixed a tiny snail from a caltrop field, he said, "Look, Sen Lo Shih. This snail is lowly, but I believe he carries a disease which poisons and kills many of your people."

Sen Lo Shih politely took his place before the microscope. He saw this almost infinitesimal snail. The interest which all Chinese had in the Ten Thousand Things of the universe, gave him interest in this snail for its own sake. The snail, confined thus, in the effort to escape, came forth from its shell, displaying head, neck, foot, and tentacles. The snail transparent as glass, could be seen breathing—life going on in it.

So, thought Sen Lo Shih, had his father regarded the pine tree, studying its significance hour after hour. "It is beautiful," he said, raising his head from the microscope. "It would give me pleasure to record the significance of the snail." He bowed, his hands folded within his sleeves.

As day after day he slipped the slides under the microscope, observing and recording every movement of the snail in hours of silent concentration, Lo Shih began to see science as learning. Before this he had been an unwilling pupil, trying to acquire this bastard education of the West, so that he might become the new type of official. That strong woman of his clan, Sen S Mo, widow of his dead brother, had contended that better than through death could he bring back the honor of his house by becoming a modern official—officialdom was the crowning mark of success in the New China as in the old. He began to desire Western learning for its own sake.

And now that he saw science as learning, he began to give to Peter the traditional respect due to a teacher. Gradually a new and strange emotion took shape in his heart—the relationship of pupil to teacher, one of etiquette and respect, changed to something warmer. Dimly he perceived some greatness in this doctor. He brought to him one day a present—the curved mace so much coveted as the mark of the official under the old régime.

"My father's," said the young man proudly. "I should like the honorable teacher to have it."

Peter had had many gifts in his years in this country. It was the custom of the Chinese to give presents, and he had received them from high and low. Only this very day an old peasant had come bringing him a few peaches. For five years he had come thus, on the anniversary of the day when Peter had saved his life. And there were the jade cups and the embroidery with the grey cranes, which the father of Lo Shih had given him. Yet Peter hesitated to take this present, not because of its costliness, but because of its personal value.

"This thing that was thy father's——" he began.

"Honored Teacher, it is nothing." Lo Shih's straight eyebrows, which looked as if they had been drawn in black ink by the sure hand of an artist, contracted a little.

Peter saw he would mar the relationship so recently established between them, if he refused. He took the mace and
placed it on the mantel between the jade cups.

Fired with the idea of making Lo Shih a doctor and a research worker, Peter asked him if he would like to take up a
course of study in preparation for it. "Science you get at the
school," he said. "I will tutor you in the rudimentary principles of medicine and research work. Later, we'll try to find
a way to send you to a good medical school. Think it over,"
Peter ended.

Five, seven days passed. Sen Lo Shih did not come to the
laboratory. Peter could not find him when he searched the
dormitory. He asked Sen S Mo.

"I do not know," she answered, and neither the calm mouth
of Sen S Mo nor the deep black pools of her eyes gave any
betrayal of knowledge.

Had he been too sudden in suggesting to the boy that he
study modern medicine?

Then, one day, Lo Shih appeared as usual, making no explanation of his absence. Soft-slippered, he came quietly into
the laboratory, taking up the conversation where they had left
it a week ago.

"If the honorable teacher wishes it, the unworthy one will
take up the new healing."

He said nothing of his week's vigil in the deserted courts of
his father's house, watching the pine against the wall, drinking in contemplation. Neither did he speak of how Sen S Mo
had come to him saying, "There is money in the new healing.
The house of thy father might be bought back from the new
government." Thus through the years had she cunningly
stirred ambition, keeping him from the pact of death laid upon
him by his grandmother.

VII

THAT October, doctors of China gathered in Shanghai. They came from every province, every Mission—German, French, English, American, and Chinese—for the conference of the Medical Missionary Association.

It was a journey of double interest for Peter. By waiting a day or two after the sessions were over, he could meet Diana and Mei Mei, returning from the northern seaside resort. In the back of his mind through the days of the conference, hovered romance. Diana was coming home. Each morning he felt alive to his finger tips as he walked into the great hall.

Working alone as he had, Peter had not realized how the science of medicine was taking hold in China, nor how many Chinese were now qualified doctors. Most of them men who had gained their first training in Mission schools, they had gone to England or America for their last years of study. Some day, Sen Lo Shih would be a member of this group, thought Peter with pride. He wished Lo Shih were here now, to see his fellow countrymen take their places among the other doctors.

At the last morning's session, a young Chinese doctor read a paper on the plague epidemic which had occurred in the north, three years before. Peter saw that the "new medicine," as China called Western medicine, had then, for the first time, lost its isolated foreign entity. East and West had worked together. Both had sacrificed life in the effort to learn the cause of the plague. There had been such acceptance of Western scientific methods, that the Manchu Government had actually sanctioned the burning of the dead in order to stop the spread of the plague. The important dead!

And yet, at present, no Chinese student could get any first-hand knowledge of the human body unless he went away to

study. It offended deep instinct in the Chinese deliberately
to dissect the dead—the important dead!

Vivisection, also, was denied to the Chinese because of the
Buddhist belief. Who knew when in the Karma wheel, a man's
spirit might enter the body of an animal?

"But, after all," reflected Peter, "was this so different from
what took place in Europe a century ago?"

He realized something else, too. The whole trend of the
conference was toward preventive medicine. Had he, separate as he was in his work, after all been a part of a new forward stride in Western medicine? The romance of his profession came over Peter. He saw it held daring vision, the
spirit of adventure, and—startling thought—tacit acceptance
of suffering.

The day of Diana's return had come. The coastwise ship
was due any time. Peter and his friend, Dr. Smith, walked
together on the Bund, watching the hands of the clock in the
Customs' tower creep slowly around from two to three.

This treaty port had changed a great deal in the years since
Peter had strolled thus the day after he had taken his first
examinations. Finer buildings now fronted the river. Among
the rickshas and low broughams were handsome motor cars.
The pattern of the city was in Peter's mind—its two faces
forever opposed, compassion and greed. In this "tribal war,"
as the Chinese called the World War, Christendom had forgotten a little her promises about opium. She wanted all the
money possible for fighting. The ghost of the old opium
struggle with its hate and suspicion never could seem to be
laid. It was walking again in the land.

"The conference certainly showed we're making progress,"
Dr. Smith broke into Peter's musings.

"When I think of my own station and the vast territory
my hospital still has to serve——" Peter paused, at a loss for
words to express just what he did think.

"Yes, I know," said the other. "Medicine hasn't yet taken
root in China. It won't, until China supports her own hos-

pitals. Look," he added. A Chinese coolie, passing the bank, reached up and touched the paw of one of the bronze lions flanking the entrance. "That's still the Chinese idea of medicine—strength from the lion's paw."

"But that's just superstition, such as we all have—like walking under a ladder," said Peter.

"True. But when one of my Chinese doctors, trained in America, was sick recently, he went to a native doctor."

"Sometimes I find their remedies good," answered Peter. "They're careful observers. Didn't you hear the paper read at the convention on their remedies?"

"To change to Western medicine," Dr. Smith went on, ignoring Peter's remark, "means the uprooting of the whole structure of Chinese thought. Medicine, like everything else with them, is rooted in some queer creative notion."

At his friend's words, Peter glimpsed anew the philosophy behind the remarks of countless patients, peasants, tradesmen and scholars—the philosophy often alluded to by Lo Shih during the summer. The *yin* and *yang* took on deeper meaning. Although science had not found it usable, philosophically it held profound significance. Man, as the Chinese said, is within himself a microcosm of Earth and Heaven, negative and positive, passive and active. And then a sudden thought struck him. What about this recent theory among Western physicians that a balance of vital forces in the human body was necessary for health? "Basal metabolism" modern medicine called it. Could it be that Chinese philosophy, unscientifically but truly had foreshadowed this centuries ago?

The black, red funneled steamer made its way through the jumble of junks and sampans. Peter's heart leaped when he saw his wife and child standing at the deck rail. Health in their faces and both beautiful, he thought. Diana was wearing the shade of blue he liked best, that clear blue which set off her hair and skin. "Because I like it," he thought delightedly.

The gangplank was in place. Peter, his friend just behind,

struggled through the mass of coolies. At last he was on the
main deck, very near Diana now. He could see the lovely tan
of her skin. It gave an odd effect—her skin darker than her
hair—but it gave her distinction, too. Then suddenly he could
not see her clearly. His vision blurred.

Diana noticed his eyes fill with tears and his mouth work
strangely. He had not cried over the death of his children.
For her alone, it seemed, he wept. She answered his kiss with
her own.

In the midst of the delight of that kiss of reunion, Peter
was aware of someone hugging his knees. He looked down
into the brown eyes of Mei Mei.

"I've brought you some shells," she whispered in his ear, as
he picked her up. "I had a lovely donkey to ride."

"Let me take the little girl," said Dr. Smith. "You protect
Mrs. Fraser from the coolies."

"Do you think she looks well?" Diana asked anxiously as
they struggled down the gangplank.

"She certainly does," answered Peter. "She's positively
sturdy, I'd say, from the hug she gave me."

Later, when they were in their room at Dr. Smith's house,
where they were spending the night, Diana asked him about
the conference. Had he made himself known to those men
who were planning a new medical school on a grand scale?

"They were there," said Peter, "for some of the sessions, but
I didn't meet them."

"I heard a great deal about the plan this summer," said
Diana. "Some American millionaires are behind it. They're
going to take the best physicians from all over China for their
two great centers—and you're one of the best doctors in China,
Peter."

He had felt a little hurt that she had asked nothing about
his summer alone. Now his heart was warmed by her faith
in him. But that night as he held her close, he felt some lack
in her response. He was realizing more and more that the
shaping of two in union was never final.

"Darling," he whispered, "let me into your heart."

Emotions over which she had no control crowded in upon Diana. Just now she wished no blending of herself with Peter. Some dark and passionate self, fed from mysterious sources, was angry with him for his devotion to her . . . that he could find healing in her for the loss of Serena and Pete . . . that he could strive for perfection of their relationship, when the children were dead! But conscious also that the sheltering warmth of his arms brought a respite from her pain, a respite which she neither sought nor desired, she wept.

"Can't I help?" he begged.

She shook her head, breaking into convulsive sobs. All Peter could do in his bewilderment was to stroke her hair.

VIII

FOR Peter, the days after he and Diana returned to the station, were days of strain. Diana seemed to want something he could not give, did not know how to give. She would rarely let Mei Mei out of her sight, but she seemed to get no pleasure in her care of the child. Sometimes he thought she resented that he did not help her more, and yet he felt, too, that she did not want his help. Entering the house one afternoon, he heard their voices, and detecting a high, thin quality in his wife's, went to the nursery door, wishing he knew whether she would like him to take Mei Mei away and let her rest. "Let me play with her, dear. You're tired," he ventured at last, and picking up the child he bore her away on his shoulder.

Diana could hear them talking together as they went down the stairs. At each step there was a jarring of her husband's voice, an expulsion of his breath because of his burden.

"You're getting such a big girl, Mei Mei," she heard him say. "Soon you'll have to carry me."

Then the delighted childish laughter at the absurdity. "Oh, daddy, I'd have to be a tall, tall giant to carry you. Why, I'd have to ride on your shoulder to carry you!"

"Beautiful idea." It was her husband's voice, faint now, from the hall below.

Both voices lost, as the two went out of the door into the garden.

Diana sat by Mei Mei's table, her tall body cramped into one of the child's chairs. She felt hurt with Peter for taking Mei Mei away, a certain sense of injury, too, that the child went so willingly. The gnawing love within her wanted to project itself into every cranny of Mei Mei's heart. The laughter of the two just outside the windows, made her feel herself the only grown-up member of the family, the only practical one.

She it was who had to plan for all three of them. Peter was more than ever immersed in his work, with this experiment he had taken up during the summer.

At last she got up, went down to the kitchen. "Is the water ready, Wang Ma?"

Wang Ma, silent and a little sullen, brought the steaming kettle. Diana dipped her knife in it, then cut a slice of bread from the loaf the old servant placed before her.

"I'd better cut another," she said to herself. "The knife's been in boiling water—it's safe, but some germs might be on the outside slice of bread." She cut the second slice. As it fell away from the loaf, it lay face down on the bread-board. "I forgot about the bread-board," she thought. "I didn't scald it. I'd better cut another."

Mei Mei's tray was almost set when Peter came in, the child dancing at his side. With alacrity she ran across the room to Wang Ma.

The native woman lifted her in her arms, murmuring, "Missie precious you, but Wang Ma precious you, too."

"Couldn't Wang Ma do that?" Peter asked gently.

Diana flushed. She had sought to hide from him her devouring fear that disease would again get under his guard and take Mei Mei as it had Serena and Pete. She would trust no one but herself.

The woman she had once been, dreaming and planning for the women of China, seemed now merely like a garment which had been rent asunder from shoulder to hem, revealing a woman she had glimpsed and thrust back that first time Peter had asked her to marry him. A fierce, maternal self, a separate self, which now tore itself free from any submission to Peter—a self bare of any dreams that falsified the utilitarian issues of life. In some strange, dark way, her maternalism embraced Peter. He, too, was her child for whom she must fight.

Autumn changed into winter. One evening, as it had been for many evenings, Diana talked to Peter of the coming opportunity for the up-to-date doctor. She was saying for the hundredth time, it seemed to him, "You must show them, you must advertise yourself. Show them what a good doctor you are." It was late, but she would not leave the delicate dress she was embroidering for Mei Mei.

As he waited for her to finish her work, Peter went over again and again his disappointment over the failure of his experiment. The weather had turned unusually cold last evening and he, busy with the sudden influx of sick, had forgotten to caution the night coolie about the fire in his laboratory. The water had frozen and killed the snails. Sen Lo Shih had brought him word only a little while ago.

"Peter," Diana said a little sharply. "You didn't answer me."

"I . . . I was thinking of my experiment. It has failed."

"Perhaps it's just as well, Peter. You work too hard."

For a moment Peter hardly comprehended what she had said. Never before had she failed to reinform him with hope in times of discouragement.

That night Diana could not sleep. All the desires of her life seemed alive with malicious obstinacy, which she sought vainly to control. The rousing of her husband to strive for position . . . Mei Mei . . . how she longed to give her every good thing! Even the making of Mei Mei's dress, the last buttonhole that she had not been able to finish, projected itself into her mind, looming large, important . . . hard unyielding matter that filled the universe. Her spirit was chained to business.

"Shadow White," the Chinese began to call Mei Mei. For wherever Diana went, the child now went, too, dressed in the white of their mourning. White, Diana had found, set off Mei Mei's beauty. But to Mei Mei herself, she was not Shadow White. She was Snow White of her fairy tales, the fairy princess living in a world peopled by black-haired slaves.

That there were no white children on the compound, that

her mother would not let her play with Chinese children at the
school, never seemed to dim Mei Mei's happiness. The springs
of that happiness ran too deep. To Peter, her joy was connected with her conception—the blossoming phaetinia, the
rose-colored clover, the dark night, the scent of lilacs, the faint
rustle of bamboos, his and Diana's consuming love. All these
elements of happiness had gone into the creation of Mei Mei.

Every growing thing gave Mei Mei delight. "She has the
Buddha heart," said Lo Shih, watching the little girl walking
carefully to avoid stepping on the ants crawling on the flagged
walk. Mei Mei, Little Sister, was a name spoken lovingly by
the Chinese.

Wang Ma rode her on her back, never carried her in her
arms as she had Serena, because Mei Mei would not allow it.
Mei Ing Perkins brought her beautiful things out of the
bundles that came to her regularly. "My mother would want
you to have this," she would say. Strange little presents—a
nut fashioned into a doll, whimsical figures carved from bits
of wood.

Sen S Mo made for her paper lanterns. Mei Mei accepted
the gifts and smiled at all the donors.

But the black-haired slave she loved best was Lo Shih. He
came often to the house on one pretext or another, in order to
practice his English. The doctor and his wife talked a slow,
careful English for his sake. At times, he resented it. He
felt certain that no one in America would speak like that.
After a little, he saw that he learned more from Mei Mei, who
chattered so fast, and always expected him to understand.

Friendship grew between these two. A childlike quality
in the slender young man drew him to the little girl and she
to him. Fairies were not make-believe with him, as they were
to her mother. He believed as she did in the fox maiden. So
did Wang Ma, but Wang Ma's stories frightened her. Dread-
ful *kuei!* But Lo Shih told her lovely stories of the weaver and
the maiden, and the one night in all the year when they met.

Lo Shih learned from Mei Mei that strange foreign custom

called kissing. This was the child's salutation to her dearest friends, and she offered it to him. Strangely sweet to him was this frank, warm pressure of his little friend's lips on his.

As spring came on, the two wandered happily about the compound. The shrubbery at the boundary of the garden was leafing out. The bamboo shoots, growing in a few days to the height of trees, were bursting their sheaths. Lo Shih, as his father and father's father before him, had stored in his senses, in a continuity of experience, the earth's spring conception. His spirit quivered to the union. Mei Mei did not understand this, but she knew that he, like herself, had plenty of time for the garden. Peter was often annoyed at Lo Shih's disregard of time, but Mei Mei was not.

IX

THE *que hua* hung its heavy sweetness on the air. In this land there seemed no dying of the year. Rather, autumn brought a resurgence of life after the heat of the summer. October was the one month when the soft haze which cloaked the mountains in mystery gave way to clarity, and the hills stood away from the horizon. You could see how shorn they were of trees, and you could see the blue shadows in the hollows. You could trace out each ridge and watershed.

It was the seventh anniversary of the New Order in China. Had Lo Shih's father been alive he would have felt his prophecy was coming true. Horses of government, no longer trained, were riding on the wind. Ignorant war lords, aggressive and greedy, were springing up here and there, fighting for power and money. The country kept from chaos only by the great and abiding discipline among the people which held man to his human relationships—duty to the clan, duty to the town father.

Peter, in such close companionship with Sen Lo Shih, felt the very foundations of the old order were cracking under the vigorous sprouting of new life. A renaissance had begun among the young scholars. They were discarding the rigidity of their classical language. They wrote in the vernacular of the people, a living language which was constantly creating words to express the new life. Peter was among those who were urging that medicine be taught in Chinese rather than in English, so that Chinese speech might grow rich with scientific terms.

The compound bustled with enterprise. The Bakers were back from furlough and Berger had returned from his short leave of absence with a young and pretty wife. He had left

270

his children in America. At last there was a foreign nurse to fill Stella's place in the hospital.

With the new interest in women's education, Diana's school had outgrown its original quarters. The old native building was now used entirely for the day pupils. During the summer, a fine dormitory in the foreign style had been erected for the girls who came from a distance.

Sen S Mo was very proud of the new building, with its glass windows, the foreign beds, the foreign desks in the class-rooms, the dining room with its many shining square tables and benches. She was more than matron in this school of a hundred girls. Gradually she had assumed one responsibility after another which Diana let drop in her need to be with Mei Mei.

In these two years since the death of Pete, hope and dis-appointment had been Diana's alternate portion. Over and over she had yearned for conception. Her passionate desire for a son led her to beg the boon of union from Peter, asking more at times than he had the strength to give. He was often tired—too much of his life force was drained away. No real union of the spirit with Diana. He sensed that all she asked of him was a son.

Now, at last, hope was changing to certainty for Diana. Now, at last, she believed she was with child. Peter watched her with pitying eyes. Strange, that desire could simulate reality.

The night of the Eighth Moon Festival, they stood together by the window, the moon's radiance streaming down upon them. Her head lay against his shoulder. He put his hand under her chin, turning her face toward him.

"Diana. Surely as long as we have each other, nothing else really matters." He looked deep into her eyes. If only he could mean enough to her, he could save her from the tragic dis-appointment that must come to her when she learned she was barren. "Do you remember," he went on, almost desperately, "that last day of our honeymoon? Oh, Diana, don't you see that not even Mei Mei, nor the child you want so much——"

For one moment the secret, separate look went out of her eyes. Her words came in a rush. "Peter, be patient with me. I don't understand myself. I'm different just now . . . I can't help it. But this child . . . I think somehow it's making me feel the way I felt before Serena was born. Be patient," she begged.

All the next day, Peter went about his work held into tight suspense. What would happen when Diana learned the truth, as she must sooner or later?

At the time for Mei Mei's nap, he opened the door looking into her garden. She often sought it at this hour. She was sitting on the stone bench. As he came near, she raised her eyes. "She knows," he thought, and went quickly to her.

"It isn't true that I am to have a child," she greeted him.

"You have Mei Mei and me," he ventured.

"You seem very certain that I can keep Mei Mei." Nervous and unstrung, she turned upon Peter. "It's I who have to see that Mei Mei isn't allowed to run the chances that the others ran. I can't do it any longer," she added, sobs threatening to stop her speech. "I can't guard her every minute. There's only one way to keep her, and that's to take her to America."

"You'd leave her with your mother?" asked Peter, trying to hold his own voice steady. Anger and hurt mingled within him. So she thought he had been careless about the children!

"No," answered Diana. "She needs me. I shall stay with her."

"That means we'll be separated for three years."

"Others have done it."

"I thought . . . once you said . . . once I promised I wouldn't let our marriage interfere with your work."

"The Mission doesn't own me. Does anything count," she demanded, "where Mei Mei's concerned?"

In that moment her desire to take Mei Mei to America, which she had not really decided upon because the welfare of Mei Mei conflicted with the welfare of Peter, became a decision. She chose the welfare of Mei Mei. It was Peter's fault. When she had spoken, it had been with a half-formed idea that when she told him she was going, he would arrange, somehow, to go with her. But he hadn't. And he didn't see what a conflict it was to choose between them.

Emotions half understood, half realized, now gathered themselves together, taking form in her mind. Words held back so long came to her lips too fast for utterance. In phrases sometimes incoherent, she poured forth her overwhelming fear of disease. As she expressed her fears, disease grew into something so definite that it became corporate. It seemed to her that she had given it material form—given it power over Peter.

It was January before Diana completed preparations for America. Peter had gone with them on the launch to the great ship anchored at the mouth of the Woosung River. The little extra journey postponed the parting another hour. But it had to come . . . it had come. The launch was putting out from the steamer's side. He could see Mei Mei leaning over the rail looking down, searching for him, and Diana just above her waving good-by.

They were gone from him. The specks that were Diana and Mei Mei blurred, disappeared. The aloneness of the moment seemed too great to be borne. He felt a sudden almost wild yearning for his work. And then he thought of his home without them——

He put his hands in his coat pockets. It was cold on the river. He'd forgotten his gloves. The launch came abreast of one of the great business storehouses on the Pootung side of the river. He saw clouds of black smoke drifting across the grey sky. Fierce flames licked up from the flat delta land. He smelled the sweet smell of burning opium. Shanghai's supplies of foreign opium were being destroyed. Christendom was ending its lucrative opium trade.

Moment of triumph for China—or was it triumph? The

opium traders had gone whining to their foreign governments
that they would be ruined if the sale of opium were prohibited.
The Chinese Government had bought the opium. Then had
come whisperings . . . was Christendom sincere? Had China
bought opium, or were the balls filled with sticky syrup? Was
the drug still here, to be sold in licensed dens?

Then had come other whisperings . . . was the Chinese
Government sincere? "The real opium had been secretly taken
away by the Chinese military. Balls of pigs' blood and fat
had been slipped into the chests in its place." A public inspection had been made—each ball in the two hundred chests
examined. Suspicion again reared its head. Why should there
be this gesture from the Chinese—the burning of millions of
dollars' worth of foreign opium, worth more than its weight
in gold, when native opium was again creeping back into
the market? So it was whispered, so many believed.

The wind carried the black smoke toward the launch,
toward Shanghai, prosperous city on the opposite bank.

Bleak and barren futility settled over Peter. Not since
the condemnation of Stella had he felt so defeated.

X

THE going of Diana and Mei Mei was felt by the whole compound. Sen Lo Shih missed the companionship of Mei Mei. Mei Ing Perkins felt orphaned indeed. For all these years she had gone in and out of the doctor's house at will. Never had the relationship between Diana and her been severed. Had Diana not had children, she would have loved Mei Ing as her own.

The Mission had given Berger's young wife charge of the girls' school. For two years Sen S Mo had been mistress of the school, but no one had acknowledged her as such. A Chinese in power! Sen S Mo accepted, with her usual serenity, the relegation of herself to the inferior position, although Mrs. Berger was little more than a girl and new to the ways of China.

Soon there began to be murmurings among the girls against Sen S Mo—she squeezed from the money apportioned for their food, they whispered among themselves. There were other, uglier, stories. Mrs. Berger listened to the tales the girls were bold enough to tell her. She thought thus to be fair to all. The ringleader had bright, wayward eyes and short hair that waved slightly. Short hair had gained sudden popularity among the new rich, when, after the revolution, the men had cut theirs. To Mrs. Berger, it made the girl look less strange than the other girls, and her bold approach she took for frankness. Diana would have known that the evils of the women's courts—love of intrigue and revenge—had crept into the school.

Sen S Mo knew it. This girl who was against her—the intricate strands of her grudge were too many to unravel, a grudge that lay far back in the history of their two families. In the end, Sen S Mo knew that this girl had the power to accomplish her purpose. Far better that she go before she lose too much face. Lo Shih no longer needed her. The younger brother of his father had come back from Szechuan, where he had lived in hiding since catastrophe had befallen the clan. He had taken his place as head of the family.

Now that her friend whom she called sister had gone, she felt more and more bewildered with the ways of this Western life. An old desire took shape in her mind—a pilgrimage, a long pilgrimage. Never had she entirely freed herself from the compelling demands of Buddhism. Now, without the solace of her friend, she sought its solace. The lotus in their round jars at the entrance to the school stirred her to reverence. The deep-toned bells of the temple—she could count the strokes in the night—stirred longings in her. Slowly, a sense of guilt crept over her. Twice she had defied the matriarch. As widow she had failed in her duty to the clan. She had kept Lo Shih from fulfilling his duty. A pilgrimage bulked larger and larger in her mind—a far pilgrimage to the sacred mountain of O *Mei Shan* in Szechuan.

Sen S Mo went quietly away in the night, closing the gate of the Mission compound behind her without regret, now that her friend was no longer there.

The next morning Mrs. Berger found an offering of flowers on her desk and a note saying that Sen S Mo had been called away on affairs of the family and could not again come to the school. Mrs. Berger was thankful, for she had made up her mind that Sen S Mo must go. She believed that Diana had spoiled her.

XI

As THE boys' school building was full and Peter's house was so empty, he suggested to Lo Shih that he occupy one of the unused rooms. At first, except when they were at work together, Peter scarcely realized the young Chinese was in the house, he came and went so unobtrusively. Often Peter wished he would bang about like an American boy, as Pete would surely have done. Run up the stairs. Slam doors. Drop his shoes. The house seemed as empty as before Lo Shih's coming. And then Peter forgot to make comparison in his growing awareness of the intricate personality of the Chinese boy.

The next year, at the winter recess, Lo Shih graduated from the boys' school with high honors, first in his class in the Chinese Classics and foreign science. Peter was proud of him, but he regretted that in the last months his pupil had been too busy to work in the laboratory, nor had he had much time for his medical studies. Peter asked him if he would like to come into the hospital as his assistant, helping him in the surgical wing, thus learning something of surgery. The rest of his time he was to devote himself to research.

"I believe," said he to Lo Shih, "it is futile for us to spend any more time trying to find the parasite in the snail. I have long wanted to begin at the beginning and see if from the egg we cannot trace the life cycle. It will be delicate work that will demand almost constant attention."

"It can be arranged," said Lo Shih.

"Our evenings," Peter added, "we can spend in the study of medicine." He welcomed such an opportunity to fill every cranny of his waking hours with work, in order to forget the void made in his life by the departure of his wife and child.

As the weeks went by, the relationship between teacher and pupil deepened. Their evenings together, when Peter often sought knowledge of Chinese thought instead of always trying to force his own upon his pupil, Lo Shih's growing interest in Western thought, brought increasing confidence in each other. The experimental work in the laboratory knit them together in shared hopes and disappointments.

In the room next to his office with its one dormer window, Peter spent all the time he could spare from the hospital, coming in often to see how Lo Shih was getting along. At first, the work was as disappointing as the work they had done on the snails. Peter had no idea what temperature was needed to hatch the ova. Warm, of course, but how warm? They bought a great quantity of cheap rice bowls. It was Lo Shih's duty, with the help of a coolie, who kept the fire going, brought water and other things needed, to maintain different temperatures in each receptacle.

Painstakingly, each day they took the ova from bowl after bowl, examining them under the microscope. They could discover no signs of incubation. Day after day they varied the temperatures, keeping records.

Their accord through these days brought Peter great satisfaction. He liked to watch his pupil in the laboratory, his delicate hands so fitted to the delicate technique. There seemed to him, too, a growing masculinity about Lo Shih, of which he had never before been conscious. At first it eluded analysis. Then he had it. It was in the shape of the head. The short closely cropped black hair, vibrant with life, was brushed straight back from the young man's forehead and temples, showing the splendid molding of his head. Then Peter realized that he had always retained that impression of Chinese men as he had first seen them, with long braided hair.

That mark of subjection the Manchus had placed on the Chinese had indeed been a handicap. He wondered if the West would ever disassociate the Chinese man from that feminine hair arrangement. Their dress, too, contributed to the feminine impression. But here in the laboratory, wearing the laboratory tunic and trousers, Lo Shih seemed a throughgoing man of science.

One grey January day, when Peter came into the low-ceilinged room, he found Lo Shih, a candle in one hand, leaning over the microscope.

"What is it?" exclaimed Peter.

For a little, Lo Shih did not answer. At last he raised his head. "I thought today as I watched, that perhaps we should not have taken the tiny egg out of its home in the water. I add like this a little water." With delicate, fine touch, he let fall from the tip of his finger a drop of water on the slide. "It seems good this way. Will the honored teacher look? It is very beautiful."

Peter looked. He saw the dead, inert substance stirring, dividing into two masses. He was excited. "What's the temperature, Lo Shih, of this water? We've got to keep it at this temperature. We'll have to watch it day and night."

For a few days, they took turns at the laboratory throughout the twenty-four hours. And then, suddenly, Sen Lo Shih could not bear the discipline, begged to be excused. As Peter was finishing the night watch, word came from him that he was unable to come to the laboratory.

Peter hurried over to his house and up to Lo Shih's room. Gently he touched Lo Shih's forehead. "Lo Shih, are you ill?" His brow was cool. His pulse was normal. "Sen Lo Shih," Peter said, a little sternly, "you know the importance of this experiment. I'm depending on you."

"It is impossible," said Lo Shih. "For many years it has been necessary to await the adjustment."

Peter accepted no such reasoning. "In science," he said, "a man works whether sick or well."

Sen Lo Shih turned his face to the wall. A frail child, pampered by his grandmother and suddenly thrown into suffering, he had grown to manhood given to fits of depression. They followed days of conflict, when the emergence of himself as a personality warred with the old law of submergence in the clan. Then he was possessed by languor and melancholy, and answered no call of pleasure or duty.

Baffled and angry, Peter returned to the hospital, determined not to fail. Somehow he'd keep the temperatures up, attend to his hospital duties, too. But toward noon, there was an emergency operation. He sent for one of the nurses and gave careful instructions about temperatures. But when he came in after the operation, he found that the man had evidently let the heat vary for a few minutes and the eggs were dead. The experiment must be done over.

When Sen returned to the laboratory and found that all his work of weeks was lost, he started patiently at the beginning again, using the same temperatures, seeking to incubate the eggs. He felt superior to Peter's rebellious disappointment, his lack of inner harmony.

As the weeks went by and the experiment demanded more and more of him, he shaped himself to the discipline of the scientist. He felt a rhythmic harmony with nature's ordered ways. He had never before subjected himself to routine.

And again, one day, he saw the inert mass moving, forming into two separate oily masses.

When Peter came into the laboratory, he found all Lo Shih's placid reserve shaken by his discovery.

"Honored teacher, look. The microscope . . . do you see the tiny things seeking a new form?"

Eagerly they watched, their brains working together as one. Again they took turns in the laboratory day and night. Slowly the two oily masses moved about the tiny embryo. It was Sen Lo Shih, in his careful watching, who discovered what appeared like a tiny trap-door at one end of the ova. Was this where the new life would come forth—this tiny new life forming in the egg. Careful, beautiful pictures Lo Shih drew of what he saw through the microscope.

Slowly, with little jerks, the embryo began to move toward

the trap-door, blocked by what seemed to be a plug. The plug lessened in size. An infinitesimal tube appeared to be forming in it.

Peter and Lo Shih hovered over the microscope. Would the trap-door open? Would a live organism emerge into the water?

Suddenly, the experiment, going so beautifully, came to an abrupt end. The egg was again inert. In a few days, it spoiled. They must begin over again. But now everything seemed to fail. They could not again bring the experiment even to this stage. The excitement passed.

XII

A HUMBLE patient who had the sickness that caused spitting of blood, so well-known among Chinese of all classes—Dr. Fraser called it "tuberculosis"—had been sent to the new Mission sanitarium out in the hills beyond the city. Quite suddenly the man developed appendicitis.

"We'll have to operate," Peter said, as he talked the case over with Lo Shih. "But it'll be difficult because of the condition of his lungs. I'll have to work very fast. We can't keep him under ether long."

Sen Lo Shih was assisting at all operations now. He had even given the anesthetic in certain easy cases, when Miss Powell, the white nurse, was unusually busy. But he liked better to do as he was doing today—hand Dr. Fraser the instruments. Then he could give his full attention to the technique of the operation. The swiftness and certainty with which the doctor cut reminded him of his father's vigorous brush strokes. He coveted such mastery of hand. He thought of surgery as an art. Today he especially admired Peter's lightning swiftness.

The operation was nearly completed. There was a little gasp from Miss Powell. Dr. Fraser gave one quick glance, leaned down, placed his lips against the patient's, forcing his own breath into his lungs. Soon the man was breathing again. Peter went on with his work.

Lo Shih was aghast. Over and over Dr. Fraser had impressed upon him that to "eat" the breath of a person who had this sickness was to eat the sickness. Had this careful scientist committed that carelessness which he so sternly preached against?

After the operation, following his usual habit, Peter took Lo Shih into his office, discussing the case with him. "In a

282

properly equipped hospital there would have been a pulmotor. In this case, it was necessary for me to act in that capacity."

A new vista opened before Sen Lo Shih. Dr. Fraser had risked his own life for this humble man, to whom he had no responsibility except as doctor to patient. The Confucian doctrine taught the relationship of son to father, pupil to teacher, friend to friend, but here was a relationship that transcended those personal ones—the doctor to his case, the workman to his task.

Heretofore, Lo Shih had accepted the popular belief of the city that Dr. Fraser was here to make money. Even according to Lo Shih's standard of wealth as he had known it in his father's dwelling, Peter showed signs of riches. This great brick house in which he lived, for instance. Now he glimpsed Peter's life as one of service. The Superior Man serving! His father had taught him that *"the path of the Superior Man leads in the end to that which even the sage does not discern."* Here was something which the sages of his country had not seen. Did this teaching of the sage called Christ take one a little farther along the hidden way? That alien symbol of the cross seemed suddenly to take on meaning.

A few evenings later, just before Lo Shih left the house for the laboratory, he came into Peter's study, sitting silently by the desk.

"Is there something you wish to ask me?" asked Peter.

"I would like to accept the teachings of Christ," answered Lo Shih.

"It is not often that a Confucianist, trained as you have been to the Confucian doctrines, turns away from them to Christianity," said Peter, a little astonished.

Lo Shih had been sitting with his legs crossed, the skirt of his gown caught over one knee. His hands were behind his head, a pose he had acquired from Peter. At Peter's words, he sat up straight. "I am still a Confucianist. I simply go a little farther along the hidden way." That Peter had shown him that way, he did not mention.

"You would like me to tell Mr. Baker that you wish to join the church?" asked Peter, puzzled.

"Join the church?" said Lo Shih. "What has that to do with me? This is a personal matter."

"Yes, it is a personal matter," answered Peter.

"We have a custom," Lo Shih went on. "As you know, our fathers or our teachers give us a literary name. I should like it if you would select for me a Christian name."

After a little, Peter said very gently, "I will give you the name of John."

"It shall be used only by the honored teacher," said Lo Shih. He rose. "If *Fei I Sheng* will excuse me, I will attend the flukes."

As the year drew to its close, both of them came to think of little else but Sen Lo Shih's future. Both realized that what he needed now was to go to a well-equipped medical school.

Peter had always thought it would be easy to get assistance for his promising pupil. Had Lo Shih been a member of the church, it would have been—there were scholarships for such. He longed to help him out of his own salary, but every cent he could spare went to Diana and Mei Mei. Even though they were living with Diana's mother, the expense of keeping them in America was a severe drain upon his salary.

One day in the very late spring, Lo Shih said quite simply, "It seems to me wise, if I am to become a good surgeon, that I study in America. Would my teacher and friend lend me the money?"

It was a hard thing for Peter to refuse. He had to tell Lo Shih that he had no money.

For a Chinese gentleman, Lo Shih was almost hasty in his reply. Eagerly he urged Peter to think no more of the matter. "There is a relative of my father who wishes to give me the money. Please, it is not important." He wanted to relieve Peter of the embarrassment of his failure to understand the

Confucian relationship of teacher to pupil. The Superior Man would have considered it a high honor to be given the opportunity to help a scholar, even if it were necessary to borrow the money.

Lo Shih did not tell Peter what obligation the loan of the money from his uncle carried—that his uncle had no children, wanted to arrange a marriage for him in order to perpetuate the family. This Lo Shih accepted. The tradition of his race to preserve the harmony of the *yin* and *yang* was strong within him. Man bowed to the mysterious forces of life and death, flowing and ebbing, making the universe.

What he did not wish to do was to take a concubine, and this his uncle had made a part of the bargain. Lo Shih was to remain six months in his uncle's house after his marriage. If there were no promise of a child, then he was to take a concubine. Only when he had a son was he to start for America.

Peter felt relieved to know Lo Shih had relatives. He had thought them all dead except for Sen S Mo, but the ramifications of a Chinese family, he knew, were great. Evidently, they had not been exterminated. In fact, Peter remembered now that an aged man had been coming, of late, to see Sen Lo Shih. Lo Shih had not said who he was, only that he had recently come from a far distant province. The old man's hair was snow white—very unusual for a Chinese— and his goatee was streaked with white. It had not occurred to Peter that he was a relative. He had not the fine, thin features of Scholar Sen and Lo Shih, nor their nobility.

Sen Lo Shih came to say polite good-by to his teacher, holding out his long slender hand, after the custom of the West.

"Please sit down for a little, Lo Shih," said Peter. "There is a custom in my country," he went on, "that a teacher sometimes gives a pupil a gift. I should like to give you a copy of our Classic, the Bible, to put beside your Confucian Classics. It portrays a finer era than any other—the Christian era."

Lo Shih had stood to take the proffered gift, when suddenly

the decorum under which Peter had seen him for all these years was rent asunder. "A finer era—your Christian era! You can say that, knowing what your opium has done to us! The Christian nations have despoiled us and weakened us. They have used their strength to force opium on us, force our land away from us. They have raped us!" Lo Shih was trembling from head to foot.

Peter had listened spellbound to this outburst. Then, suddenly, he, too, was angry. "Sit down," he said. "Calm yourself. Do not think you can shirk your responsibility like this. The blame is not all to those who exploit the weak. Why are you weak? What right have you to be weak? What right have you to harp on equality if you are weak? You praise yourself for your submission. In your submission, you have been the accomplices to what you so dramatically call the raping of your country. At Geneva in the conferences over opium your countrymen have made impotent many a plan for control by trying to hide the fact that native opium is again being grown. Take your share of responsibility like a man!" Peter sank down in his chair. He, too, was trembling.

Across the ashes of their anger, they sat silently facing each other.

"What have I done?" thought Peter. "After all these years of careful building to gain the confidence of this lad, almost son to me, I have destroyed everything in one burst of anger."

As the minutes passed, and Lo Shih did not speak, Peter tried to think of something to say to right things. There was nothing. The evil had been done, he grieved.

And then, gradually, he perceived that this silence between them was comfortable and natural. There was no necessity for speech. The strains and stresses of two sensitive men of different races, trying to adjust themselves to each other, were over. All the stubborn nationalism of each had burned up in their separate angers. All pretense, all hidden grievances, now that they had been spoken, seemed to have lost their potency. For a long time they sat thus in the darkening room, barely able to make out the outlines each of the other, their spirits meeting in understanding. At last Lo Shih rose to go.

"You will let me know, Lo Shih, what university you choose?" asked Peter. "When I go home in a year, I shall hope to see you. Here are letters of introduction to friends of mine in America. If you are near them, go to see them." And he handed Lo Shih a packet of letters held together with a rubber band.

That Peter heard nothing further from Sen Lo Shih did not worry him. In their bursting anger and the ensuing silence, understanding had gone very deep. They both, Peter felt, needed to withdraw, each into his own people. Each should let go the other for a little. To Peter, that one spirit ever pierced its way through the accumulated layers of every-day living to the hidden centers of another human being, always partook of the nature of a miracle. That it pierced through when those layers would seem naturally to be too thick to penetrate, was indeed mysterious. But despite all the contrary forces existing between himself and Sen Lo Shih, they had reached understanding.

XIII

THROUGH all these months that Peter had worked with Sen
Lo Shih in the laboratory, in spite of almost negligible progress
with the experiment, he had never doubted his final success.
But now, without the stimulus of Lo Shih's mind and the
actual help he gave, Peter began to wonder if he were not at-
tempting the impossible. He hadn't sufficient time. But
even more, he was realizing he lacked the proper equipment
for scientific research. He could not afford a micrographic
camera to record the steps of his experiment. He needed a
thermostat for accurate temperature control.

He was lonely, too. He seemed to have no vital touch with
any human being.

The day was very hot. The Great Heat had begun. Peter
was half across the city on his way to the tuberculosis sanitarium, when he remembered he had not brought money to
pay the attendants. He was near the office of the Great
American Oil Company. The oil company often cashed
checks for the missionaries of the city, but the traditional
antagonism between business and Missions had kept Peter
from asking this favor. Today, he decided, he'd take advantage of their courtesy. It was too hot to go back.

As he turned into the Great Street where the office building
stood, he was thinking what a strange relationship Missions had
to American business—at once despised by it and made its
expression. The business men openly said that they had little
use for Missions, and yet men who had made their fortunes
in these very businesses were putting large sums into Mission
undertakings such as the centralized hospitals Diana had
been anxious for him to enter. Was it an effort to transcend
the material world they lived in, or to regiment the spirit to

business enterprise? Peter, with his continual struggle to free himself from the sterility of form, was apprehensive.

He was ushered into the manager's office. Behind a flat-topped desk, swept clean of papers except for one sheet on which he seemed to be doing some figuring, sat a neat, very businesslike American.

"Well, what can I do for you?" the man asked. His brown eyes seemed to be taking Peter in from head to foot. The doctor felt awkward, standing there under such keen scrutiny. He stated his errand, feeling the man wished him to waste no time.

"Gladly, Dr. Fraser. But won't you sit down, if you're not in too much of a hurry? My name's Chase—Stephen Chase. I've heard of you often in the city. I owe a lot to your profession." He liked this lean, tall doctor, with his sensitive face.

Peter sat down. A warm sense of companionship came over him at this disarming friendliness.

"I lived in Manchuria a long time, but I've recently come from the Upper Yangtse. Do you know that part of the country?"

"No," said Peter. "I've always lived here."

"I've heard about your work," said Stephen. "I've heard you did a good deal in cleaning up opium in this province."

"Yes, we've got it under control here."

"The sad thing about it is," said the other, "it's creeping in again. On the upper river, it's bad. The war lords find it's the best crop for their use—easily transported, brings the highest returns. Why, I've seen a hundred men at a time trekking it across country under military escort. My adviser up there, a man named Ho, says the back country is full of it."

"Just what do you think that will mean? A return to the old conditions?" asked Peter.

"It's a bad combination—the war lords are greedy, the people submissive."

Peter went away disturbed over the prospect, but stimulated, too, by the contact with this man of other experience. He had liked his social outlook.

So had begun a friendship between the two. Although never going beyond the office, it steadily deepened. Peter often stopped for a half-hour's chat with this countryman of his, who accepted him so naturally. They talked a good deal about the Chinese. Each appreciated the other's deep knowledge of this alien race. Each profited by checking his knowledge against that of another good observer. Chase spoke often of the man named Ho he knew up-river. Peter spoke often of Sen Lo Shih.

One day Chase sent a note to Peter, asking if he would come to see his wife. She was not well, he said.

At the door of his apartment above the office, Chase, looking a little anxious, met him. "I think my wife is only tired," he said, "but I've persuaded her to see you."

Peter wondered what the wife of his friend would be like.

"Hester, this is Dr. Fraser," Chase said to a woman lying on a wicker chaise-longue in the hall.

"We find this the coolest spot in the house." Mrs. Chase spoke languidly.

Peter marked that she looked frail. He noticed at once the sensitive curve to her mouth, and the expressive, well-kept hands. "These women of the business community don't have enough to do," he thought.

"You have no children, your husband tells me." Very gently, he added, "Have you ever had any?"

"Yes . . . one," was her quiet reply.

As she spoke, he saw the eyes of wife and husband meet, saw the deep understanding between them. He saw something else that he felt Chase did not know—that for his sake this woman held her own powers in abeyance because for some reason they would conflict with his.

"Are you by any chance a musician?" he asked.

"How did you know?" she asked in surprise. "I play

the violin. I mean, I did. There's no opportunity for music out here."

He went away pondering. It had been a shot in the dark, asking if she were a musician. There was about her some frustration. Was there always more cost to one than to the other in marriage, he wondered? There hadn't been, at first, for Diana and him. It seemed, as he thought of it, that they had held in their hands that perfect thing, growth of each within the circle of their union.

Except for his odd hours with Chase, Peter liked best to be with the Chinese. He was beginning to feel more at home with them than with his own people. They had that art of never obtruding their personalities, and Peter was seeking solitude. He did not miss Diana so poignantly as he had at first, although the wound of absence was always there. Not only in his moments on the city wall did he seek solitude, but even when he was in the midst of his crowded hospital or the intimacy of the compound, he shut himself off into some deep inner aloneness where he sought answer to a question asserting itself more and more in his mind of late.

Slowly he was coming to the conclusion that if he were to learn how the fluke infested human beings, he must make his research in America, where he could have a properly equipped laboratory. In such a laboratory, he felt certain he could complete the scientific data, give his knowledge of this disease not only to China, but to the world. The problem was to get the ova to such a laboratory. He could not take a sick Chinese to America—but he himself could enter sick.

Summer passed into fall and then winter. During his vacation, Peter had gone to the canal area and again collected snails. He'd make one more effort. For the careful incubation of the ova, he had no time, but he could study the snails. He might find the organism there, and he might yet learn how the disease was transmitted. Doggedly, he set to work.

One morning he rose early. Not wishing to arouse Wang
Ma, he made himself a cup of coffee over a native charcoal
stove he had in his laboratory. He would put in a quiet hour
of work before the hospital awoke for the day. Skillfully he
took one of the tiny snails brought from a caltrop field,
mounted it on a slide, slipped it into place under the microscope
and started to focus the lens. The lens was broken.

No one knew how it had happened. The coolie who cleaned
the room declared he had not touched it. Well, it didn't
matter how it had happened. It was broken. He couldn't
afford a new one.

He kept seeing in his mind the laboratory at his old school—
its efficient equipment. And again that thought, that he might
carry the disease in his own body. Strange, that no one knew
how to keep man from being infected, and yet easy to infect
himself with the live flukes.

Not so dangerous a thing that he need hesitate. There was
practically no chance of death. But how great would be the
ravages on his system he could not say. Recovery varied
greatly with the individual. Some were never really well,
once infected, even though the parasite were eliminated. All,
afterward, seemed more vulnerable to other diseases. A fit
body had always been a passion with Peter, and through all
the years of working with disease, he had kept his original
feeling that disease was unclean. He had already run the
chance of tuberculosis in that unpremeditated act in the
hospital. Deliberately to bring disease into his body—it was
from this he drew back. He should not draw back. Other
physicians had done far more heroic acts to trace disease,
even accepting death.

What was his responsibility to Diana? That he should consult her about this step, he did not consider necessary, as once
he would have. Love for her had come to mean care for her—
no longer a sharing of his thoughts and problems. If he
were to weaken his body, it seemed to him, he should take
extra precaution for Diana, because there was that one chance

in a million that the disease might take his life. According to his contract, the Mission would support her, but he'd like her to have a little more. He ought to arrange an insurance. How should he do it?

He thought of his friend, Chase. He would know the business end. He sought him out in his office, taking a check as a pretext for his visit. But he realized when he got there, that it was going to be difficult telling Chase what he had come to tell. Somehow the whole matter took on a different aspect here, among the things of business, where everything was checked up in dollars and cents.

When he came in, Chase was giving orders to the head of a boat *hong*. The fellow had been up to some sharp practice, and Chase was "putting the fear of God into him," he told Peter after the man had gone. For the moment there seemed to Peter to be nothing to draw them together. Why should he have come to this man for help in a matter he shrank from telling anyone? And then, he realized there was no reason to tell why he wanted the insurance. All he needed to know from Chase was how to go about it.

"There's a business matter I'd like to discuss with you," he began.

"Yes?" said Chase.

"It's a question of insurance, something more than the Mission gives in the way of protection. What would you advise?"

"Insurance is high for any man in this country," answered Chase. "At best a man out here is considered a good deal of risk. For a man past thirty, it's almost prohibitive."

"How much?" asked Peter. He gasped at the figure Chase named.

"Of course," added Chase, "you're very fit. Anyone can see that. That would lower the rate. I'll see what I can do for you . . . I've a friend in the business. I'll let you know when I've talked to him. He'll come and see you . . . examination, and so on, you know."

Two weeks later, the policy was signed.

The time of Peter's going to America was only a few days away. He had gone early to his laboratory. Through all the years of his life he had sought to know God. He never had, except as he had seen Him revealed through other human beings. At times, when he had been with Stella, he had felt close to some revelation. He bowed his head on the laboratory table. The familiar cries of the city came up to him.

More vividly than he had ever seen them in life, he saw the men, women and children of China, depleted by this parasite. The youth of China, with flat chests, thin narrow shoulders. He saw the struggle that lay ahead of these boys and girls. Only an abortive democracy had been born in this land. The agony of real creation lay darkly hidden, as all creation was. It was these boys and girls who must bear that agony.

He reached out his hand, took the cup standing on the table, and drank what he had prepared for himself. He could not fail to be infected.

Man turns away from a secret act. Even when it is wholly good, some sense of guilt goes with it. Peter was drawn as if by a magnet back to Chase. This time he found himself confiding in him. Was it because Chase seemed so entirely apart from his own life?

"But you shouldn't have taken out insurance without explaining," Chase exclaimed impetuously, when Peter had finished.

"You mean . . . you think . . . but I couldn't tell them this. No one in the world knows it. It's . . . it's my own private business."

"You've told me."

"You're the only one."

Stephen Chase felt an odd tightening in his throat. Here again was friendship, and into his mind came the memory of his friend Ho. He remembered that first drawing together in friendship, and Ho's remark, "You think of business; we think of relationship." Two standards pulling at him. It was essential that he save for this idealist his self-respect.

"I'm sorry I spoke so hastily," he said. "I was looking at it as a business man would. You've looked at it—well, as an idealist would. And perhaps you're right. It's not a thing to tell just anyone. It's quite your own business, as you say."

Chase felt oddly humble before this man, and yet he continued to be a little shocked at his business ethics. The next week, he took out a policy for himself, to average the risk.

"Strange act on my part," Stephen said to himself. "However, very Chinese . . . the way they would settle an insult, I'm settling an obligation. But neither the friend nor the insurance company knows about it." He smiled to himself.

XIV

FAR away in Szechuan, Sen S Mo entered upon the last stage of her pilgrimage. For two years she had been on the way, visiting temples and shrines, journeying happily with other women she met, who, like her, were on pilgrimage, like her, protected by the pilgrim's sanctity. A week ago she had taken chair across the plain, going alone to her final destination, the mountain of *O Mei*, Sinai of the East, watching for the first glimpse of the Light Mountain, mountain of immolation. But it remained aloof, hidden in cloud and fog. At last she reached its base.

Dismissing her chair, on foot again, among pilgrims, she started to climb, carrying her incense sticks, telling her Buddhist beads, constantly murmuring, "*O me to fu, O me to fu,* I depend upon the great Buddha." She struggled forward. Across the Double Flying Bridge. Up the ninety-nine turns. From ridge to ridge. From plateau to plateau. The way grew wilder, steeper. She could not get her breath in the thin air. Her heart pounded against her side. She sank down, her feet weak from years of binding, unable to carry her farther. She crept on, her eyes dim with weariness. The wind whistled shrilly. The way grew still steeper, still narrower . . .

The Golden Summit reached. Clouds and fog lay at her feet. From above, the sun flooded down upon clouds and fog. Below, a great rainstorm broke; lightning and thunder flared and crashed.

Then came the Buddha Glory. Her pilgrimage was recognized. Looking down into the shining, drifting fog, Sen S Mo saw her own image. Circling her head and breast, light. The great and blessed promise of Buddhism fulfilled—in every living being is the Buddha seed coming some day to perfection. This vision of herself was the sign! Sen S Mo threw herself into the arms of the merciful Buddha, dwelling in the glittering ocean of light below her. The duty to the *lao tai tai* and to Buddha fulfilled in the one act of annihilation and negation.

As evening came, the soberer pilgrims watched the Lamps of Buddha, strange green lights flickering along the mountainside—manifestation of hosts of Buddhas come to help them out of darkness into light and peace, and shelter them from the perpetual menace of disease. They looked and were comforted.

From China's far-away city on the coast, the city of Shanghai, Peter Fraser sailed for America, carrying within himself this country's seeds of disease.

XV

PETER was coming home. Diana woke each morning with some dim remembrance that all through the night, deep within her, a substratum of her being had moved out along some hidden path toward Peter. In these three years that she had been away from him, she had learned that some profound inner bond made her union with him far more real than her separation. However she might expend herself upon Mei Mei, however much she might sink herself into the comfort and security of her mother's home, the foundations of her life were laid in Peter.

And now Peter was coming to her. That passive union would become an active union. Mind and body leaped to life in intense anticipation.

As the days of their separation grew fewer and fewer, Diana's face held a brooding happiness.

"You look as if you'd just become engaged," said her mother.

"I am happier than that," Diana answered.

Peter's steamer moved slowly across the Pacific. Each day, surely and inevitably, he realized that disease was developing in him. Never before in all his life had he known pain. Now, as violent pain gripped him, he felt he had no knowledge of how to bear himself under such an onslaught. And that fierce, animal hunger that came upon him at times . . . this, too, shattered his self-confidence. Day by day, as he kept the data of the disease, he realized that he must get to the medical center as soon as possible, for he was finding himself unusually sensitive to the ravages of the parasites. He must give up all but a very short reunion with his family. But he clung to a few days with Diana. Out of the deeps of his being rose instinctive belief that she held the strength he needed.

The train moved slowly into the station. There was the name of the town, printed in big letters in the midst of a smooth green plot of grass. There were Diana and Mei Mei standing on the platform.

Mei Mei seemed a stranger to him. She had grown very tall, her shoulders drooped a little. As his eyes traveled to Diana, he forgot everything else. He was lost in his old delight in her. The prosaic station, the earth, the sky, were touched with the magic of Diana. Wonderful miracle of renewal in her presence! He no longer felt worried, no longer felt sick. He was complete in her.

In a dream of delight, he walked between Diana and Mei Mei to a little car drawn up at the curb.

"This is mother's roadster," said Diana.

"What's a roadster?" asked Peter.

"Why, daddy!" exclaimed Mei Mei, a little disappointedly. "Don't you know a roadster?"

"Well, you see, we don't have them where I come from. Don't you remember, Mei Mei, the chairs and rickshas you used to ride in? It's just the same now, so how should I know about cars?" He spoke with a note of banter in his voice, but he was poignantly aware of how far apart Diana's and Mei Mei's world was from his.

With a little show of importance, which he loved in her, Diana slid into the seat behind the wheel. "You get in next," she said to him. "Mei Mei can squeeze herself along the edge."

So there he was, sitting between the two of them, too happy to speak. China and its suffering, even his own suffering, dropped from his mind. He could feel the warmth of Diana's shoulder and thigh. He reached out and took Mei Mei's narrow, childish hand. "You haven't forgotten me, have you, Mei Mei?"

"I don't know . . . I thought I remembered you, but now you're here . . ."

"Of course you remember him," said her mother. "She's talked of nothing else for weeks."

Mei Mei flushed and in nervous embarrassment withdrew her hand. Peter made no effort to recapture it. Her shy adolescence seemed too delicate a thing to intrude upon.

They reached the house. No one was about. Peter closed the door of their room upon Diana and himself. He held her close in his arms.

"My precious," she murmured.

"Where are you?" Diana's mother called from below.

"We're coming," answered Diana.

All the rest of that day, she was removed into a world of activities which revolved around Peter, but in which he could not claim her for himself.

"Everyone wants to see you. You're a hero to them," Diana told him proudly.

One day of the two he dared allow himself to stay was gone, filled full of people, relatives and neighbors, who seemed to him to peck at the surface of his life. His spirit, coming up out of the deeps of solitude of the past year, seemed to have grown delicate antennæ that quivered to the constant touch of their curiosity, while inwardly he was crying out against the loss of those first precious hours when he and Diana should have been alone to experience to the full the subtle, delicate charm of their reunion. Even if they were not to be parted again soon, he would have mourned the waste of those first hours, when every gesture of Diana's, every word, had poignant meaning.

As the day advanced, he grew more and more apprehensive. Would Diana understand when he told her he must go away, and why? In this comfortable little town, into which Diana seemed to fit so perfectly, he did not see the meaning of his act so clearly. He was going to have to tell her without the preparation of a quiet drawing together. All day he fended off engagements involving him in a longer stay. He did not wish to declare his plans to anyone but Diana.

He was sitting in the living room, alone, he thought, for a brief interval before guests arrived for dinner. Diana had gone away through the house on some last errand. The room seemed too full of things, and very warm. He was not used to the hothouse heat of America's houses, he said to himself, as drops of sweat stood out on his forehead and in the palms of his hands. He would not acknowledge that it was pain come suddenly upon him that caused it. For a moment he longed for his bare, cold study in his house in China, the house which they had furnished so frugally in the first days of their marriage. There he would find the strength he needed.

Then he was aware that across the room from him, Mei Mei was curled up in a great chair, almost lost in its depths, watching the gold and red trees outside the window as they slowly sank their color in the gathering twilight.

The Mei Mei he knew. He called her to him. She sat stiffly on his knee. He put his arm around her, but she made no response. He let his arm fall, feeling he had no right to press intimacy upon her. Suddenly she nestled her head on his shoulder, whispering, "Please don't ever go away." Then she was gone, across the room, out the French window into the dusk.

At last he was alone with Diana in her room, nervous now over the telling of what, a few hours before, he had longed to tell her.

"I haven't had a chance to explain in all the hubbub . . . I've got to go on tomorrow night. It's a matter of business that's got to be tended to right away."

"What is it, dear, that needs you so immediately?" Diana asked, as she laced her fingers into his in the old beautiful gesture. He felt her mind, attentive to a hundred things during the day, centered upon him.

His nervousness evaporated. Then, hands laced together, they sat side by side on the edge of the bed. His words came

fast as he poured forth the story of these last months. He
desired just now neither the lover nor the mother in her.
There had been times during the day when he had desired
both. What he needed now was that other quality in woman,
which receives unto itself a man's dreams and gives them
back to him informed with feminine insight. He looked to
her to take all his conflicting emotions—this shattering effect
of suffering, this unreasoned fear that he permanently lose
his efficiency, his sense of commitment to science, his love for
the Chinese, his ideal of service, and his constant thought for
her and Mei Mei—and unify them in a harmonious purpose
that would give him confidence. He had finished.

"You mean you are sick, Peter?" She glanced up fearfully.

"A little."

"Is it . . . will it be . . . permanent?"

"I think not."

Slowly her hand fell away from his.

"You understand, don't you, dear?" he begged. "I took
the chance only because there was no other way. Scientists
do these things."

Catastrophe had come upon Diana. What had Peter done
to himself? Peter. Strong and beautiful. Grief and remorse
mingled within her. If she had not left him . . . surely if she
had been there, he would never have done this. An old terror
which had haunted her for many months after her return to
America, again tightened its clutch upon her. That day she
had first expressed her fear of disease . . . given it power over
Peter. Disease had implications she had not seen . . . the
sacrifice she had sought to avoid in taking Mei Mei away,
had been required of her. And then, suddenly, anger. Peter
had struck at the precious entity of the family she had sought
so hard to keep.

"How could you, Peter . . . ? When you had Mei Mei and
me?" The words came from her like a cry.

"But, dear, it hasn't anything to do with you and Mei Mei.

I mean . . . why, I don't know, Diana.   What else could I
have done?   I mean . . . don't you see . . . ?"   His words trailed
away.   What did he mean?   How could he explain?

Slowly the tears rolled down Diana's cheeks.

So Diana regarded his act as a betrayal of his love for her
and Mei Mei.   It gave him a strange sense of guilt toward her.
And yet, struggling with that guilt, was a knowledge of
rightness in his act which he could not explain.

XVI

THE research men at the medical laboratories of Peter's old college took his act as a matter of course. To them it was neither abnormal nor foolish. In the technique of science, such an act had its place. A group of men from various medical colleges in the city, who had specialized in tropical diseases, asked that they might have him under observation. This parasite was known to them. Doctors in the last fifty years had found it in different parts of the world, both in Europe and Egypt, but no one had made a careful investigation of it. Now had come this doctor from China with careful observations and specimens to study the life cycle of the parasite. The research men welcomed eagerly the tall, red-haired man who appeared in their midst so unexpectedly, with his bottles of snails and ingeniously constructed tin cans, glass fastened into the sides, filled with water plants.

After consultations had been held and records made, and Peter had rid himself of the disease, he set to work in the laboratory. Debilitated, his system drained of strength, the first days he did little but see that Ross, the assistant given him, kept the ova at the temperatures he had found most successful.

From the experiments he and Sen Lo Shih had made, he knew that for several days there would be no evidence of incubation. In this little respite, he felt himself really on vacation. Freed now of pain, gaining in strength as he ate plenty of nourishing food, he had a new, vivid sense of well-being. All the intricate apparatus come into laboratories during the years he had been away was his to examine and to study. He had not realized until now how separate he had been from men whose habits of thought were akin to his. Eager as schoolboys, they gathered around him, asking questions about the East, about his work.

"How on earth did you get your things past the inspectors in San Francisco when you landed?" they asked.

"Why, I told them what I wanted to do," answered Peter. "They were interested—just said to be careful to destroy my specimens when I got through with them."

"Difficult to resist you," said Dr. Thompson, an elderly doctor who had been Peter's teacher. Looking out from his own comfortable life into Peter's hard but venturesome one, he felt himself partaking of new energy. He fell into the habit of asking Peter to lunch with him, invited men to meet him, drew him out not only on his own research, but on other scientific problems awaiting investigation in the East, got him to describe the symptoms of diseases they rarely saw.

The respect these men showed for his work made it seem so right, so natural, that Peter was able to push to the back of his mind the guilt he had felt since the night he had told Diana. But there it hung, an uncertainty, an uneasiness. He and Diana would go off somewhere together as soon as he'd finished his research. Things would be right between them then.

The ova began to show signs of life. Intent at his microscope, Peter saw the little organism stir, begin to move toward the trap-door at the end of the egg. Past this stage, Peter and Sen Lo Shih had never been able to carry the experiment. He watched closely, as the embryo bored its way into the plug of mucoid matter that blocked its way to the door. As the plug thinned, he noted forming in it the tiny opening like a tube. Along this tube passed an infinitesimal, clear bubble.

"It's hatching, all right," thought Peter.

Then, before his excited eyes, the trap-door flew open. A tiny, fish-like thing swam free into the water, moving its tail in swift, graceful motions.

"Ross," Peter said in a tense, low voice. "Take my place here."

Swiftly he gathered containers, filled them with water of

different temperatures.   In some he placed snails—in some none.

Night came. He sent Ross home. The laboratory grew quiet. The roar of the city died away. Under the strong, searching electric light, Peter continued to watch. Nine hours by his records, and the tiny organisms in the warm water had died. He reduced the temperature. Still the organisms continued to die. Was it because the proper host was not at hand for them to enter, he asked himself?

Day came. Life in the laboratory hurried about him. Ross came in with coffee and rolls. Under his slide, Peter fixed the tiny snail, hardly discernible to the naked eye, which he had found clinging to submerged boats. If this failed . . . but it wasn't going to. With groping movements the organism reached out toward the snail. Then, in a matter of seconds, it attached itself. With little, eager, shivering movements, it began to force its way in. An hour. Two hours. It had entered, casting away its armored plates. In this new form, he saw it moving within the transparent snail.

So the snail that lived in caltrop ponds was the host. How many more stages there were before the organism reached the water plants, he still must learn. That somehow it did reach the water plants, he was reasonably certain.

Forty-eight hours now he had watched, and he must have sleep, but first he placed the snail in a container with the caltrop plants and turned the experiment over to Ross.

Day after day Peter watched, taking as little time for sleep as he could, having his meals brought to him. His fatigue grew greater. By a supreme effort of will he mastered it, went on with the exacting observation. Twenty-five days passed. The organism emerged from the snail in a new form. Peter photographed it time after time, for it kept changing. Sometimes its head was triangular, sometimes round, sometimes elongated so that head and tail looked much alike. Suddenly it died. He had come again to a dead end.

Peter rose from the high stool by the laboratory table. His

mind slowly emerged from weeks of concentration. Dr.
Thompson was standing near, and Ross.

"Well," Peter said, "I've gone as far as I can. I'll have to
wait until I get back to China to go on."

"Judging by other organisms of this kind, there's only one
more stage—the encysting on the plant," Ross said.

"You need to go home and rest," said Dr. Thompson, looking at Peter sharply.

Peter went out. "In the world of science, disappointments
are frequent," he said to himself, "but sometimes success comes.
The host for typhus germs after so many centuries of baffling
research has been found. And I'll never have to do the first
stages of this research over. Under any conditions, I can
recognize this last form." With the scientist's patience, he
accepted this delay in the final knowledge.

Now came Peter's hour of triumph. He was invited to
stay on at the medical center and in a series of lectures tell
of his findings. This brought him a little extra money for his
vacation with Diana. He would surprise her—give her a trip
such as she had never had. Some dim necessity to propitiate
Diana cloaked itself in these happy plannings.

Spring was here, with its fine green showing in the city
squares. Suddenly Peter wanted to get away from the city.
"Spring fever," he said. With a great languor creeping over
him, he walked into the medical center for his last lecture.
He met Dr. Thompson in the hall.

"You're looking seedy, Fraser," Dr. Thompson said. "Drop
into my office after your lecture and let me look you over."

So this was not spring fever, Peter thought dully, sitting
on the edge of his bed in the rooming house. There was a
price to pay for the using of his body as the receptacle of
disease. The inexorable law of nature could not be escaped.
He had tuberculosis. The disease was in its initial stages,
Dr. Thompson told him. A few months in a sanitarium, and
he would be all right.

He went out, sat on a bench in the park for a very long time. The spring sun gave him its meager warmth. Slowly the uneasiness, the uncertainty at the back of his mind moved forward, chilling his heart. He felt exposed, unprotected. How would Diana feel toward him now? No chance now to make things right with her. A nervous fear took hold of him. He wouldn't tell her. He'd write her simply that the doctors had sent him away for a little rest. He felt strangely alone, as he packed and started for the sanitarium.

Years of overwork and the parasites' drain upon his strength told against him in his fight. His case proved to be a stubborn one. There was nothing to do but tell Diana. After the letter was written, he lay irresolute, wishing he could put off sending it. And then, as the nurse came by, he thrust it quickly into her hand, suddenly wanting to get the telling over.

As he lay inactive, thinking by day, brooding through sleepless nights, he felt more and more guilty. Slowly he had become convinced that he had contracted tuberculosis when he had breathed into the lungs of that tubercular patient. Why had he done so foolish a thing? He was oppressed at his own folly. Here he lay, helpless and useless, because of a blind giving of himself. He had thought of nothing at the time but of the preciousness of life and that the man had stopped breathing. He was haunted now with the Eastern attitude. Man not greatly important. Only if the individual could be considered unique and important, would this act be justified. In the matter of the parasites, he was benefiting science. This other, useless act . . .

He woke one afternoon with a sense of new strength, lay for a little with his eyes closed, thinking he had dreamed of that extra strength. Well, he'd keep the dream a little longer. At last he opened his eyes. There was Diana.

"Oh, my dear," she exclaimed, and dropped on her knees at his side, taking his hands into her strong clasp. "I'm here,

Peter, to care for you. I've arranged for a separate cabin, and they say I may stay with you."

Diana. But he had no right to her devotion.

Diana struggled to reach him and could not, struggled to break through his depression and could not. At last she went to see the physician who had his case.

"Dr. Saunders," she said, "there is something that is troubling my husband. It's keeping him from getting well. If you could find it out——"

"If he won't tell you, why do you think he will tell me?" Dr. Saunders asked gently.

Diana was silent for a moment. "I would have thought so once," she said with an effort, "but I have come to think that he has some reason for not telling me. Maybe he thinks a man would understand better."

"You mean men and women sometimes see things differently?" he asked, eying her shrewdly.

"Well . . . yes . . . perhaps that is it."

The next day Dr. Saunders stayed a longer time than usual by Peter's bed, talked to him of his work in the East. He asked about tuberculosis and how much of it there was in China. At last he wrung from Peter his secret. Once started, it was a relief to pour out the story. Peter did not spare himself, sought no subterfuges, told him everything.

Dr. Saunders said nothing for a little. Then, very quietly, he remarked, "It may seem foolish to you now. As a matter of fact, it *was* foolish. And yet it's that instinctive determination to win at all costs, when we fight disease, that no doctor can afford to lose."

No longer did Peter destroy the renewal of himself by barren regrets, in a backward effort of will that sought to change a past action. With his mind free from such regrets, he began to accept sickness and the even greater pain of inactivity. That acceptance, so characteristic of the East, he found, if rightly used, aided him in getting well. Acquiescence and effort were two halves of a whole, two opposites, which like the north and south polarities of electricity, opposed but completed each other. Peter began to gain.

Diana sat with him under the pines. She was going home the next day. Peter was better. Mei Mei needed her. She was silent, going over in her mind what Dr. Saunders had told her of his talk with Peter. It took away that hurt which Peter had inflicted upon her. If he regretted this effort to save the tubercular patient, then he also regretted the weakening of his body in that wholly impersonal experiment of the parasites. It meant he had come to see that his family was his first responsibility.

"Dear, there's something I'd like to ask of you," she began, then stopped.

"If it's within my power, I'll give it, you know that." Something kept him from unqualified promise. Instinctively he guarded from her the creative spark by which he lived.

"Promise me you'll not go back to China."

"But I can't promise that, Diana!" The words seemed wrung from him like the groan of a man in pain.

"Why?" Her question was little more than a whisper.

"I don't know how to explain. . . ."

"What is there to explain, except that you'll risk your life if you go back? You'll work too hard. You'll be constantly exposed to disease. Of course you'll be cured of tuberculosis," she added hastily, "but . . . well, it's hard for anyone out there. There's the climate . . ." Her words dwindled away. She must not destroy the faith she had created within him that he would get well. But to conserve that faith was to strengthen what seemed to her his recklessness. And then for a moment, a still, cold anger possessed her. Why did he always strike at her through his work?

"Don't let's discuss it now. Let's wait till I'm well. I'll be a year yet, they say." And he withdrew into himself.

*   *   *   *   *

Soon after Diana went home, two letters came to Peter. The first was from Stephen Chase—short, a sheet of paper half filled with neat writing. The last sentence read, "When you get back to China from this sojourn of yours in the sanitarium, I should like to have you keep me posted on the final steps of the experiment and its practical application." Chase so obviously took it for granted that he would be back.

The other letter was from Sen Lo Shih. This, too, was terse. "Since the receipt of your letter," it said, "I have decided to go to Tokio for three years to complete my course in Western medicine."

Peter wondered what had delayed him all this time. Affairs of the family, Lo Shih had said. And why had he gone to Japan? But the important thing was that he was going on with his study. Peter began to figure. Three years of study. He must arrange some way to raise enough money so that Lo Shih might be his assistant, when he went back to China.

Peter's mind began to swing again in its old orbit of interest.

XVII

DURING all this time since he had finished his studies under Peter and bade him good-by that day in his study, Sen Lo Shih had enjoyed the ease so familiar to him in his childhood. By the paying of money to this and that man in the new régime, Lo Shih's uncle had regained the family lands in the western province of Szechuan. He had thrown his influence on the side of a certain war lord. Opium grown on the Sen land— a share of the opium crop given to the war lord—the war lord and he in possession of useful money.

Sen Lo Shih knew little of this. He was not interested in his uncle's intrigues. He, like his father, did not wish to spot with black the stainless gown of the scholar. Reverie and meditation fitted him better than any other garment. He lived in semi-retreat in the old patriarchal home.

His uncle had rented from the government a few of its courts. There the remnant of the great Sen family lived. An artist who occupied the favorite court of Lo Shih's father repaired old paintings there for the new rich. Sen Lo Shih spent many quiet hours watching him. At the time Peter's letter came, he was contemplating a few months of meditation in the Buddhist monastery where his father used to go. But as he followed in his imagination the steps of the experiment which he and Dr. Fraser had sought so long to solve, the keen, speculative mind of the scientist woke once more. He felt the old zest for research. He would go to America to study. He was free to do so. His wife had borne him a son.

But this time, when he approached his uncle he did not find him willing to provide the funds. In reality, the offer had been made purely as a bait to get the young man to marry. It would take a great deal of money to send him to America, money just now needed. The old man was negotiating with some of the new officials to give him back the ancestral home.

On a summer evening, the two men sat in a half-ruined pavilion in the midst of the uncared-for garden. Lo Shih's eyes wandered to the little lake at their feet. The lotus had spread their great round leaves over the whole surface, where once they had lain in lovely restraint, only suggesting abundance. Bits of balustrade from the bridge which crossed the lake had fallen away. The rockery which he had loved as a child was overgrown with vines and weeds. He could see the mosquitoes doing their strange dance in the air, their tiny bodies circling one another as they rose in clouds from the stagnant water. But they could not enter the pavilion. Lo Shih, not able entirely to put aside his knowledge of disease learned in those years with Peter, had insisted that it be screened.

"*Ai*," said his uncle, when Lo Shih told him he was now ready to go to America. "America. You would go there, after that shameful matter of treaties made at what they called the Peace Table? Our province of Shantung signed away to Japan. China betrayed by all the world."

"That makes it the more important that I learn their strength," answered his nephew.

"If thou wilt stay here, thou canst acquire greater strength. There is a powerful man in Shanghai. He has need of young men. He and a strong man in Szechuan . . . it is only whispered, now, but a little later all this part of China may be theirs. Thou couldst become an official of the new government."

"I want only to work in the new science," Lo Shih answered stubbornly.

"Wait a little. There is no hurry," said the old man. "No one works during the Great Heat."

He must see that his nephew had more pleasures. Until now, he had welcomed Lo Shih's strict way of life. The reestablishing of the family and his own affairs of pleasure were served by Lo Shih's frugality in the matter of women.

His plan of retreat—that also was economical. It brought house reputation, too. But this determination of his nephew to become a doctor did not serve the family. He must open the way for Lo Shih to experience pleasures of the senses. He himself knew how they relaxed a man's too turbulent energy. His dry old lips parted voluptuously.

A few feasts in the best restaurants, as companions some of the gay youths of the city who knew pleasure as an art. Mellow with wine, they would talk of the famous ladies of the town, women trained in the subtleties of allure, and when they went to visit them, he felt certain they would take Lo Shih with them. Once Lo Shih had seen these lovely creatures, all would be well.

He must see that Lo Shih met Glittering Purity, living in her little citadel set on the summit of a miniature mountain by a miniature lake. Glittering Purity, with her glossy black hair smoothly coiled, rich jewels given her by the most important men of the province, decking hair, ears, and fingers. The beautiful shoes encasing her tiny feet—few such feet left now to fondle. He would see that Lo Shih was taken to her.

He must instruct Lo Shih's wife. Trained in the old pattern by a mother who knew well the technique of allure, she, too, could be a detaining force.

But Lo Shih was not interested in the pleasures of the body. His mind was astir. He dressed himself carefully, went into the presence of his uncle. "If I am to reach America in time to begin the year's work, I must go shortly."

Then did the old man whine of his poverty. "All I can give thee now is too little for a man like yourself, used to the subtleties of life. Thou and the great Sen family would lose face to have a member live as it would be necessary to live on the little money I can spare!" And he named a sum that would scarcely pay the passage to America.

"I thank my honorable uncle for the sum. I will go to Japan."

"The country that has despoiled us, that has taken our

great province of Shantung!   Where then is thy patriotism?"

"I will learn their secret of power," said Sen Lo Shih.   But he was bitterly disappointed that he could not go to America, be near *Fei I Sheng,* his friend.

Curiously familiar, curiously strange, Japan looked to Sen Lo Shih.   On signs and billboards and in books the ideographs of his own language, but the language alien.   The Confucian Classics an integral part of Japanese thought as they were of his own, but the Samurai idea of military discipline was incomprehensible to him.

In Tokio, he lived in the dormitory of the huge, rambling medical school.   At first he was lonely beyond measure.   He hated the Japanese for what they had done to his country, and he held himself apart.   Now that China had come to distrust Japan, there were few Chinese students here with whom he could associate.   But gradually he came to be one with these Japanese students through the common cause of "Asia for the Asiatics."

The deep scorn his father had felt for all the barbarians come out of the West, his grandmother's fear that they were *kuei,* his own anger and frustrated ambition over the new learning crowding out the old scholasticism and his chance for officialdom, the sense of injury he always bore the foreigners for their part in the opium business—seeds of hatred and suspicion lying dormant during the years he had lived and worked with Peter, woke to life.

In a great hall full of students from every Oriental country—China, Japan, India, the Philippines, even the little countries like Siam—Sen Lo Shih spoke for China as one of the Great Brotherhood of Asiatics.   Peter would scarcely have recognized Sen Lo Shih in the vehement youth speaking for Pan-Asia.   In fiery, fast-flowing English he besought the vast audience of Asiatic youth to take the weapons of the West and turn them upon the West.   His beautiful, delicate hands he raised, clenched hard fists.

Sen Lo Shih had found a new urge to acquire Western learning. With almost fanatic ardor he sought to acquire it. In two years instead of three he completed the course, took his degree in foreign medicine. This was made possible by his fine memory, the splendid grounding Peter had given him, and his driving hatred.

Returning to China, he found a new, proud nationalism, its high duty to rid the country of the bold imperialists who had brought opium, who had forced upon the Chinese the unequal treaties. Sen Lo Shih threw himself into the work of the New Nationalism.

The leader of this Nationalist movement had recently died, had become the honored ancestor, his picture placed in the halls of the Party. Morning and evening, students and soldiers bowed before it. Sen Lo Shih dared not display the picture openly because of his uncle's loyalty to the war lords. But at night, when he was alone, he took it out and placed it on his desk, and there in the house of his father, Lo Shih's fine thin hands were laid together in the traditional clasp, as he made the deep kowtow. This new devotion took from him the last vestige of compelling duty to take his own life— the clan duty merged in the national duty.

XVIII

Two more years, Peter struggled to get well, sometimes buoyed up by hope, sometimes depressed and uncertain. He had made no contribution to preventive medicine. For all his work the Chinese were as far as ever from being rid of the parasitic disease. Every road to the alleviation of the suffering of thousands was blocked. He sick, and no one else to go on with his investigations. He had written Lo Shih, but there had been no answer. He had tried to interest Dr. Smith in the final research, but Smith had replied that he had no time.

What pattern was there behind man's activities? Blind chance, blind wasting. At such times, the sky seemed to darken for Peter at noonday. Then, again he would be fighting with all his might, so that he might go back to his work.

At last he was able to leave the sanitarium. But the doctors shook their heads when he spoke of immediate return to China. "It is too soon," they said. "A year more, spent out-of-doors." They suggested Arizona.

Peter was bitterly disappointed. At any rate, he said stoutly to himself as he packed his bags, the freedom to live his own life was his once more—or almost. That was something.

An idea took hold of him. He'd use this newly granted freedom—stop off in Washington on his way to Arizona, see what the navy and army had been doing in Oriental diseases. There was a statue there, too, he had always wanted to see. His old teacher, Dr. Thompson, in their conversations at the medical center, had spoken several times of it.

"I'd like to know what you think of it," he had said. "It's supposed to be one of the finest things St. Gaudens has done—

in fact, one of the finest things America has done. I'd like to know whether you think it's the personification of grief, as most feel, or just what. I feel its power, but I'm frank to say I don't understand it. Some say it's Oriental."

Peter longed just now for some touch with the East. Of late, his nostalgia for it had claimed him more and more.

The first hint of fall was in the air the afternoon he walked along the gravel paths of Rock Creek Cemetery. He paused often, looking up at the soft blue sky, tasting the freedom from the routine of the sick, able once more to ignore the demands of his body.

At last he came upon the crypt of trees Dr. Thompson had described to him, stepped within. He stood before a hooded figure. He looked at the still face. Grief? This was not grief. Brooding passivity. Profound withdrawal. The soul of man, silent, waiting at the secret center of life, the outer gate closed, the spirit turned inward. In Japan, on his way home from China, he had stood awed before the great Buddha of Kamakura, but then, despite that voluntary sense of awe, he had repudiated the quietude of Buddha. But he did not repudiate the quietude he found in this face.

A little wind stirred the branches above the draped and silent figure. Was it a trick of light? Something about the mouth . . . He moved to the side, surveyed the face from another angle. No, it was no mere trick of light. The artist had put his own Occidental heritage of assertion, as well as the quietude of the Orient into his creation. Man's soul, waiting silent at the secret center of life, was returning, piercing its way back to human struggle.

A girl and a woman in black sat down near Peter. "I come here often to look at her," said the elder.

Woman? Man? Peter had not thought to ask. He sat down on the stone bench, looking long into the face, studying its harmonious blending. *Yin* and *yang*—a balance of feminine and masculine. Each human being carried within himself the elements of both. His disappointment at the year

of waiting still required of him fell away—the quietude of
the East stilled a little the restless desire of the West.

In the fine, dry air of Arizona, away from the restrictions
of the sanitarium, he grew strong. Making the grade alone,
too. For it had seemed wiser that Mei Mei's school work
should not be interrupted, and so Diana stayed with her, feeling
that Mei Mei needed her this last year before going to boarding
school.

At last the summer came and Diana and Mei Mei joined
him. Peter and his daughter drew shyly together, in some
unexpressed effort to balance their needs—Peter to enrich
himself with the love of this daughter who symbolized for
him Diana's and his great moment of love, Mei Mei to steady
herself against the demands of affection made upon her by her
mother. In these last months, Diana sought to give her
daughter all before leaving her.

Mei Mei sent out little signals to this gentle man and
then withdrew them, fearful that he, also, might make too
great a demand. So the summer drew to its end. In the
morning Mei Mei would leave for boarding school, Peter
and Diana for China. That last afternoon, Peter came upon
Mei Mei among the sagebrush, still and rapt. Had she learned
this secret of renewal of herself from Sen Lo Shih? He wanted
to ask her, but there was too deep a shyness between them.

XIX

It was September. The trans-Pacific steamer began its slow advance up the Woosung River. Peter and Diana, standing together at the rail, gazed at the flat fertile delta land, quiescent under its golden burden of rice. The willows fringing the fields trailed their delicate branches in lace-like grace over the undulating grain. Between the great ship and the tawny, tranquil fields, the brown sails of junks hung motionless. Peter could scarcely bear this sharp renewal of intimacy with this country. The ship slowed down, stopped, awaiting the tide to carry her forward. Diana went below, weary of looking at the same bit of shore line. But Peter stood as enthralled as a lover.

As dusk settled over the silent land, the ship again took up its slow progress, under the guidance of a river pilot taken on board during the long wait. Apprehension and suspicion settled over the crowded decks. Letters and papers brought in the pilot launch told of growing antagonism between East and West.

Tall grey gigantic forms looked out of mist and dusk, and then, suddenly, a thousand lights sprang up, some low, some high, as if a range of mountains had been miraculously lighted. A Buddhist might have thought it the manifestation of hosts of Buddhisattwas come to help mankind out of darkness. In reality, the electric bulbs had been turned on in Shanghai skyscrapers.

Peter could see people moving on the brightly lighted Bund, the stabbing lights of motor cars. The ship dropped anchor off the new wharf on the opposite shore. They were on the launch crossing the river. The black air of night blew in their faces. They came under the hooded canopy of the Customs' House. They moved forward with the smartly dressed tourists pouring out of the huge building, into a jam of motor cars, rickshas, hotel busses. As Peter guided Diana through the crowd, a Chinese child with matted hair, loose ragged tunic, ran along beside them, begging. "Please, mister, missie, money. No papa, no mama, no whisky soda."

There, standing apart in a little group, were friends come to greet them. Apprehension on their faces, too. Bit by bit, as these friends talked, the knowledge of violent hate toward the foreigner took shape in Peter's mind. All night there beat upon his consciousness the New China, its slogans repeated over and over during the evening. "Down with imperialism. Away with the foreigner within our gates. A unified China. Nationalism." Students, newly aroused by the teachings of Christendom to some sense of the poor man's rights, added another cry. "Give us back this great city, ruled by Christendom, where under the protection of Christendom, Chinese capital unites with foreign capital, making a hell of uncontrolled industrialism. In this foreign concession, opium racketeers hide themselves from the Chinese law and ply their evil trade. Earthborn and dark forces holding us in bondage."

Unwilling to accept such a tragic divorce of East and West, over and over to himself Peter tried to explain away these cries, deny the anger and fear he had seen in the faces of both white man and yellow that day. Such things existed only in this hybrid city, he argued to himself.

They were at the station early the next afternoon. Even the old schedule of the railroad, with the train leaving at exactly the same hour it used to, arriving at their station at the same time it used to, gave Peter a little assurance.

The brass gong clanged out their departure. At the end of the day, they would be at home again. After five long years!

He and Diana sat side by side, silently looking out at the familiar scene, the squared fields, ancient arched bridges completing themselves in their reflected half-arches. Familiar stops, the noise of the passengers going away over the bridge across the tracks. The long, leisurely waits, when the hush of the fields penetrated the train. At the clang of the gong, the train moved on, deeper and deeper into the Chinese country-side. At last the low, misty hills appeared on the horizon. Soon they would see the city wall bulking against the evening sky.

"Why, Peter, you didn't tell me the wall had been torn down!" exclaimed Diana.

"It hasn't . . . I mean, it hadn't." As Peter spoke, he saw that it was gone. The city's streets ran out in a hundred rivulets over the countryside.

The ceremony of their home-coming was over. Peter closed their house door behind the last guest. Slowly he passed his hand over his brow as if to clear his mind of something. In the five years he had been away from China, he had kept his union with her. Now that he was here in the flesh, this one-ness was gone. Here in China, where he had so often longed to be, he could no longer deny her withdrawal. With the greet-ings of nurses, students, old patients, and friends still in his ears, he knew himself shut out. He had sensed it in all who came to meet him—even in Wang Ma.

"It's as if we had just left it." Diana leaned against the door-frame seeking support. "Wang Ma's fixed everything as it used to be," she added mechanically, as she looked into her study across the hall and then into the living room. The old couch in its coolie-blue cover, its springs sagging—how often she had sat there with the children. The dining room beyond—there they had had their first Christmas, and the premonition of the agony of birth had come to her.

Peter walked away into the study, sunk in his own despair, for the first time in his married life entirely unaware of Diana.

A sharp spasm of pain shot through her. The children she so passionately loved seemed to leap to life in the old house. She could see them, feel their soft, clinging bodies—Serena, gold and white against the blue coat of Wang Ma, Pete's wiry, intense little body, struggling in her embrace, Mei Mei, the tall, baffling girl left in America, who now did not seem quite hers. She wandered through the vacant rooms, in the hour before dinner, meeting them everywhere.

Then, as she and Peter sat at dinner, they left her. She felt a sudden release, a shifting of the gravitation of her interest. With a concentration which she had not centered upon Peter for many years, she studied the lines of his face, as after his old fashion he sat idly crumbling a piece of bread. Even during his sickness, she had taken for granted that he was still the impulsive, turbulent man she had married. Any physical changes, except his frailty, she had not noticed. Now she realized that his hair was no longer the familiar sharp red. It had a grey sheen, which made it strangely beautiful. His face, too, had a new arresting beauty. His finely modeled forehead was accentuated by the hollowed delicacy of his temples. She felt a tightening in her throat as she looked at his mouth. His full, ardent lips had a stronger set to them. In part it indicated his control over suffering. In one revealing moment of intuition, she knew that physical suffering was not the only suffering he had endured.

There was something in his face which made her a little uneasy. He seemed to have won through to some sufficiency of his own. As they rose, Diana went to him, put her hands on his shoulders, looked deep into his eyes. "We're back, Peter, just the two of us, as in the beginning," she said quietly.

"The children . . ."

"What have they to do with our love for each other?"

For a moment Peter was startled out of his detachment. But for him the years could not so easily be dismissed, the long, slow discipline to live without her, to solve his problems, to fight his discouragements without her, above all, the habit of sheltering his dreams from her.

He lay very still, waiting for Diana to sleep, meaning then

to fight out his battle alone. His nerves throbbed to all the unwonted sounds of the city, once so familiar—the pound, pound of the spirit presses, the distant low tone of a great temple bell, and as dawn came, overlying all other sounds, the soldiers' bugle, filling the air with a thousand notes of war.

Every fiber of his being seemed exhausted—a suffering more devastating than any pain he had ever experienced. He faced the knowledge, hidden from him in the exhilarating air of Arizona, revealed to him now in this enervating air, that his old vitality had not been restored to him. How greatly was his body impaired? He could not yet say. A body once weakened by disease was always vulnerable. Tuberculosis might again become active, some other part of the mysterious machine give way. He faced also the fact that he must expend himself to the utmost here. As before, the money available for the work was not adequate. It was cheaper to expend human strength than to buy apparatus. The rich men who were endowing research schools and centralized hospitals, were not endowing these smaller institutions. He might try for an easier position in one of those hospitals, say in a drier climate. He believed because of his work in Oriental medicine, that they would be glad to have him. But there were plenty of men for these schools. The life in the big cities and the association with other scientists was attractive. Diana had urged upon him such a step. All through the summer, this divergence of their views had held them apart.

"It's the only practical course," she had said. "You would be an outstanding figure there. You are wasting yourself in returning to a little hospital."

He did not guess that now she would have been receptive to his dreams.

He rose, dressed quietly, went down the stairs, softly opening the door into the garden. The bamboos had grown into a thicket, and the hedge at the front was tall and rank, making the spot more secluded than ever. He sat down on the stone bench, looked up at the soft grey Chinese sky, touched

with light by the dawn.   Every living thing seemed drenched
with tranquillity—a little wind, too slight to stir the leaves,
brought him the scent of the *que hua*, and with it that vivid
moment, years ago, never forgotten, when on the drift of its
scent had come the knowledge that he loved China.

If he stayed, he knew he would have to accept pain in some
form.   No imaginary thing to him now.   He had learned
what it meant to suffer.   He remembered something he had
once said to Sen Lo Shih: "Sick or well, a man does not stop
when he has started important work."   He had yet to complete the last steps in his research.   If it were to be solved, he
must be the one to do it.   No one except Lo Shih knew the
data, and Lo Shih . . . there had been no slightest word of
welcome from him.   Peter's dream of having him as his assistant was not to be fulfilled, and lacking Lo Shih, he alone
must carry on.

No need to make a decision.   The problem solved itself.
There was nothing to do but stay.

The next morning, Dr. Smith, who was living with the
Bakers, stopped for Peter.   "I suppose you'll want to see the
hospital right away.   Better not take it over for a day or two.
It'll give you a chance to get used to the changes."

Peter looked around him.   On the veranda at the Berger
house was an *amah* with a baby in her arms.   Another child
clung to her trousered leg.   Mrs. Baker was pottering about
in her garden.   Miss Dyer came majestically through the gate
of the women's compound.   "Not much change," said Peter.
He surveyed the straggling hospital buildings.   "Except that
building across the way, where I used to have my opium
refuge."

"That's the new nurses' home.   Only women nurses, now,
of course."

"Imagine," said Peter.   "In the old days we'd never have
thought we could get women to take care of men patients."

"They make the best nurses," answered Dr. Smith.   "They're

more willing to do things. But, you know, the first day after they went to live in the foreign building, they didn't clean up the operating room. When I took them to task about it, their leader said now that the dignity of the hospital had been increased by this foreign building, they didn't think I'd want it lost. Loss of face, I suppose."

They had entered the main building—as before, *amahs* toiling along the hall with cans of hot water.

"We've put in a ramp here leading to the surgical building. The X-ray machine you sent we installed over there. . . . Come into the office and I'll call in my assistant."

"Dr. Fraser, Dr. Wing."

After the two had gone out, Peter went into the old laboratory. Much as he had left it, except for bottles and glass jars arranged on the shelves, neatly numbered and labeled. Surgical specimens, evidently used to teach the nurses about various diseases.

This little respite Dr. Smith had so kindly given him, he'd use to set up the last stage of the experiment. He must send a coolie out to the canal area to bring back water plants and water from the ponds. In the afternoon, when he had got his photographs and his drawings unpacked, he called in Dr. Wing, explaining what he was doing. "I'd like you to help me with this," he added.

"Do you ask me as assistant or co-worker?"

Peter scarcely grasped what the Chinese doctor meant. For the moment he had forgotten that there was any question of race between them. The young Chinese had on a long white hospital coat like his own, which erased the differences in their dress, and long ago, he and Sen Lo Shih had found such unity of mind in the shared adventure of scientific experiment, that he had not thought to consider that new hyper-sensitiveness among the Chinese. He'd have to watch his every step in this New China. However, Dr. Wing must accept the discipline without which no experimental work could go forward.

"I ask you," he said, "as any head of a hospital would ask

a member of his staff to work with him, with equal opportunity to do original thinking."

The man's eyebrows, black as strokes of ink, relaxed, and he nodded assent.

"I must be patient," thought Peter. "In China where solidarity of family has been a strong influence for thousands of years, the emergence of individuality is a difficult thing. And it's we who've taught them that the individual is of supreme importance."

The next day Peter began to feel more at home. He went for a walk in the city, visiting various Chinese friends. In their polite welcoming of him, he forgot that first impression of hostility. He was comforted and assured as he sat with his old teacher, Scholar Wu, in his tiny garden.

"I have come," said Peter, "hearing that you no longer go abroad. I have come to pay respects to my honored teacher."

"These are the years for meditation," said Scholar Wu. "I am an old man." The serenity of both man and garden spoke to Peter of ancient China. He remembered the day Scholar Wu had said to him, "You are my friend, but I would drop all the West into the sea, if I could." Had he foreseen this strife? To Peter's surprise, now that change had come, Scholar Wu did not seem disturbed.

"This New China troubles me," said Peter.

"Things will right themselves," said Wu. "After the ebb, there is always the flow. It has happened like this before. In a hundred years we shall see what is the value of this upheaval. The universe is not constant, but variable. Creative and destructive forces act upon each other."

As Peter went back through the city, he said to himself, "The projection of the West into East is not all pain and misunderstanding. The tearing down of the city wall and the building of broad streets have let sunlight and air into the city. The clinics in different parts of the city, carried on through many years now, have taught certain fundamental principles of health to the people." This was the time of year when, in the past, the summer heat left its sinister mark on every child of the city, but today he saw only occasionally the disfiguring boils and skin diseases.

He was passing the orphanage where Stella had tried so hard in the old days to be allowed to care for the babies. He remembered his own and Stella's despair, the day they had been allowed to go through the place—the dark, rat-infested building, the unwashed, sick waifs, the ignorant, animal-like wet-nurses, who accepted the inevitable deaths of their charges with fatalistic calm. *"Mei yu fatzu,"* they had said. The place was maintained by devout Buddhists to obtain merit for themselves in heaven. That the mortality was one hundred per cent did not matter.

How quiet Stella had been for days after they had seen these children, and how hard she had worked to be allowed at least to bathe the vermin-covered mites, and to arrange some way to protect them from the rats. But the ignorant care-takers would not admit her when she had gone a second time.

He believed he'd stop—maybe they'd let him do something now. This New China was more open to the care of the sick than the old. He had a sudden desire to do it for Stella. He knocked.

"Enter," said an attendant.

As he went into the low, dark building, he braced himself for the ordeal before him. To his surprise, as he passed through into the court, he saw the rooms where the children were kept were fresh and clean. There was no wailing, sick cry, as before, which had haunted him for days afterward.

"Ai," said the attendant. "Things have changed. Will you look, please?"

Box-shaped cribs were set on rows of high-legged Chinese tables. Over each was a cage-like construction, cunningly devised, which would protect the frailest of babies from the fiercest of rats. The babies that lay within were clean and well cared-for. Each nurse proudly displayed her charge.

"Who has done this?" he asked.

"A woman with the Buddha heart," was the answer.

So the Buddhist nuns were beginning to take upon themselves the care of the sick and needy. How, he wondered, had this Christian doctrine of interference in suffering penetrated their passive compassion of non-interference? Perhaps the Catholic child refuge carried on in the city had given them the idea. Or maybe it was the work of women like Mrs. Tang. He had been told that she had established a children's clinic in the city, was supporting it herself.

A few days later he was called to the city prison. "A sickness has broken out here, and if they all die, I will lose my position," the warden said simply.

Then Peter said to him, "How did you come to call me?"

"Once," said the man, "years ago, a member of my family was cured in your hospital."

After Peter had gone among the prisoners, he said to the keeper, "This is scurvy. You can cure it by feeding your prisoners properly." And, seeing his chance, he added, "Why not let me attend the sick of this place? If they are all well, it will give you great face." The man gratefully accepted.

Thus did Peter search out a place for himself in the New China.

In the years Diana had been away, her school had entirely changed. The matron, the teachers, did not know her. The second Mrs. Berger, who had charge of the school, was also a stranger to her. Sen S Mo, to whom she had looked for so many years to explain old customs, was not here to explain the new. She wondered much about Sen S Mo. Some said she had gone on a long journey. Some said she was dead.

There was only one in the school whom Diana knew, Mei Ing Perkins, now one of the teachers. Diana gave a little gasp of delight when she realized who the pretty girl was. She had again the excited joy of the creator. The slight young girl who stood before her was beautiful as she had never thought a Chinese could be. She had a happy face, as outgoing in its

friendly expression as an American girl's. Mei Ing had never
known the non-individual life of the patriarchal family. She
had been reared to individuality.

"I think it would be nice to have a reunion of the old pupils,"
she suggested shyly.

Diana spent the morning making the rooms as beautiful as
she could. The house woke to life. Wang Ma bustled around
with her old air of brisk importance. *"Fei tai tai,* there must
be fine foreign cakes. Plenty big face to eat foreign cake."

"She treats me as if I were a baby," thought Diana. But it
was good to be cared for, these days.

The gateman brought her an armful of *que hua.* *"Fei S Mo*
always liked it," he said. The room was filled with its sweetness. He brought her, also, two pines trained as only the
Chinese knew how to train them, so carefully proportioned
that they seemed to be large trees, although they stood but a
foot high in their blue pots. Conformity carried even to the
trees, in the old régime. She went back in her memory to
those first happy years in China, when she had worked to
loosen the bonds of the ancient discipline upon the women of
China.

The girls slipped in at the side gate. Feeling ran high just now
against foreigners, and many of their husbands were connected
with the New Party. Some of them were themselves workers
in the New Party. It was a little awkward to come to the
house of a foreigner. But the old obligation of pupil to teacher
was still vital within them.

They wore the long capes, so fashionable since the days of
change. Their heads were bare and their glossy hair knotted
in the napes of their necks. Almost all of them Diana noticed
wore foreign shoes with high French heels. She was proud as
she looked upon the smartly dressed group, and saw in no face
that dull look as if the mind slept.

One among them was more charming, Diana thought, than
any of the rest. She remembered when Mo Tsen had come
to her. How ugly she had seemed, with her full sensuous lips,

her black, unspeaking eyes. Now her face was beautiful, the full lips lending warmth to her keen intelligent eyes, her strong, determined chin. Diana watched her, pride in her achievement growing. Mo Tsen, of all her girls, had been the one to win a scholarship in an American college.

"I was a funny little girl when I went to America," Mo Tsen told Diana. "I looked like this." In a moment, with a droll twist of her features, she had transformed herself into a girl of the past. Everyone laughed.

"In New York I met the man who is now my husband," she went on. "Even then I always dropped my head and said only 'Yes' and 'No' to his questions. I think he must have liked it." Her face was aglow with the remembrance of their meeting. Suddenly she fell silent. Oblivious to them all, her eyes traced out some pattern on the floor.

Mei Ing, sitting next Diana, whispered under the clatter of general conversation, "Mo Tsen's husband has just taken a concubine. Mo Tsen is mad."

Now when Diana looked closely, she saw that it was not intellect alone which had changed Mo Tsen's face. There were lines of rebellious suffering. In the face of Mo Tsen's mother, under like circumstances, would have been fatalistic acceptance.

"All the girls who are married are afraid it will happen to them. That's why some of us don't marry. We've taken a vow not to," Mei Ing informed Diana in another whisper.

Diana looked with new interest at the vivacious women. Many of their faces were marked with suffering. "So this is what I did," she thought, "when I urged individuality on these girls. I gave them a greater capacity for suffering."

But when they had gone, she forgot them, absorbed in her own unhappiness. She felt herself beating against some closed door in Peter's heart. With despair, she sensed she had waited too long. She herself had stood apart during those years when they would have won through to an understanding of the essential differences of each other. Now that the sharp, passionate need of youth was gone, male and female should have come to mean treasured attributes of the spirit.

She did not guess that many times of late Peter had reached out to her in half-conscious efforts to reveal himself. He wanted to drop his guard and let her know that he was not well, and have her reassure him. He wanted to tell her of all the discouraging aspects of his work, and have her realize the discouragements. But more than that, he wanted her to believe in the young Chinese, believe so deeply that he would not feel he were betraying them if he told her of his growing difficulties with them at the hospital.

But Diana did not recognize his signals. She had lost the habit of acquiescence of the spirit so necessary for communion. And like many others who had helped to bring about this new individualism of the Chinese, she had never realized that it would bring a change of attitude toward her. She was out of sympathy with these young men and women whom Peter asked to the house, annoyed with him that he should ignore their little discourtesies, holding them neither to Western nor to Chinese standards of politeness. She would have denied them hospitality, but Peter insisted that they should come.

The letters from Mei Mei were happy ones. Mei Mei did not need her any more than Peter did. Work! If she only had some work to do! But down in her heart, Diana did not want its exactions, its discipline. For years, her days had been set to the constant interruptions of Mei Mei—Mei Mei wanting to be played with, wanting books, wanting playthings. Mei Mei home for her lunch, Mei Mei home from school in the afternoon. No, Diana did not want work. She wanted Mei Mei and Peter. The fulness of life was withheld from Diana. Was this all there was for a woman—this shadow of living left to her?

XX

CHINA's youth were creating a new world. "Filial piety has enslaved us. The imperialists of the West have enslaved us. Buddhism, Confucianism, Christianity—superstitions enslaving modern man. All must be destroyed," they said. They would bring a new society.

Mad, brave days for the youth of China. Some had gained their conception of service from the followers of Christ, and some had gained it from the followers of Marx. That dangerous emotion, love for the lowly, was abroad in the land. With passionate enthusiasm they charged into this old civilization where the strands of privilege and non-privilege were inextricably woven together. A new life was to be born into China, with no poor, no under-privileged.

The vision which Sen Lo Shih had first glimpsed when he had seen Peter draw into his lungs the germs of tuberculosis, in order to save one of the *hsaio ren,* was daily taking on deeper and deeper reality for him. He was a leader in the work of organizing the serfs of the soil and the slaves of industry. It had been a dangerous, secret business, a subversive work, carried on at night, first in one part of the country then in another. The peasants gathered secretly around him in trusty farmers' huts. He looked into faces dulled by generations of hopeless poverty, as he told them in whispers of the new individualism which would set them free. In the close, unventilated rooms, the smell of garlic and unwashed bodies became mixed in his mind with the New Order. When he told them the land would be divided, taken from the landlords who oppressed them, that the taxes of the war lords, collected years in advance, would be done away with, hope, incredulity and greed looked out of the black eyes that ringed the table. The time came when rifles were secretly distributed to the faithful.

But more secret even than his work in the countryside was his work in Shanghai. In the country, he had only the landlords to fear. But in Shanghai there were dark and sinister forces that knew what his plans were before he had voiced them. No racial antipathy among the greedy of East and West. An opium ring made up of the worst elements of both worked here. These were against him, as well as the conservative, good people, and vested interests of both East and West. All these had raised their hands against him. Nevertheless, he went among the industrial workers.

All his life, Sen Lo Shih had been accustomed to the sight of filth, poverty and cruelty, but he had seen nothing like this city. He was sickened. As the taxes mounted and were collected ten, twenty years in advance, peasants in the interior sold their daughters into this new slavery of industrialism, protected in the city of Shanghai. Some children were sold outright as slaves, and some into contract labor. All, in reality, were slaves, working twelve, fifteen hours out of the twenty-four, going then into the loft of the factory, sleeping there rolled up in the blankets still warm from those who now took their places at the spindles. During the years of their contract, they were never allowed to go beyond the doors of the factory. Vested interests in Shanghai, both Chinese and white, fought to prevent any laws being passed to protect the workers. They used this foreign settlement to evade justice which is the basis of both Chinese and Western law. Sen Lo Shih worked secretly here, too, at last raising up fighting men.

The winter of Dr. Fraser's return, the New Party, supported by peasant and laborer, swept up from the South, making a wedge into the strongholds of the war lords. The Bakers refused to see the movement as anything but a second Boxer uprising. "The Secret Societies are at the bottom of this," the Reverend Mr. Baker insisted. "They use the same signs and symbols." The Bergers especially were loud in their denunciation of the young Chinese. Arguments at the Mis-

sion were heated. Peter alone seemed to understand the agony
of the youth's struggle, although there were times when, submerged in his own struggle to keep the hospital going, he, too,
tasted fear and resentment.

As the weeks went by, Peter's lassitude had taken on the
definite element of pain. The winter was unusually grey. He
longed for the sun. The constant effort to keep from offending the Chinese brought its own strain. He was in sharp difference with the hospital staff. Some were angry with him
for the menial tasks he made them perform. Some were
angry because they knew that he made allowances for them
in the hospital, allowances he would not have made for his
own race. And some were suspicious of the white man's
service to them—churches and hospitals they saw as means to
the end of imperialism, maintained simply to prepare the way
for the West to take over the country. And there was opium.

The day came when the staff asked Peter to appear before
them. But at the sight of the tall, dignified doctor entering
the room, silence fell among them. Who should speak?

Peter looked around at the nurses sitting primly in a row.
Behind them stood the coolies, the *amahs*. Dr. Wing, in a
long, black Chinese gown, stood at one side, very elegant, his
hand on his hip.

"What can I do for you?" asked Peter, guessing what they
wanted to say, feeling powerless to forestall a crisis.

"We cannot nurse in this hospital unless we have the right
to say who shall be dismissed for incompetence, and what shall
be considered incompetence," said a flat-nosed, heavy-set girl,
always the spokesman for the group.

"So long as I am head of the hospital, I must be the one to
decide who is efficient and who is not," answered Peter quietly.
He talked to them, seeking to explain the meaning of discipline.

"We shall strike!" they shouted in angry tones.

"Wait," said Peter. "Do not give your answer now. Think
over what I have said. In the morning you can give me your
decision."

He was spent to the point of exhaustion with the struggle. Slowly he left the hospital, following the path he had taken so often. Reached his own house door. Opened and closed it behind him. Crossed the hall, into his study. Closed that door behind him, sank down into the chair by his desk, inert with the sense of failure. With head bowed upon his desk, he battled for control—control of the pain that shot through his body, control of his fear . . . if they did strike, how should he care for the sick? . . . control of his anger . . . against all the rules of the profession to leave hospital patients unattended.

His hands lay knotted together above his head, his teeth clenched to meet that sickening throb in his body. His mind raced over the arguments of the afternoon. The nurses' impossible demand that they should have the right of dismissal of a comrade. He had allowed a great deal in his hospital, but he could not allow this. It would lead to all sorts of abuses. Into his tired mind came the vision of the irate representative, her accusations no longer veiled as they had been earlier in the winter. Bitter, outspoken denunciation of him as a man, who, under the cloak of helping them, oppressed them.

Diana opened the door, cried out in alarm. Had Peter lain on the floor, he could not have seemed more prostrate. And his hands clasped in such mute appeal.

"Peter," she cried out. "What is the matter? Let me help you."

He gathered himself together and got up. Once he would have welcomed her coming like this. But now . . . "There is nothing," he said, "nothing you can do."

For a moment Diana stood silent, her lips working. Then she turned and went out.

He hated himself for hurting her, but he seemed physically powerless to make one gesture to detain her. As the door closed, he dropped again into his chair, this inadequacy toward Diana added to his other inadequacy.

And then, suddenly, he felt Diana's arm lying across his shoulders and her cheek wet with tears pressed against his own.

"Peter," she whispered brokenly, "don't shut me out."

"I don't mean to. I've lived alone so long . . ." To his own and Diana's consternation, he was crying. All the years of his loneliness seemed to be pouring forth in that hard sobbing. And then he had himself under control once more.

"It wasn't that I wanted to leave you. I missed you so terribly, Peter."

Bit by bit he went with her through the years after the death of her children. Like the destroying of her own flesh to lose Serena and Pete . . . some unreasoned belief that if she were not separated from Mei Mei—kept unbroken that oneness of flesh of mother and child—then there would be safety for Mei Mei. It made his love for his children seem casual. For the first time he grasped the significance of Diana's motherhood. Union with her children the primary one, union with him secondary. Not so his love for Diana. His flesh felt the separateness from her as hers did from her children. Then, suddenly, he saw that his love had seemed secondary to her in that risking of his health for science. Perfect union, then, must hold acceptance each of the nature of the other. Mutely he reached out his hand, grasping hers.

In the morning, the hospital was empty of nurses. That natural docility which once had sent the Chinese in droves to the foreign schools was gone. But they had made the gesture of independence. By noon, they were back again.

XXI

A COLD spring held the land. The evergreen trees had a dullish brown cast, the winter vegetables, not yet removed from the fields, drooped their yellowish faded leaves to the ground. The willows stood starkly bare, twigs hanging from the branches like dry sticks, hard and sterile. The buds lay against the twigs. The leaves of the bamboo, so soft in their rustling when they were green, now dry and brown, made a bleak and brittle sound when the rain or the wind stirred them. The spring rains were cold, bringing no fertility. Day after day the transformation of the earth from death to life was withheld.

The New Party advanced. There was fighting along the Yangtse. Landlords, capitalists, were shot without trial. The hate was spreading to the Christians. Churches were being used for stables, hospitals and schools filled with soldiers. Business houses, schools, hospitals, all alike, the New Party considered the work of imperialists. In ever-increasing numbers, business men, missionaries, sought safety in Shanghai, fleeing before violent hate. In the long list of those injured, Peter found Stephen Chase's name. He had been hurt trying to protect the property of his company.

Day by day the Mission became more isolated. Mr. Baker called the people of the station together in his house to decide whether they should leave. It was night. The spirit presses beat out their monotonous rhythm. A decrepit motor car chugged along close to the compound wall.

"There isn't any point in my staying on," said Berger. "Hardly a boy left in my school."

Mr. Baker surveyed him with fierce scorn. "In the Boxer uprising——"

Berger fell silent, an angry flush spreading over his face.

"After all," said Mrs. Berger, "we're the only ones here who have children. It's right we should think of them. You shouldn't ask us to stay."

"We show distrust of the Chinese if we go," said Peter quietly.

"Well," said Miss Dyer, rising, putting her hands into her coat pockets in the old gesture. "There's no use my wasting talk here. I've got my up-country Christians. No time to go back on them." And she stalked out.

"Perhaps it's an individual matter," said Peter. "The hospital's full of sick. My nurses are at their posts."

He and Diana walked silently back to their house through the dark compound. It seemed wise these days to keep the compound dark. No use to attract attention.

"Sinister," thought Diana. But she would not suggest leaving as long as Peter didn't. Since that day when they had sought each to explain to the other, they had been groping their way into each other's lives.

If Diana had not recognized earlier in the winter that delicate, intangible need of Peter's, she did recognize material catastrophe when it threatened him. The hospital was deserted of nurses. They had not left, this time, just for an hour, as a gesture. They had gone with no intention of returning.

Strange and contradictory as it seemed, the sick and poor, in spite of hatred for the white man, continued to seek help from him. Diana knew Peter would not fail them. She would go into the hospital and organize the nursing, using Wang Ma and anyone else she could enlist to help her. Work that she had once refused for itself, she ran eagerly forward to meet, now that it would help Peter.

She worked with furious energy. She put Wang Ma in charge of some *amahs* she got from the city's very poor. Mei Ing she enlisted in helping after school hours. She took the most difficult nursing herself, and she assisted Peter in the consulting room. The drug department she opened for an hour in the late afternoon.

As the days went by, the pattern of Peter's life was written on her mind. She, too, knew the weariness of the long hall, the pull on tired muscles to ascend the ramp leading to the surgical building, the three steps down to the women's building, the flight of stairs and the bridge across the street. She caught glimpses of Peter off guard sometimes, leaning for a moment against his desk, sometimes even against a patient's bed. Once she came upon him standing by a window, the light full upon him. His face, his hands, had a transparency that startled her.

With a sudden intuition, she knew what he needed most. If she met that need, she felt, his half return to her would be complete. She had noticed that whenever he had a few moments he slipped into his laboratory. He didn't seem to want her to know it, though. If she could help him there with his experiment . . . She could give a good deal of her time to it now. Wang Ma, with the efficiency of a matriarch, had organized the work of the hospital, taken command even as Sen S Mo had done before her.

"Peter," Diana said, "couldn't you show me how to carry on your experiment?"

"Would you? Why, Diana! Would you?" For a moment he could say no more. Then he poured forth his difficulties—Dr. Wing leaving, the tides of the sick again submerging him, the final knowledge of the cause of the disease still withheld, the fear that violence might come to this city before he had finished his work.

"I'm certain I'm very close to it," he told her. "If my theories are correct, it's getting near the time of year for the organism to leave the snail, take final form. We could watch, turn about, to see what happens next."

Diana had gone to the house. She had taken over the housekeeping from Wang Ma.

Peter called her from the hall below. "I may not be back all night. There seems to be some unrest in the city."

Diana went herself to prepare his dinner. The mere occupation of packing the basket brought her relief from anxiety. She carried it over, setting out the things in the office—his dinner and hers.

"I'm afraid something's going to happen," he said, coming in from his rounds, sinking down in his desk chair, "as it has in other cities. Berger went off to Shanghai this afternoon, secretly, taking his wife and children *and* his curios."

"Perhaps the violence will pass us by," she said, trying to steady her voice.

Peter went into his laboratory, gathered his notes together, made a few last statements, placed with them the films they had taken that afternoon . . . laid them all in Diana's lap. "Take them home with you when you go, dear. We haven't finished, but I'm nearer because of your help. It's been good to work with you."

The watchman went by, sounding his hollow bamboo gong. The tension went out of Peter. In its place came a sudden gift of happiness. A lovely hour, they two together eating their supper in his office.

Suddenly, he paused, listening. Something gone wrong? A hurried step along the hall. The door opened. Mei Ing Perkins scurried in, shut it behind her, stood panting, leaning against it.

"What's the matter, child?" Peter asked gently.

"A friend . . . an old friend . . . has sent me to tell you this. The New Party . . . the Chinese doctors . . . they're going to hurt you if they can. They've roused the old superstition . . . foreign devils make medicine out of babies. They want proof of it. I am to say to you that even the students who will visit you tonight might believe it." Mei Ing spoke as if she had learned by heart what she had to say. "The old friend begs you to destroy every specimen in your laboratory that even looks like flesh. Do it in the fireplace in your house.

And, oh, I nearly forgot . . . you are to destroy all records of surgical cases."

Helplessly, Mei Ing stood there, wringing her hands.

Peter and Diana moved in the same moment by the same impulse, grasped the handle of the laboratory door, pushing it open. They worked like one being, pulling down from shelves the jars in which specimens had been preserved in alcohol.

"The basket!" gasped Diana. "That's the best. The *amahs* saw me come in with it. I can go through the hall with that without being suspected. Put them in it. You come in a few minutes. Then they won't guess."

"I'll look at that appendicitis patient, as if nothing had happened," answered Peter, as he laid the films and records of the experiment on top of the basket.

Diana went down the stairs, through the long hall with her basket. The *amah* acting as night nurse was nowhere about. Where was she? What was going to happen?

Wang Ma stumped along the hall, common sense written all over her features. "*Fei tai tai* should not carry a basket. It is not the work of a *tai tai*," she admonished.

Should she let Wang Ma carry it? Trust Wang Ma?

"Oh, Wang Ma," she whispered, "help me carry it home."

"Let your heart be at rest, *Fei tai tai*. Wang Ma carry the basket."

They reached the door, looked out into the dark. For a second Diana hesitated.

"Come, *Fei tai tai*."

Together they took the path to the house.

They were within. Diana stood for a moment leaning against the door, trying to quiet her heart. "Draw the shades, Wang Ma. Quick, a fire!"

No frugality tonight in the fire.

Peter's step. Thank God, he had come. Again as one being they worked, feeding the fire, holding themselves from dumping in everything at once. At last the final bit. Peter tore up some paper lying on the table, got down on his knees by the fireplace, blowing the dull fire, trying to coax it into quicker blaze. It flared and sputtered, consuming the last fragment. He started for the kitchen with the basket, saw Wang Ma standing in the doorway. "You must not be seen with us tonight," he said to her. "Go, while there is time."

"Wang Ma's children here. Wang Ma stay."

"I can smell burnt flesh. That will give us away," he said, turning from her to Diana.

"I savee, master." Wang Ma stumped up the stairs, was back, incense in her hand.

As the fragrance of incense filled the room, a sullen murmur rose outside their windows. A group of students opened the door. Boys and girls they knew!

"We are your guard. Mrs. Fraser may go upstairs and lie down. Dr. Fraser must stay here."

"Go, dear," said Peter.

But Diana had turned on them. "Shame upon you!" she cried. "I will not go. What you do to him, you can do to me."

They stood irresolute. A young man, handsome, proud and dressed in foreign clothes which he wore well, Peter marked, spoke at last. "We want to know how much you have made out of our poor."

"Nothing," said Peter.

"It is impossible. There is that great house for the sick, and this house."

"The money was sent from America."

"To enslave us. To prepare the way for imperialists and capitalists."

"No," said Peter. "Not for that."

"You are to take us through your hospital and explain what you do to our sick."

Diana rose to go with him.

"Please," he said, "stay here with Wang Ma. They will not hurt me."

They led him straight to the door of his laboratory.

"Open it," they commanded. "This is the room you keep locked."

"It is not locked," answered Peter, throwing the door open.

Some soldiers had joined them. They stormed into the room, looking around, searching the corners, overturning the aquaria of snails and caltrop plants. Something they sought and could not find.

Who had sent the message to burn the specimens? Could it have been Lo Shih? "No, it couldn't be," Peter said to himself. Lo Shih was up the Yangtse at the center of the Party activity.

They hurried him from room to room. Nothing but sick people. At last they came to the outside door. With supercilious scorn on their lips, they dismissed him.

"Go now, and go quickly. Take your wife and get out of this city, if you do not wish to be hurt!"

Outside, he found Diana, the Bakers, and Miss Dyer in a little group waiting his coming.

"Mei Ing's got a junk for us. She's told me where. Wise to go," said Miss Dyer.

"Have you brought my experiment records, Diana?" asked Peter.

"Yes," she answered, "in this bundle with some clothes."

A group of soldiers came through the gate, laughing and shooting at random. A bullet whizzed near.

"See here," said Miss Dyer, speaking in a loud voice into the darkness, "there's no *tao li* in this. It's got to stop."

Huddling together for protection, the defenseless group moved out of the compound.

All the long journey to Shanghai Diana kept saying to herself, "We can't go back. Peter will be well in America."

XXII

WEEKS later, when the hatred had died down a little, Peter went back to see if anything were left of his hospital. He felt he could not give up until he knew for a certainty. He had understood that the Chinese who had tried to run it for gain had abandoned it when they had found it did not bring them money. Maybe they had left sick there, who needed him.

To avoid detection, he had put on Chinese dress and taken a first-class compartment in the train that reached the city at dusk. But as he passed through the turnstile at the station, his cap pulled low over his eyes, the old ticket-collector who had been there so many years cried out, "It's the Buddha-man come back!"

"Hush! Would you destroy me?" cautioned Peter. Quickly he lost himself in the jostling, struggling crowd. Soon he was on the hospital street, the hollow of each paving stone known to him. The little shops—the same. Here the gate to his compound. He knocked.

"*Ai yah,* master!" cried the old gateman, drawing him within. "But you should not come back. It is not safe!"

"The house of the sick?" Peter asked.

"Spoiled. They have taken away all they can use."

"All have gone?" asked Peter.

"One is here. The girl, Mei Ing. I go to call her."

Mei Ing came, dressed like a coolie in faded blue top-garment, worn trousers.

"Are you safe here, my child?" Peter asked her.

"No," she whispered. "They call me the friend of the foreign devils. But I cannot leave the school unguarded."

"Is there no one with you?"

"Wang Ma is here." Out of the darkness came her energetic voice, a quavering note in it, and then Wang Ma herself

345

appeared. But she had grown old in these weeks. She looked tiny and shrunken. *"Fei I Sheng, Fei I Sheng,"* she kept saying, "the old ways were better."

Making use of his flashlight, Peter walked through the bare corridors of the hospital, looked into the empty rooms. He was angry. A lifetime of work destroyed. The Chinese—what did they care for progress? He came to his office. The door was locked. Mechanically, he took his key from his pocket. He saw each article was as he had left it—a gesture of their personal relationship to him. But what was his office without the hospital?

Well, he'd go away. The despair of futility that often meets man on the threshold of age, met Peter tonight, intensified by this tangible wreckage of his life work.

His ear, trained for so many days to listen for danger, caught the soft shuffling of sandaled feet coming along the corridor. He listened. Nearer and nearer. He had laid the flashlight on top of the desk. It threw its circle of light full on the door. He waited, caring little, even if someone had come to take his life.

Slowly the door opened, and a woman dressed in the grey garb of a Buddhist nun entered, turning to close it behind her. A grey hood hid her face. As she advanced, light fell full upon her hands, holding the brown rosary beads of the Buddhist. Strange hands for a Chinese. They don't have that relaxed quality of Chinese hands, he was thinking, during that moment of her advance. Oddly familiar—where had he seen them? Beautiful, in spite of swollen knuckles . . . he knew those hands! No, it couldn't be! The woman raised her head.

"Stella," he half whispered. "Stella, you couldn't have done this."

"Did the form ever matter?" There was the old ring of irritation in her voice.

He did not answer. Slowly many things became clear to him . . . Stella had never left the city . . . the orphanage . . .

Stella had been at work there . . . and other things, things which had happened through the years. The message to burn his specimens that night. Stella . . . of course. Stella, in all these years, following his work through Mei Ing.

"Peter"—her voice softened when she spoke his name— "I didn't come here to argue with you. I came to beg you not to give up."

"How did you know I meant to? But why shouldn't I? You've seen the hospital. The Chinese don't want me."

Stella poured forth her words in a torrent after the long silence of years. "Peter, if you go away, then how shall I know? If you fail . . . it's the twilight of the white man here. You've given a lot, Peter, but always it's been expecting pay- ment—the people made over as you want them, men doing as you say at the hospital. But if you stay, it will be with none of these things happening. You'll have to be as nothing."

The room was very still—more still than Peter had ever known it to be.

"Stella!" he said, taking a step toward her. "Tell me where I can find you, so I can come if you are in danger."

"No, Peter." She raised her hand, motioned him back. The gesture set him apart from her, finally, completely.

She turned and went out. He heard the soft shuffle of her footsteps along the hall.

XXIII

THE city was filled with autumn vitality. No sense of the year's dying; rather a resurrection of life after the summer heat.

New life, too, in Peter's hospital, which for many months had stood in unproductive emptiness. For two days the compound had been filled with cheerful coolies. They bore in huge bamboo poles, tied them together with hempen withes, erected a scaffolding in the space between the chapel and Mr. Baker's house, directly across from the hospital, walled it, roofed it with clean yellow mats. Now there stood forth a great canopy, such as the Chinese erect for the celebration of important clan gatherings.

Early this morning decorators had arrived, bringing loads of red paper baubles. A frail arch now stood halfway between the great booth and the hospital. Deftly the workers bound it with red paper. From its lintel they suspended intricately cut red paper balls and baskets. Over the doorway to the hospital, more paper balls and baskets. Crossed in the middle were the flags of the New Party. Above the platform, within the booth, two flags had been draped over the picture of the dead leader.

The hospital was reopening.

At noon, the gates of the compound were thrown wide. Crowds were already gathering in the pavilion. The guttural sound of their voices rose to Diana, where she stood in the upstairs window of her house. From this vantage point above the crowd, she waited to see Peter.

Out of the hospital door the procession came. First, the city's finest band, playing a strange medley of tunes, following the scale of the West, the rhythm of the East. Officers in full regalia, the governor of the province, with him the new head

348

of the hospital, Dr. Sen, wearing the bright hood of his medical degree. Behind them walked Peter, stooped forward in an evident effort to lessen his height. Notwithstanding, his fine head, with its greying red hair, was plainly distinguishable above the jet black heads of the others.

Anger rose in a lump in Diana's throat. They were tolerating him because thus they could secure the necessary funds to run the hospital. What right had they to humiliate him? Why did Peter let them? Tears filled her eyes. When she had wiped them away, she saw Peter bowing still lower in order to pass under the arch. Even so, the red baubles brushed his head. Her eyes followed him. Only a few steps more of this walk of humiliation, as she phrased it to herself. Gone from her sight now, into the great booth.

The band had stopped playing as Peter took his seat on the platform. The light was a soft yellow, as it filtered through the mats. The sea of faces before him blurred. A sigh escaped him. The worst was over. It had been hard to declare openly his loss of face, for so his lesser position would be interpreted in the city. But it was done now, he told himself.

The efforts of the last months that had led to this passed before him. Not a simple matter for him to return to the hospital. On every side he had met opposition. The consular bodies of all Christendom had withdrawn their representatives, sent word to business and missionary organizations that the interior was not safe. The Chinese had not desired his return. Foreign money they would take, but not foreign leadership. Subserviency was a thing of the past. The missionaries had always promised that when the Chinese were Western-trained, they should be the leaders. There had long been trained leaders, and yet the day of their independence had been withheld. Either the Mission schools, churches and hospitals must go, or they must be directed by Chinese, said the leaders of the New Party. Furthermore, the Chinese had stipulated that any foreigner who did come back, must come at their invitation. The Bergers had not been invited nor the Bakers. But finally he and Miss Dyer had been asked to fill two minor positions.

When he had learned that Sen Lo Shih was to be head of the
hospital, Peter felt he could have borne it better had it been
anyone but his old pupil. Then the thought had come to
him—perhaps it was Sen Lo Shih who had asked for his return.
Why was Sen Lo Shih, once a high official of the New Party,
to hold such a position? Loss of face for him, too?

Occupied with his thoughts, Peter did not notice that the
crowd below and the officials around him had risen as one man.
Yes . . . this one thing more to be done, bow before the picture
of the dead leader. The vital dead. "Ancestor worship in a
new form," some called it. How bitterly the missionaries had
fought it. Stella would not think it mattered. He had the
warm sense that Stella was in this city. He must respect that
final gesture of hers, not attempt to find her. He wondered . . .
had Stella been in disguise that night?

The ceremonies were over. Peter slipped away, losing himself quickly in the throng, entered his own house. Sen Lo
Shih was still talking with the officials. Peter would present
himself for his duties a little later, when he could see his old
pupil alone. There had been no opportunity, so far, for a
quiet meeting, just a handshake as the procession formed. At
best it would be a little awkward, at the worst, humiliating.
He had heard that Lo Shih had been one of the leaders in the
movement to force the foreigners to surrender their authority
in schools and hospitals.

From his study window, Peter watched the crowd thinning
outside. The governor had left amid a fanfare of trumpets.
Sen Lo Shih, after bowing the governor out, had turned back
into the compound. Despite the hood hanging its bright color
over the black gown, his doctor's robes looked not so different
from the habitual dress of the Chinese gentleman. Sen Lo
Shih's shoulders were bowed, as his father's had been. His
hands, quite unconsciously probably, he had folded in his
sleeves. Altogether the traditional posture.

Suddenly Peter realized that Lo Shih was taking the path

that led to his office door. Could it be he was coming to call?

The door opened and Lo Shih entered.

"This is a great pleasure," said Peter, rising to greet him.

"I have come to do honor to my old teacher," answered Lo Shih. "It is a relationship which cannot be broken. Will you act as adviser to me at the hospital?"

Peter remembered another day when Lo Shih stood there, almost in the same place, presenting him with the mace of his father's office. A greater gift was being given him now.

He was surprised, tempted by the authority thus offered to him. He had no right to exact such tribute, binding Lo Shih to the old relationship.

"I shall always treasure the spirit that leads you to make such an offer," he said at last. "That is a personal matter between us. But in the hospital you should work unhampered, be free to follow your own vision. Only so, as I see it, can you work out your country's medical future. Use me from day to day where I can be of most use to you."

At Peter's words, Lo Shih's formality relaxed. He settled himself comfortably back in his chair, his hands behind his head, his legs crossed. As upon their last meeting in this room, they felt natural with each other.

"Have you been able to do anything more, since your return, about the parasite?" asked Lo Shih.

"Yes, a little. See here, I'll show you." Peter began sketching the last forms of the organism on a piece of paper. "Have to apologize for my drawing . . . not so good as yours. But I haven't got my films unpacked yet. Look. If what I believe is so, we'll have to teach the farmers to get rid of snails in their fields. Be a big program in preventive medicine." Peter checked himself. Here he was taking the lead. "After all," he added, "we aren't certain yet."

"Let me," begged Lo Shih, "be your assistant in the laboratory."

For an hour they talked, plans growing as each contributed his ideas. But at last they fell silent. Twilight had come.

Each could barely make out the outline of the other.   At last
Lo Shih rose, saying, "Good night.   I thank you."

Peter did not guess that when Lo Shih came in he was facing
his own hour of defeat.   The mad, brave days of the revolution were over.   The New Party had abandoned its first tenets
of faith.   The voice of caution had spoken, the voice of ambition, the voice of need, saying, "We can do nothing without
money.   Poverty and defeat face us unless we have money."
In the banks of the Settlement, behind barbed-wire defenses,
the gangsters kept their hoards.   In the shelter of the Settlement the great gangsters' business went on—the business of
opium.   Opium was now grown in huge quantities throughout
China.   The outlaws of the world gathered in Shanghai buying
opium, the raw product for narcotics.
To the house of the chief racketeer had gone the young general, the pride of the revolutionists, and almost overnight the
policies of the Party had changed.   Opium, which the New
Party was to have eradicated, was now to be legalized.   Money
that the racketeer made from it fed into the coffers of the New
Party.   Labor reforms also were to be done away with.   A
secret reign of terror had followed.   The New Party purged
itself of those who had taken part in reform activities.   Sen
Lo Shih had been too active in the social reforms of the original
Party to be tolerated under this new régime, but, also, he was
too prominent to kill.   By delicate innuendo of having him
appointed to this Mission hospital, had he been informed of
his changed status.
In the months that followed, Sen Lo Shih scarcely knew
where he stood.   As the power of the new government and
the racketeer grew, the power of opium grew.   The government declared an Opium Suppression Bureau.   In reality, it
was a government tax on opium, which threw huge revenue
into the hands of the government as well as the racketeer.
The New Party said to the peasants, "We have inaugurated
an Anti-Opium Campaign," secretly allowing the local gov-

ernments to tax the land at so high a rate that only by the growing of opium could the peasants pay. When the poppy was in flower, the soldiers of the central government went over the land, threatening the peasants with penalties, in the end accepting a little money not to report the breaking of the law. When the poppy came to harvest, the local government, officially irate and offended, descended upon the peasants, confiscated the crop. Local and central government shared the spoils.

Taxation and fines were bleeding the peasants white. More and more, their daughters went to the great industrial center, Shanghai. The racketeer had his commission here, too.

Yet some of the reforms Sen had sought were coming—road-building throughout the land, government schools started in the interior. In the capital, the New Party was financing, largely with opium revenues, a great national hospital and research laboratories, the first of their kind in China. No longer only the isolated Mission hospital financed by the West.

XXIV

PETER felt himself enclosed within the circle of Chinese life.
All the houses in the compound now, except his own, were
occupied by the Chinese. Pastor Wang in the Bakers' house,
Mei Ing Perkins and her staff of teachers in the Single Ladies'
house, where Miss Dyer had a room. Nurses lived in Berger's
house. Only Sen Lo Shih did not live in the compound, prefer-
ring the old patriarchal home.

Despite the Western activities going on, the life around
Peter seemed subtly Chinese. An age-old imperative pierced
the new. The fertility of the earth as important as the fertility of man. No part of life inferior or unclean. If the
new septic tank at the boys' school was emptied, so also was
the one at the girls' school, so that the elements of fertility
might be given simultaneously to the earth. A house was
built. The *feng shui*, wind and water, was carefully considered,
that the buildings of the living and those of the dead might
be in harmony. Pastor Wang made a Chinese garden, replacing the rockery of Mrs. Baker. He was careful to plant in it
the brave and showy *yang* flower, the peony, and the frail and
faintly colored orchid, the *yin* flower.

Peter went about the hospital fitting in wherever he thought
Lo Shih needed him. He often wished he could help Lo Shih
in his inner conflict, for he was certain there was conflict, although sometimes he asked himself if it weren't simply the
strain under which the youth of China lived these days. As
he watched them, he felt they were bowed under the weight of
their colossal task. Too much for the young.

Peter was right. Sen Lo Shih lived under special strain.
There was no moment of the day or night when he was not spied
upon by the government. He, who had once been so high in

the Party, he, who had fought opium, he, who had organized peasants and laborers, they feared might turn against them, join the peasants and laborers.

Sen Lo Shih suspected there were those on the hospital staff who watched him. All his work he carried on with the constant need for caution. He never entered the wards unattended, lest someone report to the authorities that he had talked to peasant or coolie of rebellion. The first day, he asked Peter to make the rounds with him. Peter thought innate politeness had dictated this procedure. For a while, he came late to the hospital, thinking thus to give Lo Shih a good excuse to make his rounds without him, but always Sen waited for him. At last Peter accepted the situation and met him promptly.

They had arranged between them that Peter would no longer perform operations. "It is the work of young men," Peter had said. When operating, Sen Lo Shih felt a sense of harmony. The precision of his hand, the clean fine stroke, pleased him as precision of hand and stroke in painting had pleased his father.

Then there came a day when an operation was not successful. It looked for a time as if the patient would die. Immediately, whispers against Dr. Sen were started in the city. Here was the chance for his enemies in the Party to win against him. For expediency's sake, he saw that it was wise that Dr. Fraser, protected by the laws of his own country, should operate in the more serious cases. To this, too, Peter consented, when Sen Lo Shih mentioned the dangers of boycott. But not knowing all, Peter felt that Sen Lo Shih was over-timid. Surely, with the new laws inaugurated in the country, a doctor need not fear.

This was the most crowded year of work Peter had yet known. Bit by bit he began to realize that the responsibility for the hospital was his once more. At first, he thought it his own fault. It was that Western drive of his, that flaw in him of which Stella used to complain—driving forward at all costs. And yet how could he withdraw? Lo Shih was always away over the weekends, now. The weekends grew longer, the interim between, shorter.

Again the tides of sick threatened to submerge Peter. He had so little time for research, and Lo Shih helped him almost not at all. Yet this one bit of research he would complete before his health failed him utterly. His strength, he felt, was growing less.

Natural, he argued to himself, that Diana had not offered again to help him. Undoubtedly she thought Sen Lo Shih was working with him. He could not tell her he was not. His anxiety now was to shield Sen Lo Shih from the criticism of those who did not believe in the young Chinese, and Diana was one of them.

Diana knew that he had no time for research. But she felt no incentive to help him. When she had worked before, it had been in an effort to protect him—keep him from wearing himself out. Now, to protect him, she must keep him from work. Perhaps if he had no one to help him, he would finally give up research. Why had he returned, she asked herself a hundred times, seeing his frailty increasing?

XXV

THWARTED on every side against fulfilling the new life urgently pushing up within him, Sen Lo Shih found compensation in his old passivity. Languorously, devoid of purpose, he went one afternoon toward the girls' school on a little matter of a sick pupil. As he entered, the smell of chalk hit against his nostrils. Even more than the odor of chemicals in the laboratory, did that irritating, dusty smell of chalk transport him into a new world. It was associated with his first days after the woman of his house, Sen S Mo, had led him away from the grave of his ancestors, taken him to a Mission school in another province.

He sought out the woman Mei Ing, head of the girls' school, found her alone in a classroom. She looked at him as frankly as a man would, and he found it charming. Heretofore, he had held to the old ideal. Seclusion increased woman's mystery and therefore her appeal. This afternoon, for the first time, a modern woman interested him.

After this he went often to the girls' school. Gradually he came to talk to Mei Ing as he had never talked to a woman.

"I've had to stop operating," he told her.

"Yes, it would be so," she answered him, "and it is work you wished to do."

"Yes."

"Just now," she said softly, "one must wait."

They were silent, each knowing that the other understood the danger—eyes spying at them to see if they were faithful to the New Party. Mei Ing also had been in danger.

"Once," said Lo Shih, at last, "it had seemed we could build a new society."

"Yes. It seemed so once."

Her gentle understanding filled Lo Shih with a sudden new

emotion. Here was companionship, more complete than any he had ever experienced in the companionship of men. Like two halves, their two brains fitted together. He was absorbed in his discovery—why, his countrymen had of their own will deprived themselves for centuries of this subtle companionship of women.

He had thought there was no refinement of intercourse between the sexes that a cultured Chinese did not know. Woman, keeper of the family, bearer of necessary sons, man's plaything. Wife, concubine, and courtesan—his people had satisfied themselves with an infinite variety of experience. The senses satisfied to free the masculine mind for thought. Heretofore, he had considered Western-trained woman lacking in finesse. And now he had discovered that there was a union of spirit which his race had overlooked.

As the days of the spring came, daily he went on one pretext or another to the school. The bare, dusty room seemed a haven to him.

This day, the willow branches hung down outside the window, casting their shadowed selves on the white wall. Mei Ing sat at her desk. From the shoulder button of her tunic, one flower gave forth its scent. Her short, black hair was smooth and shining. Her eyes were serious, too serious, for they held the experiences of changing China—the fears, the terrors of the last years. But they held understanding of him, too.

Many of his friends of the New China, longing as he did for such companionship, had divorced their old-fashioned wives. But tradition was strong in the aristocratic Sen Lo Shih. Such a step was violation of the very fundamentals of the Confucian code, and thus impossible for him.

It was now that Sen Lo Shih began spending longer and longer weekends in Shanghai. In the aristocratic circles of Shanghai he found a place. With the smart young men from the new capital and the smart young men of Shanghai, he went in for every sensation which the city offered. To add the indulgence of the West to the indulgence of the East was very fashionable. Pretty, modern girls went in for "Western liberty." They were more interesting than the old-fashioned sing-song girls. Sen Lo Shih was beginning to value intelligence in women, he said a little bitterly to himself.

XXVI

By the wide new road leading from Shanghai, the willows swept their long, delicate fronds down toward the yellow rape. The pear blossoms floated in white clouds above the thatched roofs.

Sen Lo Shih was returning in his motor car from a weekend in Shanghai. He was early. He could make time. Only an occasional peasant trundling his heavily laden wheelbarrow— for these Sen Lo Shih did not slow down. They cursed him for the dust that obscured the road for them. Occasionally, a peasant hating the dust which fell on his field from the fast moving car, threw a handful of fine stones which rattled against the tonneau. Sen Lo Shih's driver had his orders. He did not slow down. Sen Lo Shih lounged on the back seat, glancing now and then through the gauze curtains of the car's windows. His mind was upon the city behind him. There was a young woman with whom he had spent much time of late. Her brother was an important member of the Party. Last night there had been overtures. They had asked him to fill an important position in the new National Health Movement. Once more an official! Desire for officialdom ran in his blood. Now he could cast off this expediency of the Mission hospital—a "face-losing" position. The official position was one of service, too. The high-sounding word reconciled him with that ideal of serving the people he had once had.

The countryside flew by, a mist of white plum and swaying green willow. He tapped on the window with his long, thin fingers. The car slowed. His taut nerves relaxed, and he sat for a little, acquiescent to the growing earth.

Then again his mind took up its racing train of thought. He looked at his watch. Yes, he would find Dr. Fraser in his office. He would tell him now about the new position, and then leave this little hospital forever. Dr. Fraser would be pleased with his opportunity for service. Dr. Fraser believed in service. Dr. Fraser would see nothing but the service open to him in this position.

Peter looked up as Sen Lo Shih came in. "I'm glad to see you, John," he said quietly. Only occasionally now did he use that name. It struck with a hard, not altogether pleasant sound on Sen Lo Shih's ears.

"I have come to tell you that I have been offered a very fine official position with the government, where all my knowledge of Western medicine will be of service." He was about to add that he had decided to accept it, when to his astonishment he found himself saying, "I've come to ask your advice."

For a long time, Peter sat without speaking. Lo Shih shifted uneasily, and then, unconsciously, by an old habit long in disuse with him, he folded his hands in his sleeves and let the moments of quiet flow over him. As he did so, intuition, sensitive in the Chinese, told him that as nearly as man ever attained it, there was no self-interest in this foreign man. His scientific knowledge told him also that his former teacher was fragile to the point of death. "I can hardly call it sickness," he was thinking. "The spirit is too strong to let it pass into sickness."

Then, for the first time in all the years he had known men of the West, he saw beauty in one of them, and in this man who had once seemed peculiarly ugly to him, his hands too large, his hair, his eyes, too light, his body too bony, his height too great. Proportion of color and line ignored in everything about him. Now as he watched Peter leaning over his desk, seemingly intent on the blotter beneath his hand, Lo Shih saw repose and harmony in every line of face and body. His white hair was brushed vigorously back from his temples like a strong brush stroke of some artist of China. There was serenity in the set of the mouth. The lowered eyes suggested calm.

Peter looked up. "You have asked my advice. No man can tell another. Of the opportunity for service in this position, there is no doubt. But if you think they are asking you for that reason, I can tell you they are not. They are asking you so that they may use you. You must pay your own peculiar price. That price you know. I am speaking frankly, John, disregarding that great matter of face." It was the first time that Peter had ever spoken openly to any Chinese of the matter of face. "I have never alluded to the wiping out of your family or its causes, or to your position since. But I know there is some special price they ask of you in going to the capital."

And for the first time in his life, Lo Shih looked at himself with the mask of face removed. It gave him a curious feeling of intellectual vigor, which cut through the subterfuges of his present life. Influence in far-away Szechuan was what they wished to buy from him. He did not hide the fact now behind the high-sounding word "service." Through him they wished to gain control of the revenues of that center of opium, the province of Szechuan. They wanted his influence with his uncle, living now in that walled city given over to the turning of opium into "white drugs." They wanted, under cover of the Anti-Opium League, to participate in that business. Wherever "white drugs" were found, they could blame it on Christendom, for the nations of Christendom were the original importers. Who could prove they were not still the sole manufacturers of these drugs? The far-seeing racketeers had a scheme to smuggle "white drugs" back into the West. The circle complete. Original opium brought from the West debauching China; white drugs debauching Christendom.

Once Lo Shih entered that intrigue of opium and narcotics which stretched its tangled net over the country, he could not find his way out. One step farther, and he could never draw back. Even now it was dangerous. He had touched the fringe of the net. For one moment, he saw distinctly the man of officialdom he would be if he accepted. Power on the surface, and dignity. Within he would be honeycombed with expediency. Favors given and taken, big and little services bringing him money, which he would put away in the safe banks of Shanghai, until, at last, whatever happened, he would be secure and rich.

If he refused, he lost his last chance to be other than an obscure Mission doctor. Hard, grinding labor for the *hsaio ren,* the little men, would be his lot.

Peter, watching, saw the conflict that warred behind Lo Shih's restless eyes. He knew something of the subterfuges of Lo Shih's life and guessed at its sensuality.

"I have decided," said Sen Lo Shih at last. After a little pause, he added, "I shall decline the offer. There are many for the offices in the capital. And there is our research problem."

"Yes, there is our experiment," said Peter.

"Suppose I get together the latest data," Lo Shih suggested, "what you have done alone, of late."

Together they bent over the drawings and slides.

"It must be done quickly," said Lo Shih to himself, "if we are to complete it together." Aloud he said, "I see it is almost completed. Any but the true scientist would say it was. The last step is a certain guess, is it not?"

"Yes," said Peter. "But we must know. We must see the organism attach itself to the edible plants. Only then will we be justified in planning an extensive program to rid the fields—sixteen hundred square miles in area—of snails. I will not give up until I have proved it."

"Will you leave it to me?" Lo Shih spoke very quietly. "I will try to see that the government undertakes this education of the farmer in its new Health Movement."

All the doors and windows stood open to the night. A soft breeze swept through the hall and through the open door of Diana's and Peter's room in swift waves of scent and sound. Peter slept lightly, as if he had found a new meaning in sleep— an acquiescence that made him part of the sentient universe, himself sentient. As the night passed into dawn, he awoke into clear consciousness, and his mind, since he had lain down, had shaped itself into a decision. He must leave Lo Shih to construct his own world, hand over to him the experiment, trust him to complete this work for his country. If Peter stayed longer, he would only weaken Lo Shih. He remembered Diana's remark about going to America and Mei Mei. Yes, Mei Mei would need her mother.

The pale dawn was in the room. On his cheek and hand he felt the soft touch of the morning breeze. How beautiful the garden would be in the dawn. Something seemed to await him there. He got up and dressed, then stood for a moment looking down upon Diana lying asleep, detained for a moment by profound delight in contemplation of her. Diana would always be beautiful. The bone structure was so perfect that age would never destroy the classical set to her head, the fine brow. As he stood looking down upon her, he stooped suddenly and touched his lips to the palm of her hand. Perhaps she would waken and share the garden with him. She smiled faintly, but did not open her eyes. After all, why should he waken her?

As he descended the stairs and looked down on the rooms below, his home with its clean frugality seemed a beautiful receptacle for the wind and the coming day. There was no clutter of furniture or curtains to shut them out. The fine, hard varnish of the floors mirrored the early light. Just below him in the hall was the balanced Chinese arrangement of straight chairs and square tables. Across the highly polished top of a table the wind rippled the light in rhythmic movements. Beyond the door, he could see Diana's enclosed garden. The stone bench stood white against the bamboos, faintly touched with spring green.

He walked across the grass and lay down upon the bench, his hands under his head, looking up into the sky. "The sun must have risen," he said to himself, "the earth and sky are drenched with light." He drew in his breath, so that he might smell the fragrant breath of the garden. That black, crumbling earth used for so many centuries, gave forth its own peculiar odor of fertility. The bamboos close at his side were piercing the earth with their cone-shaped sprouts. Those that had pierced the earth on yesterday stood tall, but still sheathed. Then one, two, three, cracked their sheaths with faint staccato sounds. Deep within him he felt the indestructible core of his being vibrating to some eternal pulsing vitality, spirit drenching every minutest particle of the earth. That fertility of spirit he had sought.

Diana roused from sleep, urged by some need to guard her loved ones, lest she lose them. Peter was not there. Often she woke and he had gone, called by some early morning emergency at the hospital. But there was some urgent demand within her that she find him, today. She snatched up a dressing gown, hurried down through the house. His study was empty. And yet she was certain he had not gone to the hospital. He was near her. Did he want her to join him? As she passed the door leading into the garden, she saw him. He must not lie there on that cold stone. That was it—he was in need of her care, as her children always were. Something always told her when they had thrown the covers off, or had wandered from their beds.

"Peter," she called, hurrying across the grass, "you mustn't lie there." But he did not answer her or move. Was the morning light playing a trick on her? As it fell upon his face, his features took on transparency. She was beside him now. "Oh," she exclaimed faintly, and sank down upon her knees. Slowly she raised her hands to his shoulders, looking long into his face, searching for him, but he was not there. Slowly she felt her union with this man dissolving. Agony entered into her, as the process of separation went inexorably forward. Her flesh itself seemed to bleed as the personality that was Peter was torn from her. And then a new anguish gripped her. This care of him . . . some snapped nerve vibrated with the habitual response to his physical well-being. Blindly she rose, entered the house, brought his coat.

"It is threadbare. He should have a new one," she thought mechanically, as she laid it over him.

It was the hour for his burial. Out of the hospital dressed in the white garments of their service—the traditional garb of Chinese mourning—came the nurses. A single male figure moved on ahead. It was Sen Lo Shih. "Even in modern China," he said gently to Diana, "it is lonely to die without sons. We of his hospital would be his children, and I would stand in the relationship of eldest son to him, following behind him on foot."

THE END